THE RISE
OF THE
WESTERN KINGDOM

THE RISE
OF THE
WESTERN KINGDOM

BOOK TWO OF THE SWORD OF THE WATCH

A NOVEL BY
JOHN MONTGOMERY

The Rise of the Western Kingdom
Book Two of the Sword of the Watch

Chapter Artwork by John Montgomery

Copies of series are available from major retailers or by contacting:
IMC Studios Incorporated
901 Deerfield Court
Russellville, Arkansas 72801
(479) 880-8802

ISBN: 979-8-9999009-3-7 (pb)
ISBN: 979-8-9999009-5-1 (hc)
ISBN: 979-8-9999009-6-8 (ebook)

Print information is available on the last page.

IMC Studios Incorporated Rev Date: 1/6/2026

For Mom & Dad

CONTENTS

ILLUSTRATIONS

Acknowledgments

To my wife Bobbi, who doubles my joys and halves my sorrows.

To all the fans that stopped at a tradeshow booth, a book signing, or an author coffee, or just wrote an email to say how much you loved the story of *The Sword of the Watch*: know that your encouraging words provided the spark I needed to bring *The Rise of the Western Kingdom* to paper.

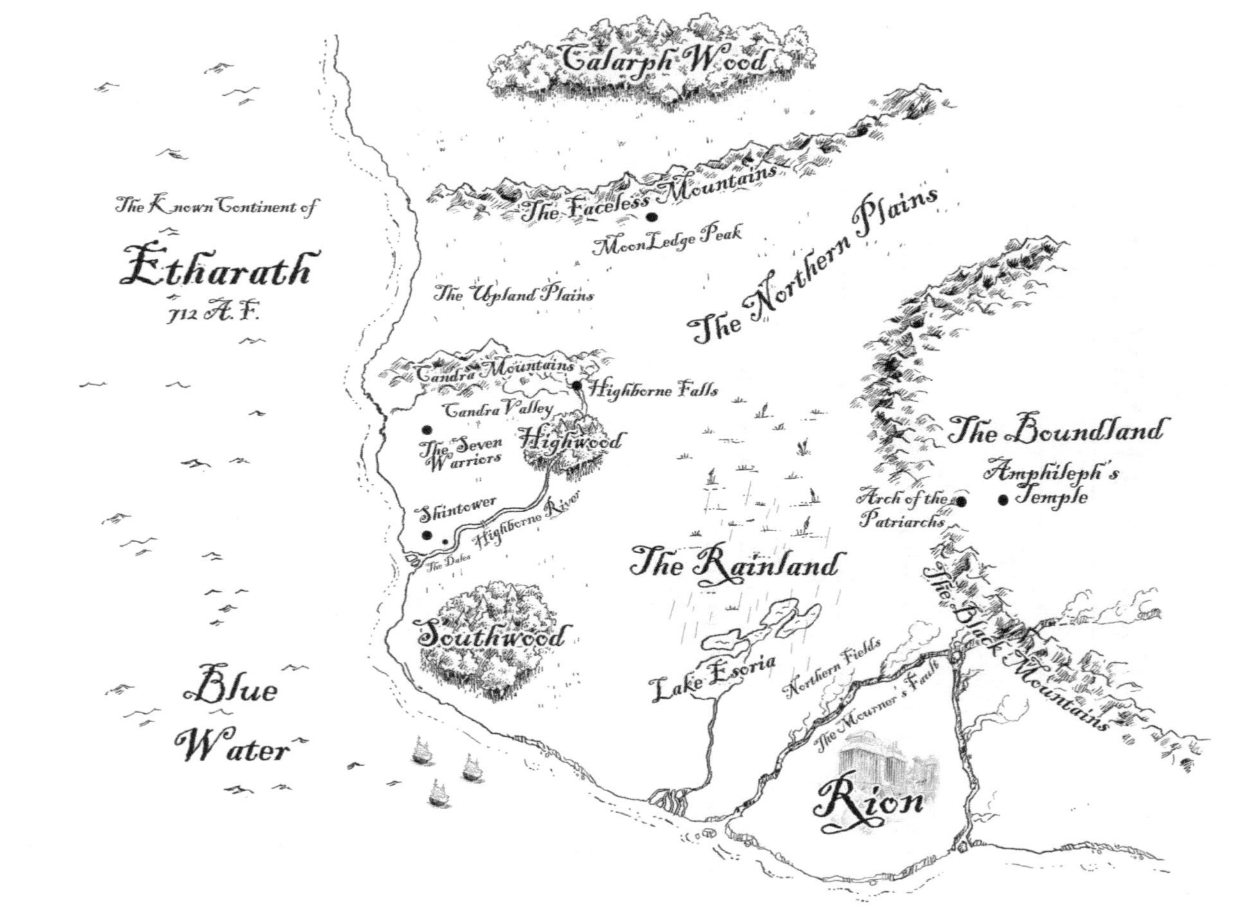

Calarph Wood
The Known Continent of
Etharath
712 A.F.
The Faceless Mountains
MoonLedge Peak
The Upland Plains
The Northern Plains
Candra Mountains
Highborne Falls
Candra Valley
The Seven Warriors
Highwood
Shintower
Highborne River
The Dales
The Boundland
Amphileph's Temple
Arch of the Patriarchs
The Rainland
Southwood
Lake Esoria
Northern Fields
The Mourner's Fault
The Black Mountains
Rion
Blue Water

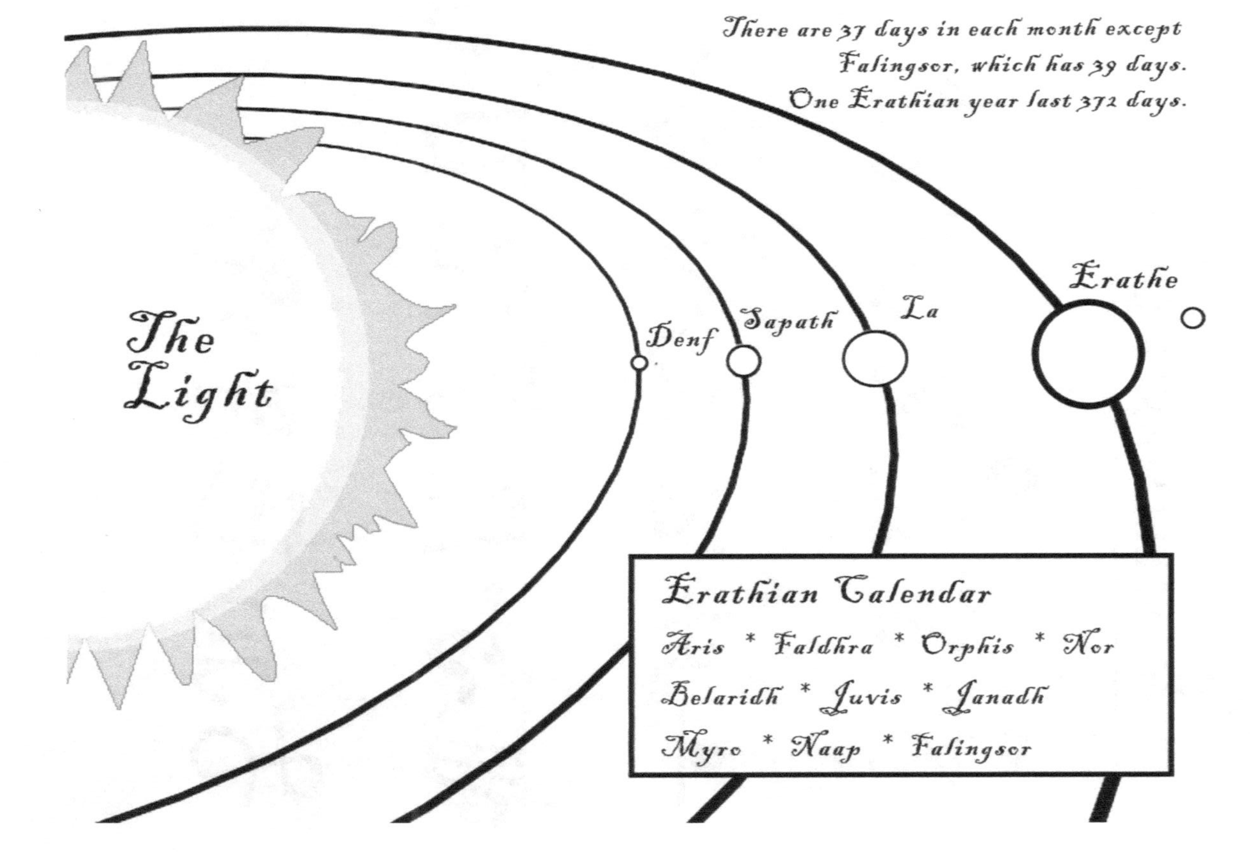

There are 37 days in each month except
Falingsor, which has 39 days.
One Erathian year last 372 days.
The Light
Denf
Sapath
La
Erathe
Erathian Calendar
Aris * Faldhra * Orphis * Nor
Belaridh * Juvis * Janadh
Myro * Naap * Falingsor

SPELLMAKER GLYPHS

THE SONG OF ISHA

Creator, let your Watchers know that patiently we wait,
We pray to have great strength of heart before it is too late.

"Rion! Our hearts, our homes, our loves!
Where are your temples great?
All gone!" decried the bard in song, "but why this awful fate?"

"Failed grace" did take the tongue of most
Who spoke of such a thing,
Begged we the Guard to make riposte,
Lest heads find Camon's ring.

Now rages Watchers' war on them beyond the nearest gate,
While Rion's Guard, our holy guard, a chance for us create.

We fled Rion by craggy coast,
That fateful day of Spring,
We swear it now and drink the toast!
They'll feel The Sword's good sting.

Oh, Book, my Holy Book of Time,
did not you once narrate
That Men one day would indeed proclaim
that they with Him equate?

Creator, let your Watchers know that patiently we wait,
We pray to have great strength of heart before it is too late.

PROLOGUE

In the time after the Foundation of Rion, the people flourished under the guidance of the immortals—the Watchers—led by the prophet Evliit, who shaped the destiny of men through one holy weapon: the Sword of the Watch, forged by the Bhre-Nora in the Third Domain, the realm of the Creator himself.

War and pestilence were unheard of. Yet by fate or by works, some prospered more than others, and envy soon turned to anger, and anger to murder and pillage, until man was set against man. The Elders, ancient followers of the Watchers, reined in the chaos by creating an army of paladins known as the Rion Guard, taking Rion's young and disciplining them in the arts of battle, music, and philosophy while instilling in them a deep love for their Creator. For a time, peace returned to Etharath—but as with all societies that live by the sword, even the poor found a blade and the hatred to wield it, and the world again teetered on the brink of chaos.

A division formed among the immortals. Some saw humankind's corruption as incurable and sought radical change through their mastery of alchemy and wizardry. Evliit named them Spellmakers and strove to temper their vengeance.

The Spellmakers would hear none of it. They demanded that Evliit reshape man's destiny through the power of the Sword of the Watch. When he refused, Amphileph, their leader, commanded the *Camonra* to destroy mankind so he might repopulate Erathe with a race worthy of the Creator.

Thus began the War of the Watchers. As Amphileph threatened the southern kingdom of Rion with extinction, refugees scattered across the continent in search of hope — and a rallying cry.

PART ONE

Chapter One

Harm's Way

Galbard walked toward the main temple of Amphileph, dwarfed by the jailer ahead of him. Slavery had both tattered his shirt and filled it with a muscular frame, and his wrist chains thumped against his leather loincloth in syncopation with the slap of his sandals on the stone path.

He kept a few paces behind, eyes fixed on the jailer's back or lowered to the ground — the posture demanded of a slave. The jailer was a Camon, one of the race collectively known as the *Camonra*.

They were the warriors of Amphileph, master of the Spellmakers, and he held absolute dominion over them. Though they shared many human traits, most stood over seven feet tall. Their slow gait, broad sloping shoulders, and thick limbs were deceiving — when they chose to move, they were as swift as they were strong. That three Camonra had rousted a human slave in the middle of the night told Galbard that Amphileph himself had taken some kind of interest in him. And that was frightening. It was better for a slave to remain unnoticed.

Two Camonra walked behind Galbard, and the jailer led the way through the encampments toward the immense temple at their center. The group stopped before the entrance, and one of them exhaled his boredom onto the back of Galbard's neck. The warm stench surrounded him, and Galbard curled his nose. He wanted to step away, but did not dare move.

He had rarely seen the Camonra without their helmets, so he stole glances when he thought no one was watching. The jailer's hair had been roughly shorn — short, jet black, exposing one ear crumpled from a blow. The other ear had a pointed tip that flopped slightly with each step.

His wide-necked chainmail revealed his upper back, where whip marks crisscrossed the bared area at various widths and depths, some of them edged by the dots of scar tissue that a coarse needle might leave.

When the Camon turned, Galbard could see deep frown lines that made his face look as though it might never have smiled. A large scar ran from the crumpled ear to the edge of his chin.

"Enter!" a voice called from within the temple.

The Camon in front of him snorted through his snub nose and motioned with his head for Galbard to enter, and Galbard momentarily looked at the Camon's face. He did not seem to notice Galbard's mistake, and Galbard quickly looked at the floor again, but the flash of an image stuck in his mind: the bloodshot eyes under the heavy brow, the flat square face, the pug nose and large carved chin, and the gold beads that adorned some of the dreadlocks in the creature's beard.

When the Camon turned to face the temple door, Galbard looked up at him again. The massive creature raised his thick, somewhat elongated arms and slowly pushed open the heavy door of the temple entrance. His tree-trunk legs lumbered ahead of Galbard through the temple doorway, and his chainmail *chinked* with each step. Galbard tried to walk in time with the Camon's steps, but he had to take two steps for each of his.

The two other Camonra took their posts on either side of the entrance, and Galbard followed the jailer inside. He heard the doors closing behind him, and then his escort pushed him forward through an arched opening, an entryway into the domed temple sanctum. They shuffled to a halt at its center.

The domed ceiling had a central opening, allowing a column of moonlight to illuminate the temple floor, and when Galbard stood still in its light blue beams, the walls of the room seemed to sink away into the darkness.

"Father, I have brought you the human," the Camon said.

Out of the darkness, a thin man in a long, flowing red robe appeared. Galbard caught his breath. It was Amphileph! Amphileph looked at his fingernails, cocking his head to one side, his long, jet black bangs hiding his eyes. He leaned his head back and pushed his bangs back with both hands. His skin was pale, and his dark green eyes were piercing.

"You are the one called Galbard?" Amphileph asked.

The Camon swatted Galbard to the ground. "Bow down before the Father, dog!" he thundered.

"Yes, master," Galbard managed.

"Now, now, let's not mistreat our guest," Amphileph said. "Help him to his feet."

The Camon's massive hand grabbed Galbard's shoulder and lifted him up, dropping him back upon his feet.

"I am told that you can speak the old language, Galbard. Is that true?" Amphileph asked.

"Yes, master," answered Galbard.

Amphileph circled him in the shadows. "A slave's life is unbecoming to such an educated man. Wouldn't you like to go free? All I need do is speak it, and it will be so," Amphileph said.

A chill crawled across Galbard's skin, the fine hairs at his nape prickling as Amphileph's words coiled around him. "Yes, master, of course."

"Then you must do something for me. You will find a man in the foothills of the Black Mountains, asleep under the Arch of the Patriarchs. Do you know this place?"

"Yes, master," Galbard responded.

"Kill the man and bring me his belongings, and I will set you free."

Galbard's heart raced at the mere thought of freedom, but he drew a sharp breath and forced himself to remain silent. Killing for freedom would bring him only a new prison of guilt, but refusing Amphileph meant certain death. Silence was the better option.

Amphileph's hand emerged from the shadows, a single finger pointed in Galbard's direction. His nails were manicured and his red garment shimmered in the moonlight.

"*Ara Libre Cudhara*," Amphileph said, and the shackles fell away from Galbard's hands and feet. Amphileph raised his hood, his face vanishing into shadow. From the shadowed hood, two green embers burned, fixing Galbard in place as if the darkness itself had eyes. "Run, and I will find you, no matter where you go."

Amphileph turned to exit the room and waved them away. "Dress him properly and see him to the western gate," he said, before disappearing completely into the darkness.

Galbard exhaled, but before he could relax even slightly, the Camon's large hand grabbed him up and dropped him facing the opposite direction. He flicked his fingers against Galbard's back, pushing him toward the exit.

The three Camonra escorted Galbard to the western gate as Amphileph had commanded, stopping just long enough to remove the large timber that barred it. The Camonra gave him clothing fit for traveling: leather boots and a long coat, a dagger, and a pack with a day's supplies. Galbard waited for them to say something, but instead, the largest jailer pushed him out of the gate rather unceremoniously, and the Camonra turned and walked away. Galbard picked himself up and watched them push the gate closed. The timber fell back in its place with a great crashing sound.

Galbard was momentarily stunned. After more than a year of imprisonment, they had just left him at the western gate without even a second thought, like so much trash. He pulled his hood over his head, tightened his belt, then turned and walked toward the Arch of the Patriarchs, a holy place of prayer west of Amphileph's temple and high in the Black Mountains.

He had always told himself that he would do anything to escape his enslavers. He had often thought of killing one of the Camonra and escaping, especially when they had been unusually cruel, but he acknowledged to himself that it was only a crutch, a way to keep some thread of hope alive in his hopeless life. Still, a Camon was one thing; never once had he imagined killing a human being, and it was unthinkable in a holy place where the Creator himself watched over them. It was not in him to murder, or at least that's what he had thought, but failure to do as Amphileph asked was toying with death, and likely a horrible death at that. He repeated Amphileph's words in his head, *Run, and I will find you, no matter where you go,* until in the distance, he could see the arch above the horizon, about two-thirds of the way up the Black Mountains.

Galbard climbed higher still, and when he pulled himself onto the arch's plateau, he could see a man, just as Amphileph had said, motionless, leaning over the large, flat, knee-high stone table centered under the arch. His hair and robes were dirty and disheveled. It appeared to Galbard that the man had been kneeling in prayer, perhaps throughout the night, and had fallen asleep from exhaustion.

Galbard approached the prayer circle. The man's shoes sat beside a small bag and an old sword. Staring at their worn soles and the dusty bag, he wondered what guilt this man carried that qualified him for death, especially death at his hand.

He stood there for what seemed an eternity, wrestling with the repercussions of not doing as Amphileph commanded. Galbard put his hands on the sword and removed it from its scabbard. He tried to remove it slowly, silently, but the blade seemed to scrape the scabbard along its entire length, making Galbard sure the man would wake. His heart raced, and he moved closer to the prone man's head, raising the sword above him. Its tip pointed precariously toward the man's temple.

Galbard couldn't move. Sweat beaded on his forehead.

What am I doing? he thought. "Creator, forgive me," he whispered, looking to the skies above. He lowered the sword and backed away, and then he returned the sword to its scabbard, his hands shaking so badly then that the length of it made a *tink, tink, tink* sound sliding into the scabbard. He tried to regain his calm, but the noise seemed as loud as a dinner bell. He stopped for a moment and closed his eyes, exhaling deeply.

He turned and looked down the mountain toward Amphileph's temple.

"Under penalty of death, I'll not bring this shame upon my forefathers," he said. "When I stand in judgment in the Third Domain, my soul will blacken with things for which I am ashamed, but this will not be one of them."

He carefully placed the sword back where he had found it and returned to the man's side. To Galbard's relief, the man had not awakened throughout the entire ordeal. "I don't see a bottle, my friend, but whatever it was that you drank, you should probably not drink it again."

Galbard shook him, attempting to awaken him.

"Wake up!" Galbard said. "Wake up!"

The man's eyes flickered open.

"You must run! Run away, far from here!"

The man looked dazed. He didn't seem fully aware of what was happening. Galbard stood back from him and yelled, pointing to the temple in the valley below. "Listen to me! Sober up! I don't know what you've done, but the master of that temple wants your head on a spear. I was sent to kill you, and now that I haven't, I've made my own doom! Flee before I come to my senses!"

The man's facial features suddenly began to shift and his clothes changed in a flash of blinding light as he slowly rose before the stunned Galbard. The pauper clothing had transformed into white, flowing robes that floated around the holy man.

Galbard stumbled back and fell to the ground. He knew immediately who it was: the great prophet Evliit, the leader of the Watchers, who could consult directly with the Creator and call down his favor or his wrath.

The former slave spat on the ground in his misfortune. "How can it be that I've angered both a Spellmaker and a Watcher in a single day?"

Evliit hovered above the ground, his face shining. He raised his hand, and the sword flew from its scabbard into it. The sword began to glow, giving off such an intense heat that Galbard had to cover his face. He braced for his doom. The winds gasped like the gods drawing a breath, and the light suddenly dimmed.

Galbard dared to look again. Evliit and his robes slowly sank back to the earth. He was teetering as though he might fall.

"Help me," Evliit managed, reaching out to his would-be killer.

Galbard hesitated in bewilderment, but then instinctively moved to catch him as the prophet fell forward.

Evliit clutched Galbard's arm to regain his balance, searching his face with what Galbard thought was a mixture of sadness and terror in his eyes.

"It has come to this," Evliit said. "The Spellmakers would take the Sword of the Watch from me by force?"

Awkwardly, Galbard helped him to sit on the edge of the altar table, and then he looked away. A slave should not have even touched the same ground as a Watcher, especially in a prayer circle.

Amphileph had sent him to kill the prophet of the Creator! His soul was likely cursed, just having agreed to make the trip to the Arch of the Patriarchs. His mind reeled with the thought that the actions of the past few minutes might actually have doomed him forever.

"Your things, master," Galbard said, and then he hurried to bring the prophet his scabbard, bag, and shoes. Galbard stopped and knelt at the edge of the prayer circle, and he placed the shoes so that Evliit might slip them on immediately upon his exit.

"I accept my fate," Galbard said, entering the prayer circle with his head down and Evliit's scabbard and bag outstretched before him. He waited for Evliit to take his things, and then Galbard quickly backed away from him outside the prayer circle.

Evliit placed the sword back in its scabbard. He removed a small vial from the bag, drank it, and put it away, and then he heaved a deep breath and slowly looked over the length of the sword.

"Come here," Evliit said. Galbard moved to kneel some ten feet away.

"Closer, come closer."

Galbard glanced up at him, and then kneeled at Evliit's feet, expecting the worst.

"You are Galbard, a slave of Amphileph," said Evliit.

"Yes, lord."

"Stand up, and hold out your hands."

Galbard stood up and looked into Evliit's eyes then, extending his hands. To his astonishment, Evliit placed the sword in them, walked past him to the edge of the prayer circle, and slipped on his shoes.

Galbard could not move. A strange tingling sensation ran from his hands throughout his body. The tingling intensified. The golden color of the scabbard and hilt began to blur together, becoming luminous. Memories raced through his mind — of Rion and the life he once had there, and then flashes of the rolling grasses in the fields north of the city. His head began to pitch slightly, and his eyes flickered closed. He was sure the Watcher could see his expression change from surprise to concern, and when Evliit spoke, the words seemed to pierce Galbard's soul.

"I can wait no longer," Evliit said. "My brethren and I have one last chance to confront the Spellmakers. We will bind them to the lands beyond the Black Mountains, and I will send the sword away from here with you. It has chosen you."

With those last words, the intense pain stopped. Galbard's arms relaxed, and he nearly dropped the sword. He immediately motioned to Evliit to take it back.

"Send the sword away with me? Oh no, my lord, please don't set this task upon me!" Galbard pleaded. "I have no business in the affairs of Watchers. I am nothing, and I must go to ask the Priests of Rion to cleanse me for the evil that I have already done. I swear to you that my eyes were covered by a strange spell, and I did not see you as you were." He lowered his head and held the sword out toward Evliit.

Evliit shook his head. "You didn't see a Watcher, and yet you spared my life. This is not the act of an evil man." Galbard felt Evliit place his hand on the sword and gently push it away. Galbard fixed his eyes upon it and accepted Evliit's charge. A surge of energy coursed through his body, as if every nerve was firing at once. It was exhilarating, and when Galbard looked up, he saw the Watcher's gentle face smiling back at him.

"You are worthy," he said, and the words seemed to melt away Galbard's anxiety.

Evliit turned away and looked westward. The winds began to stir up, and dark clouds formed above the Black Mountains valley. Evliit stared down at the valley for the better part of a minute, his eyes piercing, unflinching in the wind, his beard and hair blown back wildly. Galbard thought him sorely vexed, and he waited in silence for the Watcher's next command.

"Your former master has grown strong. A spell to bind him will come at great cost, consuming the life force of all but the strongest among us. We can take no chance of the sword falling into his hands, for with it,

Amphileph would surely end the time of men. You must take it far away. My brothers and I will not be able to bind the Camonra who already move upon Rion, and Amphileph will give them no rest until they have captured the sword for their master."

"I understand," replied Galbard.

"Your heart is true, Galbard. The Creator has crossed our paths for a reason. Take the sword far away into the western lands, throw it into the depths of the ocean that lies beyond if you must, but keep it safe from the evil of Amphileph! I have said my prayer for you. I have asked the Creator to show you the path and give you sanctuary. Go now and pray for *us*. Pray that we can still bind Amphileph!"

Evliit began to chant in the ancient tongue then, and the hair rose on Galbard's neck. There was power in each utterance. The clouds above the valley began to turn slowly. Beams of light shot out from between their wispy turnings. There was a flash from within them, and a great clap of thunder.

Galbard felt a wave of energy pass over him, moving inward toward the valley. It almost pushed him over, and then there was a second flash and Galbard saw it—a sphere of energy was closing in slowly from miles above and around the valley, converging on Amphileph's temple.

Galbard took the Sword and ran, ran as fast as he could northwest to the crest of the Black Mountains on the northern side of the valley. Far below him, he saw the battle for Rion unfolding. Ten thousand Camonra poured across the northern fields toward the city. There were five, maybe six columns of the Rion Guard's cavalry rushing to meet them, flags flying in the wind, and then suddenly, the entire mountain began to shake violently.

Galbard lost his footing and fell against the mountainside, holding onto the stone with all his strength. The Black Mountains Valley split open. A fiery rift crossed southwest through the Black Mountains, where it forked west across the battlefield and south around the east side of Rion. The sky filled with plumes of lava and jets of superheated air, magma, and ash.

Galbard struggled to his feet to look toward Rion, but black clouds of ash and smoke obscured the horizon. The battle drum and the trumpet were silenced. Gone were the long battle lines of the Camonra. Gone were the ordered battlements of the Rion Guard who opposed the sacking of their beloved city. In mere moments, it seemed that everything Galbard knew of his world had changed.

CHAPTER TWO

THE END OF THE FIRST AGE

Cayden beat his hands together to knock the dust from them. He loosened the dirty rags that he had tied around them to protect them from the unfinished stone he'd been working into the base of the railing surrounding one of the lower temple's verandas. Masonry work in Rion had thinned since the evacuation of the outer city, and rough stone or not, Cayden's hunger made him happy to have the work.

It had been especially hard to stay focused when he had started setting the stone around the side of the veranda closest to the market. The sounds and smells and the constant flow of people there kept dragging his attention away. The middle of the morning always seemed to be the best time to take a short break and watch the spectacle unfold on the cobblestone streets of Etharath's largest city. Now was close enough to mid-morning for his taste. He removed his leather apron, wrapped his chisels and short-handled sledgehammer in it, and set the bundle just out of sight behind the railing. He pushed his sandy brown hair out of his eyes and lifted up his shirttail to remove the coin pouch tied to his leather belt. He dug around in it and found a small coin, put a smile on his face, and walked toward the marketplace in hopes of buying a couple of apples or possibly some bread.

Cayden made his way toward a little stand where he'd found apples the day before, basking in the carnival atmosphere of Rion's central market. Traders making their way through the causeways between the temples shouted out their barter in almost barbaric cries.

Suddenly, above the din, there was a clap of sound so thunderous that the marketplace came to a standstill. Faces turned to the skies in amazement, and a deep red sunlight cast an eerie shadow over the traders and their customers.

"What is this?" one asked, pointing out the blood-red and blackening sky. Before Cayden could answer, a second burst of energy swept across the land. This one pushed them all from their feet in a wave.

The great Temple of Rion rocked on its foundations, breaking the relief of heroes stretched across its pediment from its mounting. The huge stone relief flipped over in midair, and crashed upon dozens of onlookers with a sickening thud. It sank in the cobblestone face up, carnage spraying from beneath its weight.

Cayden staggered to his feet. He felt something warm and sticky on his cheek and looked down at the splatter of blood on his boots. Everything inside him said to run, but he could not move. Those fleeing zigzagged around him in a blur, but he could only look across the horizon at the toppling structures that signaled the end of an age.

Someone collided with Cayden and nearly knocked him off his feet, but the force of the collision seemed to snap him back to reality. He spun around, disoriented, and then a crowd moving toward the temple swept upon him.

"No! Get away from the temple!" he yelled, trying to dig in and hold his ground. But the wave of bodies, almost knocking him down, continued pushing him toward the temple steps until a loud popping sound made all of them freeze where they stood.

Sandy dust sprayed his face from above. The columns on either side of the temple entrance were cracking under the stress. Before he could make a sound, a large shard of marble broke away from the column, ricocheted off the temple steps, and cut effortlessly through the crowd, narrowly missing him.

Bodies pinned him to the ground, almost smothering him. He had always been a little claustrophobic, and the weight of the bodies was crushing him. There was crying and moaning, and the knot of people writhed on top of him. He heard a voice yelling to get up; it might have been his. Using all his might and will, Cayden pushed a limp body out of the way. He pushed his head out into the air, clawed his way out of the pile, and crawled over stunned, wounded, and dying people to get to his feet. He began running toward the southern side of the city with abandon.

On either side of him, the great architecture of Rion was falling like wheat to the great scythe that was the fury of the Mourner's Fault. A billowing cloud of ash rushed in from the north and engulfed them, and Cayden had to feel his way along in front of him, blindly stumbling along the path between the row houses. To his left, a mother screamed for her children. Somewhere south of him, a man was shouting curses.

There was suddenly a clearing in the haze and Cayden could see where he was.

"The end is upon us!" a man with his hands raised to the sky cried. "Our sins have convicted us!"

A second man appeared beside him and fell upon his knees. "We are doomed!" he yelled. "We have forgotten our heritage with the Creator, and now we reap our penance!"

Cayden darted past them in a dead run, screaming, "Run you fools!"

The two men tore their clothes, ignoring him. They pounded their hands against their foreheads in repentance, never seeing the massive column that silently lumbered forward on its pedestal, crushing them where they knelt.

Another rolling spasm of the land threw Cayden in the air. He skidded to a landing on his back and opened his eyes. The blood red skies were streaked with smoky trails of flaming magma shooting into the air north of Rion. *I must make it to the sea,* he thought, forcing himself to get up and run south again.

Molten stone began to drop around him. A small piece landed on his shoulder and burned through his leather vest, searing his skin. He kept running, scratching and clawing at the incredible pain coming from the burning hole in his vest. He scraped the small, greyish stone out with his fingernails, oblivious to the burning sensations in his fingers, and he flew toward the cliffs of Rion.

Exhaustion slowed his pace, and then the sound of the masses exiting Rion behind him became deafening. Cayden pushed himself even harder to avoid them trampling him.

Rifts suddenly split the ground. Some were tiny cracks, but others were almost three feet across, spewing hot gases from within their depths into the fleeing masses, the intense heat searing their lungs with a single breath.

Just when Cayden began to believe the burning in his lungs and side would overcome him, he came upon the servants' quarters that lay southeast of the city, near the sheer cliffs leading down to the sea. He thought he might stop to catch his breath, but he kept moving. There were stairs that zigzagged down the side of the cliffs. Cayden hoped to find a vessel in which he could move away from the destruction and out to sea until the quakes ended.

Cayden stopped once again to catch his breath. The fishermen and stone masons whose livelihoods came from the quarries and seas to the south stood among the rubble of their shanties, watching the great city fall. Their mouths hung open in disbelief of what they were witnessing. Mothers covered their distressed children's ears so they could not hear the cries of agony that echoed from the north.

"The whole world is running toward us, Mommy!" one of the children cried just as one of those fleeing ran into his mother and knocked her to the ground. Cayden started toward her, but one of the men grabbed her and helped her to her feet. The fleeing mob was forcing them closer and closer to the sheer cliffs of Rion's southern border.

"You've got to get out of here!" Cayden yelled.

"But our masters . . ." one began.

"Wait no more!" Cayden interrupted. "I've come from the city. All is lost!" They themselves looked lost at his saying this, and Cayden grabbed the man closest to him. "To the docks! It is their only hope!"

The man appeared to regain his senses and called out to the others, "Flee! Flee to the docks!" Several others took the cue and surrounded the women and children, walking, and then grabbing up their children and running to the cliff stairs.

Cayden reached the staircase landing and looked over the railing. The sea itself seemed tossed in the turmoil. He could see the Rionese galleons straining against their moorings in the docks some three hundred feet below.

There are so few boats, he thought. He looked back toward Rion and saw a seemingly endless flow of people evacuating the city, and then he bolted down the stairs.

He rounded the second turn in the long staircase that cut into Rion's sheer cliffs and glanced up. Above him, the stairs were flooded with all walks of life—the rich, the poor, laborers and gentleman—all rushing down in hopes of boarding the ships below. Some stumbled on the narrow stairs and fell past him to their deaths, others collapsed on the stairs in exhaustion. Cayden ran with every ounce of energy that he had left into the third and final turn and managed to make his way to the head of the pack.

With each rumble of the earth, the staircase cracked and split, and he heard the collective screams of the crowds in response. Crumbling pieces of stonework were falling all around them, but the crowd choked the steps, and now some of those caught up in the knots of fleeing people screamed against the crushing weight of the vastly overcrowded staircase.

When Cayden finally reached the docks, he ran down the long central pier, away from the cliff walls. Several of the ships had already moved out to sea.

There was suddenly a strong aftershock, and Cayden again heard loud screams from behind him. He turned back toward the cliffs in time to see the upper section of the crowded stone stairs tearing away from the cliffs, the volume of screams increasing with its descent toward him. The massive upper section of steps struck the next lower section, and that rubble caught the center of the lower third. Bodies fell into the sea or burst upon the wooden decks of the harbor, and debris buried the four ships closest to the staircase. The decking broke loose from the shoreline in several places, but Cayden managed to leap onto the rope ladder thrown over the side of the nearest ship. He pulled himself over the side as a second wall of stone collapsed into the sea.

"Come on!" Cayden yelled, waving the terrified people toward one of the boats. "We have room for more here!" The throng scrambled into the boat, falling over each other in their panic. "Hurry, we must clear the harbor!" he yelled. "Move to the front! More can get in!"

Cayden could see a young woman on the dock scanning the expanse of the staircase, her panicked eyes dancing back and forth, up and down their length. Her baby was crying, screaming even. They met eyes, but she looked at the thickening throng attempting to board the larger ship Cayden occupied, and she hesitated.

"Come on, lady!" he yelled to her, but her face appeared as if she thought that she'd no chance of getting on it. She turned and moved toward a second boat across the docks, where a small group was throwing off the moorings in preparation to leave.

Cayden continued pulling others into the boat when he heard a man in the opposite boat shriek, "Get back!"

He turned to see the woman fall back upon the dock, her child screaming in her arms. The quakes rippled the docks beneath her, several boards ripping loose with the great strain of the sea's surge.

"Get out of the way!" he heard someone yell from behind him, and several men were pushing long wooden beams into a capstan in the middle of the ship.

"Warp her!" another yelled and several of the men began straining against the horizontal beams, turning the capstan ever so slowly, pulling tight a heavy rope that ran along the deck and out the rear of the boat.

"Wait!" Cayden yelled, but the boat had already started back from the dock, and the deck was jammed with people. He scanned the deck for another way across and saw that there was a longboat suspended on ropes just over the railing. He jumped upon the railing and tip-toed across it before jumping into the longboat, but he couldn't figure out how to lower it.

Her shrill scream made him look over the side. She held the baby at arm's length toward the man. "Please, sir, take my child!" she begged.

"Get back!" the man yelled again. He and three others used oars to push against the dock, and their small ship drifted away from her.

The woman drew her child to her chest, and she fell back upon the sea-smoothed wooden slats that made up the dock, trying to comfort her screaming child. People were jumping over her into the ocean in chase of the departing boats.

Cayden was still fumbling with the winches to lower his boat, when he and the man in the other boat met eyes. The man dropped his gaze in shame. Cayden was looking right at him when a great piece of stone fell from the cliff walls and struck them amidships, dragging the wreckage to the bottom of the harbor.

The crash of the stone surged the waters of the harbor, tearing away the dock, carrying the woman and child away from the shore with a great wave.

Three other men jumped from the deck into Cayden's longboat and began helping him work the winches to lower it. The section of the dock turned slightly and Cayden could see her face for a moment. She had closed her eyes, and it appeared to him that she had exhausted her will to live, but the sound of her son's choking on the water snapped her back into action. She rolled over and pushed his head above the water, and her own face sank beneath the waves. She grasped him beneath his armpit, and he writhed in her hands, his tiny fingers pinching the skin of her arm with all their tiny might.

"Come up!" he yelled, but the woman's arm continued to sink, until the baby's feet splashed the water furiously. Cayden's longboat had just reached them when the hand relaxed and the baby eased under the waves.

Cayden thrust his hand into the water, and though he worried that his strong grip would break the child's arm, he grabbed him and pulled him above the stirring waves. "Help me!" Cayden yelled.

One of the other men sprang to his side. Cayden thrust the crying baby toward him. "Take him!" he cried, and then he turned to the frothy ocean.

The child's mother had disappeared in the darkness of the depths, and without thinking, Cayden leapt overboard. He was not a swimmer, but the urgency of saving her overcame his fear for his own life.

The stormy sounds of Rion's destruction left his ears for the deep hum of the ocean's weighty water. He opened his eyes to their salty sting and caught the wispy movement of her dress descending into the darkness. He kicked with all his might, pulling the water toward him with the sweep of his arms. His boots and clothing seemed to fight his movement toward her, his exertions forcing the air in his lungs to bubble from his nose. His eyes widened with the thought that he was descending beyond his ability to return, and his kicks shortened. He was sure he was going to gasp, going to fill his lungs full of water.

Suddenly he saw her kick spasmodically. Her body turned in the water, bringing one of her legs just within reach. He grasped it, and the weight of her body made him continue to descend against his efforts to pull her to the surface. The pressure of the water pushed some of the air from his lungs, and panic gripped him. Only the outline of the boat's hull stood out against the bright surface of the water above, its ghostly shadow leading back to his salvation.

He looked at the distant hull and resolved that his strength was no match for its distance, and he stopped struggling and pulled her toward him, wanting to look at her face before darkness overcame them.

He brought her upright, and a *thunk* vibrated the water. The longboat's anchor came rushing toward them, narrowly missing them and disappearing past them in the darkness below.

The anchor rope snapped taut before him. He grabbed it and struggled with all his remaining strength to pull them upward, when suddenly it began to move in his hand, burning even his rough palm with its gnarled fibers. In response, he clutched it even tighter, a death grip on life itself, and he zoomed toward the surface with the ascending rope. He could almost make out the men, their broken image dancing in the rippling waves, but he could take it no longer, and the gasp he had fought so hard came involuntarily. The sensation of water filling his lungs made him convulse, and his own survival instinct overwhelmed him again. He lost his grip on the rope. Three or four splashes and bursts of bubbles appeared in the water, and then everything went black.

*   *   *

Cayden awoke on the deck of the ship. He coughed the seawater from his lungs and choked on the air that replaced it. There was a blur of faces over him.

"It's a miracle!" someone said.

"Stand back! Stand back! Let the air come to him!" another yelled. They turned their attention to the woman, still lifelessly sprawled on the rough deck of the ship.

Cayden rolled to his side, his focus returned just in time to see water issue from the woman's nose and mouth. She too gasped for air.

"The Creator be praised!" one woman said, but attention instantly shifted away from them. Her voice was drowned out by the needs of the boat itself.

"Man the sails!" the sailors cried.

"The kedging anchor is up, captain!" one of the men yelled.

"Secure the capstan! Out to sea!" another responded. "Away from the cliffs!"

Cayden watched the young mother's face roll toward the deck. Her nose crumpled against the hard planks. He coughed again, and remnants of the seawater burned his nose and throat. Through his bloodshot eyes, he could see that she was alive, her chest rising and falling sporadically. It was enough, he thought, and he rolled to his back and watched the sails blossom against the stormy clouds, and the makeshift crew blurring past him in all directions.

Cayden's head bobbed with the snap of the sails. He could actually feel the boat's lurch forward, straining timbers connected to the mast beside him. Faintly, he could hear the slap of water against the bow. The cool breeze rushing over him brought the strong smell of fish and sea. He didn't have the energy to turn his head toward Rion, but he could still hear its loud explosions over the orders being shouted by the seafarers among them.

Another young woman sat down cross-legged on the deck between him and the rescued mother. Her simple tunic told him that she was likely a servant in the temples, but she tucked one side of her long brown hair behind her ear, exposing her rosy cheeks and comforting smile. Cayden thought her face shone. She carried the small child Cayden had rescued. The baby was sound asleep in her arms, and she was focused on his every movement.

"Is the baby, alright?" Cayden managed.

As if noticing Cayden only then, she adjusted her skirt to cover her legs and smiled. "Yes, thanks to you." He struggled to sit up, but she placed a hand gently on his chest. "You must rest."

He lay his head back against the deck. "I'll be fine," he said.

"What's your name?" she asked.

"Cayden." He folded his hands behind his head, but he found no comfort in them, so he rolled over on his side and wiped the water from his face with one hand.

"I am Nara," she said. "You're from Rion?"

"Yes. I am . . ." he began. "I *was* a mason there." He looked toward the cliffs of Rion. Smoke and ash could still be seen rising into the air, though they were now miles from shore. "I'm afraid there will not be a Rion to which we may return. Even if there were, my father's fathers spent many years carving out the stairs to the ocean. Without them, there is no way to ascend the steep cliff walls."

"The captain says that we must round all of Etharath in the west, where the cliffs turn to shores," Nara said, looking west. Her face suddenly stretched tight with anxiety. "I've never been on a sailing ship before." She pulled the swaddling cloth tightly around the child.

The rescued woman stirred, and Cayden attempted to prop himself up on one elbow. "You gave us quite a scare," he said.

The woman's eyes closed slowly and then shot open. She struggled to rise. "Where's Ronan?" she asked. "My baby!"

Nara moved closer and lowered the sleeping child by her side. "The baby is fine. He sleeps."

The woman sighed deeply and pulled Ronan tight to her bosom, and then suddenly, burst into tears. Nara stroked her fine, blond hair, its wet braids slowly unraveling to her shoulders. She had a thin, gold chain around her neck that the baby was toying with in his sleep.

"Everything's going to be fine," Nara said. She nodded to Cayden.

"Your baby's safe and you as well, thanks to . . . Cayden," she said.

"I give thanks to the Creator for sparing our lives," Cayden added. He smiled and looked to the sky. "I should not want to test his mercy in that way again," he said. He rolled his head back to face her, and their eyes met. Cayden smiled. "Now Nara and I know your *child's* name, but not yours."

She did her best to stop her tears. "I'm Jalin," she said.

With a sudden, girlish giddiness, Nara called out, "The boat's leaving the cliffs. We're heading for the western coast!"

Jalin's eyes sprang to life. "I can't leave Rion!" she cried. She attempted to stand up, but her legs were still too weak. "My husband—wait! I have to wait!"

Cayden looked at Nara. "Oh, no," he uttered before he had realized it.

Jalin saw the strange look on Cayden's face. "What?" she asked.

Cayden couldn't lie to her. "There's nothing left of the stairs in the southern cliffs. There's no way back to Rion that way. We are going west, where the cliffs end."

Jalin stared at him, speechless. She glanced from Cayden to Nara, shaking her head in denial. He reached out a hand to comfort her.

She pulled away. "No!" she screamed. "My husband works off our debt north of Rion. How will he find us now?"

Cayden let his hand drop. "I don't know. I'm sorry."

Jalin doubled over as if she'd been punched in the stomach. Her mouth opened, but she made no sound, and then deep within her, a moan worked its way to some volume, loud enough that several of the sailors paused to see what was happening.

Nara picked up the baby and rocked him, but the sound of his mother's voice stirred the child to crying himself.

"Oh, Jalin!" Nara said. "I'm so sorry."

Though Nara was able to calm Ronan after a short time, Jalin cried for nearly a solid hour. An hour more, and Jalin became quiet. She stared into the distance, watching the horizon rise and fall just over the port rail. "My actions shame me. When the water covered me, I just gave up. I always thought I would struggle until the very end, but I just gave up."

"Feel no shame," Cayden interjected. "Even the bravest warriors ran for their lives today."

"Thank you for saving us," Jalin responded. "Saying it is not enough. I've no words to tell you how thankful I am."

"I'm glad that you both are safe. Forget about it. Anyone would have done the same."

"I wish that were true," Jalin said. "But you saw that madness at the docks. Even with a child in my arms, I was turned away."

"They paid for their cruelty," said Cayden.

"Some have said the evil of men has brought the Creator's wrath upon us," Jalin said. "That we have brought all this upon ourselves."

"I don't believe that," Cayden said. "Evil and good alike died today."

"Enough talk then," one of the men said, and then he rose from the deck's hatch and crossed the deck toward them. "Your philosophizing won't bring us to the Western Shore."

"Leave 'em be, Tadhra," another responded. "We've enough men to raise the sails—that's good enough for now. Captain's got to shoot the stars."

"Well, he'd better be about it," Tadhra replied. "There's little food on board, and sailing or no, this bunch will want to eat."

"Yeah, yeah, why don't you tell the captain to 'urry then. But call me first—I want to be there when he beats the fool outta ya," the man said. He laughed deep and hearty, much to Tadhra's chagrin. The sailors among them laughed loudly, but Cayden, Nara, and Jalin remained silent.

"Drag the nets as we go!" the captain yelled from the stern, and the sailors pulled the nets from the stowage chests.

"Drag the nets as we run!" the order repeated round the ship.

"These nets are only big enough to slow us down!" Tadhra complained.

"Watch yourself!" one of the other sailors yelled, ignoring Tadhra.

Tadhra drew the nets up on the short starboard mast that swung out over the side, watching the bubble mounted on the side of the bow upper deck. "Get the port mast out! Keep the bubble!" he yelled. The bubble slid starboard with the movement of the nets and the starboard mast.

"Aye!" came the response, and the port mast swung into position and the bubble slowly recentered.

"Let 'em down!" the first officer yelled and the nets were released. The winches whined and spun. "Not too deep!" the officer yelled and two of the sailors applied the winch brakes. The officer watched the bubble. "A little deeper on the port side!" he cried, and the sailors hand-cranked the port winch in response. Again, the bubble came to the center. The first officer raised his hand. "Lock 'em down!" he yelled.

The officer moved past Cayden. "Ever been on a ship?" he shouted.

"No, sir, but I'm willing to help," Cayden responded.

He pointed the bubble out to Cayden. "Watch the bubble—that there. If that changes, you yell out!" he said gruffly, and then he paused to check for Cayden's understanding.

"I can do that," Cayden responded. The first officer said nothing in reply, but walked quickly toward the stern. Just as quickly, he ascended the three stairs rising from the amidships deck to the stern deck and approached the captain. Jalin and Nara sat with Ro against the port railing, and Cayden watched the bubble intently as he had promised, but their position amidships put them right in the middle of the action, listening intently to the sailors around them trying to understand what all was happening.

"Nets are running, captain," the first officer reported.

"Very well, Markston," the captain said, and then he turned to a young lad at his side. "Fetch me my sextant, boy."

The young one scrambled. "Yes, sir!" he said, practically jumping down the stern deck stairs and bolting into the cabin below.

"We make our way round the cliffs, Markston," the captain said, pointing to the west. The boy reappeared with his sextant, his small chest huffing the air.

"Thank you, lad," the captain said, and then he scanned the sky.

"Give them nets an hour and bring 'em up. Perhaps the women can make themselves useful with the catch," he said. "Don't leave much to the land dwellers and my bubble."

"Aye, captain," Markston replied.

"And watch the tension on those nets' masts. Snap one off, and we go hungry."

"Aye, captain," Markston replied. He made his way back toward the bow and Cayden's intent watch of the bubble. "I've got this. Help the women until the nets come in."

"Of course," Cayden responded, and he, Nara, and Jalin made their own way back amidships, joining the group of townspeople standing there. Jalin was struggling with Ro, and Cayden thought that she was not looking very well. She was turning a green color.

He placed one hand on Jalin's shoulder. "Feeling any better?" he asked. "This is madness." She smiled weakly. "The baby is doing fine, and I feel as if I'm going to be sick."

"Let me hold him," Cayden said. He nodded to Nara. "Perhaps Nara can help you?" he asked. "I think there's some privacy on the bow of the ship, behind the mermaid."

"Mermaid?" asked Nara.

"That wood carving—on the front of the ship."

"Yes, of course. Come, Jalin," Nara said. She took her hand, and they made their way forward, around the starboard side to the wooden trellis that wrapped around the bow.

Cayden sat on the deck with Ronan in his arms, admiring how the rocking motion of the boat did not seem to bother him in the least. There had been times when Cayden had felt a bit of dizziness, especially when the sea kicked up and sloshed the boat about, but it had passed.

He touched the baby's cheek and marveled at his tiny fingers. Suddenly the little hand grasped Cayden's finger tightly, even though the baby was still fast asleep.

A smile formed on Cayden's face. "You're a strong one," he said. Out of the corner of his eye, he saw Nara helping Jalin back across the deck toward him. Jalin held one hand out in front of her. She carefully made her way back to Cayden and sat down.

"Any better?" he asked.

"No," Jalin said. "I feel awful."

"You're all wet," Cayden said.

"We stepped on the slats, and water shot up through the trellis."

"The rocking motion got the better of me, and I got very sick," said Jalin. "Thank you for holding my dress back."

"Of course," Nara replied.

A belch slipped out of Jalin's mouth, the taste of which seemed terrible. "I'm sorry," she said. "Oh, this is awful. I've nothing more in my stomach, and I still feel as if I must retch."

"Seasickness—they say it's the worst of all," Nara said.

"See if you can sleep. Nara and I can watch the boy," said Cayden.

"Well . . ." she said almost cautiously.

"It's okay, really," Nara added. "We'll be fine."

Jalin looked at the baby cuddled tightly in Cayden's arms. "Well, maybe for just a little while."

"Sure, then, just for a little while," Nara said.

The first officer walked back by them and pointed to the deck hatch. "Why don't you take the women below?" he asked. "There are hammocks in the galley area. The missus looks a little under the weather, and there'll be fish on the deck soon. I'll need you out of the way for the catch to come in."

"Yes, sir," Cayden answered, and then he moved to the deck hatch with Ro and nodded Nara and Jalin over. "Hold him, Nara," he said. He handed over the baby and lifted the heavy hatch, holding it open for the women and the child. They descended into the depths of the boat, and Cayden let the heavy deck hatch fall back into place.

The first officer squatted down to look through the deck hatch lattice. "Latch it and stand back," he added. "Lest you want to get wet. All men will be on deck to bring in the nets, and the captain will expect all the women to work the fish. The missus with the child and her friend can take turns below with the child. Don't bring him on the deck then—too much going on then, you know."

"Yes, sir," they responded.

The cargo hatch let a little light around the middle of the galley, and it took a minute for their eyes to adjust to the dim light. Cayden noticed the hammocks piled in the floor next to the Healer's quarters. He grabbed one up and hooked the ropes' eyes to two hooks in the ceiling.

Jalin climbed in the hammock and closed her eyes. The hammock gently resisted the motion of the ship. "Yes, that's much better already," she said. Cayden and Nara sat down at a small table bolted to the floor of the galley. She glanced at Ronan once or twice as if confirming Nara was attentive to him, and within minutes, Jalin and Ro were asleep.

Cayden's curiosity got the better of him, and he began looking around the galley. "You'd think with all the water I just ingested, thirst would be the last thing on my mind, but to tell you the truth, I'm parched." He meandered over to a barrel next to the iron stove in the center of the ship's galley, opened it, and the smell of hops hit him. "Well, here's something," he said. He eyed a ladle and scooped up a bit of the fermentation. He found a mug along the side of the mess area oven, filled it with the ladle, and took a long gulp. He grimaced and let the remainder of his mouthful spill back into the mug.

Nara giggled at his expression.

"This is nasty!" he exclaimed, and then he looked for a place to throw it out, but seeing none, made his way to the Healer's quarters, a small room on the port side of the ship.

The small quarters smelled rank indeed, but there was a small porthole. He thought to unlatch it and pour out the ale—or whatever they called the concoction—but when he entered the cabin, his eyes adjusted to the even dimmer lighting within. He saw implements of the Healer—saws and clamps and a leather-covered mallet. He noticed a darkly stained bench along the wall and conjured up images of the gruesome medical attention provided there. He quickly opened the small porthole and tossed out the remainder of his mug.

Through the porthole, Cayden could see a number of boats with people scattered throughout the rigging. They were apparently clueless of its operation, and their ships were drifting dangerously close to the rocks that lined the Rionese cliffs. Ropes connected two of the boats, and there appeared to be an all-out fight occurring on their decks. He could faintly hear the men shouting and the women screaming. He closed the small porthole and returned to the galley.

"Stay here," Cayden told Nara and Jalin, and then he made his way up the stairs back to the deck. Upon emerging topside, he called out to the first officer. He pointed to the warring boats in the distance. "Sir, those people are in trouble!" he said.

"Best that you go below," the first officer said firmly.

"But sir, we should help—"

"You see the size of that boat, sir?" the first officer retorted. "Do you see that their men outnumber our own?" he asked. "What would you do? Would you be willing to lose our ship to them as well? I'm sorry, sir, but these are desperate times. We'll not be moving off our course for the western shores. This is a fishing vessel and no warship—we've no weapons, save the few we carry ourselves. We run fast, as fast as we can to the western shores."

"I should speak to the captain," said Cayden.

The first officer looked him in the eye. "I'll not be bothering the captain," he said. "He's fully aware of what is transpiring around us. If he wanted us to board her, the order'd been given before now. So I'll be asking you again to go below, sir." With this, his face hardened and his open palm pointed the way back to the galley hatch.

"Very well," Cayden said, wishing no more quarrel. He looked around once again at the mad scene of the ragtag Rionese flotilla with its infighting, sinking boats, and general insanity. Feeling absolutely overwhelmed, he descended the stairs into the ship's galley without so much as a glance back.

Chapter Three

Boundland

Amphileph had taken more time than he would have liked to lock down the temple and direct the Camonra to stand guard. The slave, Galbard, had been gone for nearly half the day. His jaw tightened, and his fingers drummed a sharp, irritated rhythm against his robe. He wanted to join the other Spellmakers in the catacombs below the temple, where the coven had combined forces in the altar room constructed directly below the temple floor.

The catacombs' stench nauseated him, but he had ordered the Spellmakers' coven deep within their walls so they could focus on casting the spells of *Ponto Lethargus* and *Absconditus* on Evliit. His head pounded from hours of intense concentration. Distracted, he stepped in what he could only hope was water, soaking the leather of his left sandal before he jerked it back out of the puddle. Cursing, he looked around, eager to vent his frustration on the nearest slave.

The entire temple suddenly began to shake violently. Rubble and mortar trickled from every joint in the stonework. Dust filled the air in the catacombs.

Amphileph held up his hand to shift the micro currents in the air and the polarity of the particles. The dust parted, revealing the load-bearing arches in the crisscrossing halls. The massive stones still held firm, so he stood his ground. He could hear other Spellmakers yelling, but before he could make his way to the room they occupied, the quakes' crescendo suddenly ended.

He stood perfectly still.

Something monumental had taken place—the shift in spiritual energy was unlike anything he had felt before. He could no longer sense Evliit's life force. It was as if he could feel only the *absence* of Evliit.

Surely the great quakes signaled Amphileph's victory! Now the great city of Rion—the patron city of the Elders, those human ingrates who dared challenge his right to determine the future of humanity—yes, Rion would also fall. The Rion Guard had risen against his creation of the Camonra, and for this, he would destroy them.

Amphileph hurried to the other Spellmakers, whom he was sure were still huddled in the altar room, frightened for their lives. They barely had the stomach to do the real work required to correct the course of Etharath's history.

He passed one of the alchemy laboratories where several of the Camon jailers were attempting to put out a fire, apparently caused by some glass tubing and beakers shattering during the quake. Slaves were screaming for release from their cages before the fires consumed them, but he had no time to deal with that either. He could rebuild the lab, and there were always enough slaves to go around.

At last, he arrived at the conjuring room in the innermost section of the catacombs. The Spellmakers were scattered among its ornate wooden kneeling rails and prayer rails, most of them wearing their white prayer robes. Some had collapsed across the rails, but most still knelt at them, elbows up and hands clasped, head lowered to the image of a sword etched into a large stone altar at the far end of the room.

"Do you feel it, brothers?" Amphileph asked, entering the room, smiling broadly. "What we have accomplished in the darkness will soon be known by all! Soon we'll have the Sword of the Watch!"

Amphileph grabbed Clogren, his trusted student, by the shoulders. "Rise, my brothers!" Amphileph said. "This is a glorious day!" He thought Clogren looked especially weak; the conjuring that had overcome Evliit had been strong magic indeed, and Clogren was committed to him to the death.

Clogren struggled to his feet, pulling up the oversized sleeves of his prayer robes. "Master, you have shown them once and for all that your power knows no limits. The evil of men shall pass away! Now we create the world that should have been." Clogren looked around at his brethren Spellmakers, and then his gleeful look faded. Many of them looked confused and terrified. "Soon everyone will know of our great sacrifice, brothers! The new Erathe will give great honor to the Creator!"

"Yes, yes, of course," Amphileph replied. He reached down to help another to his feet. "Come, let us go to Rion. Let us wear the six colors of tartan and our embroidered robes! We will watch our Camonra destroy the Rion Guard and carry us to the steps of the Elders' temple."

Amphileph turned and exited the altar room, Clogren close on his heels.

They made their way through the twisted catacombs deftly, entered a laboratory, and pushed aside everything cluttering the table. Amphileph poured water into a brass basin. He pointed for Clogren to stand near the end of the table. "Watch and learn," he insisted. Clogren hurried to his assigned spot and leaned over to see the basin.

"*Aperio*," Amphileph said, waving his hand over the basin. The torchlight seemed to dance in the water for a moment, but then the water began to change shape. Figures rose from its surface and slowly took on the forms of the Spellmakers, who one by one lifted their heads and looked at each other. The basin sprang to life, showing Amphileph everything that was happening in the altar room.

"What have we done?" Ardidhus asked. "The slave was only to take the sword while Evliit slept. I have seen a vision of the slave poised to kill Evliit with the Sword of the Watch, and now I do not sense Evliit at all! What have we done?"

"Master . . ." Clogren whispered, then quickly covered his mouth, fearing the basin might somehow allow the other Spellmakers to hear him.

"Quiet!" Amphileph replied. He leaned in slightly closer to the basin.

The other Spellmakers looked away from Ardidhus, moving to one side of the basin and leaving Ardidhus on the other side alone, but he would not stop. "I know that mankind has fallen away from the Creator, but I did not agree to kill Evliit. My mind is clear that I did not speak that spell," Ardidhus said.

With each word, Amphileph felt his anger rising.

The tiny figure of Ardidhus turned in the basin. "We may have agreed to help Amphileph end the evil of man, but we did not intend for Evliit to be injured. His stubbornness notwithstanding, Evliit has not wronged us."

Ardidhus hung his head and spoke softly. Amphileph thought he saw the image wipe away a tear. "Our intent was to prove to Evliit the great good we can do with our alchemy and conjuring," Ardidhus said. "The Creator has given us this knowledge. He intended it for us . . ." His voice trailed off, and he looked away from them.

"Enough!" Amphileph said, and the figures disappeared with a splash. He swatted the basin across the room.

"Come with me!" he said, grabbing Clogren's clothes and hurrying out of the laboratory. "The others are coming."

Amphileph and Clogren quickly made their way through the catacombs and exited the temple, squinting in the bright sun. To the south, in the direction of Rion, Amphileph saw the other Spellmakers exiting the temple. They looked back at him, then began murmuring among themselves. They had done the same after the previous attempt at stealing Evliit's Sword, when Citanth, their fellow Spellmaker, was drained of his powers by merely touching it. The skin of his hand had bubbled and fallen off like hot cheese, leaving it useless, and Citanth had barely survived the encounter.

They knew he had sent the slave to *kill* Evliit this time. They were talking about him, he was sure. And they were gathering against him, Ardidhus at the forefront.

Amphileph drew in a slow breath. "Even with most gone to Rion, the reek of the Camonra still clings to this place," he said. He looked back at the group and thought to himself how they had always envied his abilities.

"I ordered all but the temple guard to move to the northern camp near the Black Mountains. Let Citanth bathe in their stench."

"Our brother is delirious with pain, master, he worries not for any smell," said Clogren with a chuckle.

"He has failed me!" Amphileph shouted back. "Let the Camonra females care for him! I don't even want to see his face! Let him tend to the fires with the old and the pregnant!"

A Camon runner approaching from the north interrupted them.

"Father!" the runner said, bowing at Amphileph's feet.

"What is it?" Clogren retorted. "The master cannot be bothered now!"

"Forgive me, but you must come toward the northern camp!" the runner said.

"I should strike you dead!" Clogren yelled. "You do not say what we must do!"

"Calm yourself, Clogren. What is it?" Amphileph interrupted.

"Father, there is no path to the northern camp!"

"What is that you say?" Clogren asked.

"I have no words for what happens, Father. I can only show," the Camon replied, shielding his face from the wrath of Amphileph.

"Show me now!" Amphileph commanded.

"Yes, Father!" the Camon responded and immediately turned and headed toward the northern camp.

"The other Spellmakers have noted the commotion," said Amphileph, nodding toward Ardidhus and the others. Other Camon runners appeared as if bearing news, but stopped to clear a path for Amphileph and the other fathers.

About a hundred yards from the temple, the Camonra camp came into view. A second group had formed on the southern side of the camp.

They looked perplexed, pacing back and forth across the path.

Clogren and Amphileph suddenly slowed to a stop some ten feet from them.

"Father, we cannot pass!" one of the Camonra cried out to Amphileph. Stepping back and taking a knee with his comrades, the lot of them lowered their heads. Amphileph paid them no mind and moved toward the northern camp with purpose. In mid-step, Amphileph stopped and put his hands out before him, then stepped back. "What is this?" he asked.

"Master?" Clogren inquired.

Amphileph's hands began to glow red, and he thrust them forward before his body, but it was as if his hands hit an invisible wall, the red glow of his hands dissipating across its unseen surface.

"No!" Amphileph shouted.

Ardidhus and the other Spellmakers stopped behind him, giving him some space. Amphileph stepped back and paced parallel to the barrier. "No!" he repeated, and then he suddenly thrust his hands against the barrier. The aura around his hands burst forth a bright red light that spread throughout the barrier, momentarily giving it some opacity and form. He could see the energy crawling along its surface, arching upward and back over them nearly fifty feet in the air.

"So Evliit's followers mean to bind us, do they?" Amphileph asked with a grating laugh. "Fools!" he said. He summoned one of the Camonra. "Have your soldiers determine the extent of this barrier," Amphileph ordered, and then he stormed off toward the temple, almost colliding with Ardidhus and the other Spellmakers.

"Amphileph, we need to speak with you," Ardidhus said.

"This is not the time—" Clogren began.

Ardidhus cut him off. "This *is* the time!" He stared menacingly at Clogren, and the latter moved back. "Can you not see that the Watchers have gathered against us? Can you not see the irony in it? Those whom we could not convince to make spells have cast a spell of Binding upon us!" he broke into nervous laughter. "They have bound us in our own temple!"

"What do you need, Ardidhus?" Amphileph asked.

"What do I need?" Ardidhus demanded. "Let us begin with this question, Amphileph: where is the Sword of the Watch?" The group of Watchers closed in behind him. "Where is this man, this slave, Galbard, and where is the Sword?"

Amphileph's jaw tightened. "Are you questioning the path you've chosen, brother?"

"It is true that we chose to join with you, to end this fallen race of men, and it was we who stood beside you when Evliit questioned the creation of the Camonra. We were the ones that believed we could bring honor to the Creator with the purity of a new race. We *all* agreed that it was time to bring about that new beginning, but . . ."

"But?" Amphileph moved in closer to Ardidhus.

Ardidhus pulled at his clothing as if he began to feel heat rising around the collar of his cloak. He glanced back at the other Spellmakers to renew his confidence. "We have seen the man Galbard standing over Evliit with the sword poised over him—ready to kill him, Amphileph! Why would we see such a vision? We never agreed to any violence against our own."

Amphileph almost smiled at how terrified Ardidhus looked.

"'Against our *own*?'" he shouted. "'Oh, what have we done? I can no longer sense the spiritual forces of the Watchers!'" said Amphileph, mocking them. "Step back, Ardidhus!"

Ardidhus held his ground. "Not 'what have *we* done,' Amphileph, it's what have *you* done?"

"He would never have joined us!" Amphileph shouted, causing the group of Spellmakers to jump at the sound. "Evliit has forfeited his right to command me by his siding with this heresy called *men*!"

Ardidhus stepped back. "This causes me great sadness. We've all been wrong. This is no great prophet, but merely a man consumed by his own desire for power. Amphileph . . . brother, we were wrong to do this," he said. "We must pray for forgiveness from Evliit and the Creator!"

Ardidhus turned away from Amphileph to seek a response from the other Spellmakers, unaware of the bright glow erupting from Amphileph's hands.

"Wrong?" Amphileph screamed. A burst of energy shot Ardidhus through the air with violent force. In horror, his fellow Spellmakers watched his body smack against the temple stone nearly a hundred yards away. He slid down the temple dome and off onto the ground, crumpling into a pile.

The other Watchers gasped in unison. "No, Amphileph!" they yelled.

"I knew you would turn on me!" Amphileph shrieked.

A blue aura formed before the other Spellmakers just as a second blast of Amphileph's fury struck it in an explosive mix of greenish red plasma, its splatter blackening the dirt it touched. They struggled to maintain their footing and to hold the protective aura with their combined energies, but Amphileph's onslaught began pushing the lot of them back.

"Amphileph, please stop!" one yelled from behind the aura. He thrust his hands downward, raising them with a grasping motion. Roots exploded from the ground and wrapped around Amphileph's arms and waist, squeezing him.

"You will not stop me!" he shouted, but fear welled up in him as the branches curled around his arms and neck, slowing his furious strikes against the aura and then stopping it altogether. Root after root sprang from the ground and latched onto Amphileph until the knotting foliage engulfed him.

In the darkness, Amphileph could still hear the muffled sounds of shouting over the closer creaking of the tightening vines. It was becoming harder and harder to breathe. He imagined the Spellmakers sighing in relief, their fast, heavy breathing telling of their struggle. He could not move at all, but he imagined that several of them were bent over, placing their hands on their knees and catching their breath, allowing their protective aura to dissipate. Panic rose in his throat. He had to think. *Where was Clogren?* He focused his thoughts on his closest disciple.

"Master!" he thought he heard Clogren yell, and then a heavy thump. He was sure Clogren was crying for him. There was more shouting, and Amphileph felt the roots stop their squeezing action. Amphileph moved his arm, and the embrittled roots broke free.

The roots stretched and snapped, and suddenly Amphileph burst forth, sending Clogren flying.

"You would kill me?" he screamed at his associates.

Five of the Spellmakers scrambled back together, re-forming the aura with their combined strength, but a sixth stopped short. Amphileph's energy shot through the man's body.

"He's gone mad!" the Spellmaker cried, grabbing his chest. His face broke out in a cold sweat as he looked at the others, remorse etched across his face. Then he collapsed to the ground.

"You will join him soon enough!" Amphileph cackled at the cluster of Spellmakers, releasing a burst of energy that nearly broke their aural shield.

Amphileph caught movement out of the corner of his eye. A group of Camonra pacing nervously along the outer wall of the Binding. "Father!" they cried repeatedly. One of them trumpeted a call to battle.

"They're summoning the other creatures in the eastern camp!" another of the Spellmakers shouted.

"Do what you can!" another cried. "We can't hold this defense much longer." Two of the Spellmakers stepped back and knelt in prayer, attempting to ignore Amphileph's unending attack.

The dirt at Amphileph's feet began to rise up and take form. With a wave of his hand, Amphileph sent a chunk of the mass splattering into the binding spell's force field. It slowed to a stop before being expelled back out of the field and onto the ground.

The mound of earth sprouted appendages and lashed out at Amphileph.

"You've improved, brothers!" Amphileph shouted. He jumped aside, and the golem's massive arm burst through the tree trunk just beyond the place where he stood.

A second golem rose up from the dirt, and together they seemed poised to neutralize Amphileph's attack, but the Camonra from the eastern camp ran to his aid. They pounced upon the golems without hesitation, stabbing and slicing, clawing and tearing at their earthen bodies. The golems seemed impervious to their attacks, wading through the Camonra in an effort to reach Amphileph, crushing them and batting their lifeless bodies aside. Amphileph rolled away from them and yelled at the Camonra. "Fools! Destroy them!" he said, pointing to the small remaining group of Spellmakers. A blast of energy tore away the upper half of one of the golems, and then the Camonra turned on the Spellmakers themselves.

In terror, the Spellmakers commanded their golems to protect them. Amphileph brushed off his clothes and watched the onslaught. The Camonra swarmed the Spellmakers, jumping back and forth to avoid the golems' attacks. Their scimitars hacked into the Spellmakers' aura, cutting deeper with each strike.

"I cannot hold them!" one of the Spellmakers cried.

"Enough of this!" Amphileph said. He closed his eyes and held his palms together at his chest. The energy engulfed his hands, tinting his face red with the glow. He pushed the energy away from his body with a scream, and a huge energy wave struck the aura, shattering it in a violent explosion. The Camonra quickly closed on the defenseless Spellmakers, their golems disintegrating with their final screams for mercy.

As the commotion ended, Amphileph heard a whimpering sound. "Master!" cried a gurgling voice from Amphileph's left. Amphileph pushed aside the Camonra to find Clogren sprawled upon the ground, fragments of the exploded roots stuck in his face and chest. A large sliver was lodged in his neck like a stake. He was bleeding profusely. "Master, help me!" he said, his wide eyes staring intently at Amphileph.

Amphileph suddenly felt numb. His ears rang. In an afternoon, his plan to dominate the Watchers had not only gone awry, but now he, Clogren, and Citanth alone remained in their pact, and Citanth was in the northern camp, outside the Binding.

"I am here, Clogren. I will save you," Amphileph responded. He closed his eyes and rubbed his hands together, trying desperately to recall a healing incantation, but the words eluded him. He turned and looked at the bloody streak down the temple dome. "Ardidhus?" he called out, and then he turned away from the sight of it, only to recoil from the bloody mess that was once his beloved followers, piled among the dead Camonra. "They challenged me, Clogren. I had no choice. I cannot allow such insurrection. Insurrection cannot be tolerated." He began pulling on his hair. "Clogren?"

Amphileph turned back to see that Clogren struggled for life no longer.

The grunts of the Camonra filled the room with the stench of their breath. "Leave me!" he shouted, but when they moved toward him in concern, he screamed again. "Leave me!" The remaining Camonra ran from him, heading back toward the eastern camp. Within seconds, he was alone, and he sat down on the ground beside Clogren.

Clogren's lifeless eyes gave Amphileph their full attention, and Amphileph continued to talk with him until the sunlight faded from the sky.

CHAPTER FOUR

DISCOVERY

Black soot blotted out the sun at times, choking breath from the air, making Galbard's frantic run to the west even more unbearable. His side burned, and he couldn't summon enough saliva to keep his tongue from sticking to the inside of his mouth. The pounding rhythm of his running droned on, each step vibrating his frame. His joints ached, and the skin on his face and lips had gone numb. Galbard tried to think of anything but the running.

Stopping only to keep his footing during the aftershocks that rippled through the slope, Galbard had descended the mountain's western face with all the speed he had dared attempt, dodging falling stone and dirt that slid off the mountain in whole sections.

When he reached the western foothills of the Black Mountains, he kept running. Sheer exhaustion would have dropped him, but every noise, every crack of a branch, every movement in his peripheral vision drove him onward, fearing that the Camonra were on his heels. Slowing only as he came upon a clearing, he would pause to look this way and that for his pursuers, but then dashed across to the safety of the jungle on the other side. If they discovered him, he was finished.

When he did stop, his legs wobbled or just gave out, and he often fell to the ground. Once, he rolled to his back to catch his breath, but the soot fell like snow, and it made him choke. He was sure he heard the Camonra yelling in the near distance, and he was terrified that any noise might alert his would-be captors. Galbard wiped away the black mud formed from his tears, and he blew black soot from his nose and cleared his throat as quietly as he could. He looked around for any reaction to the noise, but thick, dark smoke hung close to the ground, and his visibility reduced to only a few feet.

After about six hours heading west, he turned southward, hoping to find some relief from the smoke and ash, but found none. *Creator, help me,* he thought. Everything looked so different from he remembered, and he felt so completely lost. Despair was close to overtaking him, but he heard movement in the high grass. Panic surged up to replace it, and he frantically looked around for cover, ducking behind an ancient live oak.

Blackened figures emerged from the foliage. They moved closer, and Galbard could see the dazed look in their bloodshot eyes. Ash muddied their faces. They walked without purpose, barely seeming to notice anything but the larger aftershocks that upset their footing. When they were nearly upon him, he slowly came out from behind the tree and called out to them, hoping not to startle them.

"I mean you no harm," he said. "I am Galbard, from Rion." One of them came to an abrupt stop, while the others completely ignored Galbard and continued north.

"I am Jaradh," said the one who noticed Galbard's presence. He stared into the distance in a way that reminded Galbard of the faces of soldiers he had seen returning from war. "You cannot go that way. The world has opened up and its boiling blood meets with Blue Water—there are great explosions and the land gives way without warning."

"No!" Galbard shouted. His desire to return to Rion had kept him alive when he lived as a slave of Amphileph, and now to learn he was yet denied his return took his breath for a moment. He stopped and stood there, staring at the billowing smoke that blocked his view of Rion.

A young woman stopped beside them. "It is as he says," she announced. Tears streaked her cheeks. "We've no way of returning home. I will never again see my children."

"Have hope," the man said, as if her sadness snapped him from his shock. "You don't know that," he encouraged. "We must find shelter now, and then we'll find a way around them."

"Around them?" Galbard inquired.

"The Inferiors—they were everywhere. The Rion Guard had marched from Rion to meet them in battle north of the city, and then the sky grew red and Erathe shook and ripped apart! It was as if the land fell away . . ." The woman broke down in tears before she could finish.

"You're from Rion, then?" Galbard asked the man. He had not heard the term "Inferior" in a long time. It had been coined by the Rion Elders to describe the Camonra when they first learned of Amphileph's plan to replace humankind. It was not a term of endearment.

"Yes, yes, a fisherman," the man replied. He pointed to the growing number of Rionese who were appearing out of the haze. "Most were servants to the Rion Guard," he said.

Galbard was just beginning to realize the sheer number of people who had fled the city.

The fisherman's eyes grew wide. He blinked with every other word. "The Elders sent large numbers of us to the west and north out of the city before the battle began. Another larger group left about eighteen days before us. They were told to head to the mountains far to the north.

We were to hide in the wood far to the northwest—'Highwood,' it is called—where a clear river splits the ancient forest. But just as we left the city, the Inferiors attacked, and we ran for our lives."

"Erathe split open and swallowed them all!" the woman said, and she burst into tears again.

The man tried to console her. "I am afraid that nothing is as it was," he said to Galbard.

"It is a dark day upon us," Galbard said, wishing he hadn't said it the moment it left his mouth. "It is important for us to keep moving." Even here in the clearing, Galbard felt the searing heat from the ruptured earth in the south. "We need to do as the others—go northwest to Highwood."

"Yes, of course," the man answered, and he talked to the others, very few of whom were armed. They decided it was prudent to follow Galbard, and they set out together toward the northwest.

The thunderous boiling of Erathe and the thick black smoke lessened, but the rain had not. It beat down on them, and after they had walked about twelve leagues, Galbard noticed that their group was falling behind with fatigue.

"Let us rest!" Galbard called out to them, settling beneath an enormous live oak tree to block the stinging rain. He rested his head against the moss-covered trunk of the tree and closed his eyes, listening to the raindrops tapping on the leaves.

The group said nothing, but each one stopped and found cover from the rain, some sitting in the protection of the interwoven ferns and young maples in the understory, some leaning against a stand of bamboo. The exhaustion had stolen their speech. For a few minutes, there was just the rain and their heavy breathing, and then nothing but the rain for nearly an hour more.

After too little rest, the group struggled to their feet and proceeded northwest, but upon arriving at what should have been the lakes, they found that the waters had gathered to overflowing, leaving a single land bridge slightly to the southwest.

Galbard didn't like the thought of moving further south at all. Closer to the Camonra was not a direction he wanted to take. "Where is the fisherman?" Galbard asked.

"Here!" the man answered.

"How far is it around the lakes to the north?"

The man held his hand over his eyes and studied the horizon. "It looks so different," he said. "The northern lake was the largest of the group. If it has overflowed, then it has likely engulfed the smaller lakes and streams. The higher ground to the north would be much closer."

"Let us be about it," Galbard said. He did not like this one bit.

They made their way southwest for another hour, and the pounding rain began to slow. This alone was heartening. They continued west until nightfall, setting watches for the Camonra.

Galbard had not slept in almost three days. His ears had begun to ring, and pain throbbed behind his eyes and temples. The sheer act of lying down without the rain pouring on his face was all it took to send him into a complete blackness that lasted, dreamlessly, until he was awakened for his turn at watch. He wiped the sleep from his face with one hand, jumped up, and took his place.

They had not chanced firelight giving away their position, so Galbard could do nothing but stare out into the black night and listen to the others sleeping against the sounds of the wilderness. Though he felt somewhat renewed after the short sleep, the deep darkness reminded him of his old cell, and it turned his thoughts inward.

He would not tell his fellow travelers that even now, the great good of Erathe, the Watchers, had likely departed. It would break them, and they already stood little, if any, chance of surviving the Camonra who sought to destroy them. He would keep them moving and keep their hope alive.

The sun's pre-dawn light crept across the night sky from the eastern horizon and began its slow illumination of the darkness from deep purples and reds to golden yellow. Galbard was hoping to see the green landscape, but the sunlight instead brought nothing but grays and blacks. As he scanned the brightening panorama from this high point, though, it became clearer that the worst of their travels was behind them to the southeast.

"Two or three days, I figure, to make it to Highwood," one of the refugees said. The fisherman was there, too, smiling and cheerful. Galbard wanted to share his cheer, but that would not happen until they were safely tucked away in the woods with their kinsmen.

"We should take advantage of our good fortune," Galbard said, holding his palm up to the sky.

"No rain is good fortune indeed," said the fisherman. "And the wind picks up at our backs. We should make good time today." He began rousing the weary travelers one by one.

Galbard looked to the east and thought he saw a sudden movement in the far distance. "Wait here," he said to the fisherman, and he walked south. Once he had separated himself from the others, he drew Evliit's sword and continued south for a few minutes more, but he saw nothing.

As he turned around, Galbard noticed the Sword's blade. Along its length, the inscription read: "Vigilant is the Watch. Fearless is the Light. Darkness falters before it."

Courage filled him. "Give me a powerful hand that I might wield your mighty sword," he said quietly. He held the Sword tightly to his body. *I would welcome the Warriors of Light right now,* he thought.

Galbard felt a warm sensation run through his body, its traversing energy making him quiver.

What was that? he thought. He stared at the blade intently. "Camonra na Flodh," he whispered in the old tongue, and the energy wave passed over his body again, emanating from the Sword through his hands and passing up his arms into his chest, and then outward to the top of his head and the bottom of his feet. His eyes widened, locked upon the Sword.

The energy that passed through his body was purifying. He felt energized, revived. *What mysteries have ethereal blacksmiths folded into this blade of Evliit?*

He looked at the dark sky to the southeast and turned his gaze northwest, where a small patch of blue sky still fought against the creeping darkness. It was a sign, he thought, a sign that they needed to move northwest to rejoin the remaining Rionese refugees.

He made his way back into the clearing and walked through the group, making sure the whole group had caught up, and then they all heard a horn in the distance. Galbard recognized it immediately.

"I know all of you are tired, but we must move with all speed to find the remaining refugees from Rion. I don't think that the Inferiors will follow us into Highwood," he said, pointing to the forest in the distance. "We need to move farther north of the fault line, and we need to do it now."

"What was that sound?" a woman asked.

"We need to move," he said. "Now."

Galbard turned and walked briskly toward Highwood. The group assisted each other in rising to their feet, following Galbard in single file or small clusters of two or three, each falling in line behind him. They managed to make it across the open plains, but Galbard kept a close eye on the jungles to the south.

The overflowing banks of the small tributaries made the grasslands a muddy bog, and the footing only improved after they had traveled the remainder of the second day. Sleep was still a luxury they could afford only in shifts, and twice, Galbard was certain he saw lights in the distant jungle. He didn't want to panic his fellow travelers, but he was sure someone was watching them.

On the third day, a rider approached from the west. He wore the armor of the Rion Guard, and he rode toward them with abandon.

"You must hurry. We've spotted the Inferiors' scouts to the south!" the rider said. "You've the better part of a day to reach the woods, but many of us are hiding there. We've food and sanctuary."

"We give thanks to the Creator for you!" one of the refugees shouted.

"Thank him later!" the rider said. He looked to the south. "Get your people to the woods!" he shouted, and then he turned his horse and rode southward.

There was a general frenzy of activity among the group, but Galbard tried to keep the group moving toward the wooded area ahead.

"Men, let the women and children move to the front!" Galbard shouted. "We'll bring up the rear, those with weapons in the very back!" The group's fear quickened their pace. "Look sharp!" Galbard yelled to the men at the rear.

About four hours later, the rider they had seen previously topped the rolling hill just behind them and flew toward them, yelling. "Run!" he said, flying past them. The rider clutched an arrow just behind the tip, which had passed through his right side. "Inferiors!" he screamed between gasps for air. The rider shot toward Highwood without looking back.

The refugees looked back at Galbard, their faces stretched with panic. Galbard assumed that the majority of them had only heard the hair-raising stories of Camonra. Those from the city had likely never actually seen a Camon, but the stories were terrifying enough, and when there was a roar from just behind them, it jolted them all. The entire group, without saying anything, burst into a dead run for the woods.

Galbard sprinted through the high grass toward Highwood, and one of the women fell. "Get up! Keep moving!" he yelled. He was sure he heard at least three distinct Camonra voices closing on them, and he knew they would make swift work of the weary travelers. He pulled her up, and she took off running.

In that moment, Galbard stopped and looked at her turning back in her panic and seeing the Camonra. His mind raced so quickly that she seemed to move in slow motion. He could see her wide-eyed expression and her blanched face with sublime clarity. He turned and looked in the direction of her gaze. There were three of them for sure, coming toward them. They bound toward the fleeing refugees, their heads bobbing above the grass.

"I am your slave no more!" Galbard shouted. He drew Evliit's sword. "I will stand firm here and now!"

The Sword suddenly felt almost weightless, and light converged on the blade and traveled its length.

One of the Camonra screamed his sighting of Galbard to his fellow warriors. Galbard saw them take notice, and he just had time to flinch before an arrow zipped past his head.

A second arrow sprang from the Camon's bow and sped directly toward Galbard's left eye. He turned the blade out from his body, and the arrow's trajectory curved around the Sword and whizzed by in a long, looping arc behind him, gathering speed. It turned back toward the archer, its speed increasing until it became fire.

Galbard swung the tip of the sword around toward the Camon. The bolt of fire shot through the soldier's midsection effortlessly. The Camon fell to his knees, and his leather tunic caught fire around the hole.

The other two Camonra stopped, yelling in ancient Rionese. They moved slowly around the smoldering flames rising from their downed comrade, and they split up. The first circled to his left and the second to his right. The first Camon jumped through the air and swung down upon Galbard's head, the arc of his blade bending around Galbard's Sword to Galbard's left, slicing into the ground with incredible force. The surprised Camon quickly pulled it from the ground, and then Galbard attacked. The Camon raised his sword across his face to parry. Galbard's sword arced downward, its glow intensifying, and then passed through the Camon's blade without slowing, parting his face and jaw, and cutting halfway down the front of his chest armor. Galbard pulled back on the Sword, and the

Camon fell away from him into the grass.

The third and last Camon shrieked and closed on Galbard, but Galbard pivoted around the attacker like a trained swordsman and swung, opening the Camon's chest diagonally. The Camon stopped instantly and fell. Galbard heard him moan and then heard his final breath leave him.

Silence fell. Far off, the Rionese refugees still cried for help. He waited a heartbeat more, but no other Camonra emerged. With a sharp flick, he cast their black blood from the blade and eased the Sword back into its scabbard.

The wind stirred the grass around the motionless bodies. Had it not been for the moments leading up to this, Galbard might have thought the gentle breeze peaceful.

He knelt beside the last attacker and studied his face. The man's eyes were wide, his expression almost surprised — as if even he had not expected the ferocity of the Sword's power. Galbard cast a quick look around and then started running toward Highwood.

He caught up to the group about a hundred yards from Highwood, his breathing heavy. Four of the Guard's cavalry galloped out from the tree line and moved between the last of Galbard's group and the high grass to the east.

"Did you see them?" someone asked.

"Yes," Galbard responded, still debating what to say . . . or whether to say anything.

"How many of them?" a soldier asked, pulling his horse back toward Galbard.

"I saw three."

"You saw them?" the soldier inquired.

"Yes," Galbard said, but the soldier's anxiousness made him stop at that.

"You're to stay here until the captain arrives. Your companions can go."

"He's with us," said the fisherman called Jaradh. "Let him go with us to the forest. We are all exhausted."

"He stays here."

"I'm fine," Galbard said to the fisherman. "I'm right behind you."

The fisherman looked at the soldier's face and relented. "We'll see what shelter we can put together in your absence." The fisherman pursed his lips with dissatisfaction. "Take good care, Galbard," he said, and then he joined the others going into Highwood.

The group looked back at their detained friend. Their hushed conversation faded from earshot. Galbard waved them on and turned his gaze back to the east.

Shortly, several other horsemen rode out of Highwood with their long spears. They and their horses also wore the battle gear of Rion. The soldier who had stopped Galbard yelled to the others, "This one says that at least three are coming!" His fellow soldiers stopped just a few yards from Galbard and shifted nervously in their saddles. They spread out in a short line, and Galbard was thankful that the focus had moved off him and onto another rider who strode toward the group.

"Any sign of them?" the approaching rider asked. Galbard recognized him as a senior officer, the braided mane of his mount visible beneath its faceplate armor.

"No, nothing," the first rider responded.

"Where did you see them?" the officer asked Galbard.

"They were there," Galbard said, pointing to the exact area where in fact they lay dead in the high grass. However, the riders could not see them.

"Ready, men!" the officer said. "Assemble and charge. Keep your spears down and in front. Use the weight of the horse and keep moving," he said. Galbard noticed some of them practicing the maneuver when the officer wasn't looking, and Galbard thought they did *not* look sure of themselves.

"If they will not come to us, we will go to them!" the officer shouted. His voice caused the other riders to tighten up their line and press ahead slowly. "You had better leave now," he shouted to Galbard. "Best if you made your way to Highwood."

"Sir, I have to tell you—" Galbard began.

"No time for that now," the officer interrupted. "On to Highwood now, if you know what's good for you." The riders pushed into the higher grass, and he turned his horse and rode into position at the rear of the group.

Galbard began to run after them to tell the officer about the Sword and his encounter with the Camonra, but then something stopped him. What would he say?

He had drawn enough attention to himself. As much as he wanted to find some comfort with his kinsmen, his primary objective had to remain clear and unwavering: escape with the Sword of the Watch. It was unmistakably clear to him that Amphileph had meant for him to kill Evliit and return the enchanted weapon to him. It was also clear that, in

Amphileph's hands, this weapon would change their world forever.

He hoped for the Rionese warriors' sake that these Camon scouts were alone, but Galbard decided it would be best to take the officer's advice. He turned and ran toward Highwood.

After covering a little over half the distance to the tree line, Galbard could see people emerging from Highwood and joining the other Rionese refugees. Many embraced them, and then they ushered the newcomers quickly into the protection of the forest.

Galbard was within ten yards of the tree line when the soldiers on horseback returned from the field.

"Stop!" the officer yelled. He leapt down from his horse, moving quickly toward Galbard. "I must speak with you!" Galbard noticed the other soldiers bringing their horses between him and the woods.

Galbard looked around at the other refugees who were staring at him. "Yes, of course," he said. The officer took him by the arm and led him into Highwood with an escort of three soldiers, who dismounted and followed on foot.

"Please come with me to my quarters," he said.

They walked along a path of patchy grass and flat stones that ran between the massive trees of Highwood, some of which Galbard estimated to have trunks that were fifty feet in circumference. Patches of moss crept through the cracks in the stone paths where the trees had spread their roots, and on either side of the path, there were twenty-foot-thick hunks of granite jutting upward at various angles between the trees. The canopy began about seventy-five feet overhead, and he couldn't really see how high the treetops rose. The underbrush was a mixture of ferns and young oaks, with a sprinkling of slender maples. Where paths split the foliage, the depth of the forest was lost in the misty haze that hung in the air.

There were refugees working everywhere, carving and cutting, sawing and shaping the woods. Many of them stopped what they were doing and talked among themselves as Galbard passed.

Galbard followed the officer up a short grade toward the base of one of the trees. The bark had been cut laterally and pushed upward and outward with posts and rails, forming a covered porch. The moss along the porch "roof" gave it an appearance of shingles of living green, and elaborate carvings decorated the entryway and windows. They proceeded up a short set of wooden steps and onto the deck of the porch, which cut into the tree's huge girth. Galbard saw what seemed like a thousand rings of growth in the porch floor, circling outward from the doorway carved into the side of the tree. The officer turned and signaled the soldiers, who stopped at the foot of the porch steps. Galbard noticed that they were eyeing him with an interest that, quite honestly, broke a sweat upon his brow.

"Where are we going?" Galbard asked.

"We need to speak in private," the officer responded. "Please follow me." He turned and followed the curvature of the porch around the tree trunk. Galbard continued behind him.

At one end of the porch, a wooden staircase spiraled upward around the great tree's trunk. It led to a platform that bridged to another wooden structure intertwined with three great trees rising high off the forest floor. From there, Galbard could see the entire forest floor beneath them. The wind whispered in the leaves. The breeze slowly rocked the branches at some distance from the trunk, but the massive trunk itself stood unmoving some sixty feet below.

The officer removed his helmet. "I am Ariden, captain of the Guard," he said.

"Galbard," the escaped slave replied.

"You must know why I have sought you out," Ariden said, staring intently at Galbard. "I must know what happened out there."

"I was attacked, and I defended myself," Galbard began, concerned about where things were headed. This was no time to draw attention to the Sword.

"Defended yourself?" the captain questioned, nodding. "I see. My good friend, am I to understand that you, alone, fought off three of the Camonra? You parted their weapons and armor as if without effort? They look as if they were killed where they stood. I mean no offense, friend, but you don't have the appearance of a warrior. This is what my soldiers are asking."

"Yes, I understand, and I assure you that your first impression is correct. I am no warrior," said Galbard. "I was once a mason, but even that was some time ago."

"A mason, you say?" probed Ariden. "Why would a mason have the prisoner's mark?"

Galbard looked down at his arm. He hurried to pull his sleeve down over the tattoo on his outer forearm. "None too lucky with masonry," he said. "I borrowed for my tools, but I wasn't very good at the trade, and I couldn't pay my debts. Debtor's prison was my reward. I served my masters in Rion for six seasons, but in the seventh season, I sought to pay my debt by harvesting the Soru bush near the Black Mountains. En route, the Camonra killed my owner and took me as a slave."

"You've been to the Black Mountains in the east?" the captain queried suspiciously.

Galbard's jaw tightened. "Terrible fates awaited those the Camonra took as slaves. A more meager existence you cannot imagine. I'll ask you to forgive me, but I don't wish to speak of those things."

"Of course, of course," said Ariden.

Ariden moved closer to Galbard, eyeing Evliit's sword for a moment before looking directly into his eyes. Ariden gestured at the surrounding buildings. "But might I ask what brings you to our small sanctuary in the forest of Highwood?" he asked. "I've done as the Guard has asked of me. I've brought the people to Highwood, while my fellow soldiers have faced the Inferiors, and now? Now the earth has opened up and swallowed them, my friends, my brothers, while I but watched from a distance."

Galbard began to feel uncomfortable with the tone of things. "These are difficult times . . ."

"Has the Guard sent you?" Ariden interrupted.

"No, sir," answered Galbard. "The Guard?"

"I know the people are worried about all that they have seen," Ariden said, ignoring Galbard's perplexed expression. "I have kept them occupied for now with building these structures, but this is not their home, and I fear these tasks will not sustain them for long. They grow restless and ask for news of Rion."

"I have no news of Rion or the Guard," said Galbard. "I have been in the east, right up until the great quakes."

"The east, yes," said Ariden. He stared back at Galbard as if he expected him to say more.

Galbard changed the subject. He pointed to the series of bridges and homes, intricately interlaced among the trees themselves. "I am amazed by what I see. The Rionese are incredible builders, that is sure," he said. Galbard took a step back from Ariden and leaned on his elbows against the wooden railing.

"Wood, bah! 'Tis a pity that this material will never last like stone. One would have to truly love to work with such stuff as this, for after but a few seasons, so much will have to be replaced. Stone and steel are for the craftsmen of Rion."

"Stone and steel, indeed," echoed Galbard, but he noticed that Ariden was looking at his sword again. Suddenly, Ariden turned to some soldiers waiting attentively on the deck just across the rope bridge from them. They moved toward him with concern on their faces, but he raised his hand to wave them off. "Leave us," Ariden said, and the soldiers removed their hands from their swords, bowed, and descended the spiral staircase, disappearing around the tree's trunk.

"Walk with me, Galbard," Ariden said. He led him away from the main encampment crossing three other rope bridges until they neared the northern edge of the forest.

"I suppose you didn't want to talk in front of the other men," said Ariden.

"I don't know what you mean," Galbard responded.

"This weapon, how did you acquire it?" he asked.

Galbard thought Ariden's eyes were slightly bulging, but the look on his own face must have made an impression, because the captain regained his composure and looked away.

He looked down at two soldiers sitting beside a campfire, far below them on the forest floor. "This is the last outpost of our little village. There is no one out here but us and those two soldiers, and they do not even recognize it," he said.

"Recognize it?" Galbard replied.

"Did you not think I would notice what you carried?" Ariden asked. "Did you not know that an old soldier of the Guard would recognize the Sword of the Watch? These young ones are ignorant of the lore, but in my day, the Rionese teachers taught these things."

"Of course," Galbard answered. "I'm sorry, I didn't want to deceive you."

"No, I thought not. Though I am curious how any man could acquire Evliit's sword," Ariden said. "This is it, is it not?"

Galbard drew a deep breath. "Yes, this is Evliit's sword," he said. He instinctively tightened his grip on the Sword's pommel. "I would not bore you with the full tale of my acquiring it, but suffice it to say that I have been tasked with keeping it from the hands of Amphileph himself."

Ariden's eyes widened. He wiped his mouth with his sleeve. "What is it like to draw that weapon?" he asked.

"I have drawn it but once, and you have seen the result."

"The Sword defends its bearer," Ariden said. He looked around at the forest floor and then back to Galbard. "Come this way," he said, leading Galbard around the deck surrounding the largest dwelling. Galbard noticed the dwelling blocked the view of the soldiers below. "This weapon could save Rion," said Ariden. "With this weapon, a great warrior could destroy the Inferiors once and for all!"

Ariden reached out to place his hand on the Sword, but Galbard moved away from him.

"What are you doing?" Galbard asked.

Ariden stood up straight and looked away. "Forgive my forwardness, but you must know what it would mean to Rion to end this war, Galbard."

"Yes, yes, of course," Galbard responded.

"Then you must know the Sword of the Watch should be given to a great warrior, to someone who can wield it with might against our enemies!"

Galbard stepped back further. "What are you saying?"

Ariden suddenly drew his sword. "You are not that warrior, Galbard. Evliit's sword requires someone of strength to wield it rightly."

Galbard held up his hands and backed away again. "Ariden, I have no quarrel with you. Put away your sword."

Ariden raised his sword with one hand and held out the other. "Give me the Sword, Galbard! I do not wish to hurt you!"

"Test me not, Ariden. I will leave this place in peace."

Galbard began to turn away, but Ariden swung — the blade missed him by inches and severed one of the bridge's rope supports. The boards of the bridge fell away, but Galbard held on to the remaining rope. Ariden dropped his sword and grabbed for the remaining rope as well, and the two of them hung precariously over the forest floor. Ariden swung up his foot and kicked Galbard in the side, causing him to drop one hand. He quickly grabbed the rope again and began to move toward the opposite tree structure, hand over hand. Ariden gave chase, and almost two-thirds of the way across, he caught up to him and kicked him again.

Galbard stopped to defend himself, and Ariden reached over him to grasp the Sword's hilt, but his fingers recoiled reflexively as if from heat. Flames burst from his fingers, consuming his hand and wrist and crawling up his arm. He beat the flames frantically, but they crawled up his chest and face, catching the remaining rope on fire. Ariden screamed and fell, but the flames completely consumed his body before hitting the ground, a rain of ash falling among the leaves.

Galbard tried to move quickly, but the rope suddenly broke, and he swung across the forest floor toward a gigantic live oak's trunk, letting go in time to tumble hard upon the thick layer of needles, leaves, twigs, and fallen branches that littered the ground. Had it not been for the thick carpet of mosses, leaves, and a patch of huckleberry shrubs, he would surely have broken something. He lay there smarting and felt for the sword, but it was gone. He heard soldiers shouting.

Fighting through the pain, he rolled to his knees, frantically raking the leaves with his hands in search of the sword. A horn sounded.

Suddenly, he felt something. It was the Sword's hilt. He sheathed it and listened, rising to his feet slowly. A clamor arose from the direction of the main camp. It was hard to breathe—he realized Ariden's vicious kicks might have cracked a rib—but he pushed on, limping, walking, and then running, stopping only when a break in the trees revealed the mountains in the distance to the north.

CHAPTER FIVE

JOURNEY TO THE WESTERN COAST

Moonlight was a welcome sight to Cayden, for sailing these many days on the *Nurium* had felt eerie in the swallowing darkness of moonless nights. The ocean had a way of seeming completely dimensionless in the absence of the moonlight, revealing nothing across the horizon except the torches of the larger ships. Cayden thought they danced on the horizon like fireflies in the fields of Rion.

He had developed a bad habit of waking up around the third hour, an anxiety growing in him with each passing day on the sea. He missed the land more than he could say. Long gone was the uneasy feeling of the ocean moving beneath him, but it had been replaced with an insatiable desire to set foot on dry land again.

On those nights when the anxiety got the better of him, he would ease out of his hammock so as not to wake anyone and make his way up from berthing and onto the deck. Out there in the dead of the night, he'd noticed that the sailors tended to clump tightly together, smoking and talking in low voices, interrupted at times with a quiet chuckle or muted belly laugh. He had never felt comfortable enough to enter their circle, but he had become addicted to the smell of the tobacco smoke drifting by on the night air.

The ship moved almost imperceptibly forward. Even in the dim moonlight, the sea's vastness made distance impossible to judge without star and sextant, and though he'd watched the captain on several occasions shooting the stars, he'd no faith he could do it himself.

Maybe it was that utter reliance on them that spurred his intense desire to get off their ship and back to land, but the gentle murmur of the sailors and the sharp smell of their pipes was somehow reassuring. Cayden would sometimes stand the remainder of the night with them until the first mate or captain would appear, usually just before or after dawn. They would walk down the *Nurium's* deck, inspecting the ship's activities on their way to the helm. When they passed amidships, Cayden always felt like he was in the way, no matter where he was standing, and he had made note of the fact that the sailors always found something to busy themselves with at that time

Cayden started to go below. One of the older sailors looked at him and winked. He was deeply tanned and weathered, belying a cheerful nature. "You learn quick that it's better to find something to do than 'ave it found for you," the sailor said with a smile.

"You're right there," Cayden laughed.

"I heard the woman with the child call you Cayden, 'sthat right?"

"Yes. Cayden."

"Salmos," the sailor said, extending his callused hand. Cayden shook it. "Rough hands, I see. Not a sailor . . . so I'm thinking you're a stoney."

Cayden laughed. "A mason, you mean?"

"Sure, yeah, a stoney," Salmos replied, and then he grabbed a bucket and started cleaning the portside railing, never realizing how much Cayden's pride lifted from having someone in the sailors' ranks speak to him. With a big smile on his face, Cayden descended the stairs to see what the girls were doing.

Berthing converted to the galley shortly after dawn, with the cook stoking a small fire in a small, brick-hearth stove. Nara was folding the hammocks and placing them on the wall hooks. Jalin was sitting on a barrel, breastfeeding Ronan.

"Beautiful day outside," Cayden said.

"Up early again?" Jalin asked.

"Yes," Cayden responded.

"We are beginning to worry about you, Cayden," said Jalin, repositioning herself and Ronan's head. He seemed determined to roll away from her.

"Yes," Nara added. She finished with the last of the hammocks.

"Don't worry for me," Cayden said.

"Who'll worry if we don't?" Nara quipped. "You?"

"Now don't start with me," Cayden said with a smile. "Come and see the day. It *is* beautiful."

Jalin adjusted her clothes and brought Ronan to her shoulder in one practiced motion. "Yes, Nara, don't waste your time with this one," she said with a laugh. "Ronan could use the fresh air."

"Oh, very well, you're right of course," Nara said, laughing. "Can I carry Ronan for you?"

"No, no, just make sure Cayden catches the hatch!" said Jalin.

"I was raised well, ladies, I assure you," said Cayden. He pushed the hatch open for the three of them to go topside. "After you."

The clear day was striking, and Cayden noticed that many of the ships were closer than usual. The seas were calm, and the water and sky met on the horizon in beautiful shades of blue. There were the soothing sounds of gulls overhead and canvas sails billowing in the gentle breeze. The sailors were at work in the rope ladders, letting down the three largest sails.

"Let's get a little wind at our back and then steady as she goes, Mr. Markston," the captain called out.

"Aye, sir!" the first mate called back to him.

By midmorning, smoke was rising from the galley, and there was the smell of beans boiling. Word had it that the cook was going to break out some dried bread in honor of coming to the end of the cliffs, and the thought of food had Cayden's stomach growling. He saw the deck of one of the closer boats was dotted with emaciated, weary-faced passengers that seemed to be staring back at the three of them. "They look like they're starving," he said.

"Yes, that's a bit scary, I'm afraid," Nara said. "I hope that we find port soon."

"Surely soon," Jalin responded, but the nervousness in her voice made the words unconvincing.

"I overheard the captain and the first mate," said Cayden. "They spoke of being close to our destination."

The girls perked up, which was much more to Cayden's liking. "Did he say *when* we might arrive?" Nara asked.

"Oh, please, please say that he did!" said Jalin.

Cayden looked around them. "They kept saying to 'watch the starboard bow for land,' so it should be soon."

Salmos came down the deck toward them. "They watch for the Witch of Southwood," he revealed. "To the north, there." He quickly added, "Sorry. Didn't mean to butt in, but cleaning this here rail for the four-hundredth time isn't keeping my interest."

"A witch?" Cayden asked. "Why do they think a witch lives there?"

"They're not thinking it, sir—they're knowing it. Been known to attack anything comes near to her, sailors say."

Cayden looked northward but could see nothing.

"We've given her a bit of distance," Salmos said. "But as for land, should be seeing it today," he said with a smile, and then he picked up his bucket and threw the water overboard.

The girls looked at each other, and Cayden thought they were ready to squeal with delight.

"I want no part of any witch, but the land—just to see it!" Nara said. "Oh, that would be a fine sight indeed."

"I'd second that," said Jalin.

Salmos stowed the bucket and rag and moved on to checking the knots on the mizzenmast tie-downs.

"Have you ever been this far west?" Cayden asked him.

"Oh yes, sir," Salmos said. "Great fish wander in this part of Blue Water. Sometimes we would come this far out to find large schools of them, fill the hold, and return to Rion. Good money to be made."

"Have you been round the cape, to the western shores?"

"No, sir, I'm not thinking there are many that 'ave been to the west coast of Etharath, at least not that I'm knowing of. The old sailors' maps say the coast turns north ahead there," said Salmos. "But the maps I've seen 'ave nothing but blank canvas when it comes to the western shores," he added. "Right then… I've got to be about me duties." With that, he turned and headed up the rope ladders toward the sails.

About three hours later, they finally heard it—what they had been anxiously waiting for. "Land! Land, ho!" one of the sailors shouted from the crow's nest. Everyone on board turned to see the great cliffs of southern Etharath just becoming visible in the distance. The sheer cliffs came more clearly into view, and the call echoed in the surrounding ships as well. The ruddy face of the southern shoreline rose far above the crashing spray that pounded the outcropping of jagged stone at its base.

"No getting near that," one of the sailors said. "Break up your boat like a child's toy."

About an hour later, Cayden saw the captain and first mate talking.

Then the captain turned the ship's wheel a quarter turn to starboard.

"We're moving in a bit," a sailor said. "We'll follow the coastline around."

They spent the rest of the day watching the coastline draw nearer each hour, until nightfall, when the rhythmic crash of waves finally wore down the excited travelers. Jalin and Nara's wide eyes eventually tired, and the two of them went below. Cayden watched until sleep tugged at his eyelids, and then he too went below, slipped into his hammock, and fell fast asleep

* * *

Around the second hour, Cayden awoke to hurried footsteps on the deck above. A heavy thud shook the deck above him, jolting him upright. He moved toward the galley door just as Salmos stumbled down the stairway and collapsed at his feet.

Cayden caught him. "Salmos!"

"They've killed me," Salmos gasped. His shaking hand pressed desperately against a deep wound in his abdomen. He grabbed Cayden's shoulder. "They killed me!" he cried. Hammocks stirred behind them.

"Cayden?" Jalin whispered.

Salmos thrust his sword into Cayden's hands. "Take this!" "Take this!" he said.

"Don't know... how many..." He sputtered, exhaled a long, shuddering breath, and went still.

"Salmos!" Cayden whispered desperately. Voices grew louder above, and Cayden braced himself. The footsteps stopped at the entrance to berthing. A burst of whispers followed, and Cayden's heart hammered so hard he thought it might burst.

He opened his mouth to warn the others — but the hatch swung open. Two men forced their way into the hatchway, one jumping down the stairs, catching the tip of Cayden's sword under his chin. Everything happened so fast, and before Cayden realized it, he felt the resistance of his blade pushing through skin, startling him. The attacker's scream drowned in his own blood.

Jalin's scream, however, rang out sharply. Everyone in berthing jolted awake.

Cayden pulled back his weapon, and the man frantically grasped at the wound in his neck, collapsing backwards on the stairs. The second man tripped over him and fell face-first onto the galley floor. An off-watch sailor tore the sword from the man's hands and struck him squarely in the face with a massive fist. The man moaned, his head bouncing off the floor from the impact. The sailor raised the sword high above his head. Nara screamed again as the sailor swung the cutlass toward the intruder's neck. The man was beaten, terrified — Cayden couldn't let the sailor butcher him.

Cayden's sword intercepted the blow inches from its mark, sparks flashing in the dark galley.

"Wait!" Cayden shouted. "Someone get a flame from the hearth and light a lantern!"

"You don't order me!" the sailor snapped, backhanding Cayden to the floor. "This one dies!" he cried.

A lantern flared to life toward the back of berthing, revealing the attacker's frail body stretched across the galley floor, the angle of the light casting odd shadows that sharpened his already gaunt features.

"Please," the attacker whispered. "They made us do it! We didn't want to hurt no one, but we couldn't take it no more! My family—my kids—we were starving!"

"Tell that to Salmos!" the sailor yelled, driving the sword into the man's chest, killing him.

"No!" Cayden yelled. "He could have told us how many others are on the ship!" Cayden wanted to shout again, to stop the madness, but the moment was already gone.

"Shut your trap!" the sailor replied. "You men—grab those swords and follow me! Put out that light! You!" he barked at Cayden. "You and Tadhra stay with the women!" Footsteps scattered across the deck above them, skittering in all directions — and then suddenly... nothing.

"I'm coming with you!" protested Cayden. "Salmos was my friend."

"Don't make me tell you twice," the sailor growled. "They'll kill the women same as him — or worse."

Everything went dark again. Cayden's eyes adjusted, and he saw the sailor peering through the galley hatch. Starlight spilled in, and the sailor signaled all clear before heading up the stairs. He exited the hatch with two of the other men.

Cayden moved to the middle of the galley and looked up through the grate over the stove, trying to see anyone topside. After a few seconds, he heard shouting. "I'm going above," Cayden told the others, and then he made his way to the galley stairs.

Two of the men moved to follow him, though they were unarmed. "We'll come with you," one said.

"Go with him, and you're on your own!" said Tadhra.

"No, stay here and protect the women and children. "There's a mallet and a saw in the Healer's quarters. Look for anything else that could be a weapon and give it to the women."

"Very well," he replied.

"Cayden, no!" Nara said, but Cayden held his hand up to stop her.

"Stay here," he said, then moved slowly up the stairs.

He eased the hatch open as quietly as he could, and he cracked it open enough to look for movement, but the bright moonlight revealed nothing across the deck. Crates blocked his view of the stern, but he could hear men fighting.

He slipped out onto the deck, lowering the hatch as quietly as possible. He ducked behind the crates and peered between them just in time to see someone swinging toward him. Cayden tried to duck, but the force of the man's swing slammed the crates into him, knocking him across the deck and sending his sword skittering away.

"Get him!" someone yelled, and several other voices sounded out around him.

He jumped to his feet and scrambled for his sword. It had slid into one of the port drains, tip first, but caught on the hilt. He bent over to grab it, but his assailant's shout made him look up just as a sword came swinging down at his face. Cayden flinched and ducked; the blade stopped just shy of his brow, burying a good portion of the blade into the deck railing. The assailant braced a boot on the railing to free his blade, but Cayden seized it first. Cayden jumped back and slashed across the man's right hamstring, dropping him. The man howled in pain.

The deck hatch rattled under attempts to open it, but the crates held fast.

"Another one! Here!" someone shouted from above. Two voices answered from the bow behind him, and Cayden ran toward the stern.

A bear of a man jumped down from the wheel deck, and another rushed up behind him. The burly man thrust his sword at Cayden's chest, but Cayden dropped to the deck. The man behind him couldn't stop and tripped over Cayden, the tip of the larger man's sword passed through his shoulder. The larger man yanked his blade free as the injured man cried out. Cayden swung with all his strength, but the attacker deflected the blow, the impact nearly knocking the sword from Cayden's hand. When his attacker raised his sword to strike, Cayden kicked downward upon his knee, hyperextending it. The large man collapsed, shouting curses.

Cayden leapt onto the ladder to the wheel deck, but as his head rose above deck level, he saw nothing but the bottom of a boot. The boot struck his forehead, a bright flash exploding behind his eyes, and he toppled backward off the ladder, hitting the deck hard enough to knock the wind from him.

He rolled to his side and saw the captain lying face-down on the deck, unmoving. The sailor from the galley was dead, lying in a pool of his own blood. Grappling hooks and a boarding plank connected the *Nurium* to a larger ship that had the name *Merrius* painted upon the bow.

Cayden could now see the other ship's passengers clearly. They were a frightened, ragged bunch — thin, desperate, wide-eyed. He could just see their thin faces moving behind crates of pottery on the *Merrius*. They looked as though hunger alone might finish them, and it filled him with a strange mixture of anger and pity.

But the pirates standing over him and the captain were another matter entirely. These fellows were stout and well fed. The man looming over him wore the mark of Rion on his clothing.

"We are from Rion!" Cayden said. "We are your kinsmen!"

"Shut up!" another snarled, kicking Cayden in the face with the top of his boot, catching him in the upper lip and nose. Tears filled Cayden's eyes as he grabbed his face, fingers searching to see if the gristle of his nose was loose.

"Grab up the women and anything you can carry! Kill the rest!" one yelled. "Drop the anchor! We'll come back for 'er later!"

A line of pirates charged across the plank onto the deck of the *Nurium*. Cayden blinked his vision clear just in time to see the pirate above him raise his sword over his head pointing the tip at Cayden's heart before placing both hands on the hilt, as if to drive the sword through his chest.

Just over the pirate's shoulder, Cayden thought he saw a star cross the sky — but to his amazement, it arced around and came toward them. A blue light began to wash over everything, and Cayden's attacker turned to look at what was happening. Cayden shoved the flat of the blade away from his chest, and it stuck into the deck. He grabbed his attacker's clothing and yanked him down, trying to keep him from dislodging the sword tip, and struck him twice across the face.

The star fell upon the ship with a tremendous crunch of splintering wood, its blue flames folding inward into human form. The impact rocked the ship, and a concentric ring of energy burst forth from its landing, hurling men into the dark waters on either side before it dissipated. Cayden and his attacker were thrown against the wheel deck wall next to the entrance to the captain's quarters. The pirate pulled a dagger and slashed toward his face, but Cayden moved just in the nick of time.

They wrestled to their feet, and Cayden tore the dagger from his grip with sheer strength. The pirate lunged for the sword, but Cayden jumped in front of him, and the collision knocked Cayden back against the captain's door. He shook the impact from his head and looked back to see his assailant grab the sword's hilt. He pulled the sword from the deck and turned, and Cayden saw the dagger buried in his chest. He raised the sword to swing, then stumbled and collapsed.

The ghostly figure rose slowly from a crouch and moved toward the stern with purpose.

"The Witch!" one yelled, and the pirates regrouped and turned all attention to her. They struck at her wispy cloak, but it drifted around their blades in the night air. Cayden saw the apparition reach toward them, pulling ether from their bodies. They fell instantly lifeless to the deck.

One by one they fell, until only the captain and Cayden remained on the deck, and then the ghostly apparition turned about and drifted in their direction, reaching out her hand.

Cayden lay against the door, motionless. It was as if Death itself had come to take him, but inexplicably, she stopped and drew back. She cocked her head to one side and flipped her black hair over her shoulder, moving her face close to his. There was sadness in her dark brown eyes, and Cayden felt it wash over him in a wave.

She broke her silent stare, snapping Cayden out of a dreamlike trance with a start. "Cayden of Rion! You must help the man Galbard in his quest," she said. Her voice was distant, though she stood just before him, its volume rising and falling in waves that washed over him. "Go to the western shores. There you will find the bearer of the Sword!" She moved back from him slowly, her face fading again into the wispy blue aura that moved around her like a flowing robe. The apparition lifted into the air and then shot into the sky, its glowing light fading with its ascent.

Cayden lay in the darkness, his mouth hanging open. He watched the creature's trail of light turn toward the northeast and then descend over the coast of Etharath, disappearing behind the ship's hand railing. In the silence that followed, he thought he heard the captain's labored breathing. Then came the sound of others pushing open the hatch, followed by footsteps. A group of men appeared from below decks, followed cautiously by several of the women, including Nara.

"Thieves! Murderers!" one yelled, seeing the body of one of the assailants.

"Check the captain's quarters! Find the captain and the first mate!" another cried, and they fanned out around the deck. Markston appeared in the doorway of the captain's quarters, his head bleeding.

"Here!" Cayden said breathlessly, though he could see they had already spotted him. The group ran to Cayden and the ship's captain, and they saw the *Merrius*, the ramp, and the grappling hooks.

A young girl stepped out from the shadows of the *Merrius*. "Help!" she cried. She jumped when she noticed the men approaching, and then she burst into tears. "Please don't hurt me!" she said.

"Get the girl!" Markston yelled. "Board the ship! Now!"

They stormed the *Merrius*, returning shortly with men, women, and children they found in the holds below.

"They were malnourished and hunkering in the darkness," the sailors said as they brought them aboard. "They are well stocked. We weren't the first of their conquests."

"We were their slaves!" one cried out. "We didn't visit this evil upon you!"

Cayden gathered his strength and stood up at the railing. He called out to the sailors who remained on the *Nurium*, pleading. "Those that have wronged us have paid their penance. Let there be no more of this killing. Have we not enough misery in our lives?"

For a moment, everyone seemed to stop and hear his words.

"We could help them reach the western shores. We have plenty of food to make it that far!" Cayden said. "Surely some of you could command this ship?"

The sailors talked among themselves. "Two ships and plenty of stores.

It's a smart move."

"Light a lantern on the stern!" Markston ordered, and then he turned to the sailors boarding the *Merrius*. "Follow our light! Give us a ship's length and follow us in to shore."

Nara burst through the crowd gathered amidships and ran to his side. "Cayden!" she cried. "Are you alright?"

Cayden thought again of the apparition and sat down with Nara's help.

"Yes, I'm fine," he said. "Just give me a moment."

The ship's Healer pushed past them, and the sailors lifted the captain up. A clump of them began to move him below decks. "Gently, men — to my quarters!"

The remaining sailors scrambled across the deck, shifting the sailcloth and turning the ship toward the Western Shore.

"Jalin is fine?" Cayden asked.

"Yes, she's with Ro down below."

"Good."

Nara suddenly wrapped her arms around Cayden's neck. "I was so worried about you when you left us, and when that awful sound shook the entire ship, I feared you dead. Oh, Cayden, when I thought something had happened to you, I was beside myself."

Cayden's squirm was reflexive; her affection caught him off-guard. The Rionese masonry trade allowed little time for families, and it had made him more than a little rusty when it came to such affairs of the heart. He cautiously leaned in, and she quickly closed the distance, kissing him, pushing him back against the ship's railing.

He pressed his lips to hers, and the sensation consumed him, but suddenly the face of the Witch flashed across his mind's eye, and he recalled the apparition's words and pulled back from Nara.

"Nara!" Cayden said.

"What is it?" she asked. She looked genuinely surprised by his abrupt withdrawal.

"I'm sorry, Nara," he said. "But I *must* tell you something." He leaned close to her ear. "The great crashing sound you heard — it was a creature that fell from the skies." He pointed to the circular burn mark on the deck. "The pirates scrambled to attack it, but they were helpless against it. I heard one of them call it the Witch of Southwood."

"The Witch of Southwood? The demon-woman the sailors spoke

about?" she replied in a hushed whisper.

"What's more — she spoke to me."

"The creature spoke to you?"

Yes. It was like a ghost — she was like a ghost — drifting across the ship, striking down all who got in her way. But when she came to me, she spoke of me helping someone when we arrived at the western coast."

Nara searched Cayden's eyes.

"She said to 'help the man Galbard,'" he said. "She told me to protect him."

"Protect him?" Nara replied. Saying the words curled her face into a puzzled look. "Protect him from what? Who is Galbard?"

"I have no idea," said Cayden. "The entire thing seems a bit… surreal."

As they spoke, Jalin appeared with Ro and several others.

"I thank the Creator that you're all right," Jalin said. Ro awoke hungry and fidgety, and she prepared to feed him.

"What happened up here?" Jalin inquired.

Cayden and Nara looked at each other. "Come closer," said Nara, and Cayden recounted the night's events to Jalin.

"What can this mean?" Jalin asked, looking confounded.

"I'm not sure," Cayden began, but then he noticed Jalin's expression. "What's the matter?"

"My husband's name is Galbard," she replied. "It's an unusual name, you know. Don't you think it's strange that she said you needed to protect Galbard?"

Cayden and Nara looked at each other. "Yes, that's very strange. I thought you said he had gone north of Rion to pay a debt," said Cayden.

Jalin looked down at the deck, her face flushing. "He was indentured," she said.

"Your husband was a slave?" said Nara.

Jalin nodded, and a tear ran down her cheek. "It had taken over a year, but he'd worked off most of our debt. His master said he could pay the last of the debt much faster if he harvested the Soru bush that grew in the northern fields, but the Inferiors had been seen there, and I told Galbard not to go anymore — that it wasn't worth it. He said he was going, even after I begged him not to, and I—well, I panicked, I guess. I was so afraid that something might happen to him. I didn't know it, but I was pregnant with Ro, and I was very emotional. We had a huge fight, and I told him he cared more about the money than me. I told him that if he left, I never wanted to see him again, and then he left and never came back. I've waited for him every day since then, hoping and praying he'd return, hoping for a chance to tell him I hadn't meant what I'd said, that I wished it had never happened, but he never returned. He's never even seen his son." Jalin began to cry openly.

Nara held her. "Oh, Jalin, I'm so sorry."

"We have no way of knowing if it's even the same person, this Galbard," said Cayden.

Jalin sniffled. "You're right, of course," she acknowledged, and she did her best to put on a happier face. They talked of other things until dawn approached.

Nurium's deck remained alive with action. Cayden had to compete with the shouts of sailors, the rustling of sails, the creaking deck planks, and the squeak of ropes under the strain of *Nurium's* turn northeast toward the sloping line of the shore. The new light brought a few ships into view in the distance, with the *Merrius* just off their stern.

Jalin and Ro were standing near the bow. "Cayden! Nara! Look!" She pointed excitedly toward the shore, hopping and swinging the child firmly planted on her hip.

"I don't think that I've ever wanted to see a shoreline more than I do at this very moment!" said Nara.

"I couldn't agree more!" added Jalin. Even Ro giggled his approval.

"Coming through!" shouted Markston, and Cayden moved to the side. In the captain's absence, Markston had performed double-duty directing the two ships. "The cliffs end," Markston said. "We should make landfall somewhere over there. Notify the captain. Signal the *Merrius*." He hurried toward the helm.

"Are these other ships to follow us?" Nara asked.

"They seem scattered to the four winds," Cayden replied. The ships did indeed appear to be crisscrossing the ocean before them. Some appeared to be continuing north along the coast.

"But they will follow us, won't they?" Nara repeated.

"I expect some will, Nara," Cayden said. He noticed the look on Nara's face as the vast wilderness passed before them. "Something troubles you?"

"This land, to be sure. The journey we'd need to make to return to Rion — well, through a wilderness like this, numbers would be in our favor. We could gather all of our food and make for Highwood or the mountains, surely . . ."

Cayden had stopped listening. The deep, foreboding wilderness made him think of the Witch. *What of this man Galbard?* he thought.

"Cayden? Have you heard *anything* I was saying?" Nara asked. She smiled and hit him on the shoulder.

"I'm sorry. I still struggle with the night's events. I'd think all the ships would soon be on the western shores. From the looks of the people on the *Merrius,* they'll be more willing than we to escape the confines of their ships."

The sun was low in the western sky when the *Nurium* slid into the sands of the western coast of Etharath, followed shortly by the *Merrius.* Cayden had picked up a few things about sailing from Salmos, and he pitched in to help the sailors. They saw several of the *Merrius's* passengers jumping overboard and rushing onto the shore with abandon. The sailors tying off the *Nurium* growled under their breath

"Awful thankful, to be sure," one of the sailors said.

"Don't you worry your pretty little heads, we'll take care of the ships," mocked Tadhra.

"Be about your business," said Markston. "Secure the ships, and let's get an inventory of our supplies. Let down the rope ladder so these fools don't break a leg."

Cayden and Nara helped Jalin and Ro get their things together, and then Cayden helped the sailors toss the rope ladder over into the neck-deep water. Tadhra climbed over the side, and people began to storm the rope ladder almost immediately.

"Wait a blasted minute!" Tadhra shouted.

"Let's give them room," Cayden said, picking up the bags and moving away from the starboard railing toward the port side of the *Nurium.*

He set the bags down and turned to say something to Nara. He noticed she had stopped upon crossing the bent and burnt deck planks where the Witch of Southwood had landed.

"I feel strange," Nara said. She lifted her hands, and Cayden saw they were shaking. "I've got a tingling sensation in my fingers."

There was a sudden change in the skies. A swirling blackness above the *Nurium* rustled the canvas of both ships.

"Nara?" asked Cayden.

Nara looked at him, fear in her eyes — then her head snapped back, and light burst from her eyes and mouth. Several people jumped over the ship's railing, and the rest doubled their efforts to climb over, screaming and shouting. The crowd pushed Cayden back toward the bow railing.

"Nara!" Cayden cried, attempting to get to her. He forced his way toward her, but she suddenly rose into the air above the ship's sails. Blue bolts of energy shot out from around her body, vaporizing patches of ocean water and lifting sand into twisted patterns of glass.

"Hear me!" a voice boomed from Nara's mouth.

People were dragging themselves onto the beach and running inland in a panic.

"The Witch!" Tadhra yelled and started back toward the ship, but he stopped and threw his hands up before his face. A large bolt of energy turned the sand at his feet into jagged glass.

Nara raised her hand, and Cayden lifted into the air. He tried to grab the ship's railing but failed to get a handhold, and he drifted slowly toward the crowd. "Arise!" said the voice. It echoed up and down the beach. "This one is to build a temple to Evliit and the bearer of the Sword of the Watch! See that you help him in every way. Do as he says, or I will visit vengeance upon you!"

"Get back from us, you witch!" Tadhra screamed, pulling a knife from his belt. "Come a little closer, why don't you? I'll gut you like a fish!"

Nara moved toward Tadhra. The unseen forces that lifted Cayden from the ground suddenly released him, and he fell hard onto the sandy beach. He rolled over, winded, and saw Nara's shape flicker into the wispy form he had seen upon the ship, the form of the Witch of Southwood. She pointed at Tadhra, and a great burst of blue energy shot from her hands, blinding everyone.

"Protect the Sword!" Her voice boomed in all directions, amplified by their blindness. The echo resounded through the surrounding hills.

Cayden heard Nara's body fall beside him. "Nara!" he cried, feeling through the darkness to find her. His eyes began to adjust, and then he saw her unconscious on the ground. He scrambled to her side and rolled her over.

"Nara?" he whispered into her ear. "Nara, are you all right?"

"I think so," Nara muttered. "What is happening?"

"I'm not sure," he began, but stopped when he noticed the remaining sailors and passengers closing in.

Look," one said. Cayden realized they were pointing past him. Cayden adjusted Nara's arm over his shoulder and turned. Tadhra stood behind him, still pointing at the sky, his wide-eyed stare frozen within the glass that had sprung from the beach sands to encase him.

"We'll do whatever you ask!" the group said, sheepishly looking to Cayden — unaware that he had no more idea than they did of what to do next.

CHAPTER SIX

THE NORTHERN FIELDS

Tobor, the Camon General, surveyed the remnants of his once-great army strewn across what had been the northern entrance to Rion. The battle in the Northern Fields was meant to be the deciding victory over the Rion Guard — the final obstacle in his conquest of Rion — but everywhere the land roared defiantly, making it nearly impossible for his captains to hear his orders. He had never once seriously considered retreating from an enemy, but this — this tearing open of the land and the storm of fire and smoke — made it appear as if the land itself had turned on them, and it had become obvious to him that moving forward toward the rift's edge was mere suicide.

"Retreat!" he cried, hoping desperately that the chain of command could hear him over the chaos.

The very mouth of the underworld appeared to have opened up beneath their feet, and a vast chasm now separated them from the Rion Guard. Jets of gas exploded upward through the stony ground ahead of them, hurling three and four Camonra into the air at a time. They combusted in the intense heat, and what remained of them swirled upward like ash from a campfire.

Tobor looked toward the horizon where, moments before, he had seen the Rion Guard — columns of archers and infantry — but the massive column of soot rising from the fissure now blotted out everything. His army scrambled back from the smoke, fire, and molten rock in sheer terror, and Tobor realized they might trample him if he stood his ground.

He pulled upon the reins of his mount, an Azrodh, and the great lizard reared and turned. Its front legs crashed down, nearly crushing two Camonra as it bounded forward and lumbered northward away Accelerating, its tail swept back and forth, knocking several more of the

Camonra to the ground.

The remaining captains saw the general's retreat and attempted to do likewise, but the entire concept was foreign to the Camonra. Amphileph had created them for war and domination, and the retreat's execution was an exercise in confusion.

The Azrodh brayed at a Camon whose movements stuttered ahead of them, unable to interpret the mount's direction. "Out of the way!" Tobor yelled — but a large chunk of molten rock fell on the Camon, taking half his body with it. A splattering of lava seared the neck and face of his lizard mount, spurring it instinctively to jump away.

The sudden turn sent Tobor flying. He hit the ground and skipped on one shoulder, rolling face-down in dust and ash, the impact knocking him senseless. Years of battle had taught his body to rise quickly, and reflexively he rolled over and tried to gather his footing.

He did so at his own loss. His recent wounds burned, his bruises ached anew, and the crudely stitched gash on his shoulder popped its thick thread and began to bleed. He screamed his defiance of it all, rising to his feet and drawing his great sword.

"This way!" Tobor cried, waving them on. He turned and ran through his exhaustion, outpacing the nearest soldier and fixing his gaze on the ground before him. He ran what seemed like a full league before he looked back again, and then fell like the others to the ground. His eyes closed. Fatigue consumed him.

*　*　*

Tobor awoke to a gray world. A heavy rain fell, and most of his men lay in the thickening mud formed by ash and water. A gray mud was everywhere, and a puddle of milky water submerged half his face.

He pushed himself up with effort and looked to the skies for his bearings, but the gray ash blotted everything out. After some time, he got a feel for the light and dark of it, and determined that they had generally run north. Turning south, he saw the ash's origin — still spewing great mounds of lava into the air with thunderous force.

It was hard to breathe, and the taste of the ashen water bit his tongue.

"Captain!" Tobor yelled, but there was no reply. "Captain?" he called again.

There was movement to his left. Tobor thought he heard Idhoran cough.

"Captain!" he called a third time.

Idhoran's upper body shot up from the ground, shouting, "Yes, my liege!" Idhoran kept his head shaved high above his ears, and Tobor could see a decent-sized cut starting in the stubbled scalp over his left ear and running into the short hair on the crown of his head. The captain seemed to struggle to maintain his balance.

"Rally the Camonra!" the general shouted. "Count heads!"

"Yes, my liege!" said Idhoran. He placed his hands on the earth beside him, forced himself to his feet with a quick thrust of his mighty arms, and found his helmet among the bodies. "Camonra, ready!" Idhoran shouted, the gruffness of his voice being enough to roust all but the dead.

His subordinates found their feet in similar ways, the order rippling through them.

Tobor walked back from them to higher ground a hundred paces north, hoping that he might rise above the storm of ash that hovered over the plains, but to no avail. He coughed, spat, and blew muddy ash from his nose, but he could not get the taste of it out of his mouth.

Amphileph's fury will be great, he thought.

Idhoran approached him. "My lord, eighteen companies of the Camonra remain. We have forty slaves and some supplies, but few of the Azrodh remain."

Tobor winced and motioned Idhoran closer. The two of them turned away from the other Camonra and ascended a small hill. Tobor waited until Idhoran came around him so he faced away from his warriors. "I have failed," he said.

"No, my lord," Idhoran interjected.

"Look around you, Idhoran! Little remains of Amphileph's great army—*my* great army!"

"My lord, reinforcements come. Amphileph will know of these things and send our brothers to our aid. The great kingdom of Rion will still fall."

Tobor pointed to the south. "The men of Rion have fared no better than we."

"We have need of water, my liege," said Idhoran. "The water in this place assaults the tongue and turns back out the meal. The Camonra despise it. Let scouts determine the fate of the Guard while we move north. We will determine the fate of Rion and report it to our master."

Our master, Tobor thought. *Amphileph will not care that no one could have foreseen the land tearing apart; he will be furious.*

"You are right," Tobor said instead. "We must have water and clear our nostrils of this air. No Camon can breathe this air for long."

"Yes, my liege."

Idhoran strode down the hill and closed the distance to his soldiers. "We march north, Camonra — away from the sickness Etharath spills upon our heads!" he bellowed.

Tobor watched them pass, the rhythm of their sloshing feet helping him organize his thoughts on how best to proceed. With Rion possibly crippled by the great quakes, he would need to find a way around these new fire gates to the city's entrance.

Idhoran drove the Camonra northeast until the rain fell clear or not at all. The winds carried away the ash from the great chasm in a north-by-northwest direction.

"We will make camp here!" announced Tobor. "Sound the drum. We must recapture the Azrodh that have scattered to the winds."

* * *

That night, Tobor summoned Idhoran and waited for him at his tent. He watched moonlight filter through the holes in the entrance fabric, and he remembered their reckless escape from the rain of molten rock.

Idhoran pulled back the entrance sash and entered. "My liege?"

"Please, at ease, my friend," Tobor said, and Idhoran removed his helmet. "I have need of your counsel."

"I am your servant, lord, but what help could this old, scarred head lend to your wisdom? I'm afraid I'm good to you only as a warrior."

"Sit… sit," Tobor said, gesturing to the crudely hewn chair. "A warrior's head is clear of many meaningless things, Idhoran. Life and death is never clearer than it is when swords ring."

"Battle alone makes our eyes see," Idhoran said.

"Yes, my friend. Battle is the fire that cleanses the soul. Let us drink to this!" Tobor grabbed a goblet and tossed it to Idhoran, then picked up a flask and a second goblet, filled them both, and struck them together.

"To the end of men!" Tobor said, and then he turned up the goblet.

"To the end of men!" Idhoran echoed, drinking as well, though his face grew stoic. He put down the cup. "My liege, if you have heard complaints from the ranks, I will kill them myself."

Tobor grunted. "They know who to challenge if they wish to lead!" he said. "It's not the troops, Idhoran."

"What troubles you, my lord?"

Tobor looked around, ensuring no one was within earshot. "Amphileph sees the future; he created us," Tobor began. "Why would his lordship wish to challenge our loyalty this way?"

Idhoran looked confused. "As I said, my lord, I am a Camon. I don't know of such things."

Tobor looked him in the eye. "Why would Amphileph lead us to our deaths? Have we not done whatever he has commanded of us, whenever he commanded it?"

"Without question," Idhoran answered.

Tobor rose and paced around the tent. "Let me ask another way, Idhoran: When does a general lead his men to certain death?" Tobor asked.

"When all is lost, my lord," Idhoran responded. "A Camon general will lead his men into certain death so that they may take as many of the enemy to the Underworld as they can."

Tobor moved close to Idhoran. "There is another time, Idhoran."

"Yes, my lord?"

Tobor hesitated, drinking again from his goblet. "A general will lead his army to certain death when he does not know that it awaits him."

Idhoran stood abruptly and looked around the tent, checking for anyone who might be listening, and then saying in a hushed whisper, "To say our master, our Father, Amphileph did not know these things—my liege, forgive me, but this is wickedness! Amphileph is all knowing!" Tobor had been in many battles with Idhoran, but it was the first time he had ever seen Idhoran genuinely troubled. "I beg of you, my lord, speak no more of this!"

Tobor poured the remainder of the goblet down his throat and slammed it onto the table. "That will be all, Idhoran!" he shouted.

"My lord?" Idhoran probed, a look of pain crossing his face.

"That will be all!" Tobor repeated.

"Yes, my liege," Idhoran said, slamming his fist to his chest before turning to leave.

"Tomorrow we begin sending scouts to find a new passage to the men of Rion," Tobor said.

Idhoran stopped and turned back to his general. "As you wish, my lord." Pushing the thick cloth of the tent aside, he exited.

Tobor felt a mixture of excited abandon and guilt. He waited for the tent folds to settle behind Idhoran's exit before he turned to the small wooden cabinet from what remained of his personal effects. The adorned case his attendants once carried so carefully behind his army had been crudely reassembled after being partially crushed in the frantic dash from Rion. He opened the small doors that protected the even smaller likeness of Amphileph. As he had a thousand times before, Tobor lowered his head to pray for guidance. He began with the prayer Citanth had taught him long ago before he had entered the vicious training of the Camon.

But this night, something was different. Before Tobor could grunt out even the first word, he stopped and slowly raised his head, opening his eyes to focus on the idol. "You should have known," Tobor said, and then he carefully closed the small cabinet doors and rose. He stood there as his guts twisted, suddenly doubting everything he had come to believe about the world around him.

*　*　*

Tobor rose the following morning still cross with himself. Idhoran was waiting just outside his tent.

"My liege," Idhoran greeted him.

"A new day, Idhoran," Tobor replied. "Make ready the scouts. If a path exists for us to pierce these fiery gates of Rion, we must find it before reinforcements arrive."

"More of our great army comes any day," Idhoran grunted. "The humans will find no comfort in their city soon, my liege."

"Send forth the scouts!" Tobor shouted.

"Yes, my liege," Idhoran responded.

Tobor watched the scouts ride their Azrodh mounts to the forefront of what remained of the Camon army.

"Search them out!" Tobor cried. "Find a way into the temples of Rion!"

The Azrodh roared in unison, joined by the howls of the scouts. They rumbled away south toward Rion.

For weeks, the scouts came and went from the deadly chasm, twice returning with fewer members of their party. Though Idhoran implored them to find the path to their victory, it was not to be, and the expanse of the chasm prevented them from discerning the state of the city beyond. Disgusted, Idhoran met with Tobor in private once again.

"The great chasm ruins our approach, my liege," Idhoran told Tobor. "We have searched its length, but no way is found around it."

"You are sure of this?" Tobor asked.

"Under threat of death, the scouts have found nothing," Idhoran emphasized. "There is no passage, my liege."

Tobor stared in silence at the map Amphileph had given him, then shoved over the table on which it lay. "This makes no sense, Idhoran! How can it be that we are given the honor of being the ones to destroy the Guard's stronghold, yet we cannot take the battle to them? And why have no reinforcements arrived?"

"Something is wrong, my liege," Idhoran answered. "Father should have arrived by now." Amphileph had *declared* he would stand in the ruined temples of Rion within three days, yet nearly five weeks had passed with no sign of him.

"We must send a runner to him, my liege," Idhoran said.

"And report what?" Tobor retorted. "That our army is destroyed, that we have found no way to carry our master's banner into Rion?"

"My liege, something is wrong," Idhoran said again, the exasperation clear in his voice.

Tobor, too, was beyond frustration. This latest round of bad news shook him to his core. *How can this be Amphileph's will?* he thought. *Do you test me, my master?*

"Send the runners to Amphileph, Idhoran, but know that the master may require our deaths for this failure," said Tobor.

CHAPTER SEVEN

POWER REVEALED

Galbard ran through the seemingly never-ending trees of northern Highwood with breakneck abandon. Branches slashed him repeatedly; he tripped twice, and on the third fall he hit so hard it took him several minutes to rise, even in his panic. He was sure he heard the people of Highwood just behind him to the south, but whenever he looked back, they were nowhere to be seen.

Galbard was a slave and a stoneworker. He was no stranger to enduring mental and physical pain, but even his stout constitution was no match for days of running, sleepless nights, and the gnawing anxiety that made him jump at the slightest sound. Fatigue found him and settled squarely upon his frame until his knees gave way, and he slept the silent, black sleep of exhaustion where he fell.

He woke with a jolt in the darkness, thinking a Camon had found him. He frantically felt for the Sword until his hands found it, gripping the scabbard and hilt tightly.

Galbard was not sure how long he had been out, and he steeled himself for another run. For a moment, he thought it was too quiet, and he strained to listen to every sound. He opened his eyes wide to clear the sleep from them, then closed them again to listen even harder.

There was no sound but the wind and the birds. He took note of his own heartbeat pounding in his chest, and he gave thanks to the Creator for smiling on him another day. His heartbeat slowed, and he leaned back against the rough wood of a tree stump as if it were a pillow of feathers.

* * *

For three days he marched north, and the last stand of the great trees of Highwood parted, revealing a deep, cold stream and the foothills of another mountain range to the west. In the distance, Galbard saw a hundred-foot waterfall pouring over the eastern end, its misty droplets lifting to the winds and drawing his eyes to another great mountain range to the north. The nearer range was much more inviting, but much too close to Highwood. He would have to move farther north, to the cold gray stone that shot into the clouds in the distance. They looked barren and bleak, but it was another chance to reunite with people, and his supplies were all but gone. "The mountains, then," he said aloud, and he left the cover of Highwood to head north.

The plains were wide open and tough going. The wind was so strong it seemed to throw off his balance. He was hungry, and the pain in his stomach rolled around under his ribs ferociously. Fatigue was omnipresent, always tempting him to stop and turn back. *Remember,* he thought, and the images of the dungeons of Amphileph's city snapped back into his mind.

Remember the silence of true despair. Remember reaching for the scattering of food scraps the Camon jailers had tossed into your cell only to hear the rattle of your own chains and the scurrying of tiny feet all around you. Remember the dank smell of the dungeon, its musty odor broken only by the acidic smell of excrement and the choking smell of death.

These memories gave him clarity. The Camonra meant to search him out, to kill him, and retake the Sword. He didn't need to understand everything—just that one thing. He had accepted the charge of Evliit, and he meant to make good on this second chance at life outside those dungeon walls.

He rose then, renewed, and refocused. The far mountain's ominous look seemed to change, its sheer stone now appearing as a new refuge. It would give them pause to follow him into the crevices of its jutting rock, and that pause might be his saving grace.

Galbard made his way toward the Faceless Mountains, as he named them. The ever-decreasing distance and sharpening angle brought him more hope for their crossing, revealing pathways he might take in ascending its jagged rock.

The slow rise of the northern plains to the mountain foothills had given him some appreciation of the destruction that had occurred in the south. He could clearly see a tear in the earth stretching from the Black Mountains to the sea. The ash and smoke flowed into the atmosphere with unending fury, causing huge storm clouds that came in from the sea and spread their lightning throughout the debris. Large white plumes of steam rose far to the southwest and southeast, on either side of Rion, and rumbling thunderheads continued to pour down rain and lightning upon what had been Rion's beautiful northern fields. He could only turn away from such a sad and terrible sight, for he knew that it served only to discourage him.

That night, he lay back in a crevice and pulled his long coat tightly around him, trying desperately to seal out the frigid wind that raced over the mountainside. He could see fires burning in the plains to the south. Some were clearly wildfires sparked by lightning, but others were more ominous — smaller, and gathered too symmetrically. These, he was convinced, were his pursuers.

In the solitude of his climb, Galbard had devoted more and more time to controlling the power that seemed to emanate from the Sword. He sensed something when the blade was drawn, something like a quiet voice, and he could feel the energy coursing through his body intensifying. The link between him and the Sword was growing stronger. He pulled down his hood, and clutching the Sword tightly, he closed his eyes and slept.

He woke the next morning to a dusting of snow. He shook it off and started up the mountain, but something caught his eye in the distance. He dropped low to the ground and cautiously closed the distance between himself and the place he thought he had seen some movement.

For several moments more he waited, thinking he heard whispers on the wind, and then one head slowly appeared, followed by another and another. The foothills suddenly revealed many men and boys hiding among the rocks.

"I am Galbard of Rion!" he shouted, rising slowly. "I am alone, and I mean you no harm."

They closed on him in a wide circle, and then one of them stepped forward. "I am Illian, also of Rion! Have you news of Rion, brother?" one asked, his voice betraying a near-desperate sadness on the subject.

"No, my friend, I have not set foot in my beloved city in over a year," Galbard answered.

"It has been months for us," another said. "We were in the third wave that the council sent away in preparation for the war. We've been hiding in the ca—"

"Silence!" yelled one of the elder men of their party. "We do not know this man!"

"Does he look like an Inferior to you?" retorted the younger.

"The Spellmakers do not look like Inferiors either, you simpleton! They look like you and me, but they could kill us all with a wave of their hand."

Several squatted back behind their rocky hiding places at the mention of Spellmakers, keeping a watchful eye on Galbard.

"I assure you, I'm no Spellmaker," said Galbard.

"Show us your hands!" cried another.

"Of course," answered Galbard, raising them both.

"Have you seen our brethren?" asked one of the boys. The tone in his voice tugged at Galbard's heart.

"Yes. Others fled just before the attack. I met them on their way north from the city. They're hiding in the woods near the mountain range southwest of here."

Galbard did not see fit to share more of his adventure there. He parted his long coat, allowing the sword's hilt to be visible. He studied their faces, watching to see if they recognized it as the Sword, not wanting to repeat the events of Highwood, but no one seemed to give it a second glance. They appeared to be peasants, not soldiers, and Galbard let down his guard.

"What of the Inferiors, then?" one asked. "Has the Guard defeated them?"

"I don't know, my friend, but I've seen them in fields north of Rion, so I don't think that is the case."

Questions came at him in a flurry. They crowded around him, hungry for news of Rion.

"Friends! Friends!" shouted Illian. "Give the man a chance!" A hush slowly fell upon them then. The speaker slung his bow across his body and put out a hand, which Galbard grasped, grateful to see a friendly face. Illian wore a fur collar and a leather shirt covered with chainmail, with a leather long coat over that. The light peppering of snow blended with his graying hair and beard.

Galbard told them of meeting the refugees in the northern fields. But of his encounter with the Camonra, he said only that they had all run for their lives, and he had wandered as far away from them as possible, and ended up here.

"Many Rionese were sent to the woods west of the northern fields," Illian said. "We were to find our hiding place within the mountains. There are caves beneath the highest peak of this mountain range. We've taken refuge within them."

"There are many of you?" Galbard asked.

"Around four thousand. It's been difficult, but the mountain has kept us safe these many months." Illian nodded toward the distant fires. "What do you know of this tear in the land? We want to make our way home. Rion awaits our return."

Galbard looked at the ground.

"It's not good, is it?" Illian asked.

Galbard hesitated. "There's no passage back to our fair city, friend. The people I met in the northern fields coming from Rion — they said the great chasm cuts off all passage to the city."

A collective cry rose from the group.

"We'd seen the fire and smoke in the distance, but hoped for the best," Illian said.

"I'm afraid, for the time being, we're separated from our people — exiled to this great mountain." Galbard watched their spirits break, the brightness in their eyes fading with the realization. Many of the men hid tears from his searching gaze, and Galbard felt compelled to give them purpose.

"If the Inferiors' army has not been destroyed, then we cannot spare time for such sadness, my friends. We must prepare for the battle to come."

Fear replaced the sadness in their faces, and oddly, Galbard took some comfort in it. Fear, at least, could serve them well.

"Yes, yes," they answered. "You're right."

"If Amphileph's temple still stands, then the Camonra will come from that direction," Galbard said, pointing southeast. "But take heart! Do you not remember? We are men of Rion! The builders of the great temples! We have worked the fields and the oceans to feed tens of thousands! Surely, we can make a stand in the protection of these mountains!" The hand Galbard rested on the Sword's hilt felt warmth beneath it. Its energy seemed to charge him. *Perhaps the Sword counsels me,* he thought, and the sensation increased, driving the volume and strength of Galbard's voice. "You must accept that we will remain in exile for but a short time, and you must do what is necessary to protect the children of Rion!"

Again, all eyes focused on Galbard, and the truth of his words changed them. Galbard saw a flicker of hope and a steely determination.

"Yes!" they shouted. "May the Creator sustain us in our time of need!"

"He sustains you even now," Galbard answered. "Be faithful stewards of the good he has granted. Ready the mountain. Raise a stronghold against whatever evil Amphileph would cast upon you."

One of the men stepped forward. "Would you not eat with us? You look famished."

"Yes, of course, let us break bread together, brothers. I am indeed travel weary."

The men led Galbard through the paths in the foothills of the mountain toward the caves they had made their home. The sheer size of the rising wall of stone, its snowy peak disappearing into the clouds, continually amazed him. He caressed its surface. "This is good stone," he said. "This stone will stand against even the Inferiors' army."

"Yes, my friend," Illian responded. "And we have just the tools to mold it. A true stonemason never leaves the tools of his trade behind, even when fleeing the very city he builds," Illian laughed.

Galbard laughed as well. "I do remember the cost of a good hammer and chisel!"

Illian waved Galbard forward into the opening in the mountain. "Watch your head," he said. "Keep a good eye," he remarked to the others in his party, and they fanned out to keep watch on the entrance.

Galbard's eyes strained to adjust to the darkness at the cave's entrance. It was tight for a man to fit, but he squeezed in behind Illian.

"Tight for us, but impossible for Inferiors," Illian remarked. "We are blessed to have found such a place."

"Indeed," Galbard responded.

Illian lit a torch, and the spark's sudden flash in the darkness made Galbard flinch. His eyes adjusted to the light, and he turned his eyes up slightly, looking away from the flame. He could see that the brown stone above them was blackened by torch smoke where others had also raised their torches to fit through the opening, and they worked their way through the passage's varying widths for some time.

Galbard thought he heard voices ahead. Illian turned his head carefully in the narrow space and shouted back. "Almost there."

The voices grew louder, and suddenly the passage opened to a great cave, its flat ceiling at least sixty feet high. "Watch your footing," he added.

Galbard noticed the ground was nothing like the smooth ceiling, but covered in pebbles and rocks of every size. The floor began to drop away, its grade steepening with each step, and the voices quieted as they moved deeper into the mountain.

"It is I, Illian!" the group leader yelled. The torchlight revealed an even more expansive room.

"Who is with you?" a voice replied.

"A brother from Rion, a man named Galbard," he yelled.

There was a sound of voices again, and Galbard saw hundreds emerge from around the columns of rock that rose from what looked like piles of mud, though they were as hard as the stone outside. It was an eerie place, and the folds of stone hanging from the ceiling danced in the firelight, appearing almost like moving wings or flaps of stony skin. He had never seen anything else like it.

Here the masons had chiseled out a walkway of sorts, and the group gathered on the far side of a crevice, connected to the area where Galbard and Illian walked by, a natural bridge. Galbard saw steps and elaborate rooms carved into the surrounding stone, torches and candles by the thousands revealing an expansive cavern whose true size could not be judged in the dim light.

Illian noticed the look of amazement on Galbard's face. "It is not Rion, but we have made do."

"Impressive, brother," Galbard said. "You bring honor to the very name of Rion with this effort!"

Illian placed one hand on Galbard's shoulder. "We must inform the council of your arrival," he said. "Follow me."

They moved past the crowds and deeper into the cave, where the stone changed color and texture. Here it appeared as if the stone was softer, smoothed by running water. They passed through another opening where a shaft of light illuminated their surroundings, and Illian extinguished his torch. They entered, and a group of men in long white robes came up to greet them.

"Greetings," one of them said. "We are the Council of Moonledge Peak. I am Caratacus, and I was assigned by the Rion Guard to oversee our time in this place."

"My name is Galbard, son of Gulbrand. I, too, was a citizen of Rion."

"I know the name of Gulbrand—he was of my time," Caratacus said. "Did your father make the journey?"

"No, my lord. My father has returned to the Creator, eight winters past."

"I rejoice in his return," Caratacus said. "My friends, the right good members of this council, wish to know what fortune has brought you to us. Would you endeavor to endure our questions?"

"But of course, my lord," Galbard responded. "Please, ask what you wish."

Galbard found that Caratacus and his companions had many questions, for they were very curious of the progress of the war. Galbard apologized yet again that he had very little news of the war, and recounted once again his journey to the mountains, but beyond that, Galbard said little.

"You are a mystery," Caratacus said. "A man alone in this wilderness is a curiosity to the council, but we can find no harm in your staying here with us."

"I assure my lord that I will bring no harm to the good people of Rion," Galbard answered. He felt his face tighten and redden, though he tried to will it still. *The presence of the Sword may bring just that,* he thought to himself.

"Food is scarce, but enough for one more," Caratacus announced to the group. "Illian, show Galbard where he might find food, drink, and rest."

"Yes, my lord," Illian responded, motioning Galbard to follow.

Galbard turned to follow him and noticed the council drawing close together, their low voices echoing unintelligibly in the corridor Galbard and Illian used to return to the main dwelling place.

"I hope I have not intruded," Galbard said.

"You would have known it at this first meeting if they thought as much," Illian said. "The council has no issue with letting their feelings be known."

"That is good," said Galbard. "I can work for the food you offer."

"That you will," Illian responded. He waited for Galbard's face to change to something akin to concern, and then he could not contain himself, letting his hearty laughter bounce off the cave walls. "That you will!"

Illian led Galbard to a small dwelling where several women were pounding thick strips of meat with stones and hanging them inside a small leather tent to smoke. One of the women handed him a small stone platter of the smoked meat and a cup of clear, cool water from a trickle that passed through their dwelling. Galbard sipped from a polished stone cup, and eagerly ate the dried meat. He marveled at its wonderful taste, so much so that he had to consciously slow his chewing, and when he commented that it was very tasty, they giggled and fed him until he could eat no more.

Galbard thanked the women profusely, and then Illian led him to yet another cave, where several men were winding cord to make or mend nets. The room had many torches.

"There are fish," Illian said, pointing to a dark pool of water at the lower end of the cave, its surface looking almost like pitch in the torchlight.

"Fish?" Galbard asked.

Illian pointed to a strange, pale-white creature the men pulled from their nets. "Yes, my friend, there is a great cavern beneath us, filled with all manner of sightless fish. Had it not been for a small boy falling into this opening, we might never have found it. When we pulled him from its clutches, he said that he felt something all around him, touching his hands, feet, and face. He had nearly drowned from panic in the darkness.

We have since mounted these torches and ventured with a lanyard into the depths. In the light that the torches provide, we have found neither the bottom nor the sides, and though it is fairly still now, when the rains come, the currents can be quite dangerous."

"Amazing," Galbard said.

"You mentioned that you once fished the northern lake?"

"As a child, I mended nets for my father."

"I was hoping that you could help the men."

"Yes, of course. I'm glad to earn my keep."

Galbard stayed at this task for several days, and his weaving of the nets proved considerably helpful to the other stonemasons, whose experience with such things was lacking. It was the first time that Galbard felt at ease, and though he kept mostly to himself, he became fast friends with Illian and the men who worked the nets. His welcome ease brought sleep that he had not enjoyed in years, deep and restful, and Galbard thought that he might at last have some peaceful place to lay his head. However, on the fourth day, his deep sleep brought a dream that changed everything.

In this dream, he walked through the caverns alone, passing rooms now empty where the refugees of Rion had once been. The silence was menacing, and a chilling breeze moved through the passages, one by one extinguishing the torches that lit his way. Suddenly, there was naught but darkness, and Galbard stumbled and fell, fighting back the rising fear that he would never find his way out of the immense void swallowing him. He felt a firm hand clamp onto his arm, and he instinctively reached for the Sword — but it was not at his side.

"You must leave this place!" a gravelly voice said, and Galbard thrashed about from hearing it, but he could not break away from the iron grip.

"Who . . . who are you?" Galbard managed.

"I am Tophian, Watcher of the Mountains!" the voice responded, and the grip released. A magical light suddenly illuminated their surroundings. The man before him had chest-length white hair combed back, save for a single tuft that curled beside his light blue eyes. He stood there with his walking stick, its curved handle caught up in one of his fingerless leather gloves, dark crystal studs adorning their long cuffs. He turned the other palm up, and an orb of light floated above it, revealing a beard neatly trimmed around his chin, and a blue cloak that partially covered a breastplate bearing a yellow, triangular pattern and numerous belts and pouches. Ancient Rionese script was embroidered in brown thread along the forearm-length sleeves of his white tunic. "This is what is to come if you remain amongst these people, Galbard! The Sword draws the Camonra to you even now! Take it from this place, or ruin will come to you all!"

Galbard awoke with a start, striking his head on the low ceiling above his bedding so hard it dazed him. He looked about frantically for the Sword and his pack, and having put his hands on them both, he drew a deep, calming breath and exhaled slowly. He looked out through the window-like opening carved into the humble abode Illian had so kindly shared with him, and he saw the rock walls surrounding him flickered with candlelight. The panic of the dream subsided. Galbard thought with sadness about leaving what little comfort he had found on his journeys. The thick stone walls of Moonledge had become protective, peaceful, where the still of the night was broken only by the faint sound of snoring or the occasional child's stirring. He took that moment to take it all in for what would likely be the last time.

Illian woke to find Galbard stuffing his pack with some of the dried fish and goat meat.

"Galbard?" Illian inquired. "What are you doing?"

Galbard stopped and looked at the pack. "I must leave you," he said, and then he resumed his packing.

"Leave?" Illian asked. "What do you mean?"

"It's not safe for me to be here," Galbard began.

"Not safe? Why, Galbard, you're our brother! What possible harm could come to you here?"

Galbard stopped packing again, trying to think of the right words to explain his vision.

"Galbard?" Illian asked. His face was a mixture of confusion and hurt.

"My brothers, indeed," Galbard responded. "It's not what you would do to me, but what evil I might bring upon you."

"What evil you would bring upon us? I don't understand," Illian replied.

"I have had a vision," Galbard began. "A vision given to me by a Watcher named Tophian. He has told me that the Inferiors search me out, and staying here will only mean that I endanger everyone."

"Galbard," Illian chuckled nervously. "It is a nightmare. It means nothing. Stop what you are doing and let us talk of this."

"This was no child's nightmare. I *must* leave you," Galbard said, his tone causing Illian to straighten up in his bedroll.

Illian stared at him, not knowing what to say. Galbard finished packing, and he rose to leave, but Illian rose to his feet and grabbed his arm.

"Surely, you can explain yourself a bit better, Galbard. Do I not deserve that much?"

Galbard stopped and looked at the floor of the room.

"Yes, Illian," Galbard said. "You do, indeed. If I tell you something, will you swear to the Creator that you will speak of it to no other?"

"I swear it," answered Illian.

Then Galbard told Illian everything. He told him of his capture, of the vision of Evliit, and his receiving of the Sword. He told him what had happened at Highwood, and then he stopped, trying to judge Illian's somber face.

"This is much to take in at one sitting," Illian said. "I am beyond words."

"You have done well by me, Illian. I am forever grateful. What little comfort I have known on this journey, you have provided — provided, it seems, by the hand of the Creator himself. Forgive my leaving so abruptly, but know that I go because of the very fondness for my brethren that would have me stay."

Illian turned from him and rummaged in the darkness near his bedroll. He produced two loaves of bread and pushed them toward him.

"Here, take this. You will need them more than I," Illian said.

"I cannot take any more from you, my friend," Galbard responded.

"Take them," Illian insisted, reaching across Galbard and pushing them into his pack. "May the Creator watch over you and keep you safe."

Galbard wrapped his arms around Illian, squeezing him tightly.

Illian brought him to arm's length. "Where will you go?" he asked.

"I don't know," Galbard answered. "I truly don't know what I'm to do." He turned his face from Illian and moved to the doorway. "I suppose I'll follow the mountains northeast."

"Then take this as well," Illian said, offering Galbard his animal skin coat. "I stitched a hood into it when we first arrived; it was so cold here compared to Rion. I was sure I was going to freeze," he said with a soft smile. "Take care of yourself, Galbard."

"And you as well, my friend," Galbard said. He stepped through the doorway, then poked his head back in. "The Camonra live on. They are not destroyed. Prepare the people for their coming, and I pray that this Tophian, this Watcher of Mountains, may come to your aid when that day arrives."

Galbard looked one last time into Illian's face, searching his eyes for understanding. Illian's nod was enough. He turned and made his way through the caves and out onto the northern plains. Pulling the coat over his shoulders and settling his pack, he looked one last time at the cave opening in the moonlight before venturing east.

Chapter Eight

Shinetower

Days after the incident on the beach, Cayden was still grappling with the fear and distrust left in its wake. It had scared the life out of everyone involved, and those days passed with little interaction between the other refugees and Cayden, Nara, or, by association, Jalin. There were often whispers from the others, and Cayden truly began to worry about Nara's safety, so he had pitched two tents for them away from the shore, away from the other refugees.

Jalin had just put Ro down for a nap, and she and Nara were talking. Nara was complaining of the muscles in her arm twitching. Cayden was tending the fire when Nara suddenly fell onto her back, writhing in pain She was convulsing, making a choking sound.

Cayden scrambled about and found a wooden dowel that they used for pinning stone among some masonry tools. He wiped it off on his pants, thinking of using it for her to bite down on.

"Hurry, Cayden!" Jalin said.

Cayden pushed the stick toward her face, but she grabbed it from his hands, rolled over, and jabbed the stick into the dirt beside the campfire. She swept her hand wildly across the dirt, but something about the motion made Cayden think it was more than random shapes.

"She's trying to draw something!" he said. "Stay with her. I'll be back!"

He turned and headed toward the main refugee camp.

"Where are you going?" Jalin asked. "Don't leave us here alone!"

"I'm going to find something for her to write with," he said. "Stay with her. I'll be right back."

Jalin looked up at him with wide, frightened eyes. "It's going to be all right," he insisted.

"Please hurry," she whispered. She folded her arms, one hand rising to her mouth as she bit her lip and swayed anxiously.

"I'll hurry," he replied, and then he ran toward the main camp.

The refugees had offloaded a stash of all kinds of things from the *Merrius*, and he was sure he had seen a wooden pen, ink, and paper among them.

When he arrived at the main camp, people were preparing to eat the evening meal. They had formed a line to a large soup pot that he recognized from the *Nurium's* galley. He moved around them to a broad tent pitched for the supplies. The person posted at the entrance recognized him from a distance, met his eyes, then quickly looked away. For once, their fear worked to his advantage, and the post moved to the side from the entrance without saying a word.

He rummaged through the supplies and found several pieces of paper, a pen, and ink. Then he bolted back out, ignoring the looks and murmurs of the few who noticed his sudden coming and going.

He sprinted back to Nara's side, pulling the paper from where he'd tucked it inside his shirt and producing the pen and ink well from his trousers. He dipped the pen, unfolded the largest sheet he had, and laid it across a smooth chunk of wood they used as a chopping block, pressing out the wrinkles with his hands.

"Nara?" he said.

He set the pen and paper before her on the block. She rolled up to a squatting position and tossed aside the dowel. Snatching the pen, she began scribbling furiously. At one point she knocked over the ink, splashing a corner of the page with blackness.

Without hesitation, she dragged the pen through the spill and across the paper, her frantic lines bursting outward from the indigo blot, instantly folding it into whatever she was creating.

"I worry for her," Jalin replied. She looked over Nara's automatic drawing. "I pray to the Creator that these spirits will leave her."

"Soon," Cayden said, turning and sitting beside her to study the frantic drawing she was creating. He barely had time to replace one scrap of paper with another as she filled them.

"It's a building of some type," he said. "Some kind of tower, I think."

After a few minutes more, Nara suddenly lurched backward onto the ground, dropping the pen from her hand.

Nara's eyes closed. "Ah!" she shouted. Then the strain in her face calmed. She opened her eyes and focused on Cayden.

"Cayden?" she asked. "Is it over, Cayden?"

"Yes, darling," Cayden said. He caught the hint of a smile on Jalin's face at his choice of words.

"It's okay, you're with us," said Jalin, wiping the sweat from Nara's face. She leaned in close and whispered, "I believe he's quite madly in love with you." Jalin feigned coyness with a muted giggle, but then with great seriousness, added, "No matter what this thing is that haunts you, Nara, you will overcome it."

"Look what you have drawn," said Cayden. The two of them helped Nara sit up.

"I feel strangely relieved," Nara said.

"*You* were drawing this, Nara," Jalin said. "Can you remember anything?"

"No," Nara replied. "Well, I remember talking with you both, and then the uncontrollable shaking in my arm, but then nothing until now."

There was the sound of Ro's crying from their tent. "Oh, my darling," Jalin said. "Let me check on him."

"I am fine," Nara insisted.

"Yes, of course," Jalin responded, this time openly smiling at Nara. She glanced at Cayden and entered their small tent where Ro had been sleeping.

"Let me look at this," said Cayden, reaching for the largest parchment.

"Of course," Nara responded.

Cayden took that parchment and studied it. It was a drawing of a tower-like structure, and a scrawl across the bottom gave instructions to the stonemasons of Rion to cut the stone from the massive rocks by the sea. It even delineated where the tower was to be built.

Cayden studied the drawing. "These stones are to be cut thirty hands across and sixteen hands deep and wide!" he exclaimed. "And this tower is nearly two leagues away from the shore! We have no animals of burden to move such massive stones that great distance. Even the great masons of Rion could not do this!"

"It is to be done," Nara responded. "Of that I'm sure, Cayden."

Jalin returned from their small tent carrying Ro. "What have you found?" she asked. "Is there anything more . . . about Galbard?"

"No, Jalin, I'm sorry. It's a map of sorts and a floor plan. This part tells of the quarry, and this . . ." Cayden began. "Wait, look at this," he said.

"What is it?" both women asked.

"This says that we are to cut the stone and move it no further than what is needed for us to cut the next. Cut it and leave it where it lies, so that we may know the power of the Creator."

"What?" the women repeated, but Cayden was oblivious. He grabbed up the drawing. "Wait here," he said. "I must let the masons of Rion see these."

"But," Nara began, reaching out to him. "Are you sure?"

Cayden looked deeply into her eyes. He wanted her to trust him—and for him to prove worthy of that trust. "I believe in my heart that this is best, Nara. I would never hurt you."

"Yes, of course," Nara said, looking a bit embarrassed at first. "The others have already shunned us, and I must admit I'm a bit afraid that this might only make things worse. I don't want to be alone anymore."

Cayden could see that her lip was beginning to quiver. "Never alone, Nara," he said. "Not as long as I breathe."

Nara nodded. "Of course. Do what you will with it, but I don't want to be there. I'll stay here with Jalin and Ro."

"Surely. Come now, that's enough of this," Jalin interjected. "Ro would love the company." Jalin took her by the hand.

Cayden waited for them to enter the tent, and he walked back toward the main camp, holding the papers open and apart, ensuring that they were drying properly. It was getting dark, and Cayden steadily picked up his pace toward the main camp, for he felt a sense of purpose. He was sure these drawings held the secret of how he was to "protect the bearer of the Sword."

When he came upon the edge of the encampment, he stopped and held the drawings over his head. "Men of Rion!" he shouted. "I bring news!"

His excitement quickly faded. The women and children moved away from him behind the men, and Cayden noticed that the men were standing their ground as if they expected to defend themselves. He lowered the drawings.

"What is it you command of us?" someone shouted from the crowd.

"Command of you?" Cayden answered. "*I* command nothing. It is the Witch of Southwood for whom I speak. I bring a message, a way for us to satisfy our oath."

The father of a young family stepped forward. "If your message will end this curse, we want to hear it," he said. "The darkness of these days must end."

An old woman stepped toward Cayden with the assistance of her staff, and then she turned around to face the crowd. "What are you waiting for? Come let us judge for ourselves what message this one brings!"

The young family moved to join her, and then others appeared from the crowd and joined them. Someone shouted for a table, and when it was brought, Cayden spread the drawings across it for all to see.

"It is a tower fit for the likes of Rionese masons," Cayden began. "It has seven floors that rise above the wilderness." Realizing the crowd was too large to see, he stepped onto the table and held the drawings aloft. "We are to cut gears and wheels of stone, large flat plates like the segments of a circle, and there is work for the blacksmith and the carpenter, for there are great rods of steel, wooden rings, and timbers for floors and bracing."

"What are these?" one of the masons asked, pointing to trenches and pits around the structure.

"There appears to be an intricate labyrinth of square holes and ditches all around the main structure. "Maybe they are for water? A garden? I don't know," answered Cayden. "There are pipes and levers and all manner of gadgetry set in the stone."

"Show us again the drawing of the tower itself," said another.

Cayden shuffled the pages. "The top floor has an altar of sorts, open to the air, and the floors are connected by steps that spiral around a central column of stone." Cayden showed them the drawings of intricate stone and metalwork. Many of the components Cayden could neither name nor describe their purposes, but he was sure of one thing: the Witch of Southwood wanted them to build it.

"Only a Rionese mason can grasp the magnitude of such a project," Cayden said. "Look here." He held up a drawing of three quarries between the beach and the nearby fields. The plan marked the locations of thousands of stones, though it offered little guidance on how they were to be set.

"We'll use plugs and feathers to separate the stones, and then leave them where they lay for the apprentices to put the cock's comb to them. The next day we will do the same, and the day after that, until every stone that is required has been cut and shaped."

"But how do we move the stones?" asked another. "We could gather wood for the ramps we'll need to raise them, but I've seen only six head of cattle on the boats still arriving—and we may be hard-pressed to keep the villagers from turning those into steak."

Cayden sorted through the drawings again. "The tower's location itself appears to be one of the quarries, so that's not an issue." There were arrows from the other quarries to the tower's final location. "Here, brother," Cayden said. He pointed to the words under the arrow. "It says 'Bhre-Nora,'" he said with a nervous smile.

"Bhre-Nora?" another asked. "Like the little temple statues?"

Cayden stared at the drawing, but nothing came to him. "I don't know, but it is not the oxen. There is a trail marked for the oxen to use to bring iron ore from here," he said pointing to the map.

There were murmurs again, and then another of the masons spoke up. "How do we know that the Witch of Southwood does not mean to use this altar for some great evil?"

Cayden knew that this would come up, but he was not about to let them turn Nara into some harbinger of evil. "I have seen no instruction to build an image of a deity of any kind, nor credit taken by any foul names that we might recognize. There is no reference to anything but the Sword of the Evliit. I fear not the Creator's wrath so much for building it as for *not* doing so. You witnessed what happened on the beach, same as me, and for anyone that doesn't remember, Tadhra still bears witness within the glass."

The murmurs ceased, and one of the master masons spoke up. "We are masons of Rion. This is what we do. What must be done to satisfy the witch must be done, but know that we will hold you accountable for any evil that comes to us."

"I understand," replied Cayden.

*   *   *

Work began immediately, and though Cayden was very much in the middle of things, Nara did not go to the quarries, but busied herself with Ro and Jalin, away from the central encampment.

After two months of backbreaking labor, the blacksmiths had poured the iron and hammered out the metalwork, and the masons had etched the last of the stones in all three quarries. At last, they laid down their tools. Cayden had dreaded this moment, for no matter how many times he sifted through the scraps of drawing, he could find nothing about what came next. There was only the reference to the "Bhre-Nora," which gave him little more to say to the masons.

"What shall we do now, Cayden?" one asked. "We have laid the metalwork into the pits, and the stone has been cut."

"Rest, friends, let me see what more I can find within the drawings," he said. "We have finished the work we have been given," Cayden announced. "Leave the stone where it lay."

A low murmur rippled through the masons — not revolt, but far from confidence. "Leave it where it lay?" they asked.

"Yes. You may return to your camps."

For the remainder of the day, Cayden sat at the northern quarry with Nara's drawings, watching the motionless stone. The sun slowly fell over the ocean behind him. He rolled the drawings up and accepted that, for now, he had done all he could.

Cayden approached their small camp, and Nara walked out to meet him.

"Come, eat, and rest, Cayden," Nara said. "One of the snares has netted us a rabbit!"

"Excellent!" exclaimed Cayden, but as he approached her, he could see that something was wrong. "Something bothering you?" he probed.

"That obvious, huh?" Nara replied. "Jalin has had a tough day. She tried speaking with some of the others about returning to Rion, but no one would even answer her. I think it would be good for her to have a decent meal and hear what all was accomplished today."

"Yes, of course," Cayden replied.

Cayden got a cook fire going, and he laid out two blankets beside it. They had a pleasant meal of rabbit, and afterward, Cayden tried to reassure Jalin. "You should stay here with us," he urged. "We've cut the stone required by the drawings. I feel like we'll know so much more about the tower very soon, and when its purpose comes to light, you should be here with us."

She seemed about to acquiesce, but Ro became fussy, and when it seemed that he might wake, she got up with him. "Time for me and the little one to retire for the night," she said, and then she heaved him upon her shoulder. "You're getting so big," she said. Ro lay his head against his mother's neck, his thumb just managing to stay in his mouth. Jalin looked at Cayden and Nara, and she smiled. "Thank you," she said. "Thank you for being so good to us. I owe you so much, but . . . this tower will take many years to build, and I don't know if I have the faith to wait that long. I *must* find my husband. Ro needs his father. I hope you can understand."

"Of course," Nara said, though the disappointment in her voice was unmistakable.

"Of course," echoed Cayden. "Nara and I will see to the fire; get yourself some rest."

"Goodnight," said Jalin, and then she and the baby slipped into their tent.

The night sky filled with a scattering of stars. Cayden picked up the blankets and checked the fire, and then he and Nara, too, made their way to bed.

*　　*　　*

"Cayden?" Nara whispered.

Cayden rolled over, trying to rouse himself from the dead sleep of a hard day's labor. "What is it?" he responded.

"Sounds like a good wind's stirring up, and I'm not sure the tents are staked well enough to wait it out. Could you look them over? I would hate to lose the tents if the rain follows.

Cayden felt a flicker of irritation, but he shook off the sleep and rose. "Yes, of course, I'll check them both," he said as he pulled on his pants. Fumbling with his belt, he noticed that the wind was picking up quickly, and his rising seemed better timed with each passing moment.

He pushed aside the tent flap and stepped into the gusts, facing the moonlit ocean. Far out to sea, a massive waterspout raged over the waves, twisting the surface with the sheer force of its spinning winds.

A deep rumble swelled from the distance, and Cayden threw the tent flap back open.

"Nara!" he yelled. "Get up! Get Jalin and the baby!"

Nara saw the look on Cayden's face and rose immediately, moving quickly into Jalin's tent.

Cayden watched the whirlwind bear down on them, then turned to the scattered tents of the Rionese camp, dread tightening in his chest. The refugees emerged from their tents slowly at first, but when they realized the storm was bearing straight toward them, they broke into a run, fleeing east toward him

Cayden watched the waterspout turn onto the shore, and the sand drew up into the funnel. Its white funnel turned dingy as it sucked up sand, and once it crossed onto the mainland, the winds darkened to a heavy gray.

Following Nara and Jalin, Cayden began moving toward cover when suddenly he noticed something changing about the whirlwind. The cloud ceiling above it seemed to take on the shape of a face, its widening mouth coughing forth what looked like a dark mist. He stood there, frozen in his steps. The swirling mist drew closer, and Cayden realized it was no mist at all, but thousands of small creatures. Their fluttering wings rode the whirlwinds with ease, moving back and forth between the twirling debris.

He watched the whirlwind pass over the great stones they had cut from the shoreline, its tremendous winds breaking loose the stones from Erathe's grip and hurling them into the air. The small creatures seemed to swarm the rising stones in clumps, their tiny wings making a buzzing noise that added to the cacophony of the storm. Together, the swarm and the whirlwind shepherded the stones toward the southern edge of the valley.

"The Bhre-Nora," Cayden muttered in his shock. The winds whipped his hair around his head, but his eyes remained fixed upon them. Repeatedly, the tiny creatures followed the stones' trajectories, wrangling them under control, and then guiding them into a line behind their brethren like a caravan. There was a rumbling of the clouds, the flashes of lightning intensified, and suddenly, with a great clap, the fingers of electricity combined into one great bolt that shot into the ground from the swirling clouds.

Cayden saw the energy boring into the earth like a carpenter's drill, sending great chunks of stone into the stratosphere. The lightning struck the mixture repeatedly, and a slurry of molten stone formed in the air. The molten slurry spun within the whirlwind, stretching into a cylinder far larger than any column Cayden had ever seen in the Rionese temples. When the cylinder formed, the clouds began to slow their winds. The great stone column seemed to stall in the air for a moment, and then it began its fall from the skies. The whirlwind appeared to be dissipating.

The creatures were deft at corralling the cut stone, but they ignored the other debris entirely, and Cayden realized it would be deadly to remain anywhere near the base when the winds released it. "Run!" he yelled, and then he ran to Nara, Jalin, and Ro, grabbing Nara by the arm.

A large stone shot past them overhead. "Run! This way!" Cayden yelled. They sprinted for the shelter of a shallow ditch and threw themselves into the cool water. Another stone bounced once near them and crashed into the ground a second time, peeling the turf from the earth and piling up a mound of dirt, shaking them to their core. Several others saw them and joined them in the ditch.

The column accelerated to terminal velocity, and a silence seemed to take hold. Cayden looked up for a last time, just in time to see the column stick into the ground like an arrow shot, sinking at least half its length. He saw the earth ripple outward from the impact, ducking just before a wave of dust and debris swept over them. The concussive force of the shockwave sent anyone standing flying through the air, and the ensuing layer of thick dust that hung in the air blinded anyone within the circumference of the expanding wave, blocking the moonlight and stars.

Cayden tried to get his bearings, rising from the muddy water in which they lay. The top of his head felt like he had been kicked, his organs quivered as if he had been shaken violently. His hearing returned after a short while of muted ringing in his ears, only to be replaced by a humming sound in the distance, whose volume and pitch rose and fell in waves. Intermittent grating and grinding rose from the distance, punctuated by heavy thumps that shook the ground beneath him.

Cayden could hear Ro gagging for air. One of the tent poles was still standing in Jalin's partially collapsed tent, but his and Nara's tent was still standing. He hurried to help Nara, Jalin, and the baby into it.

"Stay here," he said, but Nara and Jalin just plopped down with Ro, saying nothing in return. He grabbed a shirt from inside the tent, closed the tent flaps behind him, and tied them shut. Then he tied the shirt around his nose and mouth, using one of the sleeves to wipe the mud from his eyes. He drove a stake into the ground outside the tent, tied a rope to it, and fastened the other end to his belt. He began the arduous task of looking around for people lost in the aftermath of the storm.

He found several of his people still lying on the ground, many of them exhausted from wandering in the wind and dust. "Follow my rope back to our tents and get inside!" he told them.

For three days, the winds raged, and the dust made it nearly impossible to see or travel. The refugees gathered what they could of their belongings and hunkered down in what remained of their tents and lean-tos.

On the fourth day, the winds subsided. Cayden walked back toward the massive column, but there were none of the little creatures in sight. He climbed the small knoll where he and his group had taken cover. The Rionese artisans were yelling from all directions, a group of them shouting and pointing to the west. A twenty-foot wall of stone surrounded the column at a radius of about fifty paces. Hammering and muffled voices echoed from behind the stone barrier.

Cayden walked around the high wall with the other men, but there was no way in. They waited until nightfall for something more to happen, but the strange sounds from within the walls soon unnerved them. They returned to their camps.

For seven nights, Cayden stepped outside his tent and looked at the stone column. The buzzing sounds were endless, but the moonless nights left him blind to what was happening. Each morning, he woke to find stones disappearing from the quarries and rising around the stone column, until at last, under secrecy of night, the tower had risen.

On the evening of the seventh day, a blast of wind rushed through that place, and a low trumpeting pitch rumbled through the valley. There was the sound of chains and gears, and the mighty wall that surrounded the tower parted. Cayden marveled that it did not swing like a gate; instead, the two walls slid apart horizontally, like the eyelid of a giant lying on his side.

Cayden joined some other craftsmen mingling at the opening, watching the tower for some sign of life, but they saw none.

"Should we go in?" one of the masons asked.

"Cayden should go," another piped up.

"Yes, Cayden should go," they all agreed.

"I will go," Cayden responded. "This stonework is of the Creator's doing, there's nothing to fear."

He walked alone through the outer walls to the inner court and looked around, but there was no one in sight. The tower shot into the sky, and when he moved a little to the south, it blocked out the sun, revealing the balconies stacked high above him.

His gaze drifted downward. A doorway stood open below, and three of the small creatures shot out from it — two racing toward the southern trees, the third fluttering to a stop in the grass before Cayden. It was a small, winged, man-like creature, no taller than Cayden's knee. Long hair stuck out from beneath a tight leather cap with a ridged crown, from which tiny brass goggles hung before its eyes. He had elbow-length gloves that flared at the top, knee-high boots, and a long coat. Poking out from beneath the long coat was a tiny golden rapier, and leather straps crisscrossed his vest, having strange devices hanging from them. He looked up at Cayden, his wings twitching to reveal metallic panels where feathers should have been. The wings were jointed in three places, which the little man spread and then folded behind him when Cayden approached.

"The Creator has seen fit to build a temple here," the third little creature said.

Cayden was speechless for a moment. "It is truly amazing," he managed at last. Then, almost uncertainly, "Thank you."

"My Lady of Southwood has sent us to help you protect the Sword. She has seen the labor you have put forth with the stone and has found favor in you. Prepare for its coming and she may yet find favor in you still."

The creature turned and zipped through the air a good thirty paces before Cayden yelled out to him. "But how should we prepare?" he asked.

Looking very pleased, it circled back to him. "There is woodwork and furnishing, of course," he said. "And much more stonework that you should do to make ready the way for the sword! I have left you a list. And look for the man named Galbard to bring the sword, for he has saved it from the clutches of the evil one, Amphileph!" He spun around and quivered upon uttering the Spellmaker's name. "We will make a great battlement to protect the mighty Sword of the Watch from the evil one and his creatures!" he said, with great defiance in his voice. "We must build it mighty indeed!"

The winged artisan darted to within inches of Cayden's face, making him flinch. "Build it in honor of the Creator himself!"

The little creature flipped his goggles aside and studied Cayden's face, his tiny head bobbing as he peered into each of Cayden's eyes. Whatever he found there seemed to satisfy him; he gave a single, decisive nod.

"Blessings upon your efforts, human."

He flipped his goggles back into place, and he shot away in a whoosh of air that made Cayden's eyes flutter under the force of his wingbeats.

"My name is… Cayden," he tried to call after him.

He shook his head, trying to clear the disbelief, but when he set his hand against the surrounding stone, it was solid beneath his palm. This was no dream.

He walked toward the doorway of the great tower with the same awe that he would a holy temple in the old city of Rion. He searched for any sign forbidding entry, but found none, and then he knelt on one knee before the entrance and looked up at the sky.

"Mighty Creator!" he yelled. "Please grant me entry!"

After a moment, he stood up, took a deep breath, and then broached its doorway. He stepped through the threshold, counting three paces of solid stone before the room opened around him.

As Cayden's eyes adjusted to the light, he looked around at the flawless stonework rising above him. The tower had stood for only seven days, yet its construction was so precise it might have been carved in a single breath. The great central column dominated the space, a massive shaft of stone wrapped in copper tubing that climbed through the heart of the tower and vanished into the shadows overhead. Cayden noted the narrow gap where the column passed cleanly through the floor above — a deliberate allowance for expansion, though he could not imagine what kind of heat such a structure was meant to endure.

Set against the outer wall was the stairway, ascending in both directions just as he had seen in the Nara's drawings. Six narrow windows cut into the stone cast thin beams of light across the landing. Something glimmered in the glow above.

Cayden stepped between the column and the outer wall and climbed the first turn of the stairs. There, resting on the landing as if placed with intention, lay a large scroll tied with a ribbon. He untied it and unrolled the parchment, angling it toward the nearest window.

"Oh my," Cayden whispered. "We've much to do."

CHAPTER NINE

THE HUNT BEGINS

Amphileph stared at the bloodstain Ardidhus's body had left on the temple dome. The summer heat had long since turned its reddish hue to brown, yet to Amphileph the moment felt freshly carved into memory. He could still see Ardidhus's face just before he'd hurled him through the air.

For the first time in his life, he felt utterly alone. "Creator," he said. "Why have you allowed Evliit to torture me so? I've demanded nothing but reverence for you!" He stood still, awaiting an answer, but his prayers seemed to whisk away in the wind, and silence was the only reply.

The stench of the other Spellmakers' rotting corpses clung to the air, a constant reminder of his violent coup. He could take it no longer. "Camonra!" he shouted. Within moments, three of the Camonra appeared from the western camp. He thought they smelled of wet dog.

"Yes, master!" one of them said. The three of them stayed low to the ground, diverting their eyes from him.

"Burn the bodies of the other Fathers!" he screamed. "I can't bear their stench another moment!"

"Yes, my lord," they replied, and immediately they turned to the task.

"You!" Amphileph said. "Bring my beloved Clogren to my study!"

"Yes, master!" he replied.

Amphileph walked to his temple and opened the door to his study with the wave of his hand. He entered and began rummaging through the glass jars on one of the shelves. The Camon carried Clogren in and tried to set him in the chair, but rigor mortis had already locked his limbs. When Amphileph heard the sickening snap of stiffened joints, he shrieked at the Camon in fury.

"Leave me!" he shouted. The Camon turned to go, but Amphileph hurled him out of the doorway and slammed it shut behind him. "Such incompetence! I need nothing more from you!"

He gathered several jars and set them on the table. "You, Clogren, are a different matter altogether. You alone have remained faithful." Amphileph opened the jars and arranged them in front of Clogren. "What's that?" he asked. "Yes, of course, my friend. We have much to discuss. Please, please — be seated." Amphileph rubbed herbs and oils into Clogren's body, and he soaked his joints until he was able to gently bend them and seat him at the table.

When he finished, Amphileph capped the jars, removed them back to the shelves, and sat down beside Clogren. "We will unravel the mystery of this Binding Spell together." Amphileph rummaged among the books scattered everywhere on the floor around them.

"I have mapped the exact shape of the spell's effective area — its height, its depth, the objects that failed to pass through its field — every scrap of information that might prove useful."

"Yes, I have punished the Spellmakers that did this to you. Now they wish that they had sided with us rather than with Evliit!" he laughed. "They fully expected to foil everything that we had worked so hard to achieve. The Creator's holiness demanded more than the simpletons of the human race could provide, and I have moved to make things right."

Clogren's mouth hung open, as if in reply.

"You are right. Evliit lacks the discipline to remove these worthless sacks of meat from this world, and in his arrogance, he stands against me, his poison costing us everything, and now—now there is nothing left of the Spellmakers save that impossible Citanth! He will never serve me as you have," Amphileph cried out.

"We see what you are," said a voice.

"What?" Amphileph replied. Instead of Clogren, Ardidhus's battered corpse sat slumped in the chair. "We see what you are," Ardidhus repeated, though the crumpled left side of his face lagged behind the right side.

Amphileph stood up and screamed aloud; his heart felt like it would burst. He instinctively cursed, and the chair blew apart.

Clogren's body scattered about the room while pieces of the chair's stuffing slowly drifted down around him, but Ardidhus had disappeared. He bent over and picked up Clogren's severed arm, staring around at the splattered ruin in disbelief.

"No!" he cried. "Clogren!" He dropped the arm as tears welled in his eyes. "Ardidhus! Show yourself!" Amphileph screamed again. "I will… I will…" he stammered. The volume of his voice quickly fell to nothing, but the thoughts screamed inside his head: Ardidhus is dead! Ardidhus is dead!

He flung Clogren's arm aside in disgust, as though only now realizing what he held. The Camonra watch me, looking for my weakness. They would not hesitate to usurp me in my weakness. Amphileph looked toward the courtyard, expecting to see them crowded at the entrance with blades drawn, but there was no one there.

"Citanth!" Amphileph screamed, its high pitch revealing his terror. He waited for a moment, but no one answered. "Citanth!"

Amphileph stormed out of the library and marched toward the northern fields. He approached the stones marking the Binding's edge, and he yelled again, red faced and huffing, "You are last among us!"

Amphileph noticed movement through the windows of the small mud hut at the Camon's post just north of the Binding. A Camon appeared and then groveled before him. "Find Citanth!" Amphileph cried.

The warrior scampered away from him toward the larger tents that were pitched some sixty or seventy paces north yet. A man staggered out of one of the tents and looked toward Amphileph. It was Citanth — drunk, Amphileph thought.

Citanth tilted his head back with disdain, looking down his nose, his pursed lips pushing his soul patch forward. With his left hand he tossed his long black hair over the high shoulders of his brigandine. His right hand — wrapped in a bloodstained rag — he held tight against his midsection.

"Eight hundred years!" he shouted, half laughing, half crying. "Eight hundred years without losing so much as a finger — and now look at me!"

"Oh, spare me," Amphileph hissed.

Citanth barreled on. "I was the one when there was no one else! I convinced the others to listen to you, to take up Spellmaking, and now—"

"Shut up."

"—now in my agony you pity me not?"

"Shut up!" Amphileph roared.

Citanth only jogged toward the Binding's Edge, theatrically obedient, then stopped just short of Amphileph, refusing to meet his gaze.

"When ties with Rion unraveled, who defended you?" he snapped. "I did! I said Spellmaking alone could advance man fast enough to stem the tide of wickedness!"

"You have lain around for months doing nothing!" Amphileph shot back.

"You forget what you've done to me!" Citanth lifted his ruined hand — twisted, charred flesh and bone. "Because of you, my powers are gone! The brothers told you we could not take the Sword from Evliit, but no — you said your spells would protect me! Look at me!"

"You are nothing!" Amphileph spat. "A little man whose bravery depends on this spell that separates us!"

"I am a Spellmaker!" Citanth shouted, voice cracking. "I too was called by the Creator — and you have long lost respect for that!"

Amphileph thrust his hands forward instinctively, and the blast that erupted was so violent that even Citanth flinched. The energy spread through the Binding like ink poured into a basin, momentarily giving the Binding visible shape between them. But then it dissipated.

Citanth's indignation sharpened. "You would kill me as well? The Creator has caged you up for your maleficence! You have brought this upon yourself!"

Amphileph screamed his defiance, and energy from his hand ripped open the ground between them right up to the Binding's edge. A blackness poured out of his body, spreading outward like paint rolling down a lamppost, withering the grass around him. He reached out his hands toward a nearby tree, and its leaves withered and died from some unseen force that ripped it from its roots. It rose above Amphileph's head with the movement of his arm, and he smashed the tree against the Binding until nothing but fragments remained. Amphileph's labored breathing brought him to his knees.

When the dust settled, Citanth stood exactly where he had been — not cowering, not shaken, barely even moved. In fact, he had barely changed the stance he had taken moments before the rampage began.

"Honestly, Amphileph, you waste your energies," Citanth said.

Amphileph rose and brushed the dust from his robes. "Be aware, my brother — sooner or later, I will break this Binding. I will not forget your insolence."

"When that day comes, my dear lord Amphileph, you will have much bigger issues than me to deal with," Citanth sneered, checking the dirt in his fingernails of his good hand. "While you have been studying your incarceration, I have been doing a little thinking of my own.

"Surely you see how grandly this Binding is wrought. Undoing it might have been possible with our brethren's help — but your murderous rage denied you that. What lies within will remain. It is what remains out here," he said, tapping the earth with his boot, "that demands our attention."

"What are you saying?" Amphileph asked.

"I'm merely pointing out that I am capable of executing your plans while you are . . . well, incapacitated."

Amphileph gritted his teeth. "What is it that you want, Citanth?"

"You will name me commander of the legions untouched by the Binding. And when I return with the man Galbard, you will restore my hand — and my powers." He let his demand hang between them for a moment or two as if it too could spark along the invisible plane that kept them apart, never taking his eyes from Amphileph's. "Swear it!"

Amphileph clenched his teeth and fist. "It will be as you wish."

"You will swear it!" Citanth demanded.

His left eye twitched uncontrollably. "I swear it!" Amphileph roared.

Citanth could barely contain his giddiness. "I will gather the Camonra and return. You will tell them as much!"

Amphileph did not answer, straining his last shred of patience.

When Citanth returned with the leaders of the Camonra, they bowed down before Amphileph. "Tell them," said Citanth.

"Citanth now commands you!" Amphileph declared. "Obey him — or you will answer to me."

The warriors bowed before Citanth, an act that clearly pleased their new commander. Citanth dismissed them and walked close to the edge of the Binding directly across from Amphileph.

"I will find the Sword, Amphileph," Citanth said. "The slave Galbard cannot have traveled far. He is on foot, with nothing but the clothes on his back. If we find the man, we find the Sword. It will grant us the power to break the Binding Spell of Evliit."

Citanth unwrapped his charred hand and pressed it against the Binding. "And when I find him, how do you propose I bring the Sword to you? I'll not touch it again."

Amphileph looked over the atrophied limb and back into Citanth's eyes.

"Capture this Galbard alive and bring him to me! He will give me the Sword!"

"And what of our war with Rion?"

"Tobor knows what I expect of him. Send him word that we have given chase to the Sword's thief."

Citanth placed his hand back in its wrapping, cleared his throat, and turned to the Camonra.

"Captains!" he shouted. "For my first act as High Commander of the Camonra: send the unseasoned warriors to Rion to make contact with Tobor. Ready your finest for the mountains to the north. We go to reclaim the Sword for our master!"

Citanth turned back to Amphileph. "If you will excuse me, my lord," he said. He bowed, and then rose and marched away toward the northern camp.

"No excuse will likely come," Amphileph said under his breath.

*   *   *

Galbard struggled to dress the small caribou he had managed to corner and kill just east of where the Faceless Mountains' elevation died away and the Northern Plains opened up to the northern frontier. Blood dripped down his left cheek from a shallow cut — more annoyance than injury. The caribou's glancing blow had hit more squarely on his left shoulder before he had driven his mighty blade into the deer's charging heart. His shoulder was already turning a deep purplish blue, leaving his left arm numb and sluggish.

It was difficult to pull the meat back from the ribs, but his short blade made fairly quick work of the animal's hide. He would waste nothing he could dry and store, and several cuts already sizzled over the smoky fire he'd built.

Galbard kept a constant watch on the horizon. The long, clear view in every direction was the only reason he dared risk the heavy smoke of the campfire.

It didn't hurt that he'd done without much protein since leaving the caves and smoked meat was one of his favorite meals, either. The smell of slow-cooking meat drifting through the smoke made his stomach feel as though it might burn a hole straight through him.

He was concerned about the top of the Faceless Mountains being lost in the clouds that were moving in from the west, and having the dried meat for the journey northwest around them was an absolute necessity.

Though the rough terrain offered wild grains, roots, and the occasional small game, this meat would sustain him for what might be a long journey into solitude with the Sword. He cut off a thin slice of the meat from the spit with his knife, and then put away the blade to free his hands, swapping the meat between his fingers and then his hands; it was almost too hot to touch. When the meat was just cool enough to eat, he tore off a piece of it with his teeth, savoring the flavor.

Drawing the sword from its scabbard, he marveled again at its perfect edge and balance. He rolled his wrist over, and watched how the Sword's blade caught the sunlight. His mind drifted back to the moment Evliit entrusted it to him, and then the sun's reflection flashed across his eyes and broke the trance.

If only he could move farther north, he thought he could make himself disappear with the Sword until Evliit returned for it. To the northwest, a vast tree line looked like just the place in which to disappear. He was sure that the Camonra's confusion over their Rion strategy would soon be resolved, and they would quickly turn their attentions to him. When that time came, he wanted to be as far away as possible. If only he had more time to master the Sword's mysterious power — even a fraction of it — then perhaps, when the time came, he could stand against them.

The Sword's power was a very difficult thing to put his finger on, but he had begun a morning ritual of drawing it and clearing his mind, channeling its energy through his body. It was then he could feel the warmth in the Sword's hilt slowly creeping down his arms. He tried to remain focused. "I do your will," he said aloud. "I command this power!"

Suddenly, the world around him seemed to slow, and a deep, unnatural calm poured over him. Heat surged through the hilt, rising to an almost unbearable intensity, but he refused to let go. The fire climbed into his chest until it felt as though his ribs themselves were burning.

He focused his mind on the tree before him. The intensity faltered with even the slightest shift in concentration, yet he felt a distinct difference from his earlier attempts. He stepped forward and swept the Sword laterally across the trunk. The explosion of wood fragments startled him.

A shard struck his face near his right eye. He flinched and looked away, and before he could open his eyes again, he heard the groaning protest of the great oak, followed by the sharp crack of wood under strain. When he looked up, most of the tree's circumference had vanished on the side nearest him, and the massive trunk was tipping toward him.

He glanced up its length and threw himself backward, instinctively thrusting out his hand as if to ward off the fall. The tree's deadly descent slowed — then reversed — crashing away from him with a thunderous impact.

Galbard felt the hairs on his arms rise. The unseen energy had surged from the pit of his stomach to the palm of his hand at the exact moment the tree halted. It moved through him like a physical substance — like water — rising, gathering, and then pouring out through his hands. As the force left him, new energy from the Sword flowed into his body to replace it.

Days passed, and his proficiency with this strange power grew rapidly. The moment with the tree had been a turning point, revealing a deeper level of control. As he traveled through the valley toward the stand of trees to the northwest, he practiced whenever he stopped, learning to gather the energy within himself and release it with increasing precision.

Now, he could actually see the wave of force rippling through the waist-high grass. He concentrated, letting the energy build inside him until his skin crawled with it. Then he threw his arms outward and released it. The clouds overhead split apart, and the wave burst from him, flattening the grass in a circle thirty paces wide — and it did not rise again.

*   *   *

Amphileph cried out, "Citanth! Did you feel it?"

Citanth halted his discussion with the Camonra and slowly closed his eyes. "Yes!" he shouted, springing into action. "The fool thinks he can control the power of Evliit's Sword!" he called to Amphileph.

"Find him! Find him now!" Amphileph screamed, then stormed into his temple.

The camp erupted into motion. The commander rallied the Camonra, ordering them to make ready to ride. Their scaly beasts of burden — the giant Azrodh lizards — eyed their riders with reptilian contempt. Tamed only enough to allow the Camon soldiers to mount them, their small brains had been beaten into submission by relentless discipline.

The Camon captains mounted the Azrodh, barked orders to their foot soldiers, and the entire force surged north at double time.

Several human slaves carried Citanth behind the main column in what had once been prepared as Amphileph's victory carriage for his triumphant return to Rion. The commander parted the silk curtain and addressed his head slave. "Aldor, inform the captain that I will be indisposed until we reach the valley. I expect a progress report in the morning."

"Yes, my lord," the slave murmured, eyes downcast. "At once."

The slaves lifted the carriage onto their shoulders and moved in perfect lockstep to ensure their rider's comfort. Citanth cast one last glance toward Amphileph's temple, then let the silken curtains fall shut and slept to the gentle rhythmic sway of the carriage.

*　　*　　*

Galbard reached the Calarphian Wood by early fall, when the trees were at their most majestic. He stood at the edge of the great wood and looked back toward the snowy peaks of the Faceless Mountains.

As he looked down the ridge to the west, a sound behind him made him whirl and draw the Sword. He pressed his back against a tree and peered around it into the forest.

There before him stood an elderly man, bracing himself against a staff as he struggled to remain upright. His long white hair and beard tossed in the wind, yet his eyes stayed fixed on Galbard. His sleeves billowed beneath an animal-skin vest, and Galbard noticed several necklaces — some bearing talismans of earth and beast, and one holding a small pouch embroidered with the symbol of a tree. He wore a wide leather belt around his ankle-length tunic, with tiny pouches and an ornate ox-horn swaying from the loops as he moved.

"They are alerted to your presence," the old man managed.

"What?" Galbard said.

"Your efforts to control the Sword's power alert them to your presence," the old man explained. "They're coming for you." He leaned heavily on his staff as he closed the distance between them.

"Who are you?" Galbard asked. "Have you been watching me?"

"My name is Mategaladh. You've nothing to fear from me, I assure you."

Galbard studied him a moment longer. The old man tried to step forward but stumbled and nearly fell. "You appear to be injured," Galbard said.

Mategaladh attempted a laugh. "Don't trouble yourself with my ailments. It's you who are in great peril."

Galbard stepped closer. "Why do you say that?"

"You've channeled the Sword's energy," Mategaladh said. "Such movement ripples through our world like a wind."

"Only a Watcher could know these things," Galbard said. "Or a Spellmaker." His hand drifted to his weapon.

"Would a follower of Amphileph offer the bearer of the Sword the courtesy of an introduction?" he asked. "When Evliit gave you the Sword, ten Watchers stood against the Spellmakers' evil and forced our greater will upon them. Some were taxed beyond their strength — their very spiritual energy spent — and they were carried into the Third Domain before my eyes."

"Let them come for it now, and I will show them its power."

Mategaladh shook his head. "My friend, you play with it as if it were a toy. You draw the enemy to you as though shouting in the town square."

Mategaladh grimaced and slumped forward.

Galbard looked around, bending to peer between the trees toward the Calarphian Plains north of the Faceless Mountains. He saw no one approaching from the south, yet his heartbeat quickened. He thought of his practicing to control the Sword. "How long?" he asked. "How long until they find me?"

Galbard looked at Mategaladh's face. He needed answers, but the old man was pale and motionless. Galbard drew the Sword of the Watch before him with both hands, closed his eyes, and focused on reviving him.

When he opened his eyes, his hands glowed brightly. He placed one of them on Mategaladh.

"Be well!" he shouted, and the glowing light surged into Mategaladh's chest. The old man gasped, his eyes snapping open.

Ah!" he cried. Galbard steadied him, helping him recline against the nearest tree trunk.

"Careful," Galbard said. "You must rest. If what you say is true, my use of the Sword has likely given away our position."

Mategaladh caught his breath. "We must not tarry." He tried to rise again, but could not. "Give me but a moment, and I will be well enough to ride. We may intercept them in the valley east of here. I—"

"You are in no shape to leave this forest, nor could you stand against the Camonra — much less the Spellmakers!"

"Evliit believed Citanth was the only one not with Amphileph when the Binding was created, but it matters little. He touched the Sword with evil in his heart — that alone would have drained what power he had. It is a wonder he lives at all! I can stand with you. Others have remained here by sheer strength of will. We will come to your aid!"

Galbard shook his head. "This thing — this Binding — has sapped you. Recover your strength, for we men may need the Watchers to win the day. You must be healed and whole. I will hide the Sword as Evliit commanded, and you must gather your strength — and your brethren — to fight another day."

"Galbard," Mategaladh began, then stopped. He reached for his staff and leaned back against the tree. "You must hurry. Go down this path," he said, pointing to their left. "There is a rare Ampura tree with dark wood and roots exposed along a spring. Use your dagger to cut the roots no thicker than your finger. Keep them, Galbard — they can sustain you when other food will not. There is also a small blue fruit in that tree — it grows in bunches like grapes, but resembles a large strawberry. Pick all you can carry. Their sweetness belies their ferocity for healing. You can eat them for any ailment, and their paste can mend even a nasty wound."

Galbard did as Mategaladh instructed, but he brought the best of them back to the old man.

"If their healing is as you say, then you can use some of your own medicine," Galbard jested.

"There is truth in that," Mategaladh said, forcing a smile.

Galbard stayed with him until he had eaten three of the Ampura fruits, and indeed Mategaladh's color and manner seemed much improved.

"You need not sit with me, my friend. The herb will take time to work, and you have little of that. Go now," Mategaladh said. "A day's ride west, up the slow grade, you will find a plateau, and the mountains will rise high indeed. There you will find a boulder marked by a bright red bird — I will see to it. When you see that bird, Galbard, go due south. It is the only passage through those sheer peaks. Go south and flee Calarph. Beyond this range lies another, but it is the lesser of the two to cross. Further still lies a valley, and beyond that, Southwood. There is a woman there, and if things are as I pray, she will aid you further. For now though, you must make what distance you can between yourself and the Camonra."

"I am sorry if I have brought them upon you," Galbard said.

"They will not trouble me," Mategaladh said. "The forest will protect me. But you — you must go now, and ride like the wind!"

Galbard couldn't help but flash a confused look. Ride?

Mategaladh gathered his strength and whistled. "I have a new Calarphian stallion who can carry you to flight!" Mategaladh pointed down another path leading deeper into the wood.

Galbard thought he saw shapes in the mist, and then a loud neighing split the air. A strong young stallion, bridled and saddled, burst through the mist into a small clearing.

"Take this path, Galbard. Take it — and this good Calarphian horse. Take them with care, but hurry now, hurry!"

"My thanks to you, good prophet. May the Creator smile upon you. May you see Rion in this lifetime and the Third Domain in the next."

Galbard climbed onto the stallion and turned him with ease. He was young, but well trained. "I heard tales of Calarphian horses in my youth — oh, that they live up to their stories!" Galbard exclaimed.

"His name is Pladus. He will carry you well," Mategaladh said. "You will also find some useful items in his saddlebags. Use them wisely."

Mategaladh waved him away, and Galbard raised a hand in return before turning Pladus back down the path and into the mist, parting it with a soft swoosh. Galbard lay low across the horse's neck, wide-eyed and watching for branches. They sped north and then west with abandon.

CHAPTER TEN

MISSING SCOUTS

One of General Tobor's wives interrupted his reading.

"My lord, a runner to see you," she said, bowing.

"Send them in," Tobor replied, returning to his reading. The runner entered the room still winded, as Tobor would have expected. That, at least, was a good sign.

"My liege," the runner began, waiting for Tobor's acknowledgment.

"What news have you?" Tobor asked.

"My liege, my master Citanth wishes you to know that Lord Amphileph is unavailable to command you, and has now appointed my master High Commander of the Camonra—"

Tobor set his reading aside at the mention of Citanth as "master." "Your *master*, Citanth?" he repeated. "You would never utter such words in the presence of Lord Amphileph, young runner. What madness is occurring in the Temple of Amphileph?"

The runner hesitated, lips parting as if weighing the risk.

"May I speak freely, my liege?"

"Answer!" Tobor barked.

"Th… things are not right, my lord," the runner said. "Lord Amphileph and many of the Camonra have been… captured… in some kind of wizardry."

Tobor moved to the edge of his chair. "Go on."

"Lord Amphileph was beside himself. He has killed the other fathers — his very own brothers!" The runner looked at the ground in dismay.

"He has killed our makers?"

"All but Citanth. He was in the northern camp when the wizardry came upon the others, and he was not caught up in it."

No! Not the fathers! Tobor thought. He could barely contain his anger.

He had long suspected Amphileph was becoming unstable — like a fire fed too much wood, too hot for any to stand near — and now this news of him murdering the other fathers!

"Lord Amphileph will escape this spell," Tobor said.

"Begging your pardon, my liege, but I must tell you — Lord Amphileph has been trying since the moon of Denf was full in the west. He has not broken the spell, and he has killed hundreds of our kind in his rage."

Tobor stood. It was more than he could bear. "That will be all, runner. Stay here in our camp. I will consult with my captain, and we may have further need of you."

"Yes, my liege," the runner said, bowing before he exited.

Tobor's thoughts whirled in his head. These feelings — his mixed emotions in his worship of Lord Amphileph — tore at him like two dogs fighting in a pit. Then it all snapped into place — the simple truth that Amphileph, powerful as he was, was still less powerful than *something*. If he could be caged like the pit dogs, then simple warrior's logic told Tobor that Amphileph could not be lord of all.

Now something deeper raged in his gut. Tobor had killed for Amphileph without reservation all his life — and now this? A sickness churned in him.

A second wave followed — anger. Tobor had been fool enough to worship him like a god. This stuck in his craw like the bone of some small animal. Amphileph's deceit would require blood payment, for you could do many things to the Camonra — starve them, beat them — but you would not make them fools. Tobor snorted as if to get the smell of it from his nostrils.

If Amphileph was but a created thing, then he had a vulnerability to exploit. It might take one hundred of his brothers, it might take one thousand, but the Camonra could swarm him — perhaps even destroy him. His arrogance in thinking himself a god — that would be his downfall, Tobor was sure of it. Such an arrogant man might deserve a quick death — but to be ignored, to be made insignificant — Tobor could think of no greater insult. He threw back the tent sash and walked to the assembly of captains waiting outside.

"News, captains!" Tobor shouted. "Amphileph no longer commands these armies! I alone lead us now! The Watchers war amongst themselves; they have bound Amphileph in the east like a caged dog. Citanth and he are the only survivors. Citanth thinks himself our master — which can only mean Amphileph is powerless to escape his cage." Tobor looked at his captains. "Have the runner return to the northern camp. Bring our women! We make our camp here!"

Tobor had spread the Camonra camp along the north–south trail they'd taken from Amphileph's temple to the outskirts of Rion, but after riding to the edge of the fault himself and watching seawater surge up from the lava below in violent spasms, he ordered the camp moved farther northwest.

Cool ocean air swept north across the fault line, and the steamy collision of heat and wind produced an almost constant rainfall. The runoff pooled into rivers and shallow lakes the Rionese vegetation could not endure. Everywhere north of Rion's gates, the high grasses and trees withered away, giving rise to marsh reeds and leafless, twisted trunks visited only by the occasional waterfowl.

With the fault keeping his Rionese enemies at bay to the south, and reports from his scouts that the Rionese refugees remained hidden in the trees to the west, the wide-open spaces of the northern plains presented Tobor with a unique opportunity for peace. Two weeks after being sent, the runner returned with a great host of young Camonra, their females, and their children. Though witnesses confirmed that Amphileph was unable to escape the area surrounding his temple, the Camonra had still fled the northern camps during the night in fear of him.

It was the first time the Camonra had reunited with their families without fear of Amphileph's heavy hand, and the celebrations brought Tobor a happiness he had never known. The females cooked, the males wrestled for sport, and their offspring ran through the common square between the mud huts and timber structures without fear of Amphileph's wrath — it was life-altering.

Their camp had grown into a large clump of structures almost overnight, and the only thing that gave Tobor pause was the possibility of Citanth's return, though he was convinced that he could turn the Camonra against him with little effort. He had no real fear of the humans, though a run-in with them was becoming ever more likely as they expanded their hunting and gathering. He wanted war no more, so he kept a constant flow of scouts searching the camp's ever-growing perimeter, diligently ensuring that the delicate peace of isolation remained.

And so it did, through the rest of that summer and into the time when the leaves began to change their colors.

The cooler air came down from the north, and the Camonra prepared for their first winter. As the sunlight faded in the west, Tobor walked through the camp, watching warm firelight begin to spill from the crude windows of their humble homes.

He saw Idhoran at the northern end of the camp and stopped to speak with him, as he often did when the scouts checked in for the day — but tonight Idhoran looked unusually tense.

"What bothers you, old friend?" Tobor asked.

"The headcount of scouts reporting in was short," Idhoran answered.

"The scouts from the plains east of the forest?" Tobor inquired.

"Yes, my lord," he said. "I'll look into it at once!"

"Very well," said Tobor.

Idhoran bowed to him and entered the small barracks used by the scouts.

Tobor knew the humans had sought sanctuary in the distant forest to the west. It was tall and dense — the kind of forest that granted both height and stealth, stripping away much of the advantage his warriors held in size and strength. It was only a matter of time before they had fortified their position and concentrated their numbers there.

Idhoran raced back and took one knee.

"What say you?" Tobor inquired.

"Three of our scouts from the west have not returned!"

"Is that so?" Tobor said. "Much is reported by their absence. Ready a hundred of our best. We march on the high wood."

News of Tobor's orders spread like wildfire. The Camonra, emboldened by their newfound freedoms, stirred rambunctiously for war. Tobor rode out before them to meet with his captains.

"The Camonra are excited to find the enemy, General," one said.

"What are your orders?"

"We'll march through the night so we may look upon the forest with the light at our backs," Tobor began. "If they've killed our scouts, we'll take blood from them as payment — enough to remind them they do not dictate where we go or what we do."

"Are we not to kill them all?" another captain asked.

"No," Tobor responded. "What threat do these humans pose to the Camonra?" He noticed a flicker of confusion on their disciplined faces. "Are not the Camonra superior in every way to these humans? We need no war with them."

A general grunt of acknowledgment quickly came in answer.

"Ready the march!" Tobor ordered, and they returned to their mounts and rode back to their respective charges. With only a hundred or so soldiers in their company, the Camonra carried none of the pageantry shown during the march on Rion. No banners, no war drums, no catapults. This company would move quickly and silently upon the men of Highwood.

They crossed the distance under cover of darkness, careful to use the rolling hills to hide from the watchful eyes of the Rion Guard. In the fields across from Highwood, they found blood in the high grass. The sword of one of their brethren lay close by. No Camon would ever have given up his sword.

"Then they have killed our brothers," Tobor said. "Let us bring swift and terrible vengeance upon them!"

They hid in the high grass through the night until Tobor saw the faint glow of dawn rising behind them. He ordered the Camonra to stop. Dawn's light pierced the trees at a sharp angle, revealing archers placed high in the limbs — a height advantage that was problematic.

The last hundred yards or so to the tree line was fairly flat, so Tobor knew they would have to cross that distance at a dead run. It was hard to tell how many archers filled the trees, but if he could draw the humans from their hiding places, Camonra strength could easily overwhelm them. Before they could charge, however, Tobor saw a group of riders breaking from the cover of the trees.

"Ready!" Tobor said in a hushed yell. The captains relayed the order and moved to their mounts; the foot soldiers readied behind them. Tobor spurred the Azrodh's ribcage. It hissed in acknowledgment, and they raced out from the long shadows where they hid.

It seemed that the instant Tobor's large frame appeared in the morning light, a horn blew a long tone that echoed through the hillside.

Tobor rode toward the riders. "Now! Follow me!" he bellowed. The Camonra battle cry boiled out from the foot soldiers, and they fell behind the captains in double time. The Rionese cavalry shuffled in disbelief. "Inferiors!" they cried. Their riders formed two rough lines, the first lowering their long pikes alongside the polished armor shielding their horses' faces and chests.

The Camonra weaponry varied greatly, some with clubs and axes, and some with nothing more than their bare hands. Arrows whistled past them far more quickly than Tobor had hoped — one struck his mount in the shoulder, another in the lower left leg. A third he deflected with his shield, skipping it over his head — only for it to strike a foot soldier behind him in the eye. The soldier's body folded in on itself. The other foot soldiers parted around him or leapt over him. The Camonra battle cry was deafening, and the Rionese horses appeared as if they would bolt at any moment.

"Charge!" the order rang out from down their lines — and bolt they did, directly into the charging Camonra.

Tobor's heart pounded in his chest with the thrill of war. His great reptilian mount flew into their midst, its head passing just to the left of one rider's pike and directly into the path of another. They crashed together in a thunderous clap of armor and the crack of splintering wood. Tobor's mount slowed only a little, and the Rionese rider slammed into his shield and bounced away. His horse stumbled backward and fell on its side, its stiff legs pointing skyward. The second rider Tobor had narrowly missed tried to pull up his pike, but it rammed into the ground with great force and hurled him backward off his horse. His helmet flew from his head with the concussion of his fall and bounced off the shoulder of one of Tobor's captains who was coming just behind him.

Suddenly four arrows hit the bugler in the neck and chest, and the Camonra battle horn ceased. He fell from his mount, his limp body skipping into the legs of the oncoming horses. Two horses toppled forward to the ground, and their riders plowed face forward, eating their share of grass. Tobor leapt from his mount and slashed at two other horses, crippling one with a hobbling cut and slicing across the upper leg of the other's rider and its ribcage. The Rionese rider screamed out. A spray of blood from his leg temporarily blinded Tobor in the right eye. The horse spun away in pain, and Tobor ducked beneath its rider's clumsy thrust.

Tobor raised his hand to wipe the rider's blood from his face when he felt a tugging sensation below his ribs. Another of the rider's pikes had pierced his side. The tip barely protruded through his thick skin, and Tobor spun away before the serrated edge could tear him open, his own sweeping blade catching the attacker in the chest. His foot soldiers flew upon the riders then, and one of his captains called for Tobor to fall back.

"Kill them!" Tobor cried in return, and another arrow struck the chain mail on his chest. He skillfully moved to keep the riders' horses between him and the archers. Arrows rained down around them, and his foot soldiers sprang upon the remaining riders.

"My liege, they prepare another attack!" his captain yelled again, this time pointing toward the wood. Other humans were moving to mount their horses.

He surveyed the tremendous price they had inflicted on the humans. "Back, my brothers!" he said. "Back!"

Tobor grabbed his Azrodh by the saddle horn and struck its rump with the flat of his blade, turning the creature toward the south. He held on tightly as it sprang to a gallop at Tobor's prompting, lifting him off his feet. Arrows struck its side twice, and it slowed, but Tobor used these lulls to throw one leg over its girth, breaking the arrow shafts off with his shin. He mercilessly spurred it onward, turning southeast toward their camp, the foot soldiers and riders rushing in behind him. They flew back across the marshy plains eastward and moved beyond the range of the archers.

Evening fell before they were welcomed back at the encampment. The females had a large fire burning. The wounded dismounted with their help, and the others rested at the fires, waiting for food and drink.

Tobor surveyed his wounded troops and took count of the lost mounts. His guerrilla tactics had been only moderately successful, killing around twenty of the Rionese. He had lost four of his own soldiers, and though it was a good five to one, he was dissatisfied with the outcome.

One of the females stitched his side, and he considered how to give the humans more than the little sting they had felt this day when next they met.

CHAPTER ELEVEN

IRRECONCILABLE DIFFERENCES

Mordher had seen every battle of the Watchers' War from the frontlines, and the battle for Rion had been no different. His father, Mordhonar, had served in the Rion Guard before him, and when Mordher was seven, he sent him to be trained in the family business — the art of war — under the tutelage of the Elders of the Guard. Twenty-one years later, Mordher was battle-hardened like steel to flame and quench, but the Battle for Rion had tested the Guard's training as no battle ever had.

Mordher sat down upon what had been the cornerstone of the Temple of Evliit and pulled his old, scarred helmet from his head, letting his hair fall around his muscular shoulders. He dropped the helmet and stared at its red plume, singed almost completely away. He loosened the strap of his shoulder armor, removed the pin of his draping red cloak, and lifted the molded iron chestplate over his head, flipping it before him. He ran his fingers over the gashes in the dark brown paint and the golden symbol of Rion, and then he tossed it on the ground before him. He leaned over, his practiced fingers making short work of the straps on his greaves, and freed his shins from their armor. Then he simply sat there in his skirt and tunic, staring at his sandals, feeling the breeze move across his sweat-saturated body.

Mordher looked over the rubble of the small homes that once surrounded the great temple, and his hard expression softened. Before he could even grasp the feeling rising in him, a single tear fell — strangely unfamiliar to a warrior of his mettle. He lowered his head and ran a callused palm down his face to scrape the tear away. When he closed his eyes, the images of the battle returned to him.

He had been on the frontlines once again when the massive eruption beneath the Rion Guard and the Camonra hurled them all in every direction. The stampede of warriors fleeing the bedlam crushed many comrades; the underworld that opened beneath them burned others alive. The eruption had thrown Mordher high into the air, backward toward Rion, where several of his fellow soldiers had broken his fall. They recovered their senses only to feel the intense heat pouring out of Erathe itself, singeing their hair. He remembered the smell of it. They had run for their very lives to escape it, and the memory of the screams and chaos snapped him back to the present with a jolt.

He lifted his head to watch what remained of the Guard as they returned from the northern front. They were distant and speechless, shuffling in no particular groups or order through the city streets. One of the Elders stood in the main square in his full regalia, his purple robes dingy and torn. He attempted to corral the soldiers back toward the main temple to prevent the inevitable looting that comes when desperate men roam the streets, but his voice had little impact. He seemed oblivious to the small child clinging to his torn robes, crying at the top of his lungs.

Mordher looked around the horizon, his head pounding. The destruction of Rion's temples was nearly total. The massive temple at the southeastern wall, the heart of the Rion Guard, was one of the few exceptions. *How had the Creator allowed such destruction?* The very ground beneath their feet had consumed nearly two-thirds of the armies of Rion *and* Amphileph.

It was like some kind of cruel joke. The Guard had dedicated their very lives to the defense of the Creator's teachings. What unbalanced fate — to die in equal or greater numbers than the very ones who declared contempt for the Creator's holy army? The Guard had proven beyond any doubt that they were willing to die for their cause, yet the Creator had destroyed their great city, taking his brothers into the abyss of lava and flame — these things were impossible for Mordher to fathom.

When he could stand to look at it no more, he rose and walked toward the small adobe home he had built for his family in an alleyway off the main thoroughfare. People everywhere dug through the remnants of their homes, and Mordher found himself quickening his pace as the true depth of the city's destruction settled upon him. In short order, he was running down the alleyway toward his dwelling, pushing aside rubble and debris, leaping over bodies and mourners. He cried out for his wife and daughter. A sinking feeling grew in the pit of his stomach, telling him something terrible had happened to them.

He found their bodies trampled in the street just outside their home, and the sight of their dirty, broken faces drove him to his knees. Memories surged through him — flashes of moments that had shaped every happiness he'd ever known.

Something inside him snapped. *He would have protected them if he had been there.* A high-pitched ringing burned in his ears, numbing him with its relentless whine. He felt unmoored, as if watching from somewhere outside himself. None of it seemed real.

Through brimming eyes he looked down again at their gray faces, praying he would not see them — but they remained, motionless, save for the hot breeze that gently stirred their hair.

He drew his sword instinctively; his body flexed tightly, veins bulging in his face, neck, and arms. A scream exploded from deep within him — a sound that terrified the remaining townspeople even through their shock. Several stopped where they stood to look at him as his body slowly relaxed and his sword fell from his hand. He made no effort to pick it up, but reached instead for a shovel that lay next to a fresh grave and walked toward their bodies with new purpose.

When he had buried them near their home, he returned to the place where his sword had fallen and picked it up, squeezing the hilt with his mighty hand. He slid the sword into its scabbard and lowered his head slightly. Then he fixed his eyes on the temple of the Elders in the southeast part of the city and moved with a new purpose: to kill the ones who had sent him away from his family. Nothing else mattered anymore. There were no gods, no devils, no afterlife, and no theology. There was only the cold vengeance that flowed through his veins and calloused his heart.

He made his way down the city streets toward the temple. The destruction grew less severe, but everywhere people cried and shouted, digging through the remnants of their homes, gathering small piles of dishes or clothing they might still salvage. They passed through his peripheral vision without a second glance.

When at last he reached the steps of the great temple, his foot fell upon the first step — and he stopped suddenly. "Elders!" he shouted. "Elders of the Guard!"

Several of the young warriors made their way to the temple entrance, looking down upon him with fear and respect. Others slowly formed a wide circle around him at the foot of the temple.

"Elders of the Guard!" he screamed again. A lone, robed figure stepped from between two of the young warriors.

"Great warrior, Guardian of Rion, what brings you to the temple in anger?" the acolyte asked.

"I seek answers from the Elders!" Mordher yelled.

"The Elders are seeking the face of the Creator in prayer, brother. May I be of assistance?"

Mordher drew his sword, and a ripple of movement passed through the encircling warriors as they tightened their ranks around him.

"*You* cannot," Mordher responded. "Tell the Elders that I will speak to them now!"

The young acolyte shrugged, and his tone changed.

"You do not command the Elders, great warrior."

Mordher flew into a rage and bounded up the stairs toward the acolyte.

"Stop him!" the acolyte commanded, retreating behind the closing line of warriors.

Mordher's sword rang off two or three of theirs, and then a dozen of his brethren tackled him to the ground. In his struggle, another dozen still fell upon him, and they pried the sword from his hands. Even with three of them holding his arm, he managed to break free and strike the nearest one in the side of the head, instantly robbing him of consciousness. Before he could break free, one of them stood over him on the steps and struck him repeatedly in the face with the pommel of a sword, bouncing his head off the stone with each blow. The first blows slowed him very little, but by the third or fourth he felt the warm flow of blood down his face and neck. His left eye swelled shut. He could still see his clutched fists with the other, but the sound of his attackers drifted farther and farther away — and then everything went black.

*   *   *

Mordher awoke in a small, low-ceilinged cell that was little more than a cage beneath the rear of the temple — a place where the Rion Guard had once kenneled their war dogs. The old bars were rusty red, partitioning ten or so cages that faced the ocean, exposed to the elements. The wind off the ocean gave him a steady diet of dust, but he was already regaining the strength his attackers had beaten out of him.

"You're the one that threatened the Elders, eh?" a voice chuckled from somewhere around him.

Mordher tried to stand, but struck his head on the marble ceiling and buckled to his hands.

The chuckle increased. "Too big for that, warrior—sit or squat's about your only options," the voice said. Mordher's eyes were squeezed shut from the blow, but one managed to open enough to scan the cages around him. Two cages over was another warrior of the guard, dirty and thin, his forehead resting on the bars with a hand on either side. He was smiling broadly.

"Who are you?" Mordher asked.

"Ardhios, at your service my friend," he replied. "It is good to meet someone else who is brave enough—or foolish enough, one might say—to threaten the Elders."

"My motivation will not change the cut I make," Mordher said. "They can ponder such things while they bleed."

"Still hostile, I see," Ardhios said. "Good. You'll need that."

Mordher opened the other eye to get a better look around.

"Yes — nine of us, caged like dogs. A fitting end for dedicated servants of Rion, wouldn't you say?" Laughter rose from the other cages, and Mordher saw the men shifting to the edges of their cells to get a look at him.

"You are Mordher," another said. "We know of your great deeds battling the Inferiors."

"Mordher?" asked another. "Mordher of the Guard?"

Mordher sat down and set his back against the rusty bars. "I fight no more for the Guard," he responded.

"Neither shall my friends and I," Ardhios chuckled. "Our crime is sedition, same as yours. They mean to put us all on the tree."

"I don't want to hear that," said the man in the cage to Mordher's right. "They'll not nail me up! They will have to kill me first."

"They will bring one more than is required to put you on the tree, Borian!" another laughed from down the line.

Mordher had heard enough. He crawled toward the cell door and shoved against the lock.

"Save your strength, Mordher," Ardhios said. "They may not feed you for days, and we've all tried the locks."

Mordher's face reddened. He worked his hands across the bars until something caught his eye, then rolled to his side and gripped the bars closest to Ardhios. With one kick, he snapped a rusted bar in the front of the cage and then rolled to his knees. He held the bar next to it with one hand for leverage and bent the broken bar up and outward with the other hand. The lower portion of the bar was a sharp break, too short to bend away from the cross-member that strengthened it, but Mordher braced his back against the cage and pushed with all his strength, bending the upper portion up and out.

"Impressive!" Ardhios said. "You'd better be about getting out of there now. The Guard won't be too thrilled with your attempting to escape."

Mordher ignored him and sat on his knees, grabbing the two bars to either side of the broken one and shaking them furiously. For nearly five minutes, Mordher pushed and pulled with no effect — until a tiny bit of stone fell onto his forearm from where the ceiling anchored one of the bars. Mordher smiled, then pulled back and forth with renewed fury on the bar that had shown the slightest weakness. A crack began to form in the stone, and granules of dust fell in Mordher's face. There was suddenly some movement in the bar, and Mordher placed both hands on it, straining with all his might. The marble capstone broke free and the bar jumped outward. Mordher pushed it down beside the other bar and turned sideways, attempting to squeeze his oversized torso through the tight opening.

"Well," Ardhios exclaimed. The other captives began a quiet encouragement of Mordher's efforts. Mordher pushed against the bars, his ribcage catching on the jagged lower bar, stabbing him repeatedly.

"You've got a nasty cut there," Ardhios commented. He sat back against his own cage's bars to watch the spectacle of the large man struggling to escape. Mordher simply grunted each time the jagged bar struck his chest, blood now freely dripping down his side, his pants, and his leg. With one last effort, Mordher squeezed through, cutting his upper thigh on the same stubborn bar. He stood, glanced both ways for a guard, and turned to run.

"Mordher!" Ardhios shouted. "Take us with you."

Mordher neared the cage. "What advantage are you to me?" he asked.

"I have means of escape," Ardhios said. "You won't get far without such knowledge, and the Guard won't make the mistake twice of letting you escape again."

"I'll take my chances," Mordher replied.

"I have a boat," Ardhios gambled. "Let me and my brothers go with you, and we will leave this place together."

Mordher considered the offer. He had seen what had become of the land north of Rion — there was no escaping that way. He had lived in Rion his entire life and knew the docks were the only way out.

"I will find my own boat," he replied, and he turned toward the southern cliffs.

"The stairs are gone, Mordher," Ardhios said, and Mordher stopped. "What did you say?"

"The cliff stairs were destroyed by the quakes," Ardhios elaborated. "But I know another way. Take us with you, and we will sail away from this place."

Mordher looked perplexed, then stepped close to Ardhios's cell and leaned in. "Lie to me, and I will wring your neck like I did those bars—except with less effort." Mordher grabbed the bar that was bent outward and pushed it back and forth, snapping it off in his hand.

"I have no trouble believing that," Ardhios replied. "Behind you!" he added, pointing to a guard rounding the temple base. He turned his head slightly to shout his discovery to his comrades, but managed only a deep sigh. Mordher had thrown the piece of bar hard enough to pierce his chest.

"Quick! The keys!" Ardhios yelled, but Mordher had already pounced upon the dying soldier, taking his shield and sword and extracting the keys from his belt. The guard struggled helplessly, but Mordher seemed oblivious to his dying gasp. He pushed the body aside and tossed the keys into Ardhios's cell, who quickly unlocked the gates of all the cages.

"Follow me," Ardhios said. He and the other men moved toward the southern cliffs.

"I follow no one," Mordher responded.

"Come with us," Ardhios rephrased, and the eight others echoed him. "Come with us!" they cried, waving Mordher forward. He grumbled something under his breath and fell in behind them.

They made their way to the southern cliffs, and Mordher saw that the stairs that once made their way to the sea below were indeed gone.

"This way!" Ardhios yelled. He ran west along the cliff's edge, then cut north toward the servants' watering well. Behind them, the temple alarm rang out in a shrill, urgent peal.

"They will not be long behind us, now," Ardhios said. He picked up a stone and threw it into the well. "Quiet!" he yelled, and then he listened for the splash in the well below. The stone hit the water with a hollow *g-dunk*, and Ardhios nodded, satisfied the waterline was low enough. "We've but one way out. We jump in here," he said, pointing them down into the well.

"What?" one of them inquired.

"Trust me!" Ardhios said. "About ten feet below the surface there is a tunnel that opens to an underground cave. The caves go to the sea."

Ardhios glanced west, where the evening sun turned the sea gold. "Yes!" he said. "We are in luck — the sun is at just the right angle to light the cave." Listen to me, listen closely: dive into the waters of the well and feel for the walls. There's a narrowing of the walls just after the last well stone and just before the cave entrance. "Before you jump, breathe like this," he said, then deliberately hyperventilated.

"You'll need to hold your breath for some time before you make it to the cave. Below the last of the stones in the wall of the well, you'll turn through the darkness. Pull yourself forward—keep moving, and don't panic! The cave will open to our escape!"

Mordher looked at the others. They stared at Ardhios as though he'd lost his mind.

"This is your plan?" another asked.

"My cousin drowned here when I was a child. Several of my kinsmen and I climbed into the well to retrieve his body. I am telling you — there is a cave below the surface to the west!"

The Rion Guardsmen were approaching from the east.

"Do you see them?" Ardhios cried. "They outnumber us ten to one. Even Mordher cannot fight them all!"

"All right! All right! I'm going!" one yelled.

"Wait, the best swimmers first!" Ardhios responded. "We all drown if anyone blocks the way!"

Suddenly, an arrow struck one of their companions through the chest. He lurched forward onto the stones, still clawing to make the jump, but collapsed dead before he could pull his weight over the edge. Other arrows began to fall around them.

"Now!" Ardhios screamed. "If you can swim, now would be the time to prove it!" They all began hyperventilating.

"To the south, right?" one asked.

"Yes, the south, the south!" Ardhios cried.

Two of them dove over the side, and the rest waited, trembling with impatience. The Guard grew ever closer. Mordher deflected an arrow with his sword — one that came dangerously close to his face.

"Now!" Ardhios screamed, and the others continued to dive into the well one after another, until only Mordher and Ardhios remained.

"Go, Ardhios!" Mordher said. "I'll hold them off!"

"You cannot hold them off, Mordher!" Ardhios replied. "Jump now!"

"I cannot swim!" Mordher growled.

Ardhios looked a little stunned. "What?" he asked.

"I cannot swim!" Mordher yelled. "You must go now! I release you from your promise to lead me from this place. Go now!"

Ardhios kept hyperventilating. "Look out!" he yelled, and Mordher turned instinctively. Mordher felt the impact of Ardhios' shoulder striking him in the side, and the two of them went over the well's edge.

Mordher barely kept hold of his sword as he plunged through the light and into the darkness with Ardhios. Mordher's huge body burst through the surface and then rose back again, the panicked look on his face unseen in the darkness. His sword struck the stone wall, sending a brief spark of light that revealed Ardhios beside him.

"Put that sword away!" Ardhios yelled. Mordher raised it as if to strike him — then felt himself sinking beneath the surface. He wanted to curse Ardhios, but the water entered his mouth and fear won out over all other emotion.

"If you want to live," Ardhios began, but paused to spit water. "If you want to live, put away the sword, and I'll help you through the caves!"

Mordher flailed in the water, sinking again and again. His free hand scraped desperately at the smooth stones of the well wall. He fumbled to put his sword in his belt. "Help me!" he cried. Above them, the outlines of soldiers leaned over the well, their voices echoing down the shaft.

"Take a deep breath!" Ardhios yelled.

"Yes!" Mordher replied, and he gasped loudly.

"Now!" Ardhios yelled — and Mordher heard the *thwap, thwap, thwap* of arrows punching into the water around them.

Mordher dove beneath the surface of the water and clumsily felt around for Ardhios in the dark, cold water. He felt Ardhios grabbing his shirt, trying to pull him deeper into the well's blackness. With his free hand, Mordher felt along the wall — stone, then mud where the well lining ended — and Ardhios jerked him deeper.

Mordher was beyond panic when he first saw the faint light of the underwater cave. He clawed toward the light, but struck his head on the stone wall and gulped water into his lungs. He lost all hope of reaching the caves when something pulled on him again.

He could just make out the forms of the others in the dim cave light when the water burst from his lungs and he collapsed, coughing, into the soft dirt.

"Which way?" one of them screamed in their panic. There was the strange sound of muted voices on the water.

"Toward . . . the . . . light!" Ardhios managed to say.

Mordher struggled to his feet and joined the motley group as they pushed through the twisting cave — smooth walls, rich red mud — moving toward the faint evening light that signaled escape. When they finally reached the cave's exit, it was nearly dark. The men gulped the dank air in great gasps after navigating the winding, slippery, erosion-sharpened stone. The old cave had taken them up and down through the bowels of the stone cliffs of Rion, and from the exit in the cliff walls, they saw that the ocean was still some sixty feet below.

"Jump as far away from the cliff as possible!" Ardhios said. "And wait until the wave is going out to jump!"

"Going out?" Mordher probed.

"All of you, watch!" Ardhios said. He broke a chunk of stone from the cliff wall, watched the waves crash below, and dropped the stone when the water ebbed. It fell toward the exposed, jagged rocks at the foot of the cliffs.

They watched without blinking as the ocean surged over the jagged rocks just before the stone struck.

"Going out!" Ardhios said. "You must swim away from the rocks as quickly as possible!"

They stared at Ardhios as if he were mad — until the grim realization settled that there was no other choice.

"Wait for each other!" Ardhios shouted. "Wait until the person before you has cleared the tide and the rocks and swum clear!" Ardhios scanned their faces — fear on some, near contempt on others. Then he looked down in time to see the water falling away and jumped.

The group watched his descent intently. Coral and stone lay exposed below him, and for a breathless moment it seemed he would strike them — but the sea surged in ahead of him, flooding the rocks. Ardhios's body plunged a white arc into the deep blue water and surfaced in the wake of the outgoing wave. He swam hard with the outgoing wave, gaining as much distance from the rocks as he could before the swell returned. Then he moved parallel to the shoreline where it shallowed, and the current pushed him roughly upon the sandy shore with a crash of frothy water and seaweed. Ardhios staggered to his feet, wiped the water from his face, and drew his first full breath since the jump.

"Come! You can do it!" he yelled, and no sooner than he had said it, they followed, one by one crashing into the sea and mimicking his pattern to the shore. Even Mordher, terrified of the water, managed to dog-paddle into position for the tide to carry him to shore.

"Follow me!" Ardhios said. Several of them rested their hands on their knees, and they were all winded. "Come on, now!" he said to them.

They rounded the short beach and spotted the dock. They ran as fast as they could, but the warm knee-high surf pushed the sand around their feet, sapping the speed from their escape.

As they neared the docks, several archers appeared on the broken staircase above, descending as far as the sturdier rock would allow. From that distance, they could watch the arrows for what felt like several seconds — blurring only at the last instant before sinking into the sand around them.

They scrambled for a single-sailed cog that they thought they could manage, with the sound of the arrows striking the wood all around them. They manned the capstan, kedging the little cog out toward the southern sky. When the boat finally caught the rising tide, the open sea claimed it, and the cliffs of Rion faded into the distance.

*　　*　　*

Like the *Nurium* and the *Merrius*, the boat carrying the seven warriors followed the shoreline around the western end of Etharath — until a sudden storm forced them farther out to sea. After eleven days at sea, the seven warriors came ashore some thirty leagues north of the refugees that were tending to the building of Shinetower.

Finding nothing aboard their stolen ship but hardtack and a little fresh water, they abandoned it — dehydrated and desperate for food. They found themselves just south of a mountain range dividing the northern plains from a beautiful valley — a place that reminded them of the peace ancient Rion had once offered. They happened upon a little stream and drank, but they were all still very hungry.

"Those leaving Rion were to hide in the woods to the east or in the mountains to the north," said Ardhios.

"There are soldiers of the Guard accompanying them," Mordher grunted. "I will never bow down to the Elders again."

"The world has changed, my brother," Ardhios replied. "The Elders will never leave the Temples, and the land between us is no more. Their words will fade quickly from the people's ears."

"My sword is closer than the words of the Elders," Mordher said. "Let us see which they choose to follow."

"Now, now, my friend," said Ardhios. "We are free of the Elders. What is there in Highwood that interests us?"

Mordher looked toward Highwood and frowned. "I am done with Rion and the Guard. There is nothing in Highwood I wish to take from farmers and slaves. Let them wait on the Elders to close the great fault so they can go home. Let them wait on that."

"Then it is done," Ardhios said. "We make our camp here."

As evening fell, they saw fires in the valley below, and Mordher refused to sleep until he knew who warmed themselves so close to their camp. Six warriors followed him into the valley, moving around the base of the mountain that lay to their north. Ardhios called the peak "Candra," meaning *haven* in ancient Rionese, for it seemed to him they had found a new home — and the days of the Guard were truly behind them.

They made their way close to the fires, and Mordher could see that the people around them were haggard and weak, their dress giving them away as refugees from Rion. He made his way into the light at the edge of the encampment.

"Who goes there?" one of the men asked.

"I am Mordher," he replied, stepping into their midst, his immense form taking them aback. "You are from Rion?"

"Yes, of course," the man said, and Mordher could see a little calm come across the faces of the crowd that moved him. "You have news of Rion?"

They examined his clothing. "You are a warrior of the Guard," one said. A woman, keeping her distance, pointed to the pin on his cloak. "You carry the mark of the Guard."

"I am marked by the Guard, that is right," Mordher said. "But not by this pin," he said. He pulled the pin from his cloak and threw it into the fire. "This pin pierced only my cloak—the Guard has pierced my soul."

For a moment, there was only an awkward silence.

"Have you heard news of the Inferiors? Do they attack Rion?" another asked.

"Some say they are coming for us!" one of the women said.

"If they are coming for you," Mordher said, snatching a staff from one of them with ease, "then they will take you." He smiled and tossed it back. "You cannot fight the Inferiors with staves and rocks."

"What do we do then?" another asked.

"We will protect you!" Ardhios said. "But to do so will require our strength, and we are famished from the trip here. Pray, have you something to eat that we might recover?"

"Yes, yes, of course," they replied, hurrying to gather what appeared to be the best food they had. Mordher and the others tore it from their hands and ate until they were completely stuffed.

Each of the seven warriors took their share and built their own fire some twenty paces from the townspeople. As Mordher and the others finished, Ardhios sat beside him, picking over a plate of food.

"We could have taken what we wanted!" Mordher said.

"Oh yes, my friend, you could have done just that. You might even have killed a few of them in the process," Ardhios smirked, glancing at the watchful refugees.

"I can do what is necessary," Mordher said. The other warriors quieted, watching the exchange with interest.

"I am sure you can do pretty much whatever you put your mind to, Mordher," Ardhios said. "But why kill them when they can feed you, follow you—fight for you?" There was a low rumble of agreement from the group.

Mordher did not answer, but the idea pleased him. These townspeople were no more warriors than he was a cook, and their food rightly belonged to the warriors. *In fact,* Mordher thought, *they might be willing to part with much more.*

CHAPTER TWELVE

WITCH OF SOUTHWOOD

Rendaya landed just outside the deep Southwood forest. Her face was taut with regret for the lives she had taken on the *Nurium* moments before, but her resolve remained unshaken. Nothing must stop the Swordbearer from finding sanctuary in the west. To do less might mean the end of humankind — a chance she would not take.

She walked for about a league into the darkness of the forest, finally seeing the familiar glow of a fire through the bubbled window glass her husband had made with his own hands for a wedding present. He had used no conjuring — though he had been an incredibly gifted conjurer — but had made it with the sweat of his brow in the heat of a makeshift glass furnace. Winter or summer, sun or rain, the old window glass always reminded her of him and the great effort he had put into providing her with some level of luxury that Rion once had.

She could see the shifting shadow of her cat, Bellows, moving dimly through the panes — more translucent than transparent. Bellows moved to greet her entry, and when she opened the cottage door, Bellows was right under her feet, his tail brushing her leg with each step she took.

"Bellows! Out from under my feet!" she said, more worried she would step on him than angry. He looked at her with those eyes of his, and she melted. "Oh, come here. I bet you're hungry!" she offered. She checked the stew pot on the small fire in the hearth, ladled a bowl for Bellows and one for herself, and plopped down in the old rocker.

"My bones hurt, Bellows," she reported, but Bellows gave her only the slightest look before returning to his soup.

"That good?" she asked, feeling a faint smile forcing its way onto her face. Bellows listened intently to every word, slurped the bowl dry in record time, and then jumped into her lap. She set aside her own bowl, half eaten. He turned on her lap twice and, finding a comfortable direction, fell into a clump, placing one paw on her hand. Then he looked at her with his big black eyes. She rubbed his head behind the ears, and he let out a loud *purr*, flipping onto his back and playfully biting and swatting at her hand. She took the look on his face as absolute devotion.

"I needed that, Bellows," she said. "It's been a very long day."

A long day indeed. She had come to grips with the fact that the Camonra were here to stay. They had camped near the great fault that now separated Rion from the rest of Etharath, and the Creator alone knew how long it would be before they declared all-out war on the refugees who had fled to Highwood. And with a slave named Galbard carrying Evliit's mighty Sword of the Watch somewhere to the north, the situation had all the makings of a catastrophe beyond imagining.

"What will we do with them?" Rendaya asked her cat.

Bellows answered with a flick of his right ear and a quick pass of his paw across his face.

"You are right, of course," Rendaya responded. "We will do whatever is necessary to protect the Sword, won't we?"

Bellows stopped perfectly still and locked eyes with her.

"You know what I'm saying, don't you, Bellows? They will *never* have the Sword." Her serious tone prompted Bellows to spring from her lap onto the floor in front of the fireplace. He turned, glanced back at her, arched his back, and darted across the room onto Rendaya's quilted bed.

"Yes, of course; we must rest," Rendaya said. She pushed herself from the rocker and checked the fire. Its tamped coals would keep the soup warm, so she removed the wooden cook spoon and settled the pot lid. Then she threw herself upon the bed and watched the warm red glow of the fireplace dance on the ceiling until sleep overtook her.

For the next few weeks, she and Bellows tended the garden in the clearing down the path. Rendaya used the time to reflect, while Bellows explored the woods surrounding the garden.

She kept a large assortment of herbs and vegetables, and out of no necessity other than her own pleasure, she had planted a flower garden where she often sat for hours when the sun was gentle, thinking of simpler times before she knew of Watchers or Spellmakers.

Today, she was in that flower garden, and the sweet perfume of the flowers faintly scented the air all around her. She enjoyed the scent so much that she produced a small vial from her garden apron and spoke the word, *Captus*. The flowers' mingled scents visibly raced into the vial, concentrating into a golden liquid. She corked it at once and slipped it back into her apron pocket. Now when the cold of winter gripped Southwood, it would take no more than a drop of golden liquid to remember the warmth of summer and her beautiful garden.

She wiped away a bit of dirt from her face and noticed the distinct smell of tomato vines still on her fingers. She looked over the basket of tomatoes, okra, and peppers she had gathered and thought of a soup she hadn't made in some time. She was fairly sure there were still some cloves of garlic in the pantry. With fall coming, there would be no more tomatoes for months, and she wanted to make that tomato-and-okra soup once more before the long Southwood winter.

The next morning, Rendaya left the cottage early, much to the chagrin of Bellows, who sat in the window and stared at her, motionless except for the occasional swish of his tail.

Rendaya saw her breath on the crisp cold air. She pulled her wrap across her head and walked northwest. With the Camonra camp growing ever larger, it was time to ensure the Bhre-Nora's plans for the tower were coming to fruition. Though it was a long walk, she wanted to conserve the energy required to take flight.

She crossed the Fields of Hannington and entered the rolling hills before the tower site, but even before she left Hannington behind, she looked toward the setting sun and stopped. They had done it. And now it was as if the sun itself rested upon the tower's crown, its blazing light like a fireball atop a torch stand

"Shinetower," Rendaya said under her breath. "Stand strong, great tower, preserve the hopes of mankind." She stood there for several minutes, a prayer of thankfulness forming somewhere between her heart, her head, and her lips, and a peaceful feeling washed over her. *We will reclaim this land for the Creator,* she thought. *There will be a new beginning, a Third Age.*

Rendaya carried that peaceful feeling with her as she crossed the remaining distance to the tower and moved among the people working the land around it.

*   *   *

In the two months since Cayden had returned from the tower, the people had taken the message to heart that the Witch of Southwood was pleased with their efforts. When he presented the Bhre-Nora's list to them, it had been life-changing. The list had set an end in sight for fulfilling their oaths, and urgency had taken the place of fear. When the list had dwindled to a few items, there had even been an air of victory among the Rionese refugees. It was as if a new *certainty* were growing — a feeling that the worst might finally be behind them.

Being the messenger had finally worked in Cayden's favor. As the news improved, the refugees' opinions of him shifted quickly, and they welcomed him — and Nara, Jalin, and Ro — back into the fold. He took down their tents in the eastern fields, and they moved back into the main encampment. In celebration of the turn of events, he had asked Nara to marry him, and she had accepted.

The rise of the tower had also been a tipping point for Jalin. Galbard had not appeared as she had hoped, and it seemed to break her spirit. Cayden and Nara had pleaded with her to stay and help with the wedding, and that pleading might have been the only thing that kept her from taking Ro and heading east. She had reluctantly stayed, and she seemed to drop the conversation about her husband altogether. Maybe that had been best.

The small refugee encampment, once nothing more than the passengers, tents, and cargo from the *Merrius* and *Nurium*, had grown almost overnight. Builders who finished their work on the tower turned to the encampment itself, and together they raised a combination tavern and store within the first few weeks. Everyone pitched in on raising the structures, and modest homes steadily began to replace tents in the hills and valleys that rippled eastward from Shintower's higher, flatter terrain.

Scouts from Highwood had seen the tower from leagues away, and before long traders found their way to the flourishing little village. With the Highborne River separating it from the east, traders considered the village a safe haven and gave it the name "the Dales," a name that quickly stuck with the locals. The sheer number of construction projects kept the Dales lively, and a trickle of traffic began to flow from Highwood and as far away as Moonledge Peak.

Cayden was working with several other men on the massive oak door for the entrance to the tower's base. They had rigged eyelets with ropes and were straining to set the door on its hinges. The door swung into place with a great rumble that echoed through the glassless windows above them, and they could just hear the men inside attempting to set the pins. They waited expectantly, and then the muffled hammering stopped, and the door slowly swung open to the large smiles of the men inside.

The sweat poured from their faces. "It is set!" they yelled, slapping backs. In the midst of the celebration, a cold shiver ran down Cayden's spine, and he suddenly recalled that fateful night on the *Nurium*.

"A draught! A draught for all!" the men shouted. They started toward the Dales.

"I'll catch up!" Cayden shouted.

"No, you won't!" one of them answered, laughing. "Unless you've got a drink in each hand!"

Cayden pretended to inspect the tower doors. When the celebrants were finally out of sight, he strained his eyes toward a dark figure, her silhouette almost lost against some trees to the southeast. It merged with the long shadows of the ending day that stretched across the rolling hills.

The Witch! he thought. The urge to call out made him cough and clear his throat, but he did no more than that, for he was mysteriously drawn to her, as if his fate had become somehow inexplicably intertwined with her own.

Except for the gentle movement of her hair and her long coat, her dark-hooded figure was motionless against the tree limbs that stirred in the sudden cool breeze.

He looked around for anyone watching, and seeing no one, approached her — stopping just across from her as the last light slipped below the horizon. The darkness engulfed them, and he could see her eyes glowing within the recesses of her hood.

"Are we not doing as you have said?" Cayden inquired. "See? The tower rises as you have commanded."

"Yes, you do as I have commanded," Rendaya responded, "but I have come to show you what must be done next."

Rendaya bent down and touched the ground with one finger.

A golden glow flowed from her touch and traveled across the ground, etching an intricate design that encircled the tower. "You have until spring to build another curtain wall that rings the base of the tower. On the eastern side, you will build a great gate. When the wall has been constructed, close the outer gates and lock them, and tell no one to enter until La and Sapath cross in the northern sky, for in this time, the Bhre-Nora will do a mighty work."

"It will be done," Cayden replied.

"You must protect the Sword," she said. "Do not think that you have escaped the wrath of Amphileph."

"It will be done," Cayden responded.

"Be about it then," she replied. "I will return again." Rendaya turned from him and walked back toward Southwood. Cayden's resolve reminded her of her late husband. That memory rekindled her anger toward Amphileph, and she suddenly wanted to be home. When she was some distance from Cayden, she shot into the night sky toward Southwood to be with Bellows and those surroundings that gave her comfort.

She neared Southwood quickly, but thoughts of Amphileph clouded her mind with anger. Her flight faltered. Had she not refocused in the final instant, she would have crashed—and with enough force to do herself great harm. As it was, the landing was bad enough, and she tumbled through the high grass just outside the trees, rolling to a bruised and battered stop. She cried out in pain, and after lying there for some time, she managed to pick herself up. Her left wrist was obviously broken, and she had a nasty cut above her right eye. She squinted at her right shoulder, where a hole in her clothing revealed raw flesh, already bleeding freely.

"Creator, let me be strong," she managed, and she pushed herself to limp home. With a great deal of effort, she opened the latch on the door and entered the house. Bellows moved around her frantically.

"Not now, Bellows," she begged. But Rendaya's obvious pain made the cat circle her repeatedly, his ears standing straight up and his eyes wide with concern.

"Bellows! Stop!" Rendaya cried.

Bellows's ears fell back. He quietly curled up on the large pillow on the loveseat by the window. When he looked away and licked his paw, Rendaya felt a twinge of guilt.

"I just . . . need . . . a minute, Bellows," she said, though he appeared to be ignoring her.

Rendaya lowered her head in prayer. She raised her one good hand to the heavens, her palm open as if to receive the gift. She raised her head then; her eyes remained closed. Her palm grew hotter, the heat spreading across her hand and then up her arm. She silently gave thanks to the Creator, placed the heated palm upon her wrist, and winced as the bones shifted back into place. When the last of the carpals had popped back into place, she moved the palm down and across her fingers. She raised her hand to her eye, cupping the cut, and it immediately stopped bleeding. No sooner had Rendaya removed her hand than the skin had mended, leaving only the dried blood to hint at the injury there had been.

Rendaya pressed her hands together for a moment, then gingerly set her left hand on the torn shoulder. It also stopped bleeding in an instant, and the lump on her collarbone slowly disappeared. She opened her eyes and carefully crawled into bed.

"Now, you," she said to Bellows, whose head popped up at the welcoming tone in his mistress's voice. Rendaya groaned and blew out her lantern, curling up with her blanket. Bellows gathered in a knot at the small of Rendaya's back, and in no time, they were both fast asleep.

Chapter Thirteen

The Faceless Mountains

Citanth had rounded the Faceless Mountains and tracked Galbard to Calarph forest, but the thick, dark woods hid too many unknowns, and horse tracks led west, so he chose not to venture deep inside. He was unsure whether the Watcher Mategaladh had survived the Binding Spell, but if the old man was somewhere in this forest, the brush would give him far too great an advantage—he would unleash his fury on their company, even at the cost of his last strength.

"Move along, commander. My old *friend* Mategaladh—if he is even alive—is in no shape to ride, so the man we seek rides west," Citanth replied when the commander told him of their findings. "Send your fastest riders west!"

Far in the distance, Galbard pushed Pladus, his new horse, relentlessly. He had to draw the Camonra away from Mategaladh and distance himself from his pursuers.

The horse's speed was frightful—Pladus ran like no mount Galbard had ever seen. He held on with white knuckles as they shot across the Calarphian plains north of the mountain range where he had once huddled in the deep caves with Illian and his kinsmen.

When he looked to the south, the peaks of the mountain range appeared to go on forever into the west, and the thought occurred to him that he might be trapped. As far as the eye could see, there was only the tundra to the north.

They were streaking past the mountains when Galbard suddenly pulled back on the reins. "There, Pladus!" he shouted, guiding the horse toward what appeared to be a goat trail up the mountainside. They galloped along the trail until the narrowing passage scraped Galbard's leg against the rock wall, nearly knocking him from his mount and sending him tumbling down the slope. He pulled Pladus's reins until he recovered his seat, then they crept along the trail until they found a small landing, where he dismounted and began leading Pladus up the ever-steepening path. After hours of struggling, there was a break in the steep grade, the trail widened, and Galbard decided to ride again. He stepped into the stirrup and threw his leg over Pladus, but then he thought he heard voices in the distance. He leaned forward to whisper into Pladus's ear.

"Hold, Pladus," he said, stepping back down. Galbard wrapped the reins around an outcropping of stone and squatted to look back over the terrain they had covered that afternoon. He watched and listened for several minutes, but there was no sign of his pursuers. A light powdering of snowflakes evaporated in the air, but higher up Galbard could see the small flakes sticking, and farther still, where the long path climbed toward the high ridges, the snow lay deeper. The cold was clearly something that would affect him more than the Camonra, and if he could not find a crossing, they could easily wait him out until he starved or froze to death.

Galbard's stomach reminded him of Mategaladh's saddlebags. He stood back up and walked around to Pladus's side.

He worked the aged, soft leather through the buckle with worn ease and opened the saddlebag flap. There Galbard found small packages and vials within, some unlabeled. One, however, was labeled with the single word, "Traveler." There was smaller print that read, "Use sparingly." He opened it, intending to assess its taste, and instinctively sniffed its contents. His nose burned from the intense fragrance, and he quickly eased the cork back into the vial. A wave of lightheadedness struck him, but he managed to replace the vial in the saddlebag and make his way around Pladus back up the trail before he had to sit down.

Struggling with nausea, he felt a strange rush of blood to his head, and with what might have been a momentary loss of consciousness, his surroundings changed. He lifted away from his own body, the clouds raced across the sky with the sun, and then everything came to a sudden standstill.

He could see himself, frozen in time, a mixed look of concentration and anger on his face, hiding behind a large outcropping of stone.

Suspended in mid-leap, the scouts were making their way up the hill in front of him.

"It looks pretty dire, doesn't it?" a voice said.

Galbard jumped, startled. "Mategaladh?" He could barely make out the old Watcher's face in the strong light that seemed to surround his body.

"I see you have found the Traveler potion that I put in the bag," Mategaladh said.

"What's happening to me?" asked Galbard.

"You're seeing the future," Mategaladh answered. "Be quick and take note of their attack, for the effects will not last long."

"Are you here with me?"

Mategaladh let out a little laugh. "That's a little Connection tincture that I mixed in—my own special blend. We can talk but a short time, so be quick."

Galbard shook his head. This whole experience was surreal. He looked again at the scene before him. Below him, at the far end of the valley, he could see an army of Camonra approaching. "I am completely outnumbered."

"Yes, it looks so, but it is said that the righteous warrior is always outnumbered," answered Mategaladh.

Galbard crinkled his nose, then his expression settled into calm.

"If I am not to be, then I go to the feast of my ancestors in glory. They will see that the son of a mason has done great things, and they will be proud of my brave passing."

Mategaladh's image appeared to shift on the wind for a moment.

"What's happening?" Galbard asked.

"The connection is ending," Mategaladh replied. "What will you do?"

Galbard turned his back to Mategaladh and, drawing the Sword, held it high. "Let them come for me!" he shouted, then closed his eyes and listened to the echo of his words ringing throughout the mountainside below. "If I must, I will die in the service of my oath! I have given my word to Evliit!"

There was a second rush of blood across the top of Galbard's brain. He snapped back into the present, certain he still heard the echo of his defiant shout in the valley below. He drew a deep breath, sat up, and tried to get his bearings on the time of day, but it seemed as though no time had passed at all. Pladus dipped his head and shook his mane, displaying his boredom at being tied off to the mountain.

Galbard crawled on his belly to the edge of the stone ledge, and just as he had seen in the vision, three scouts were closing on him. They were hunters, the skulls of *men* hanging from their belts. One of the Camon scouts saw him then, and he shouted up to him.

"We have seen you, little man!" the younger scout barked. He suddenly changed direction and moved quickly upon Galbard's position. "You are surrounded by the Camonra!"

Galbard moved back from the edge and rolled to his back. He held the Sword tightly in both hands, the sweat on his palms making the leather-covered hilt feel slippery. He stood up then and looked over the edge at them. "Come to me, bastards of Amphileph! I will end you!" He felt the temperature rising in the hilt of the Sword, and a blue flame engulfed it.

"I am Pras!" The elder Camon bristled. "*You* would challenge *me*?" he screamed. The other Camonra appeared from behind their cover. The one called Pras turned to the younger scouts and growled, "He is very brave hiding on that ledge. Let him come down from there and say such things to me!"

"Your master could not take this Sword from Evliit! What makes you think his lowly servants could?" taunted Galbard.

One of the younger Camonra had heard enough. He came up from beside Pras up the hill, but Pras knocked him aside with a wave of his great shield. "Hold your ground, Dahran, and wait for Citanth! This one is going nowhere!"

"Enough of this talk!" the younger Camon said. "We can kill this little fool of a man!" He burst forward, and Pras moved to stop him, narrowly missing his leap to a thin perch of stone.

"I'm coming for you, little man!" Dahran shouted. He leapt again to a second perch.

Pras put his horn to his lips and blew loudly, sounding to all that the bearer of the Sword had been found.

Galbard was amazed at how quickly the Camon moved up the face of the rocky mountainside. He stepped back from the ledge just as Dahran leapt over it.

The Camon pulled his large scimitar from its scabbard and walked toward Galbard with something akin to a smile on his face. "Time for you to die, little one!" he screamed and leapt at Galbard, bringing his sword over his head in a death strike. Dahran's blade descended with enough force to knock the Sword from Galbard's hands, but instead it parted where it touched the Sword, the last six inches whizzing past Galbard's right ear.

Instead of recoiling from the impact, Galbard's parry continued upward and met the chin of his opponent's unchecked forward motion, passing effortlessly through his jaw and out the back of his head, the two halves of his helmet clanging to the ground. The scout fell forward upon Galbard in a lifeless, bloody heap, knocking him from his feet.

He stared in disbelief at the blue flames that danced around Dahran's parted skull and the red molten half of the great scimitar he still held in his hand. The Camon's weight pinned Galbard down.

"Get off me!" Galbard yelled, and Dahran's body flew away from him over the ledge as effortlessly as tossing the last of the ale out of a cup. It burst into blue, then yellow-red flames for a brief moment, arcing through the Calarphian skies before disappearing over the mountainside.

Galbard jumped to his feet. He could hardly control the power that surged through his body. "Leave now if you want to live!" he cried. He forced a deep breath, and a wave of energy emanated from deeper in his gut. The blue plasma began to radiate from his body, lifting him off the ground.

As the second Camon scout topped the ledge in chase of his zealous brother, Galbard pushed the plasma toward him, incinerating the scout in a flash of yellow and red flames. Galbard topped the mountainside and looked down for the remaining Camonra. He could not see the one called Pras at first, but then the Camon poked his head out from around the mountainside, eyes widening at the sight of Galbard, before fumbling for his horn and ducking back behind the stone.

Galbard heard the horn's signal, and he cried out again. "Come if you dare!" A wave of blue energy passed down the mountainside, and the horn's note just stopped. He raised the Sword and jumped down to engage the Camon—only to see him motionless, still holding his horn in the air. The Camon's ashen form held for but a moment more before the winds of the Faceless Mountains swirled him skyward.

At the foot of the mountain, Citanth's warriors heard the familiar battle horn's long tone cut short, and they knew that could only mean one thing. The human was within their grasps!

"Master Citanth!" an acolyte yelled. "The alert is sounded! The human has been found!"

Citanth peeked out from the curtain of his carriage to see what the ruckus was. News of the man Galbard was welcome to his ears.

"Master Citanth, the scout's horn sounded just up there," the acolyte repeated. He pointed just up the mountainside ahead of them.

"We stand ready to do your bidding, lord!" one of the captains shouted.

"Take your men and bring me the man called Galbard," commanded Citanth. "Leave only the slaves—take all the rest. Capture this man Galbard at all costs! Capture him and bring me his weapon!"

"Yes, my lord!" the captain responded. He pulled his battle horn to his lips and blew it loudly. The other captains surrounded him within seconds.

"Bring our High Commander the man Galbard and his sword! Even now, our scouts have found him out. Capture the sword at all costs!" The resulting rumble of warriors was deafening. The Azrodh riders led the way, and the foot soldiers followed behind them, creating a dust trail that remained in the air for minutes after their departure.

Galbard heard the second horn from the valley below, and readied for their assault. "I will not fear you," he told himself. A peace came to him then. Galbard looked back at Pladus for a moment, then moved over the edge of the ridge, falling directly toward the oncoming horde in the valley below. The blue plasma hugged the terrain, descending rapidly down the mountainside.

When he reached the base of the mountain, the plasma set him gently on the ground. Galbard could feel the ground shaking at their approach, but he kneeled before them.

"Creator, grant me your grace once again. Help me to destroy my enemies."

The Sword seemed almost white-hot, and fingers of blue plasma licked the air around him, illuminating his body like a blacksmith's bellows stoking the coals. He rose to his feet, and the Camonra moved to within moments of crashing down upon him. He pointed the Sword in the direction of the oncoming wall of warriors, and there was the sound of air drawing in toward him, followed by a burst of energy so great that the sound lagged behind its fast-moving wave. It devastated the Camonra ranks, vaporizing the vast majority of them in wisps of flame and ash, while the remainder flew through the air away from him.

Silence hung in the air like the ash. The grass around him was blackened or burning, and the bodies of the Camonra were scattered across the valley before him. His attack struck terror in the hearts of the few Camon survivors, and those that could not walk clawed the ground to escape from him. Those that could run did so without looking back.

Galbard felt drained. The plasma disappeared, and he fell forward to his knees, just catching himself with one hand to prevent falling upon his face. He lifted the Sword with great effort, pushed it into its scabbard, and turned to struggle up the mountainside toward Pladus.

When he reached the ledge where Pladus waited impatiently, Galbard climbed onto him and spurred him hard enough to trigger a flight he could barely control.

Pladus bolted past the snow line, and still showed no sign of slowing. They had nearly topped the mountain before Galbard knew it. He saw an opening up a steep grade.

The angle of the terrain had him nearly lying on Pladus's neck. The great horse dug in his hooves in his attempt to ascend, but slid repeatedly, dangerously tempting the edge more than once.

When at last Pladus neared the mountaintop, they came upon a large patch of ice on the plateau. Galbard pulled on the reins, trying to halt Pladus's momentum. The horse straightened his legs, sliding across the ice-covered plateau until his front hooves caught traction, but his rear footing slipped out from under him, and the reins slid through Galbard's cold hands. He fell to the frozen ground with a loud thud, knocking the air out of his lungs.

Galbard tried to regain his wind. He slowly rolled to his side and watched Pladus struggle back to his feet, then lay on his back and let the snow land gently on his wind-burned face.

Out of the corner of his eye, he saw a tiny red bird flittering across the snow, jumping and turning this way and that. It twitched its head and looked at Galbard, and then it darted away. Galbard's eyes followed it through a passage in the mountainside. He stood and struggled along the little bird's path until he saw the southern valley below through the snow-filled winds held at bay by the passage walls

"To the south then," Galbard said. "We are saved, Pladus."

He had found a passage that he could use to put some real distance between him and whatever remained of the Camonra. Galbard called to Pladus and struggled to gain his mount again, both of their breathing strained by the altitude. They made their way down the twisting path of the mountainside toward the smaller mountain range to the south.

*   *   *

Citanth shifted nervously in his coach. He had heard the booming noise from the mountainside and felt the wave of energy dissipating around him.

"Master!" one of his slaves said. "Master, the Camonra return!"

Citanth bolted from his coach with great anticipation, stepping down upon the slaves' shoulders and backs. There were no more than a handful of the Camonra left, and even those seemed startled and confused.

"Where are the others?" Citanth inquired.

"They are . . . gone, my liege," one of the Camonra announced.

He dragged what remained of one of his comrades and dropped him at Citanth's feet. It folded in a heap upon the ground, spilling the organs from the half that remained.

"I do not know what happened, master," the Camon replied. "I was at the rear of the column when the order came to attack the man-creature. I heard a shout from in front of me and then a push, like a great wind, master. Then the dust blinded me."

"Stop!" Citanth yelled, looking over the dead soldier. "Speak no more of it!" he cried, raising a hand to strike the soldier's face. He turned and attempted to climb back into his coach. Stumbling slightly, he managed the steps and entered what privacy the curtained coach provided. He put his arm to his face, muffling his gasp with the sleeve of his coat. Everything was gone, erased by this man, Galbard.

"I will have my vengeance," he muttered and then sprang to the curtain and pulled it back. "Back to the Temple!" he screamed, and then he threw the sash closed again. The slaves looked at each other.

"We cannot return to Amphileph in defeat!" one of them whimpered. "He will kill us all!"

"Shut up! Grab your part!" another yelled, and they each seized the horizontal supports and lifted the coach into the air. "To the Temple!" the slave cried, groaning under the weight.

CHAPTER FOURTEEN

AUTONOMY

A corps of twenty or so Camon soldiers had gathered outside Tobor's tent to celebrate their victory over the humans in the raid on Highwood. The females had prepared a feast in honor of the warriors: a Camon favorite, Rudh-Oric, a spiced roast of the less-than-agile Azrodh lizard, the beasts the Camonra preferred to ride into battle.

Tobor had coined the phrase "less than agile" after watching the female Camonra that very afternoon running through the Azrodh pen with their mallets ready. The Azrodh had been quite aware of why the Camonra were in the pen, and they were scrambling in all directions.

Tobor never failed to note the ruthlessness of the attack, either. When the females cornered an animal, one moved before it to distract it from the real threat, while another struck it down with a single swift blow from outside its peripheral vision. *Never let them swarm you, Azrodh!* he thought to himself, and the image it conjured made him shake with laughter.

One of the females tried to pull his parted side together with her stitch work. "Be still, master, please," she said. A slicing wound ran horizontally along his ribs, and she had paused mid-stitch, the skin stretched to a point on the thick thread.

"Of course," Tobor replied. He tolerated a certain amount of backtalk from the concubines that traveled with him. Many times he had returned from battle a mess of injuries, any of which might have infected and killed him had the females not nursed him back to health within the secrecy of his tent. Hidden away from the eyes of the other soldiers—they remained within the confines of his tent's inner quarters at all times—they had seen him at his best and worst. They had never once shared the secrets of his inner sanctuary with even his most trusted captains, even when, in his weakness, his rivals might have torn control of the clan from his grasp. Not even then had they betrayed him, and Tobor valued their loyalty highly.

The ripping open of the land before Rion and the binding of Amphileph had changed everything; now the exodus from the Third Quarter was almost complete, save only for those completely faithful to Amphileph. The Camon females had never been so close to the battlefield, but now they settled in with the males on what could only be called a "new frontier" of their own making.

The great rift to the south had prevented the Rion War from continuing, and the Binding of Amphileph had taken away the terror that seemed to drive his people. Tobor could only feel good about these changes, even if Rionese were scattered to the west and north. Humans didn't seem to want this land of rumbling rain clouds and quakes, and for the first time in his memory, there was a small spot of land that the Camonra could call their own. So tonight would be different, for Tobor had announced to his concubines that they would be allowed outside for more than just preparing or serving the feast, and they were clearly excited by the prospect.

The afternoon had been quiet, interrupted only by the chatter of the Camonra females. They sorted the largest Awira insects to crisp in a pit of coals. The scent of the slow-roasting Azrodh wafted among the tents, mixing with the strong odor of the baking Awira, an insect that the Camonra prized for the juices in their lower thorax. The heat of the coals made the sac-shaped stingers swell as if they would burst, and when a clear liquid began to ooze from the tip of the tail, the cooks pulled them from the pit and rolled them across a special stone made for extracting the juices. The juice from the Awira's tail made a potent drink that the Camonra would fight for—well worth the hard efforts the females might spend making it. Since squeezing Awira tails was normally a morning duty and they had started the process later in the day, the constant chatter seemed a requirement for speeding the process along.

Tobor removed the high-back chair from his tent that he reserved for such occasions and sat back in the afternoon sun, watching the clouds pass overhead. The misty warm air from the southern storm clouds seemed to soothe his nasal passages. Several soldiers were working on a table for the feast, using their short blades to plane planks for the top. The noise of the woodwork combined with the females' chatter was relaxing in an odd way, and Tobor dozed off.

As night fell, Tobor sat outside his tent with a mug of Awira and a plate piled high with Rudh-Oric. The celebration was in full swing.

"Rudh-Oric! More Rudh-Oric!" one of the Camonra yelled. "The only animal you can ride into battle or eat if you have to wait for the fight!" A roar of grunting laughter followed his pronouncement.

A bonfire blazed, its light dancing across the soldiers' happy faces, lit as much by drink as by flame.

Tobor listened to the loud carrying-on by the soldiers with little comment. For him, there had been many battles, and many celebrations had followed. Over the years, the memories that followed the drink were of fallen friends who had once shared their stories with him, as these younger ones did now. He could almost see them again, charismatic and brazen, shouting at him from another time. He watched the young Camonra retelling the day's events. *A rite of passage*, he thought, this retelling of the battle. His eyes swept the crowd, noting the older soldiers quietly eating, smiling now and then at one story or another.

Tobor reached for his cup and felt the stitches in his side pull. It made him wince a bit. He silently raised his cup to one of the older soldiers, who nodded ever so slightly in response — but in whose eyes Tobor saw the stare that countless years of war had darkened forever. Deep within his being, a sadness welled with the realization that this had been their lives.

His mind raced with thoughts he had never dared before. Had they ever known anything but war and death, and the ever-pressing demands of Amphileph? When would there be a time to raise the young, to grow old and die?

Tobor could remember only a handful of warriors who had seen the number of winters he had seen. Was it beyond their hopes to live out their lives in peace? Hadn't they sacrificed enough for Amphileph's seemingly never-ending conquests?

Tobor moved his hand to touch the coarse thread that held his wound closed. It was still tender to the touch, but a bruised sensation around the entire area had replaced the sting of the cut. He was thinking of turning in early.

"The humans will not challenge us again!" one of the Camonra shouted. He raised a cup into the air, undeterred by the sloshing of the drink down his arm and across the table.

Another Camon jumped upon the table. "We should kill them all!"

"What say you, General Tobor? Should we ride back and finish them off?"

There was a roaring response to the suggestion. The cheer had just begun to settle when another rose out of it, the soldiers yelling, "To-bor! To-bor! To-bor! To-bor!"

Tobor could see that the drunken soldiers were not going to let it go. He could see the wild look in their eyes, and he recognized the frenzied release of pent-up emotions that can overcome soldiers after a battle. With the drink and the camaraderie, it had fallen over the lot of them like a spell. He stood up, and they went crazy with shouts and grunts.

"Settle down, young ones!" Tobor said. The crowd took a moment, but did just that after a few more slaps on the back and individual roars of fierceness. "I too celebrate avenging the death of our brothers," he began. There was another roar from the group, and his mind wandered to the statuette of Amphileph he kept in the prayer case in his chest — the same chest he had carried from his hut in the village that had sprung up around Amphileph's temple. His mind wandered to the old warrior and the years of war already past. "Amphileph would be proud . . ." Tobor began, but he could not find the words to finish the sentence. He looked at his soldiers, and again his words failed him. The group seemed poised to hear him revel in the moment, but Tobor did not deliver the expected goading for drink and blood. Instead, he put his cup back down on the table and took a serious tone that passed through the room like a cold wind.

"I have thought long about how the Camonra should deal with the humans," he started again. "I have fought many battles against them, and as many of you have also found, what they lack in stature they add in determination. I have looked hard at the human 'threat' we have been assigned to eliminate, but I have found little threat at all."

There was a surprised look forming on the faces of several of the drunken soldiers. Many struggled with what they heard.

"No one will go into the forest again. We will not war with the humans unless they bring it upon themselves. Let us have no more of the humans, for what have they that the Camonra require?"

"Lord Amphileph would have them all killed!" one of the warriors yelled.

Tobor did not flinch. "Lord Amphileph would sacrifice every warrior among us if it suited his purpose."

There was a sudden silence. All eyes were upon him.

"This is blasphemy!" one of the Camonra burst out. He jumped onto the table and drew his sword. Cups and bowls flew as his upward swing lopped off the tip of one of the general's chin-dreadlocks. He recovered quickly while Tobor drew his own sword, swinging downward a second time. Tobor leaned to the left, and the attacker's sword narrowly missed his head, removing the upper corner of Tobor's high-backed chair. Tobor's swing, however, was unaffected by the drink, and his blade crashed into the young Camon's helmet, crushing its side with the force. Blood sprayed from his nose, and the would-be insurgent flew from the table to the floor.

A second attacker stepped over the body and leapt at Tobor's retreat from the table. Tobor moved back toward his tent, and the circle of troops widened. A second and then a third attacker joined him, and Tobor's back brushed against his shield hanging from one of the tent's outer supports.

"Our lives for Amphileph!" they shouted and moved in on him.

"If that is your choice, then I will oblige you!" Tobor shouted back at them. He grabbed up his shield in one hand and blocked the first thrust with his mighty sword in the other. He swung around, striking the one at his right with the edge of the shield just at the bridge of his nose, the sound of it ringing through his shield. That one crumpled instantly. Tobor reversed his hips and flipped his blade in his hand, running through the second attacker with the familiar sound of punctured leather and the thump of his hilt stopping against the attacker's chest. The stitches in his side broke loose with his exertion, but Tobor was oblivious to it, allowing nothing to detract from the movement of his sword and the sounds of battle.

As the last of the attackers struggled to pull away, he tried to cry out, but no sound came out of his mouth, and his struggle slowly ended. He slid backward off Tobor's sword and collapsed to the floor. Tobor looked around the room for any other challengers. No one moved.

"Challenge me now, if you dare!" Tobor screamed at them and then drew in a great breath and bellowed. "*I* command you!"

Several of the elder soldiers dropped to one knee, lowering their heads, and a ripple effect passed over the entire group of soldiers.

Tobor's labored breathing was more from the excitement of the battle than his exertion, and it quickly subsided.

"Go not into Highwood! I command it!" Tobor shouted. "Find your wives! Build your dwellings! If the men of that place wish for war, the Camonra will show them no mercy! They are not welcome here, nor us there, so will we keep our distance. If men have brains enough to leave us be, then we shall do likewise!" There was what seemed to Tobor a long silence before a grunt of acknowledgment rumbled back from the group.

"Throw these rebels on the fire!" he yelled, and several of the soldiers moved to carry away the dead.

Chapter Fifteen

Altar for the Sword

For two months, Galbard wandered the wide-open plains north of the second mountain range he had seen from atop the Faceless Mountains, moving first west toward the beaches of the Western Shore. He longed for the warm air that blew in from the sea there, the warmer temperatures helping to thaw the Faceless Mountains' chill from his bones.

Galbard's prayers were single-minded: asking his Creator to remove the threat that had stalked him since the day he set foot outside Rion. It had seemed to him that his prayers had been answered, for he had not seen a soul since the encounter with the Camonra in the mountains to his north.

He wandered along the shore letting the ocean's waves crash upon his pant legs, their baggy leather saturated and sagging. He stood on the beach and looked to the sea, allowing the sand to trickle between his toes with the tide. He slung the thick boots he had received from the refugees in the Faceless Mountains over his left shoulder; the wool coat he had tied atop the pack Mategaladh had given him. It had doubled as a bedroll quite nicely.

He had made his way around the second mountain range that lay south of the Faceless Mountains, and after most of another day, he came upon an abandoned sailboat big enough for ten or fifteen men. He glanced over the contents and immediately recognized the tattered flag of Rion snapping in the strong ocean winds, and that alone was enough to spur him onward. He wanted no more encounters like Highwood, no more chances to tempt the Rionese with the power of the Sword. There had been so much death surrounding it that at times he thought it best to cast it into the sea, and had it not been for his strong belief in Evliit's return, he would have done it.

Half a day more along the beaches, and he saw it—a structure that towered over the hillside. It resembled the oldest structures in Rion, and whatever its age, the architecture was unmistakable—Rionese hands had surely built it.

The tower's magnificent height must also have taken many years to construct, even with the latest techniques of the greatest builders in all of Erathe. How it could have been built without all of Rion knowing of it, he could not imagine. More importantly, a Rionese temple would likely have a contingent of Elders, and surely they would take the Sword of the Watch for safekeeping until Evliit returned for it. This thought made Galbard immediately begin a march in that direction.

*   *   *

In the fields east of Shinetower, Cayden stood on a flat, circular stone about ten feet in diameter at the center of a little amphitheater. The stone was set upon two similar stones, each larger than the previous, forming a slightly raised platform in the concave excavation of the hillside. Jalin was trying to finish weaving flowers in a wrought iron arch beside him.

The amphitheater had stone seats surrounding it, and flowers lined four paths leading from the center platform. Pillars stood on either side of the four paths leading out from the circle, each topped with an oil basin. Jalin had made a hanger with wooden dowels and some string, and she had hung some silky white fabric from each of them. It tossed lazily in the gentle breeze of that beautiful day.

"Sometimes I can't believe how much this place has grown," said Cayden. From the little bit of elevation the platform afforded, he could see a line of fifty or sixty people coming toward the wedding circle from the Dales. "And this wedding circle—it's really nice. Your decorations are beautiful, Jalin. I can't thank you enough." He stood on his tiptoes and craned his neck, but even with the platform's elevation he couldn't quite see the oil level in the basins atop the eight-foot pillars.

"They're bringing some oil for the basins, right?" asked Cayden. "I'm expecting the celebration to go into the night."

Jalin stopped what she was doing and looked toward the coming crowd. "I'm pretty sure some of those girls are carrying jars of oil," she said.

"I hope we have enough food," said Cayden. "That's a lot of people."

"To think we could even have a wedding in the Dales," she said. She used the back of her hand to wipe her forehead. "People are so fickle. One day they hate you, the next, they're dancing at your wedding."

Cayden looked down at the ground. He had worried his wedding to Nara might strike a nerve with Jalin. As the date approached, she had talked more about moving on, getting past the loss of her husband, but the drive to reconnect with him had been replaced by a tinge of bitterness. He hated that.

"What can I do to help?" Cayden asked.

"Ro's exploring is making me crazy," Jalin said. "I keep thinking he's going to fall on the steps or run headlong into one of those benches."

"Ro!" Cayden said. "You need to settle down, little one." Ro stopped and looked at him. "Into the grass with you!" Cayden added, scooping him off the stone steps and patting him toward the lawn.

Ro chuckled and ran into the grass.

"Thank you, Cayden," Jalin said, sighing.

"Oh, when they learn to walk!" Cayden laughed. Ro started back up the steps, and Cayden grabbed him up, tossing him up in the air. Ro's funny face shifted to a flash of panic until Cayden's strong hands caught him, and then a giggle bubbled from his lips.

"I've got you, little man!" Cayden laughed. He turned his gaze to Jalin, and his smile faded. She was fighting back tears.

"Men and boys," she said, batting her eyelids. She caught a tear falling from the corner of her eye with one shaking finger. "I miss his father so much, you know, I . . . . ." She stopped and shook her head. "No, no, I'm sorry. I refuse to let anything spoil this wonderful day."

"Hey, it's okay," Cayden said. He looked at Ro and back to her. "Keep your faith, Jalin."

Jalin forced a smile. "Come here, Ro!" she said, reaching for him, and then admonished Cayden, "If you don't stop all this excitement, he'll never sit still during the ceremony!"

"That will make two of us," Cayden replied, but his laughter was cut short when the crowd coming from the Dales neared the wedding circle. They were abuzz with laughter and talking. Some carried stools and tables; others brought baskets of food and instruments. Two young men walked around the stone benches and placed a table just outside the wedding circle on the hill closest to Shinetower. The musicians roosted on one of the benches, tinkering with their instruments, while the hooded clergy stood along the circle's edge, watching the procession and speaking quietly among themselves. Some of the men began pitching two wedding tents, one on either side of the circle along the paths that lead to the platform.

Two young girls approached him and Jalin. Cayden was amused at how seriously they carried themselves — and their baskets of summer sausage, crackers, and cheese. "Excuse us, please," one of them said.

"Excuse *me*, ladies," Cayden responded. He watched them skillfully weave among all the others that were busily decorating.

"It's time to go!" Jalin said, grabbing him by the arm. "Nara doesn't want you to see her before the wedding!"

*　　*　　*

Galbard had slipped behind the pillar marking the path from the wedding circle to Shinetower. He had seen the crowd of people coming from the village, and the sounds of celebration drew him in. It had been so long since he had heard laughter. In the chaotic jubilee, he had moved toward the wedding circle unnoticed, but when he saw Jalin, he was overwhelmed with emotion. She carried a child and was arm in arm with another man. He was confused, furious, and crushed, and could think of nothing but getting away from there — away from them. He pushed off from the pillar and headed directly for the tower.

She's gone on with her life, had a child, and settled down, he thought, wrestling with the revelation.

For over two years he had replayed the day he left her for the Soru plant harvest — how certain he'd been that the money he earned would save their marriage, how certain he'd been that she would recant her rebuke of him. That hope had driven him through his enslavement by the Camonra, through the long journey to return the Sword to Evliit.

Now that hope lay shattered, and he struggled to understand what any of it meant. He had believed that delivering the Sword would finally tip the scales of fate in his favor, that this one great act of bravery would somehow bring him back to the one he loved. Now he was sure of nothing.

Perhaps the Sword's commission had been a penance all along, and the journey to return it nothing more than time granted to savor its sting.

"No!" he shouted, stopping mid-stride and lifting his face to the sky. "Give me strength!"

This is beyond my relationship with Jalin. Amphileph must be stopped from destroying all I have ever known. The Sword must be returned to the Elders — to Evliit.

He tried to clear his mind and focus. A Rionese wedding could last for days, and with the custom of inviting the entire village for food, drink, music, and dancing, the tower would be as unguarded as it would ever be. It might be his only real chance to take the Sword into the tower in secrecy.

Galbard moved around the southern side of the tower's outer wall and confirmed that indeed, the guards were few. Several of them had moved to the eastern side of the walled courtyard to see the procession. He slipped silently into the courtyard through the western entrance and moved to the massive first floor door.

He was contemplating how he might enter, when suddenly the door creaked open. Two of the guards pushed open the great doors of the tower. This was his chance.

"The wedding's today?" he heard one of them ask.

"Yes, yes," said the other excitedly. "Lots of food, and I heard that Isha will be there."

"That's all for you, then," the first laughed. "How can you be expected to stand your post when Isha sings?"

"We could stand watch at the eastern gate—you could give me your horn, and I could watch while you go for a bit, and then I could go when you come back."

"Yes, that could work," said the other. "First one to the eastern gate gets to go first to the party!" he said, laughing as he took off running.

The second guard quickly gave chase toward the eastern exit of the courtyard. The great doors began to close, and Galbard waited until the last possible moment for the guards to get far enough away, then slipped inside just before they shut.

The Swordbearer pressed his back to the wall and listened, glancing up at the vaulting that crisscrossed the tower's first-floor ceiling and its skyward-leaping walls. A large stone column stood in the center of the room, and a spiral stair wrapped around the outer wall, rising so high that Galbard could not see its end.

Scattered about were mason and carpentry tools of all types, apparently supporting any number of projects in various stages of completion. He saw what appeared to be a prayer room off the main wing, and across the way, beside a six-inch-thick locked door, a weapons armory visible through metal bars.

There were alcoves with slotted windows along the rising central tower and outer walls, allowing light to fall lattice-like on the structures within. Galbard held the Sword and its scabbard tight in his left hand to prevent any noise as he ran across the main floor to the staircase.

He thumped his back against the wall—the lack of sound from his impact hinted at the massive thickness of the walls themselves. Galbard had seen the newer structures of Rion rise up, their construction requiring the resources of the entire city for a decade.

How could they have built this just since the quake?

Galbard rounded the staircase quietly. The tower door moved again. The two guards returned inside, followed by another soldier, who was shouting a reprimand of some sort.

"We're sorry, sergeant," one of the guards responded. "We wasn't trying to do no harm."

"You stand your watch!" the sergeant barked. "You stand it *here!*"

"Yes, sir!" they answered, and when the sergeant exited, Galbard could hear them still bickering.

He moved with swift stealth up the steps that spiraled around the stone column of the tower, branching off to landings with floors and rooms upon each. He searched several rooms, but he found no Elders anywhere. In fact, most of the rooms had no furnishings at all.

At times, Galbard could hear singing and clapping, and when he neared a window slit, there was music in the distance, the faint sounds of fife and fiddle, drum and tambourine—he could even make out the melodic percussion of a hammered dulcimer.

Finally, Galbard reached the top floor. The wind whistled through the slanted opening to the sky. Cautiously he poked his head up at the upper deck level, looking for another guard post. He saw nothing but a neatly swept pile of sculptor's chisels and stone.

Galbard stepped onto the tower's roof. He chanced a look upward, but the tower's height gave him a little vertigo. The upper deck formed a stone ring about twenty paces wide around the tower's crown, enclosed by thick battlements whose merlons rose to his shoulders while the lower crenels dipped to his waist, offering both cover and a clear view of the world far below. From the deck's surface rose two structures: the central column and the square mouth of the stairwell, the latter's stone walls extending up to his waist like the open top of a small turret. Wind swept freely across the height, tugging at his clothes and reminding him how little stood between him and the vast drop beyond the battlements. Above it all, the sky was deep, the heavens' thick black canvas broken only by the stars' tiny points of light showing through like needle pricks.

At the upper deck's center rose the top of the great column that ran the tower's full height. It protruded about waist height, the crown cut at an angle and highly polished. At its center, the shape of a sword was etched in its face. Instantly, he recognized the shape as that of Evliit's Sword.

This must be it! Galbard thought. *This must be the place that I was destined to find.*

This was no coincidence. There was no mistaking the painstaking detail. The sculptured stone was a perfect match. Surely this was the Sword's final resting place, this high perch where Evliit himself might reach down and pick it up.

He drew the Sword and held it before the etched outline, then turned away, daring himself to test the fit. He walked to the edge of the steps leading back into the tower, and hearing nothing, he walked again to the edge of the deck and looked over. He could see the wedding party and a crowd of onlookers far below, and then he walked back and examined the stone cradle again. Gently, he placed the Sword into its marble top. It fit perfectly.

"I've made it," he said. He placed his hands on either side of the Sword and called upon its power to signal Evliit of its return. The stone's face began to glow, heat rising from beneath its surface and forcing Galbard to step back. Inside itself, the very tower rumbled, the structures' vibrations making him lean over the Sword and steady himself on the altar. Air rushed all around him. Galbard tried again to look to the heavens, fully expecting to see Evliit as before, but the movement of the tower beneath him made looking up even more unsettling.

*　*　*

"How can this be?" Aleris, the leader of the Bhre-Nora, demanded. "Someone's activated the tower's defenses!" He adjusted his goggles and flew around the stone column that rose from the bedrock far below, up through the cavern's center, through a hundred feet of stone, and into the tower to the very altar where Galbard had placed the Sword.

Here, deep beneath the tower, a flurry of activity filled the airspace of the cavern. Here the Bhre-Nora lived, tending a monstrosity of copper piping, valves, and tanks of every shape, all fed by a coil of piping wrapped around the now-glowing stone column.

Off the central cavern was a labyrinth of arch-ceiling tunnels, stairwells, and catacomb-like anterooms opening into other rooms. The Bhre-Nora's simple dugout dwellings lined the cavern walls, and the busy sprites buzzed between rest and work in their goggles, leather caps, long coats, elbow-length gloves, and tall boots that protected them from jets of steam and scalding water. They were an exceptionally nimble race of beings, zipping between the twisting piping in coordinated groups like birds in a flock, working together to tackle valves, chains, and levers that required their combined strength.

The stone's heat radiated through the coil, and the temperature in the room rose almost instantly. Movement began to occur seemingly everywhere at once. Counterweights, slides, and pistons sprang to life, turning a series of gears and belts of a myriad of sizes. The pipes banged and jumped, squealed and screamed. Steam spurted out sporadically around the valves and all along the piping at almost every other connection.

The Bhre-Nora dispersed through the tunnels by foot and by wing, tightening bolts and connections with tiny tools wherever they could.

Aleris launched himself into the air and through the piping with unparalleled grace. He spotted a group of his kin struggling to open several valves as the piping rattled so violently they could barely keep hold of their wrenches.

He passed three others working on a small tank at the intersection of several tunnels. "Blow down that line! Watch the pressure!" he yelled.

"Be sure that—"

He was cut short by the shrill banshee of escaping steam, punctuated by the *pop—pop—pop* of rivets flying from a seam. With an explosion of scalding vapor, a plug blew off the tank and ricocheted around the room, damaging several pipes but narrowly missing his workers, most of whom had dropped to the ground and covered their heads. The billowing steam completely engulfed Aleris and the other sprites. A deafening roar blasted from the open hole in the tank, ending only after Aleris and the others managed to close the valve feeding the pipes from the stone core. They had been lucky, Aleris thought, that only the plug had ruptured and not the tank, for that surely would have killed them all.

"Find that plug!" he screamed. "And get it back in that tank! Riveters!"

The workers scrambled to their feet, searching the room while a team of riveters attacked the seam, beating the two pieces back into alignment. Three of them threw back the hatch into the tank, flew inside, and worked the red-hot rivets with their counterparts on the outside, mushrooming the heads of the rivets with their hammers.

Unaware of the chaos occurring beneath his feet, Cayden stood on the circular platform under the flower-lined arches in the sacred circle of his and Nara's hand fastening. Two of the women had donned robes and, to the music of a tambourine and a lute, were spreading sea salt around the wedding circle. Following them around the circle, one of the young men walked with a sword drawn, a hint back to the pagan days before the Elders forbade such rituals of white magic. Cayden didn't care much for the ritual, but it seemed harmless enough, and the women preparing the wedding feast were adamant about performing it to ward off evil, so he let them have their way. But all he wanted was to see Nara. When they had chanted and circled him three times, they sat down on the stone benches, and finally, the moment had arrived.

He watched Nara emerge from her wedding tent, and his heart began pumping wildly. He thought she had never looked so beautiful. Her eyes lit up, and a broad smile crossed her face. She walked slowly toward Cayden and reached out her hand to him. "You look absolutely incredible," he whispered.

"I thought you looked a little frightened," she said with a soft giggle. "I never imagined the love I feel for you could grow any more... but when I saw your face, it did. Right in that moment."

Cayden lifted her hand and kissed it. He opened his mouth to speak, but the loud grinding and groaning of gears turning startled them all. Behind them, the tower suddenly roared to life. A rumbling of chains and machinery launching into gear completely stopped the progression of the wedding. Steam shot into the sky from the upper deck of the tower.

"What is happening?" Nara yelled above the din. Cayden thought her face was a combination of fear, anger, and disappointment.

"I . . . I don't know!" Cayden stammered.

The ground suddenly quaked beneath them, and she fell into his arms. Chaos overtook the grounds around the tower, and guards were running in every direction. The walls of the outer court began to quake. A grinding of stone on stone shook the air as the inner ring shifted, closing the gaps between its segments and forming a solid wall of stone.

On the roof of the tower, Galbard was just as taken aback. He tried to gain his feet, but the tower shook and growled with activity. Dust puffed around the perimeter of the column where it pierced the top deck, followed by a clattering that sounded to Galbard like stone gears engaging.

Galbard fell forward and looked back over the deck's edge. He could see dust stirring on the grounds below him, and the sounds of whooshing air, ratcheting chains, and stones colliding rocked the tower to its core. He struggled to regain his feet and seized the Sword from its resting place, its mysterious link breaking into feathery wisps like dissipating gas.

The tower's altar stone suddenly dimmed.

Deep in the bowels below the tower, the Bhre-Nora leader smacked the side of his head, perplexed. "Now what's this then?" Aleris yelled.

"Stop everything! You know what to do!" The workers scrambled about, turning hundreds of valves to reroute the rapidly building steam pressure to the outside vents. The order to stop repeated throughout the tunnels beneath the tower, unheard by human ears far above them.

Three hundred feet above Aleris, Galbard could see steam shooting into the air from exhaust ports around the tower's courtyard and the upper deck's perimeter. As abruptly as it had begun, the activity slowed to a stop and everything settled back into place.

The tower's violent vibration ended with its internal grumblings, and Galbard placed the Sword back into its scabbard. He made for the stairwell, but he heard the sounds of shouting and running feet within the tower. Trying to stop, he slipped onto his haunches, scooting back from the stairs until his back pressed against the still-warm altar stone at the deck's center.

"Evliit, why do you not claim the Sword?" Galbard questioned.

Several armed guards sprang from the stairwell and surrounded him. "Hold!" he yelled, but they drew their swords and lowered their spears to his chest. "I am not your enemy! I only mean to return the Sword to its rightful owner!"

The man he had seen arm in arm with Jalin sprang through the stairwell onto the tower's upper deck and burst into the group. "Stand down!" he yelled, trying to catch his breath. "Stand down!"

The man stepped to the front of the soldiers, placing himself between them and Galbard. "I am called Cayden," he said, studying Galbard's face for any hint of intent. Galbard saw Cayden's eyes drift to the Sword, and then Cayden's jaw fell open. "Are you Galbard?" he asked.

Galbard was speechless for a moment. "How do you know my name?"

"In the name of the Creator!" Cayden shouted, unable to take his eyes off the sword. "You are the one we have been waiting for!" He turned to the guards. "Lower your weapons! At once!" He waited for them to comply. "This is the one we have waited for — the bearer of the Sword of the Watch!"

"We weren't prepared for—" a tiny, obviously annoyed voice rang out.

"Aleris!" Cayden said.

Aleris removed his goggles. He buzzed in front of Cayden's face, and Galbard saw the tiny creature's features tighten in exasperation.

"You must coordinate with us!" Aleris exclaimed — but then his expression softened at once. "Wait! Has he—"

His eyes fell on the Sword of the Watch in Galbard's hand. "The Swordbearer! He is here!"

Aleris immediately darted to the ground at Galbard's feet and bowed on one knee. Cayden and the others followed suit, leaving Galbard leaning against the stone altar, staring at them in disbelief.

"I meant no harm!" Galbard announced.

Aleris's head popped up, and he sprang into the air and bobbed before Galbard. "My lord, you are among friends of the Sword. We are at your service!"

Galbard was still stunned. "I'm not sure what's happening."

"Prophecy, sire, has brought you here," Aleris said.

"We've been waiting for you for many months," Cayden said.

"Here indeed is the bearer of the Sword!" Aleris accented his words with a quick circling in the air. "But why has the bearer of the Sword initiated its defense?"

"I am sorry to have caused such turmoil — and at a wedding, no less," Galbard said. "It looked as though the Sword belonged on that altar. I thought Evliit might return for it, that I could lay it there unnoticed and take my leave in peace. I flee the Camonra, and I had hoped my journey had ended."

"Camonra!" Aleris said. He shot up a few feet above them so that he might see over the edge of the upper deck to the grounds below.

"No, no," Galbard said. "I left them in the farthest mountain range to the north. I've been running from the Camonra ever since I was given the Sword. There seems no safe place for a weapon such as this."

Aleris returned to their eye level. "You have found sanctuary here, sire," he said. "This is Shinetower, an altar for the mighty sword. You are safe here."

Galbard let out a deep breath. "Safe? I've not felt safe in a very long time. You could not have spoken kinder words."

"Come with me, sire," said Aleris. "We have much to discuss."

"Discuss all you will later," Cayden offered. "But for now, you and I must speak to the swordbearer alone."

Aleris looked at Cayden and then to the soldiers. "But of course," he said.

"That will be all," Cayden said, signaling the soldiers, who nodded and immediately marched down the stairwell.

Galbard rose to his feet, and the three stood silent in the steady northwest breeze. "I have seen you with Jalin," he said, "but I have no quarrel with you."

It was obviously Cayden's turn to be stunned. "I was struggling to think of how to tell you about Jalin, but now I'm even more confused. I don't know what you mean."

"In the wedding circle—I saw that she was with you."

Cayden's stunned look turned puzzled, then his eyes widened. "No, sire — not *with* me," he said with a nervous chuckle. "Your wife was decorating for my wedding day."

"*Your* wedding day? But I saw you with Jalin and a boy . . ." Galbard murmured, his voice trailing off. He drew a deep breath and sat back against the altar.

Cayden approached and placed a hand on his shoulder. "This must be a great deal to fathom. Jalin has told Nara and me many times of your last day together — the argument, the harsh words. By the Creator's grace they are here; it can be nothing else. They should have died in Rion like so many others, but the Creator brought them here — and brought you as well. I can only imagine what you feel, but know this: she misses you deeply. The boy's name is Ronan, and he is *your* child."

"A son," Galbard said. He was silent for another moment, and then he looked up at Cayden and cleared his throat. "Could you tell them that I would like to see them?"

"Come then, my friend — you can tell them yourself," Cayden said. He took Galbard's hand and lifted him to his feet. "Won't you honor Nara and me with your presence?"

Aleris flew in front of them, hovering at head height. "Wait!" he said. "The Creator brought you to Shinetower for your protection. You can't simply carry the Sword of the Watch in the open. Surely you realize by now that Amphileph and his minions will not rest until they possess it."

"What are you saying?" Cayden asked. "Are you telling me he can't even see them?"

"I'm saying he would endanger them by being seen with them," Aleris replied. "Amphileph would use anyone he could reach to get to him."

Aleris drifted closer to Galbard's face. "No one should know of your relationship to them — for their sake."

"I'm sorry, Aleris, but you ask too much. I've not seen my wife for two years, and I've never seen my son before today," Galbard said.

"I know you care for them deeply," Aleris replied, "and that is exactly why I warn you. Meet them only in secret — at least until we've completed Shinetower's defenses and the escape tunnels beneath the catacombs. Then you can judge for yourself whether they're safer here with you, or far from this place."

Galbard's face tightened. "If she will come, ask her to bring the child. I must see them."

Cayden nodded. "I can tell you without doubt — she longs to see you. Tonight, after the wedding, I will tell her to come to Shinetower."

"It will be done in secret?" Aleris asked, glancing between them. Galbard nodded.

"In secret then," Cayden said.

*　　*　　*

In the distance, Rendaya stood at the edge of Southwood, looking upon the great tower. She had felt an urgent pull to walk from her home in the deeper wood that afternoon, arriving in time to watch the tower roar to life on the horizon and then fall silent again. She somehow knew that it was a good sign, and she was confident Aleris would quickly report to her the events of the night.

The past few months had been unreal, even for one that had looked deeply into the inner workings of their universe. For weeks after the Rionese refugees arrived, she had prayed for the whirlwind to come — often fasting, often fearing she had misread the signs of the Swordbearer's coming. Doubt had encircled her, and she had been unable to see what the Creator intended for her to do. The arrival of the Bhre-N ora completely revitalized her spiritually and gave her peace of mind that her vigil had altered the course of events, but it had taken a heavy physical toll.

Until she had regained her strength, Aleris had been kind enough to update her regularly in every possible aspect of the project, first at her bedside, and then daily in her garden.

She must have been deep in thought, for she had not even heard Aleris's approach. He flew upon a branch at about her eye level and sat down, looking quite winded.

"Aleris! You startled me!" Rendaya said.

"I'm sorry, my lady," said Aleris. "But I could not wait to give you the news! The Sword of the Watch resides in Shinetower!"

Aleris spoke on excitedly, but Rendaya's mind drifted. While she had rested for months, the Bhre-N ora had toiled beneath the tower, fashioning defenses that only they might build. Physical rest had barely quieted her anxiousness, but for the first time in a long while, she felt the Sword was truly safe with the Bhre-Nora in Shinetower.

A thin smile came to her face. "You have done well, my friend," Rendaya said.

"How well I've done remains to be seen, my lady."

Rendaya's smile faded slightly. "That it does, Aleris. That it does."

* * *

Galbard watched the wedding from the height of the tower's upper deck, anxiously awaiting the time when he might see Jalin and his son. It had grown very late before the wedding celebrants began to disband, but he was not tired. In fact, the closer he thought he was to seeing them, the faster his pulse seemed to race.

Sometime after midnight, Galbard heard footsteps on the stairwell. Cayden appeared with Nara, and Jalin followed behind, carrying the sleeping child. She looked frightened.

"Let me hold Ro for a minute," Nara said. She leaned into Jalin and lifted him away.

"Why are we here?" Jalin asked. "To tell you the truth, I don't like this place."

Galbard moved out of the darkness toward them. "Jalin?" he asked before Cayden or Nara could say a word more.

Jalin saw Galbard then, and her knees buckled.

"Whoa!" exclaimed Cayden. He caught her arm and held on to her. "Steady."

"Galbard?" she asked. She looked at him as if she still couldn't believe it. "Is it really you?" Tears welled in her eyes.

"Yes, my love," he replied. "I'm here."

"We'll take Ro downstairs for a moment," Cayden suggested. Galbard and Jalin nodded, and Cayden and Nara turned and descended the staircase.

Jalin waited no longer. She ran to him and threw her arms around him. Her emotion rocked him, but he wrapped his arms around her and laid his head upon hers. He stroked her hair and lifted her chin to look into her eyes. They kissed passionately, and then Jalin looked into his eyes.

"I'm so sorry," she said. "I . . . ."

"Don't say another word, I just want to hold you," he said. "I've missed you more than you'll ever know."

They stood in the cool of the deep night — her crying and thanking the Creator for his return, him recounting his capture by the Camonra, receiving the Sword from Evliit, and the incredible journey that brought him to Shintower's upper deck.

Shortly afterward, Cayden and Nara returned. Jalin went to Nara and took Ro, and she held the sleeping baby up to Galbard.

"This is your son," she said.

Galbard took him and held him in his arms. He kissed the child on the cheek, unable to take his eyes off him. "He's beautiful."

"May we never again be apart," Jalin said.

Cayden shuffled nervously. "We must talk about that."

"What?" asked Jalin. She turned to Galbard. "What does he mean by that?"

"The tower's defenses and escape tunnels are not complete," Galbard answered. "You and Ro would be in great danger staying here until we can finish what we have started."

"No!" exclaimed Jalin. "We will not leave you again."

Galbard pulled her close. "Jalin, listen to me. Amphileph himself is searching for this Sword. If word comes that he is making his way to Shinetower and our preparations are not complete, you must flee. Go to the Western Shores, then north to the second mountain range. Follow the mountains east to Moonledge Peak — many of our people are there."

"You can't leave us! We'll take our chances here with you!" Jalin exclaimed.

Silence fell. Galbard handed the baby back to Jalin. "Listen to yourself. I could never do what must be done to protect the Sword while knowing you were in danger."

"Then we're a distraction?" asked Jalin. "Is that what we are?"

Galbard let out a deep sigh. Her pained expression cut him to the core. "No, Jalin. How can I explain this? The hope of seeing you again is what kept me alive in Amphileph's dungeons. You and Ro are my life. No matter what happens, I want to protect you. And if I were forced to choose, I would choose you — and many people could die."

"Jalin, you know Nara and I want nothing but the best for you," Cayden said, hesitant to step into the conversation. "The Bhre-Nora are amazing. They'll complete their preparations quickly, and then you and Ro can be here with Galbard. Let them complete their work so that you and Ro are safe."

"You will be close, Jalin," said Galbard. "Cayden and I have arranged a place for you and Ro. Cayden and Nara will be there also, right across the road from you."

"In the Dales, Jalin. We'll be right over there," he said, pointing toward the little village.

Galbard wrapped his arms around her and the sleeping child. "We've made it this far. We can get past this."

Jalin attempted to smile. "I want to be with you now, but I understand,"she said. "You're only concerned for us." She stepped back from his arms and looked to Cayden and Nara. "We should probably go."

Galbard tried not to show his disappointment, but when Jalin looked at him, he couldn't help it. "I love you, Jalin," he said, reaching out to her, but she turned away. Fighting back tears, she hurried down the stairs. Cayden nodded, and he and Nara followed behind her.

Galbard turned away and looked east. In that moment, the burden of the Sword felt heavier than ever.

Chapter Sixteen

Imperfect Cage

Citanth's carriage stopped to the north of the Binding. Only a few warriors remained who had survived Galbard's summoning of the Sword of the Watch in the Faceless Mountains. Most had died after its powerful blast of energy had shaken the very foundations of the mountainside, and most of the remaining wounded died in transit back to Amphileph's temple.

Citanth had taken the better part of two weeks to return from the mountains, chiefly because he dreaded delivering such news to Amphileph.

He exited the valley leading to Amphileph's temple, but the situation got no better. Even from a distance, Citanth saw that no one remained in the northern camp, and the villages within the Binding seemed scarcely alive. Furniture blocked the windows of the small huts as if the occupants were trying to keep something out.

Citanth stepped from his carriage and approached the northern edge of the Binding Spell, stopping just short of the markers that outlined its boundary. "Wait here," Citanth commanded his attendants, and then he moved toward the Binding Spell. He scanned the area, but there was no sign of life. He moved along the perimeter of the force field, off the path, and east.

"Amphileph!" Citanth cried out.

There was a fire smoldering on the southern side of the Camonra huts, causing a thick white smoke that drifted lazily along the ground. A small dog seemed to appear out of the haze. It stared back at Citanth with sad eyes, but remained perfectly motionless, save for the twitch of its left ear. Its face was bloody and matted, and a sudden yelp beside it made Citanth flinch. Another dog scurried out from the smoke and turned toward Citanth, and then sat down and panted, its ears back.

There was the outline of a ditch, the dirt thrown outward as if something had exploded from within. Citanth squatted to look more closely, and his movement caused the little animal to bolt, disappearing once again into the thick smoke. "In the name of the Creator," Citanth said under his breath.

The decomposing bodies of the other Watchers still lay where they had fallen, though the dogs of the Camonra were busily scattering their remains. They nipped at each other as the pack tore the once-holy prophets apart like scrap meat. Citanth's nose wrinkled with the smell of death that drifted on the slow-moving smoke.

Glass shattered somewhere ahead, and Citanth stepped back onto the path, moving forward until the Binding's energy field pushed against him hard enough to slide his footing backward. It was a strange sensation, repelling him like the forces of magnetism he had studied with such great enthusiasm under Amphileph so very long ago.

There was cursing in the old tongue, and Amphileph appeared at the entrance to his chambers, his head down, scrawling something on a piece of paper.

"Amphileph!" said Citanth.

Amphileph gave no sign he had heard Citanth, wholly absorbed in a sprawling assembly of brass tubing and flasks — the scattered remnants of his alchemy laboratory now reconfigured in the courtyard. There was a beaten path lying between the equipment and the temple.

"Amphileph!" Citanth yelled again, holding his sleeve up to cover his nose, and for a moment, Amphileph appeared to notice Citanth.

"Could you not retrieve my property, Citanth?" Amphileph asked. "Could you not even retrieve my property from a simple Rionese slave?

Citanth stiffened. "He has learned the Sword's powers, my lord. I followed him past the woods of Calarph into the Faceless Mountains. He was cornered, and we attacked in force."

"You failed me as I knew you would, you sniveling fool!" Amphileph said. A red glow enveloped Amphileph's hand as he charged across the courtyard, thrusting it into the Binding Spell directly toward Citanth's heart. His hand slowed to a stop in the force field, and energy crackled and dispersed through the force field like bolts of red lightning skipping among clouds. The energy emanating from Amphileph's hand suddenly stopped, and he fell upon his back and burst into laughter.

Citanth watched Amphileph's reaction and felt like crying. "Do not laugh at me!" he shouted. "You will not laugh at me!" He stepped toward the spell's edge, pushing against it.

"We had him cornered, ready to destroy him!" he shouted. "We attacked him in force, and he released the power of the Sword upon us, destroying everything around him. I had no choice but to flee!"

The disgust in Amphileph's face was unmistakable. He jerked upright, supporting himself with one hand and pointing the ink-stained finger of the other at Citanth's face. "You are worthless, Citanth! You are utterly worthless!" he screamed, veins bulging in his neck and eyes. "Wasn't it you I first sent to take the Sword from Evliit's sleeping hand?" he asked, the question dissolving into a laugh that boiled Citanth's blood.

Amphileph stared up at the sky. "How can it be that the most incompetent of us all would be on *that* side of this Binding and I *here?*" he asked the heavens. He looked at the dogs fighting over the remains of the other Spellmakers. A twisted smile crossed his face. The dogs became frenzied, barking and howling and whining. "But of course! They know it, too!"

Amphileph ranted on, and the smile evaporated. "Is there anyone who does not know of your absolute impotence? You who looked upon the Sword for your own taking? How could an imbecile like you even believe for a moment that *you* could lead the Spellmakers?" Amphileph asked.

His face became deeply red, and then he burst into laughter again. "I will kill you, Citanth! I will snuff out your life without raising so much as a finger!"

Citanth looked beyond Amphileph, distracted momentarily by the tearing sounds of the dogs ripping apart the corpses' bloody clothing. The dogs' faces were suddenly horrific — bloodstained teeth bared, lips curled. They snarled with their eyes wide and wild, and they dug in their heels and jerked on the sleeve of a Watcher, his partially rotted hand flailing in the tug of war. The sight made Citanth raise his hand to cover his nose and mouth.

Amphileph's rambling stopped. He rolled up on one elbow, studying Citanth intently. Citanth slowly lowered his hand and looked at it himself, confused by Amphileph's sudden curiosity. He stared at the strips of dirty cloth, blood-stained in places — a shoddy veil covering what had once been his right hand. The memories of touching the mighty Sword began to flood his mind.

Amphileph suddenly jumped to his feet and ran toward the temple, barely noticing the intricately placed stones around a map drawn in the dirt. He plowed through the middle of it and disappeared in the smoke.

Glass shattered again in the lab, followed by Amphileph's shouting. The master Spellmaker seemed thoroughly mad.

Moments later, Amphileph appeared again in a dead run, smiling like Citanth had not seen in some time. He looked strangely happy, Citanth thought, as he skidded to a stop before him, waving the smoke aside and then seeming to cup it in his upturned hand. It feathered around him in the micro-currents of air that followed in his path.

"Amphileph?" Citanth queried.

"Gases are amazing, are they not?" Amphileph asked. "Do you remember when we spent a whole season boiling water, trying desperately to understand its properties? Do you remember when I forced the water through the cloth? How we'd purified the water of Rion for the sacraments?" he asked almost giddy with excitement. "Must make a note of that," Amphileph said, and he returned to scrawling something on the paper. Citanth noticed the parchment was nearly destroyed, and Amphileph's palm was black with ink.

Amphileph noticed Citanth's interest in it, and he quickly stuffed the parchment in a pocket and turned away, mumbling to himself.

"My lord, the Sword Bearer has disappeared in the mountains," Citanth began again, attempting to regain his composure. "He is likely—"

Amphileph snapped around to Citanth, a sudden intensity taking control of his face. "You covered your nose, Citanth!" he shouted back at him, and then he burst out in laughter.

"Yes, my lord, I was overcome by the stench," Citanth responded. "This whole place smells of death."

"You miss my point, Citanth," said Amphileph.

The joyous look on Amphileph's face made it impossible for Citanth to see any point at all.

Amphileph moved closer to him, to the edge of the Binding. "The bodies are in here; you're out there, yes?"

Before Citanth could answer, Amphileph carefully removed a small vial from his cloak. Citanth watched as Amphileph gingerly removed the intricately carved glass cap, and the red liquid inside vaporized almost instantly. Amazed, Citanth watched the vapor begin to swirl slowly in the air. When it made contact with the Binding, it dispersed.

"Watch! Watch!" shouted Amphileph. After a moment, it appeared that the vapor was recombining in the air just outside the Binding.

"My lord?" Citanth began, but the dark red vapor suddenly crossed the distance and struck him in the chest, hurling him across the temple grounds.

Amphileph laughed hysterically. The vapor raced across the courtyard, lifted the carriage out of the hands of the servants and raised it some twenty feet off the ground. It hovered effortlessly, then dropped, the impact snapping its front struts and collapsing the covered frame meant for its once-royal rider. The servants witnessed little of it, for they ran toward the western valley the very instant it had lifted out of their hands, never looking back.

Citanth lay beside the broken carriage. He lifted his head just in time to see Amphileph wave his hands, sending the red vapor rippling through the grass toward him. His body flew again through the air.

"Not all my spell-making fails!" Amphileph screamed with delight. "I can make use of this!" he said, turning back to his laboratory. The vapor dissipated, and Citanth crashed back to the ground.

CHAPTER SEVENTEEN

UNEASY PEACE

Two winters had passed since Galbard's arrival at Shinetower. Two winters without a sign of the Camonra; two winters without war or any communication from Rion. Ever vigilant, Galbard stood his post with Evliit's sword, watching over his son and wife from a distance. He had been certain the Camonra would come for him, pressing Aleris daily about the tower's defenses and tunnels. The strain had taken its toll, and Galbard was weary.

The former artisans of Rion had done anything but stand still in that time. Small shops had sprung up throughout the Dales, and a sense of normalcy had returned to their daily lives. With the days of the Witch of Southwood apparently behind them, they seemed oblivious to further danger.

Galbard listened to Cayden's regular updates about Jalin and his son. She was forging a new identity apart from being his wife, and though that separation tore at him, he remained steadfast in his duty. The distance between them had grown, and even when she came to him in secret, it lingered. Galbard feared their love was slipping away. For two winters, Galbard had kept to himself, locked away in the upper two floors of Shinetower.

Today, a beautiful blue sky stretched across the southern part of Etharath, and once again Galbard had made his way to the upper deck of the tower. He was so intent on watching the activity below that he didn't hear Cayden ascend the stairs behind him.

"I thought I might find you here," Cayden said.

"As if it has ever been difficult to find me," Galbard laughed.

Cayden smiled. "It's that difficulty I wanted to talk about."

Galbard caught the hesitation.

"Well, spit it out," he said. "You know how much I hate to see you worried."

Cayden laughed at that — a genuine, familiar sound — and moved to one of the stone seats surrounding the Sword's altar. He glanced at the others, all empty.

"We've spoken of many things here, my friend," he said. "Matters of our people's future, the workings of our great temple... even the war we once feared but never saw."

He paused. The wind brushed across the tower, cool and steady. Galbard turned toward him, watching as Cayden closed his eyes and lifted his face to the breeze.

"Something troubles you, friend?" Galbard asked gently. "Was it not you who told me on this very spot, 'You are among friends — there is nothing we cannot speak of'?"

"Jalin needs you," Cayden blurted out, and Galbard's next words failed him. "She knows that you have provided much for her and Ro, but they need *you*. She spoke of this with Nara, and Nara has asked me—"

Galbard let out a nervous laugh. "Nara sent you to speak to me about Jalin?"

Cayden's face reddened. "Do not make this harder than it has to be, Galbard. Nara and I care for you both very much, and things are different now. Aleris says the Bhre-Nora have finished their work in the catacombs, and many in the Dales would swear allegiance to the Sword if you called. You don't have to stand this watch alone." Cayden let out a sigh. "You know all these things, Galbard, but you have not brought Jalin and the boy to the tower, and that has Jalin very confused." He glanced away. "There, I've said it."

Galbard moved to the southern side of the upper deck and looked to the tall, proud stand of trees in the south. "I am about to see the leaves fall from Southwood's trees for the third time, Cayden," he said. "I never thought I would live to see her again, you know."

"She is worried that you might not be with her because of the child."

"Ro?" Galbard replied. "Nothing could be further from the truth—she should know that."

"Well, she doesn't, brother," Cayden replied. "It's time for you to make your intentions clear, I think."

Galbard paced the circumference of the deck, then turned back to him. "I have lived in fear that the Camonra were right behind me — that Amphileph's darkness would follow me here. My entire focus has remained on protecting the Sword and fulfilling my promise to Evliit."

"But what if Amphileph's attack is in the distant future, Galbard? This tower will stand long after we are no more than dust. Think about this for a moment: What if the Creator never intended that you see that battle? Maybe you have already done what you were tasked to do, for you have brought the Sword *here*."

Galbard opened his mouth, then stopped himself. He sighed deeply. "That could be the truth of it."

"Then if that *could* be the truth of it, Galbard, why should you live through this time alone? I know that you fear for their safety, but push your wife and child away no more."

A faint smile appeared on Galbard's face. "You *should* have been a barrister, Cayden."

"What message should I give her?" Cayden asked.

"No message. I'll talk with her in person," Galbard replied.

"That's excellent!" Cayden said. His face beamed momentarily and then quickly turned serious. "Wait! You're leaving Shinetower?"

"You said it yourself, my friend. It's time," said Galbard.

Cayden nodded and turned to leave, but stopped. "Do it soon, Galbard, for both of you," he said and continued on his way.

Galbard watched his friend descend the stairs, then looked out across the horizon until his eyes settled on the rising ash from the fault line around Rion. "You mourn for us, don't you?" he whispered. "Erathe, mother of us all, I pray for the Creator's healing touch."

As he turned to descend, lightning leapt from the storm clouds north of Rion, striking through the billowing ash rising from the glowing tear in Etharath's heart. Galbard stopped for a moment and watched the silent flashes' misty glow through the haze until the low booming sound covered the distance between them, and then he descended the stairs into the safety of Shintower's stronghold.

Galbard stopped at a small anteroom off the tower's ground floor, which acted as a prayer room for some of the more faithful followers of the Watchers. Its thick, tomb-like walls provided its visitors with a profound silence, and for Galbard, it was strangely peaceful—with one exception. The stoneworkers had created a tribute to his "calling" — a free-standing sculpture of him standing over the sleeping Evliit, the Sword poised precariously above the Watcher's head, Galbard's face lifted heavenward as if caught in rapture. He had never liked it, though he had graciously accepted it and its placement in Shinetower. Over time, he had come to ignore it and the terrifying memories it invoked.

He knelt and closed his eyes, attempting to lose himself in the silence. Slowly he became aware of his own breath and heartbeat. He squinted in concentration, hearing the blood pulsing into his forehead. He wanted so much to hear the Creator's voice, Evliit, or one of the Watchers, just as he had on the fateful day of his calling and at so many critical times in his life. He loved Jalin, and that love vexed him with questions about the path before him. He had known no love like his for her before, and the thought of hurting her or Ro by involving them in his life of Watchers and their war seemed selfish at best.

"Why do you speak to me no more?" he asked aloud. "Will you not tell me what is expected of me now?"

This time, the silence was not a welcome one. Galbard found himself longing for the days when the Creator had spoken to him aloud through his prophets. He waited patiently for that voice, but after nearly an hour of prayer, the silence shook him.

"Lord, is it safe to bring Jalin and Ro to the tower?" Galbard spoke up again, "Guide me not to this, if that is your will, Lord, for I know that you wish your servants no ill. Search my heart, oh Lord, that I am ready to be your servant over all else."

There was a fluttering that startled Galbard.

Aleris stopped on the ground at Galbard's side. "I am sorry, master, I did not mean to disturb your prayers," he said.

"You disturb me not nearly so much as the lack of an answer to them," Galbard replied.

"Perhaps you ask for something that has been *answered*, my lord," Aleris said.

"I'm sure I don't know what you mean, Aleris," said Galbard.

Aleris looked perplexed, then his expression shifted. "I am well-versed in the Book of Time, my lord. It would be a privilege to help you in any way I can — perhaps with the appropriate verses. And rest assured, our discussions would remain in the utmost privacy."

Galbard glanced around the room before meeting Aleris's eyes again. "I am asking the Creator to speak through His prophets, Aleris — in answer to my desire to be with Jalin and Ro."

Aleris blinked, puzzled for an instant, and then his face brightened.

"You need no verses to answer this, Galbard," he said. "Love is an inseparable part of our Creator. If it were possible, the Creator would have no one live without love."

It was no earth-shattering revelation, yet something in Aleris's words rang true, and Galbard felt his hope for love rise above every other concern.

"Thank you, Aleris," he said.

"You are most welcome," Aleris replied, and he buzzed from the room with a contented look upon his face.

*   *   *

Galbard left Shinetower and for the first time in over two years, he proceeded across the grounds toward the Dales.

"Afternoon!" said a man carrying flour from the little mill on the western end of town.

"Good day to you," Galbard responded. "I'm looking for the *Horse's Ear*."

"You on the right path, straight ahead then," the man answered. "Can't miss it."

Galbard nodded his thanks and followed the dirt alleyways between the small shacks that housed their ever-growing population. He rounded the corner and saw the *Horse's Ear*, Jalin's modest bed-and-breakfast that she shared with several older women and two couples.

Ro was with a group of other small children gathered around the doorway. A young man sat at a table in the corner, apparently garnering the attention of everyone.

"I've seen many fires burning in the Inferiors' camps in the east," the young man said. "Their numbers grow even faster than ours!"

Galbard pushed through the boys and stood with his back to the wall. There had been much talk lately about the Camonra, and he did not want anyone frightening the young ones. There had been a lot of talk lately about the Camonra, and Galbard did not want anyone frightening the young ones.

"I hope Cayden has made it quite clear about the Camonra," Galbard said.

Everyone stopped as if suddenly noticing Galbard leaning against the wall.

"Oh yes, sir, of course!" the young man said. The entire group of young boys and girls listening to him shook their heads in agreement.

"We will keep our distance," Galbard said sternly.

The young man finished his drink, and the group quickly dispersed, leaving Galbard with the older inhabitants of the inn. Ro started to follow the others out, but Galbard stopped him. He smiled and reached for him, yet it was clear Ro didn't quite know what to make of him. The realization cut Galbard to the core, and he lowered his hand.

"Ro? Where is your mother?"

"She's in the kitchen, sir," he responded.

"You grow up faster by the day," remarked Galbard. "What will you remember?"

"To keep our distance," Ro answered.

"Very good. Take off now!" Galbard said, and Ro scampered away into the alleyway and ran to catch up to the other boys.

Galbard made his way to the kitchen where he found Jalin washing some clothes in a large cauldron. The kitchen smelled faintly of hearthbread and the sharp, comforting spice the Dalesfolk added to nearly everything. Before she noticed him, Galbard stepped closer and placed a hand on her shoulder. She jumped, raising the wooden spoon as if to strike.

"I'm sorry! I didn't mean to frighten you," said Galbard.

"Galbard! In the name of the Creator, what are you doing here?" Jalin asked, wiping sweat from her face and brushing hair from her eyes. She set down the spoon and adjusted her apron.

Galbard touched her arm. "The tower is finished," he said.

She raised her hand to her face and gasped. "Are you telling me . . . ?"

"Yes," he interrupted. "It's time that you and Ro came to live in the tower with me."

She burst into tears. "I thought you'd lost your love for me." The tears streamed down, and he gently wiped them from her cheeks.

"Never," said Galbard.

"Not much to look at, eh?" she asked, and then she wrapped her arms around his neck.

"I'll have you know my tastes are quite refined, and I'm certain you're the best-looking of them all," he quipped.

"Especially right now, eh?" she replied, pursing her lips and blowing the one dangling piece of hair out of her face for a moment before it fell right back again.

"Especially right now," Galbard said. "Pack some things for the two of you. Cayden will have the rest of your things delivered to the tower."

"Yes, all right," she said. She sniffled and took a towel from the clean laundry, wiping her face. She grabbed a bag from the bottom shelf of the pantry and rustled through the clothes, stopping with a small pair of pants.

"That boy of ours," Jalin said. "He'd better be prepared to make quite a living if he continues to run through the clothes like he does." Jalin ran her hand up the leg until her fingers danced from a hole in the knee. Galbard laughed aloud at her gesture.

"Boys are hard on pants' knees," he said.

"Mothers can be harder on the seats of them," Jalin said, her head cocked to one side, eyeing him from under that troublesome bang.

"Indeed," Galbard replied, feigning a worried look. They laughed together, and before he knew it, she had closed the distance and kissed him passionately. When she pulled back, they looked in each other's eyes, and there was a moment of blissful silence.

Jalin's eyes grew wide. "It really is time, isn't it?"

"Yes," he said, taking a deep breath. "I want to share the remainder of my days with you and Ro. I want to declare publicly what I held secret these past two years: you are my wife and Ro is my son!"

"Oh, Galbard!" she exclaimed. "You've made me so incredibly happy! I'll get Ro, and we'll leave at once!"

*　　*　　*

Leagues to the east, Tobor sat beside the stone fireplace in the great room of his adobe home, a hundred yards from the main camp of the Camonra families. He often sat facing the thick wooden door, left ajar so he could watch the campfires in the night and smell the food of hundreds of cook pots in the valley below him. Packed away were the tents of the nomadic life they had always known under Amphileph's iron fist. The Camonra now built structures to accommodate the new, more settled nature of the lives they had built in the past three years.

Tobor's home was spacious even among the oversized adobe dwellings the Camonra built to suit their colossal frames. It sat upon an outcropping of rock that had apparently jutted up during the great upheaval of the land. The Camonra jokingly called it *Bern na Stydhra* after the Hill of Kings in Rion, the mount upon which the Rion Temple sat, the spot that was to be their ultimate conquest in the battle of Rion. The fault that tore the land apart between them and the Rionese had left this ridge of stone in the middle of Rion's former northern fields — their "final conquest." It had become the inside joke among the workers who had carved the sweeping curve of stone steps that led up the edge of the ridge to the entrance of Tobor's home.

In three springs, Tobor had survived two attempts on his life, but his experience and cunning still outmatched the would-be usurpers' youth and strength. There were times in the harsh, icy winters that Tobor had laughed ruefully with his wives that the assassins' success might simply have brought sweet relief from the ever-growing tension in his people.

There were often torrential rains, and they were laden with volcanic ash and seawater from the fissure. The rain's high acidity began mutating the animal and plant life north of Rion, a region now simply called *The Rainland*. Strange creatures and flora began to multiply and expand at a surprising rate, so that now the populace felt the effects here, a camp that once had been a good deal of distance west of it all.

Water was slowly becoming less potable, and there were strange sounds in the darkness. War-dogs began to go missing in the night.

A storm was brewing to the southeast. It was often the case nowadays, as the hot ash and dust from the rift in the land mixed with cool northerly winds blowing in from the ocean. It had been true for most of that day. Tobor always liked to watch this spectacle of nature, where lightning jumped from the storm clouds through the heavy ash and into the ground with spectacular explosions. He would take the razor-sharp knife from his belt, sit on a short porch stool with a hefty stick of wood, and whittle curled shavings into a pile. He never really made anything, but he found it relaxing to whittle away a hefty piece of wood into nothing. He just sat and whittled, watching the lightning crash upon the surrounding lands, lighting trees ablaze or blowing a chunk of earth into the air.

Both attempts on his life had come on nights like this, so Tobor favored the front porch, which gave him a panoramic view of the only path to his home along the curved steps up the hill. It had been a flash of lightning that had alerted him each time to the presence of assassins. So now, whenever lightning flashed, his mind wandered back to killing them; those memories always drew him back to the porch stool, even in the dead of night.

As Tobor eyed the surrounding area, he saw movement on the stairs, and his heart rate jumped up a beat or two. The figure stopped in the middle of the flight of stairs and spoke. "It is I, Idhoran."

"Good thing you chose to call out," Tobor smiled. "I'd hate to kill my best commander." Tobor released the tension on his crossbow and set it beside him. He removed his knife from its scabbard and began whittling again, satisfied that Idhoran's face showed his obvious relief at being recognized rather than shot.

"You do not sleep, my liege?" Idhoran asked.

"Things to think about," Tobor said. "And I like to watch the fire fall from the sky."

Idhoran stepped upon the porch and leaned against one of the rough wooden posts that supported the porch roof.

"Have you ever wondered why the fire falls from the sky, even though Father—Amphileph—does not command it?" asked Tobor.

Idhoran looked as though he was about to answer, but stopped. "I'm a soldier, my lord, I think not of these things," he said at last.

"I've thought about it many times, Idhoran. I sit here carving wood, questioning everything I've ever known."

Idhoran fidgeted a bit, but kept his silence.

"Soldiers do not think about such things, eh?" asked Tobor.

"No," Idhoran replied.

Tobor rolled the wood in his hand and set the blade to the bark. "As I've sat here watching fire fall from the sky, I've asked myself: how does it fall when Amphileph does not command it? And do you know what I've discovered?"

"No, my lord."

Tobor carved a wide swath from the tree limb clenched in his strong hand. "Without so much as a word from Amphileph, the fire falls—day after day, again and again. I tell you that another father lives in the skies, a father greater than Amphileph, and it is *he* that calls down the fire upon the land."

Idhoran's face spoke volumes. His eyes darted around the porch as if an answer might materialize from the air. "My lord," he stuttered. "I . . ."

Pricari, the first of Tobor's concubines, burst from the doorway, the sudden movement snapping both Tobor's and Idhoran's eyes toward her. "Master! Come quickly!" she cried. Only then did she seem to notice Idhoran; she halted before Tobor and lowered her head in submission. "I am sorry, master; I did not know that you were not alone."

"Speak freely, Pricari," answered Tobor. "What is wrong?"

"Lurenda has borne you a child," she said. "She is asking that you give the child your blessing."

"A male?" Tobor inquired, turning back to Idhoran.

"Yes, master."

Tobor rose to his feet. "It's time I name an heir, Idhoran. Let's see if the young one is fit for such a claim."

"If he is not, you will make him so, Tobor," Idhoran replied.

"I will make him so or kill him trying," Tobor said, grunting. "Can you stand watch for me while I tend to this?"

"Of course, master," said Idhoran, and then he turned his back on the doorway and fixed his gaze on the grounds in front of Tobor's home.

Tobor moved through the living area, past his bedroom, and up the short stairwell to the upper level where the concubines kept their beds. There he found them circled around Lurenda's bed. But when Tobor entered the room, they quickly moved aside.

Tobor looked at Lurenda. Her face was tired, but oddly content. Her gaze never left the tiny swaddling cloth in which the other concubines had wrapped the child. Something in her expression struck Tobor — not the look of a mere concubine, but the quiet triumph of a victorious warrior.

A tiny hand grasped the cloth, and Tobor noticed the child's fingers were a miniature of his own. Tobor reached for the tiny hand, and Lurenda opened up the cloth so that he could see the baby within.

Tobor was unprepared for the surge of emotion that swept over him, and he drew in a sharp breath. The boy looked so much like him, the tiny face curled into a cry that sounded to Tobor like a wee battle cry. A rare smile stretched widely across the father's face.

"You've done well, Lurenda," Tobor said. "You've done well, indeed."

"Thank you, master," Lurenda replied. Her voice resonated with the pride that shone in her face. "He'll make a fine member of the Camonra."

"He will be leader of the Camonra!" Tobor barked, handing the infant back. The concubines rushed back around Lurenda, and Tobor turned to leave.

"Tobor?" Lurenda said. "Master?"

Tobor turned back to her.

"He will know the peace we never knew. He will know the new life we've built here — not the bindings of servitude under Amphileph."

A hush fell upon all the concubines, and they stopped everything.

Tobor drew a deep breath and exhaled, his nostrils flaring. "It shall be so," he replied.

"Master," Lurenda said. "What name will you give your son?"

Tobor looked at the child and stroked his jaw. "I will call him Adheron, after my father's father."

PART TWO

CHAPTER EIGHTEEN

NEW PATHS

Sons of warriors, worlds apart—some born in the stormy darkness of the Rainland, others far from their homeland of Rion, exiled by the cause of that same darkness. Theirs seemed two paths divided by choice, their destinies separate and distinct. The forest and jungles of the Rainland grew thick, while the villages and hideouts of the Rionese refugees became towns and fortresses. Though all prepared for war, few but the Candrians sought it out, and fewer still dared into the Rainland's steamy wilderness. Those who ventured there were thought captured or killed, for they never returned.

Seventeen years would pass, while Ro and Adheron trained dutifully — one seeking mastery of the Sword of the Watch, the other the hardened steel of the Camonra blade.

* * *

"Again!" Idhoran directed, and Adheron snapped to attention. He carried his father's large frame, and today, he added another of his father's characteristics—battle scars.

Idhoran stood along the rim of the training pit, leaning over the wooden beam that circled it, watching Adheron's tactics closely. The boy's father had felt it best to have his captain train his son, to make it clear to all that Tobor showed Adheron no favoritism. He would learn the Camonra style of fighting in the training pits, or he would die, like all the other young males who wanted the title of Camon.

He tightened his grip on shield and sword, trying not to think of the wound above his left eye — a gash in the corner of the socket that had narrowly missed the eye itself. Each time he turned his head, the blood ran into it, effectively blinding him to attacks from the left. His opponent noted Adheron's new disability and circled in the direction of his fresh blind spot.

His opponent swung the spiked balls of his flail back and forth, building momentum to shorten his reaction time should Adheron challenge. Adheron had garnered a new respect for the flail, a weapon he had not yet mastered. It had certainly fared much better against his sword than he had expected. It could smash or tear flesh with a single strike, and from his first close inspection — his now-swelling eye — it was clear his opponent meant to do exactly that.

Adheron knew the Candrian slave had nothing to lose, for captives and Camon convicts served out their days as training partners for the young would-be warriors. It was an interesting mix of punishment and possibility, for more than once, a training slave had ended a young warrior's conquests with a single blow. Victory could earn a slave his freedom or a convict a return to warrior status.

"Watch him!" Idhoran said.

Adheron always listened closely to Idhoran, and his grating voice seemed to ring through the jeers and cheers of the trainees and Camon soldiers that had gathered to watch the son of Tobor for his first bout in the training pit.

The slave jumped suddenly at him with abandon, slashing Adheron across the cheek.

"Just a few stitches, that one!" belted Idhoran's voice. "Did you see his eyes? Watch him!"

Adheron replayed the attack in his mind, tracking his opponent's movements with practiced focus. His challenger swung at him again, and this time Adheron clearly saw it: the slight closing of his eyes right before he swung.

Adheron moved to his own left, watching the slave's eyes without flinching. *There it was,* he thought. The slave prepared to swing and feinted with his shield, but Adheron pivoted, deflecting the blow with his own. Then, with a thrust, a full inch of his blade cut into the warrior's side just below the ribs.

The slave's eyes told Adheron even more then. The realization swept over his face that Adheron had most likely struck a mortal blow. His eyes darted to his side where his skin parted. He pulled his swinging arm into his side and used his elbow and forearm to hold back the flood of red that ran from his wound. The slave's flail fell harmlessly to the ground, and he fell to his knees before Adheron.

Tobor's son ignored the crowd's bloodthirsty calls to add the slave's head to his belt. Instead, he lowered his blade and motioned to the other slaves. "This one is worthy of care," Adheron shouted. "Take him and tend to him so he may fight another day!

The other slaves scrambled to him and carried him away.

"Well done, Adheron!" Idhoran said. He dropped his massive hand on the young warrior's shoulder armor with a loud thump. "Well done, indeed!"

"I wonder if there will ever come a day when you have nothing left to teach me, Idhoran," Adheron said. "How is it you know the fight so well?

Idhoran laughed. "Why do you think the hair of my beard grows gray? It is the battles themselves that ferret out the weak and unskilled."

Adheron stopped and turned. "Do you think I should have killed the slave when I had beaten him, then?"

Idhoran stopped, met his eyes, then glanced at the crowd. "They would have liked that, wouldn't they? You chose well."

Adheron bobbed his head in appreciation. Idhoran stopped and put his hand on Adheron's head, turning it for a closer look at the cut beside Adheron's eye.

"Come with me," Idhoran said. "I know just the female to stitch that up."

* * *

"We must unify the West," Cayden said. "Your father believes the future of men depends on that unity."

"Yes, I understand," Ro said. He reached behind his head to adjust the band his mother insisted he wear to pull back his long brown hair, pushing his bangs out of his face. He was more than a little anxious to meet the envoy from Moonledge Peak.

With the growth of the West, the Rionese refugees now controlled Highwood and the caves beneath the highest peak in the Faceless

Mountains, which they had named Moonledge Peak. A band of former Guardsmen known as the Seven Warriors held the valley of Candra, north of Shinetower, and there was talk of them claiming the stretch of Highwood along the western bank of the Highborne River.

Some had even warned his father that the Seven Warriors meant to bring all the western lands under their control, but while the Seven Warriors had rejected the Elders, the leaders of Highwood remained faithful to Rion, and tensions were high. His father worried that the aggressive stance of the Seven Warriors might intensify if they discovered that Shinetower held the Sword of the Watch. He had written to Caratacus, leader of the refugees in the caves of Moonledge Peak, and over the course of several months, they had decided to ally Moonledge and Shinetower through marriage. The betrothed would meet at Highborne Falls, approximately halfway between Moonledge Peak and Shinetower, just at the eastern end of Candra Valley. He made the secret journey with Cayden by horseback in support of his father's vision of unity.

It was mid-morning in early fall, and Ro thought Highborne Falls was absolutely beautiful. The trees were a gorgeous mix of greens and reds and browns. Ro and Cayden dismounted, and the Shinetower soldiers accompanying them waited beneath the trees by the falls. Ro and Cayden walked their horses alongside the pool at the base of the falls. The pool was over a hundred feet wide, and its deep, calm waters belied the force of the Highborne River downstream, which flowed from Highborne Falls through Highwood and on to the ocean near Shinetower.

"Won't they be on the other side of the pool?" asked Ro. "Isn't Moonledge Peak about there?" He pointed to the high ridge atop the Faceless Mountains to the north.

"Yes, you're right," answered Cayden. "Beneath the peak there, at the base of the mountain."

Ro looked across the deep water of the pool. "But I mean, how do we get over there?"

"No worries," said Cayden. "Follow me." He led Ro along the mountainside where erosion had carved an indentation beneath the falls. The sound of the water striking the stone edge of the pool was impossible to talk over, but Cayden guided him through the narrow path behind the falls to the eastern side.

"That was incredible!" said Ro.

"Thought you'd like that," replied Cayden. They made their way around the eastern side of the pool and watched the northern plains for riders.

"What do you suppose she'll look like?" The question burst from Ro's mouth.

Cayden started to answer but kept walking. Aside from the falling water, it was quiet, and late-summer flowers still bloomed along the path.

"She is the daughter of the leader of Moonledge Peak. I'm sure that she's well-suited to you."

Ro saw Cayden's brow wrinkle as soon as the words were out of his mouth.

"Well-suited to me, eh?" Ro responded.

"Okay, even I know that sounded idiotic," Cayden said. "I struggle with the idea of an arranged marriage myself. But I know your father's love for you — it's unquestionable. I've watched you grow, and I've never seen a father love his child more. He honored me by asking that I escort you. He wanted to be here, Ro, but the protection of the Sword can be its own kind of prison."

There was the sound of horses to the north. Cayden signaled the Shinetower soldiers across the pool.

"I think I see them coming," Cayden said.

Half a dozen soldiers bearing the flag of Moonledge Peak rode ahead of a young lady and her entourage. They halted when they spotted Cayden and Ro, motionless for a moment except for the flags waving in the gentle wind.

A single rider came out in front of the group and dismounted, walking to Cayden and Ro at the water's edge.

"I am Trestaire, the Lady Tiamphia's escort," the man said, and then he bowed.

"I am Cayden, Master Ronan's escort," Cayden announced and returned the bow.

"Shall we let the two of them have some time together?" Trestaire asked.

"Of course," answered Cayden. "After you," Cayden motioned to Trestaire. "Master, may I take your horse?"

"Yes, please," answered Ro.

"Milady," Trestaire said, offering his hand as she dismounted.

"We'll give you privacy," Cayden added. He and Trestaire guided their entourages aside — close enough to see, far enough not to hear.

Ro looked at Tiamphia, a ringlet of flowers crowning her waist-length, wavy blond hair. She wore a silken veil across her face, but her light blue eyes drew him in, and the breeze carried the sweet scent of her perfume — sweeter even than the flowers around the Highborne Falls pool. Her silken dress flowed around her in the wind, hinting at her alluring figure. Ro felt his blood in his cheeks and butterflies in his stomach. He tried to think about what to say to her.

"Hello . . . I am Ronan, son of Galbard and Jalin."

"I am honored," Tiamphia said, looking down. "I am Tiamphia, daughter of Caratacus and Sadhra."

"Your eyes are so beautiful," Ro said. "I think… you can remove your veil now."

Tiamphia looked away, and suddenly Ro felt like he had said something wrong. "I don't mean to be too forward," he said. "You can call me Ro . . ."

Tiamphia looked up again, laughter in her eyes.

"No, that's a very nice thing to say . . ." she replied, "Ro." She removed one side of the veil and let it fall away. Her smile enchanted him.

"I kept thinking you might be like the large woman who works in the tavern," he said with a nervous laugh.

"I thought you might be a balding, potbellied fellow," she said, covering a giggle with her hand.

"You're nothing like that, of course," he added quickly.

"Nor you," she replied.

They walked along the edge of Highborne Falls for about an hour, though it seemed like minutes to them. Trestaire and Cayden walked their horses back to them.

"It is time, milady," said Trestaire. "We should return to Moonledge."

Cayden mounted his horse. "Come along, Ronan," he said. Ro helped Tiamphia to her horse and remounted his own.

"And what shall I say to your father?" Trestaire said, his eyes searching her expression.

"Give father my love," she answered. "And let him know that it's a good match."

Trestaire smiled at her; then he turned away and rejoined the Moonledge entourage. "Make ready!" he said. Tiamphia waved as they rode toward

Moonledge and disappeared over the horizon. Then she joined Cayden and Ro for the long ride back to Shinetower.

When the three riders arrived in Shinetower, Tiamphia was welcomed with open arms. Jalin took special care to make her comfortable in her new surroundings, insisting that Tiamphia have a room of her own close to hers. During the coming weeks, she would sit and talk with her on many occasions when the men were attending to their duties. Jalin was thrilled to see how completely the young bride-to-be charmed Ro. Her worries eased when Tiamphia confided that she found him "quite handsome."

For Galbard, the romance had been a distraction, and though he wanted love to blossom for his son, the importance of teaching him to control the Sword was paramount. Galbard knew that unless Evliit returned to claim it, one day Ro would bear the responsibility of protecting the Sword, and with that responsibility would be the dangers it would bring. Galbard felt strongly that it was in Ro's best interest to master the Sword, and he brought Ro to the upper deck of Shinetower with regularity to show him all that he had learned of the Sword's power. By late fall, the upper deck had grown miserably cold, but Galbard insisted the lessons continue. It was on a blustery day such as this when Galbard felt that Ro was ready for a test of his skills.

They stood atop Shinetower, and Galbard gently removed the Sword from his scabbard. He walked toward the altar at the center of the tower's upper deck and looked up at the sky. The wind was surprisingly strong, though the sun was clearly visible. At times it felt as though a gust might lift him into the heavens, and the thought of drifting on the winds to the Third Domain brought a faint smile to his face.

He glanced over at his son, Ro, feeling a sense of pride in the way his solemn stare toward the heavens reflected the seriousness with which Ro took his father's faith. It was obvious to Galbard that Ro respected him, and nothing could have honored Galbard more.

A buzzing noise announced Aleris's entrance, capturing Ro and Galbard's attention. He lit upon the deck beside them, wobbling in a sudden gust before regaining his composure. He came to attention, pulling his long coat straight.

"Is he ready, Galbard?" Aleris asked.

Galbard looked down at Aleris for a moment and then back to the skies. His gray hair blew back from the force of the wind.

"As ready as I was," Galbard said.

"I have checked the grounds again, master. All is clear. Cayden has ordered the townspeople away from the tower, and the Bhre-Nora stand ready."

"Very well," Galbard said. He thought that it was the first time that he had ever seen Aleris looking nervous. "I'm afraid my charge over the Sword must end one day, Aleris," Galbard said with a soft chuckle. "I'm getting no younger. I look to Ronan to carry on this task."

As Aleris looked up at Galbard, his face exuded the friendship that had grown steadily over their years together at Shinetower. "Of course, master," replied Aleris, but Galbard thought there was a bit of a pained expression peeking out from his disciplined response.

Galbard drew in a deep breath and exhaled. He looked at the misty covering on the mountains to the north and marveled afresh at their beauty. "This is the natural order of things with men, Aleris," Galbard smiled. "We come about our power but for a fleeting moment before we realize it was never ours to keep. We beget naught but dust in the end, save the souls of the children that carry on. The Sword will far outlast me, I'm afraid, and it will likely outlast even the Bhre-Nora."

"Yes, lord," replied Aleris. "I have seen this in men, and even my beloved Bhre-Nora must pass into the Third Domain in time."

"Then this is our duty today, Aleris: to lead Ro in the way of the Sword, to teach him the truths of Men and the Bhre-Nora, and to draw him ever closer to the Creator and His creation," Galbard said, motioning to the majestic mountains in the distance.

"May it be done," Aleris answered.

Galbard turned to address Ro. "Come, Ro; it is time."

"Yes, Father," said Ro, and then he moved to the altar of the sword beside his father.

Galbard removed it from its scabbard gingerly. Ro's breath caught as the Sword came free — not in ignorance, but in reverence. He had seen it many times, but never with its power stirring. "This is the Sword of the Watch, my son, given to me by Evliit himself. The Creator has given it great power, and Evliit himself said that it has the power to control the destiny of all humankind. It has fallen to me to teach you of its power to defend its bearer. The ability to control even a part of its power has saved me on more than one occasion."

Ro listened intently, and his eyes moved down the Sword's length, as if admiring the beautiful inscription on the blade. "I've watched your devotion to the Sword firsthand, Father, and to be allowed even a chance to wield its power is a great honor."

"It is my declaration of your worthiness as the future leader of Shinetower," Galbard said. "Kneel, my son!" he shouted.

Galbard held the hilt before him with both hands, its tip resting on the stone of the upper deck just in front of the altar.

Galbard shouted to the heavens. "Oh, Creator of everything, grant that Ronan might wield this, your mighty sword! May he stand against evil as your warrior, and let the holy power of the Sword flow through him!"

The clouds began to swirl and darken around the upper deck of Shinetower. A hum of electricity filled the air, and small bolts of energy jumped between the swirling mists and the heavy, steel rods that jutted from the stonework of the upper deck's buttresses.

"I am ready, Father," Ro said, though awe and fear warred in his eyes.

"Good luck," Aleris said, but his voice carried a tremor.

"It is your time, Ro," said Galbard, echoing Aleris' encouragement. He placed the Sword in Ro's hands, released it, and stepped back from it for the first time since Evliit's commissioning and took a knee beside Aleris.

Ro's face tightened.

"Stay calm," Galbard said. "Let the Sword's fire pass through you."

Ro rose and set the Sword into its resting place, then placed both hands on the altar. A bluish plasma outlined the Sword and spread to his hands and over his body.

"So begins the test!" Aleris shouted to Galbard. Aleris's wings snapped tight against his back. "Galbard…Anyone attuned to its power will feel this!"

Galbard said nothing, for fervent prayer completely consumed him. He knew the Sword was searching his son for his worth as a bearer of its power and that his son's life was very literally in the balance of that assessment.

Ro squeezed his eyes shut. "I feel… nauseous. Dizzy," he said. One of his knees buckled, and he caught his weight on the altar with his hands.

Suddenly the tower quaked with energy. Steam shot from the ports in the tower walls and a slow rumble began deep within.

"Keep your focus!" his father shouted.

"Wait, Galbard!" said Aleris. "Something is not right!" Aleris flew to the edge of the upper deck and looked upon the grounds below. "The walls are shifting too fast!" Aleris cried. "Steady! Steady!"

The energy of the Sword surged through the stone until the tower itself glowed a deep, molten red. Steam blasted from the relief vents. Then came a deafening crash.

"Two of the courtyard walls have collided!" screamed Aleris. One of the Bhre-Nora shot up through the upper-deck opening in a panic. "We must stop!" he cried above the din, waving his arms.

Galbard rose to his feet and ran to the altar, grabbing Ro by the waist. The blue plasma separated from Ro as Galbard pulled him away from the altar.

Galbard bent over him. "Ro!" he cried. He searched him for any sign of injury, but there was none. Ro's head slumped over Galbard's arm — limp, lifeless. "What have I done?" he shouted to Aleris.

The high-pitched scream of the blowing steam began to slow, and the clouds began to dissipate.

"Ronan!" Galbard said, and then he glanced up. "Creator, please! Have I not done as you have asked? You must spare my son!" he cried. Galbard frantically listened to his heart. "Please!" He turned to Aleris. "Get the Healers!"

Aleris flew down the stairwell, and in moments, the Healers returned with him.

"Will he be okay?" Galbard inquired.

"We do not know, my lord," the Healers replied. "Let us take him to his room where we can treat him." They carried Ro's limp body downstairs, leaving Galbard and Aleris alone on the tower's upper deck. Aleris paced around the altar and sat down at the top of the stairs, attempting to find the words to comfort Galbard.

Galbard was silent. He walked to the tower's edge. "I have done my part!" he shouted to the heavens. "I was willing to sacrifice my son!" He looked out over the countryside. "Why should I follow such a vengeful god? You are no different from Amphileph! I curse your wrath!"

Aleris's jaw dropped open for a moment. "This is only a setback. We—"

"No." Galbard stopped him. He turned to seize the Sword from the altar, but a bolt of energy blasted from it, striking him square in the chest. He skidded across the deck and slammed into the parapet wall.

"Galbard!" Aleris shouted. He flew to Galbard's side and found him conscious, but in great pain. "Galbard, what have you done?"

Galbard struggled to his feet, holding his chest. His face was a mixture of anger and shame.

"My time with the Sword has ended. The Creator will call another to bear it. I brought it to the Bhre-Nora and kept it safe all these years."

"Shinetower requires the bearer of the Sword to be present. They are one, inseparable," said Aleris.

Galbard raised his hand in witness. "I have fulfilled my promise."

Aleris flew to the hand railing beside Galbard's head. "We just need to make repairs, my lord. This is only a setback."

"Yes, see to it," Galbard said. "Evliit will return for the Sword in his own time. The Bhre-Nora and the people of the Dales have been kind to us, Aleris, but my time has passed. I will make room for the next bearer. I must go to my son. I leave the Sword in your care."

Galbard said nothing more, but descended the stairs on the way to Ro's room to check on him.

*　*　*

"Father calls for you!" the Camon said, beating upon the door of Citanth's shack. Citanth rolled his bruised body in bed, but before he could rise, the Camon shoved the door open, splintering the latch. "Father wants you now!" he said. The Camon put his massive hand on Citanth' ankle and pulled him out of bed.

"I am coming!" moaned Citanth.

It was raining again, so he pulled his hood around his face and walked to the edge of the Binding. Amphileph stood just on the other side, obviously excited.

"Did you feel it?" he asked. "The thief has used the Sword again!"

"I am injured, my lord, I was sleep—"

"Shut up and listen, you fool!" snapped Amphileph. He raised his hands, and the water running off the Binding circled and clung to it, shaping itself into the form of a tower. "The Bhre-Nora meddle in my affairs again. They have built a tower in the southwest to protect the

Sword."

The rain and lightning intensified, and the water ran off the Binding again, revealing Amphileph's face. The excitement was gone—replaced by grim hatred.

"This time, I will destroy them all," said Amphileph.

*   *   *

Caratacus and the High Council of Moonledge Peak were concluding a dedication ceremony deep within the caves of the Faceless Mountains. There had been food, drink, dancing, and music in celebration.

"We honor the stonemasons that have worked so diligently," Caratacus said.

There was loud applause that echoed through the stone chambers.

"Only the Rionese could create such a stone fortress beneath the high peak called Moonledge! You have performed above and beyond what even the High Council could have expected, and we salute you!" Caratacus yelled above the roar.

"All is not cause for celebration!" someone shouted from the crowd.

"What's this?" Caratacus asked. "Who said that?"

There was a great deal of stirring about in the crowd that had gathered.

"'Twas I, my lord!" one of the men said. He stood up, and several in the crowd booed him.

"Quiet!" Caratacus shouted, slamming his gavel upon the council table. "Speak up, man!"

"My lord, rumors are rampant concerning a strange group of creatures hunting in the fields below the entrance to the caves," he said.

"We have seen the creatures of Amphileph, my lord," another of the townspeople cried. "The ones the Elders called the Inferiors."

The room suddenly became very quiet.

"Were you seen by these creatures?" a member of the council asked.

"No, my lord, we remained hidden in the cliffs."

"Describe these creatures," another of the council requested.

"They were brutish creatures, my lord—walking on two feet like men, but nearly twice a man's height. And they rode scaled beasts, like wingless dragons!"

"They were armed and armored for war!" another cried. "And they tore a deer apart before our very eyes—ripped it to pieces and stuffed the bleeding carcass into their packs!"

"They could smell your fear, I am sure of it!" a voice rang out from their midst.

"And who is this?" Caratacus inquired of the voice.

The Watcher of the Mountains parted the crowd and stepped before the council. Though he bore the trappings of a wizard—herb bags, potion flasks, and staff—Tophian concealed his true identity. He intended to reason with them, to give them the opportunity to solve this problem themselves. "These creatures could have hunted you down like the deer they savaged," Tophian said. "But they didn't. They killed food for their kind and left you alone to spy upon them."

"What do you mean by that, good sir?"

"Only that they wanted you to see they hunted food, not men," Tophian said. "They let you watch, knowing you would report what you saw. Be assured—they will do the same."

"It's said that the creatures of Amphileph are soulless, that they roam the land in search of the spirits of men," another of the council exclaimed. "The Guard warned us of their evil."

"The Watchers have given themselves so that you would be saved from their bloodlust," said Tophian. "A new age of men and Camonra has begun."

"A new age?" inquired Caratacus. "You speak in riddles, good wizard."

Tophian walked to the center of the floor before the council's curved table. "The time of Amphileph's power over them has passed," he said. "The Camonra were created and bred to end the time of men—this is true. But we severed them from Amphileph when we bound him in the east, where he will remain until this age ends. This was done so men might live and prove themselves worthy of the Watchers who perished for them."

A druid rose up from his seat. He was ancient and blind and stood only with the help of his staff.

"The ancient one speaks truth," he said. "I am blind, but even I see as much. This one is a Watcher!"

There was a collective gasp that echoed in the council chamber's stone walls.

"Silence!" Caratacus commanded, raising a hand. He studied Tophian with sharp curiosity. "Is this true?"

"It is as the druid has said," Tophian said. "I am Tophian, Watcher of Mountains."

"Why then have you not ascended to the Third Domain?" the druid interrupted. "Has not the time of Watchers come to an end?"

"In many ways, yes — the time of Watchers is no more," Tophian replied. "I did not join my brothers because I was not fully given to Evliit's hope — the hope that men could be saved from their own vices. I would not give my life for you, though near enough to it I was."

Again, there was a rumble among the crowd.

"If you've no love for men, Watcher, what are we to make of your presence here today?" another of the council asked.

Tophian's face suddenly reddened. "My brothers cared enough for men to give up their lives!" The cavern shook violently. Dust and small stones rained down, and the council cowered in fear.

Caratacus threw up his hands. "Great Watcher of the Mountains, do not destroy us!" he cried. "We fear the creatures of Amphileph, and this fear consumes us!"

Tophian heard these words and his face calmed. "Yes, councilor, this is the truth of it." The rumblings ceased, and all eyes fell upon Tophian. "You and your people deserve to live without this fear. It is fear itself that will destroy any hope for peace — and in that, Amphileph wins without lifting a finger."

Tophian paced the room, but no one made a sound.

"In honor of my fallen brothers, I will raise up with you a great castle of men, one that even the War of the Watchers might not pierce! When you fear no attack, maybe then, you and the Camonra will war no more."

Caratacus moved from behind the council table and slowly walked in front of Tophian. "We are in your deepest debt, Lord Tophian." He fell to one knee and bowed his head. "All hail, Tophian, Watcher of Mountains!" One by one, the other councilors did likewise, until not a man was standing in the room save Tophian.

* * *

Due west of the council chamber, Ardhios and the remaining Seven Warriors huddled around a fire with fifty or so villagers and townspeople.

Mordher made good on the Candrians' oath of fealty, immediately having them raise a stone house in which the warriors would stay. Several of the men dug a pit and worked a mixture of mud within it, while the women thatched roofing from the long, thick-bladed grasses growing in the fields. By evening, the outline of the stone wall was complete, but the Candrians' diviner was upset that the structure dwarfed the round stone hut dedicated to their god. There was a great deal of shouting and arguing among those in attendance, though the warriors were themselves silent.

"We do not hold to the traditions of Rion," one of the townspeople said. "We have abandoned the ways of the Guard of Rion, for they have brought us naught but ruin. Fehamina, the spirit of the river, has led us here to this promised land!"

"Fehamina! Fehamina! Fehamina!" The chant's volume rose, calling the name of their god at the top of their lungs.

The heads of the crowd spun about looking for their diviner. "Let us hear from Fehamina what we are to do!" the cry rang out. A path rippled through their midst, and a man made his way toward the fire. He was covered in white ash and oddly painted across his body with handprints and wild slashes of black coal. He had a wooden figure with hands outstretched dangling from a leather strap around his neck, and it had the name Fehamina carved across its chest in the ancient tongue.

Mordher grunted, "Another priest? I thought we had rid ourselves of those fools when we escaped Rion!" The once heroic warrior had never regained his heart after finding his family trampled in the ruins of Rion.

Ardhios smiled at him. "A diviner? He should read your palms, Mordher!"

"He can read my knuckles if he tries," Mordher retorted.

Their diviner cut a branch from a tree, and the chant began to die down. He mumbled a prayer and cut the branches into small sticks that he marked with a short blade.

The crowd gathered around him. "What do the lots say?" one of them asked.

"Quiet!" said another.

The diviner lay a deerskin face up on the ground and pulled four sharp pegs from his waistband, driving each of them into the skin to pull it taut. He threw the sticks upon the skin and read them thrice. The diviner paused between each of the casts and took in deep breaths of smoke from an urn he swung slowly before him. After the third reading, he set the urn on a chest-high stone and fanned the smoke into his face until his eyes rolled back and he collapsed. When he did this, two of his acolytes cut the throat of a sheep and threw its body upon the fire.

The flames engulfed the carcass, and the diviner jumped to his feet and roared in a great voice. "Thrice were the lots cast and read, and Fehamina has given me truth! She speaks to me of conquerors from the south, and of a new kingdom of men."

"She speaks of the strangers," another whispered, pointing to the Seven Warriors. Mordher looked over his shoulder at the villager, and then feinted lunging at him. When the villager jumped back, Mordher laughed heartily.

"Maybe your Fehamina will protect you!"

"Enough, Mordher," Ardhios said. "We are soldiers for no one but ourselves. We did our duty to Rion — sacrificed much — and gained nothing."

"But we would swear fealty to the Seven Warriors!" the crowd cried in unison. "Protect us as Fehamina guides our paths!"

"That you would fight for us is no consolation," Mordher replied. "What more can you give that might pique our interests?"

"We will build a great hall for you, our Seven Lords! We will grow food and make crafts to give you pleasure."

"Let it be done!" the Seven Warriors said, raising their swords. "Build for us a great castle, swearing fealty to us for all time!"

"We swear it!" the crowd cried.

Mordher's eyes flashed. "Then you will need no diviner!"

Before anyone could react, he seized the diviner by the arm and drove a short sword straight into his heart. The man collapsed without a sound.

A stunned silence fell over the gathering.

Mordher hoisted the limp body high above his head, then hurled it into the fire. Flames swallowed it with a hiss.

"We are your masters now!" he roared. "Ardhios will oversee the building of our Great Hall, and my brothers and I will hunt these creatures and destroy them! Bring us food and wine! Play the lute and harp! Let us celebrate your oath!"

"Yes, my lord!" the crowd answered, voices trembling as they rushed to obey, scrambling to prepare a feast for their new rulers.

Ardhios did not move. He watched the diviner's body blacken in the flames, the smell of burning flesh rising into the night.

He bowed his head.

He prayed silently to the Creator for forgiveness — for the evil he had unleashed upon these terrified souls.

*   *   *

"You mustn't leave!" Aleris urged, but Galbard did not answer. He continued gathering his things with a grim, mechanical focus.

The Healers had worked on Ro through the night, plying herbs and chanting incantations. Jalin and Tiamphia had prayed without ceasing, but Galbard would not join them. Even when morning came and Ro awoke, Galbard's face remained drawn and tense while Jalin and Tiamphia gave thanks to the Creator.

"I'll be fine, Father… really," Ro whispered. He was weak, barely able to sit upright.

Jalin moved about the room in a panic, snatching up items as soon as she saw them and tossing them into the chest.

"My lord, please don't do this," Cayden said. "The evil one will surely follow you all the days of your life. You can protect your family no better than you can within these walls."

"Then I have built no less than a prison," Galbard replied. "It is the Sword Amphileph wants, and I will bear it no more. I will put distance between it and my family. You are right — Amphileph will not rest until it is his. I should have cast it into the ocean long ago. Perhaps that is my best advice to you now: rid yourself of it. If the Creator means for it to survive, He will send another who can control it. I have sacrificed enough."

He shoved the last few items into a chest and signaled an attendant to take it away.

"Jalin, are you ready?"

"I am coming," she said, struggling to force the chest closed.

"I wish you good luck," Galbard said to Cayden.

"I have arranged a wagon," Cayden replied. He forced the latch shut on Jalin's trunk, then lifted several bags and held the door open with his foot. Bhre-Nora entered to remove the larger items. The Healers moved Ro to a stretcher and carried him out with Tiamphia close behind.

"We'll see you downstairs," Jalin said as she left. Cayden followed her, letting the door close behind them.

Galbard moved toward the door, but Aleris hovered in front of him, blocking his way.

"But where will you go?" Aleris asked. "What will you do?"

Galbard paused only long enough to answer.

"Jalin and I have decided to build our home on the western shores. We've often watched the sunset over the ocean from Shinetower's upper deck and thought how wonderful it would be to spend our remaining years there. I'll learn to fish, and I'll forget the years lost to the Camonra. I'll make new memories of peace and happiness, and with luck, I'll live to see my children's children prosper."

Aleris looked as though he might speak, then stopped, swallowing the words. "I have said what I can say to you," he murmured. "It is a great dream, of course. I cannot deny that."

He drifted lower and settled on a small table beside the door.

"I'll wish you well then… and tell you that all Bhre-Nora hope the best for you."

Galbard shifted the weight of his bags and looked at Aleris — wings drooping, head bowed.

"Come now, my friend. This is hard enough without thinking I've wronged you."

Aleris forced a smile.

"No, of course. We are friends until the end. Be well, Galbard."

Cayden and Aleris watched as Galbard and his family loaded the wagon and disappeared into the west. "What do we do now?" asked Cayden.

"We've repairs that must be made," answered Aleris. "Walls and piping can be fixed."

"But what of defending the Sword? With Galbard gone, how will Shinetower withstand an attack?"

"Having twice activated the tower, Amphileph has surely found us out. I must contact Rendaya. She will know what must be done," answered Aleris. "Until then, tell no one of what has transpired."

"No, of course. As you wish," said Cayden.

"I will return within the hour," said Aleris. "Meet me on the upper deck."

Cayden nodded. "I'll be waiting."

Aleris flew toward Southwood, and Cayden ascended Shintower's steps to the upper deck.

As promised, Cayden saw Rendaya and Aleris approaching from the southeast. They landed upon the upper deck still speaking of the Sword. Cayden instinctively gave Rendaya a wide berth.

"If Amphileph did not discover us when Galbard activated the Sword's defenses, he surely felt its power during Ro's attempt. We must assume he has found us. We must move the Sword," Rendaya said. "It is said that the Watcher Tophian is building a fortress in the mountains to the north. It could be hidden there."

"But you could use it to power Shinetower," Cayden blurted out.

"No," answered Rendaya. "If you knew my feelings for the Watchers, you would know why I dare not touch it." Her somber stare remained fixed on the altar — then suddenly, her face lit up. "The Bhre-Nora made Evliit's sword. Though they cannot command it, they are immune to its power." Rendaya leaned down to Aleris. "Do you still have the strongbox the Sword was kept in before it was given to Evliit?"

"Yes, of course. It is a holy relic to the Bhre-Nora," answered Aleris.

"Then the Bhre-Nora will return the Sword to its case, and Cayden can take it to the leader of Moonledge. For the safety of his daughter, Caratacus would surely hide it there, and no one should know that it has left Shinetower. If Amphileph attacks, perhaps Tophian could wield it, and draw the Camonra to Moonledge Peak."

"I'll bring the chest," Aleris said, and he sped away. Within minutes, Aleris and several of the Bhre-Nora appeared with an adorned case. Aleris flew to the altar and lifted the Sword, placing it in the case and closing the hasp.

"I'll get my horse and meet you in the courtyard," said Cayden.

"No, we'll not chance taking it by land," said Rendaya. "The Bhre-Nora will take you."

"Take me how?" asked Cayden.

"We will carry you," said Aleris. "And you will deal with Caratacus."

Cayden swallowed hard as a flurry of butterflies spun in his stomach. "As you wish."

"Hold on to the case," Aleris said. "Tightly. Now raise your arms." Two Bhre-Nora slipped a wide leather strap beneath his arms, two more gripped his belt, and the last pair each took an ankle. "Ready?" asked Aleris.

"As ready as I will ever be," answered Cayden, and suddenly they lifted him off the upper deck. "Oh!" he cried and closed his eyes, leaving the upper deck and hanging precariously in the sky. The buzz of their wings was louder than he imagined.

"Relax — we've got you," Aleris called, flying ahead. "We're crossing over the Dales."

His eyes had remained closed until Aleris said that, and then curiosity got the better of him. He opened them — and saw the most astonishing sight of his life. It was as if he were a bird, soaring over the Dales. The wind blew his hair out of his face, and he closed his eyes again, feeling the cool air flowing over him. He opened his eyes again, and smiled at the sight of a flock of birds to their left.

"You see, flying is wonderful," said Aleris.

"Absolutely incredible!" said Cayden. Within minutes he could see the lights of Highwood, and farther west, the scattered glow of the Candra Valley.

Within four hours, they descended upon the fields before Moonledge Peak. Cayden blew out a deep breath upon touching the ground again. It was the deep of the night.

"We will stay out of sight," said Aleris. "Take the Sword to Caratacus, and when you return here, we will find you."

"Very well," answered Cayden.

At the Moonledge outposts, soldiers confronted him, but he explained he was an envoy of Shinetower and that he must see Caratacus at once. They passed him up the chain of command, Cayden repeating his plea at every level. When at last he had been taken to the highest soldier in charge, Cayden was taken to the council chambers. The soldiers' superiors had reluctantly awakened Caratacus.

"What is the meaning of this?" Caratacus asked, entering the council chambers. He was still buttoning his shirt.

"Sir, please forgive my intrusion, but I have urgent news from Shinetower."

Caratacus looked mortified. "Is Tiamphia all right?"

"Oh yes, sir," Cayden said quickly. "She is well — but her safety is threatened."

"Threatened? What do you mean?"

"Shintower's defenses have been damaged, and the safety of the Sword is at risk," said Cayden.

Caratacus paused and looked at the case. "You mean, you've brought the Sword of Evliit here?"

Caratacus's expression alarmed him. "Yes."

"That thing is like a magnet for Amphileph—it cannot stay here!" said Caratacus.

"My lord, please hear me out. It is true Amphileph's armies seek Evliit's sword, but I came in secrecy, telling no one what I carry. My lords ask only that you hide it in your keep until Shintower's repairs are complete. Then we will return for it. Galbard has taken Tiamphia, Ronan, and Jalin westward, to make their home on the western shores."

Cayden felt heat rising in his face. Telling Caratacus that Galbard had abandoned the Sword seemed unwise. "My lord, I beg of you. If the Sword is captured at Shinetower, will not Amphileph seek out the fortress of Moonledge on the very next day? And declaring it here could bring the Camonra away from your daughter, could it not?"

"To the very people I have been tasked with defending!" cried Caratacus. "No cast of this die favors me."

"The die favors the brave," Cayden said. "And I'm told bravery is not in short supply among the people of Moonledge Peak."

"These are desperate times, my Lord Caratacus. The people of Shinetower are calling upon that bravery now."

"I will consult the priests," said Caratacus. "Give me a moment."

"Yes, my lord," Cayden replied. Caratacus left the room, and he placed the Sword's case upon the council table. It was the first time he had taken pause to actually look at the craftsmanship of the case itself. The dark polished wood was adorned with symbols of ancient Rionese, embossed with gold. The hinges were intricately carved with flowers and vines. It was truly a thing of beauty.

Caratacus reentered the room followed by a priest and two acolytes. They looked tired and irritated — until they saw the case. Then Cayden saw barely contained excitement flash across their faces.

"My lord," the priest said. "Is this what I think it is?"

"Quiet," said Caratacus. "Make a safe place for it, and say nothing."

The priest's face immediately turned stoic. "Yes, my lord." He picked up the case and exited the room.

Cayden's anxiety spiked at the case's unceremonious removal.

"It will be well guarded," said Caratacus, apparently noticing Cayden's expression.

"Yes, my lord. Then I will ask for your leave and report to Shinetower."

"Very well. I expect every effort made to see to Tiamphia's safety."

"Of course, my lord," replied Cayden, bowing and exiting the council chambers.

He made his way through the keep and out onto the steps with the soldiers' escort. When they left him, he continued into the predawn darkness south of the temple, hands outstretched in the near-blindness. He was greatly relieved to hear the familiar buzzing of the Bhre-Nora. Aleris appeared carrying a small lamp, shielding its green light so that it only illuminated his face.

"We must hurry!" said Aleris. "Lift your arms!"

Cayden complied, and his stomach turned over as he soared into the dark night sky.

Chapter Nineteen

Amphileph's Revenge

Ardhios was frustrated. He lay in his bed looking at the ceiling. The woman lying beside him touched his cheek. "My lord, what troubles you?" asked Portina, the woman he had met during his travels to Highwood. His life had been loveless before her, and her decision to ride back with him six winters past had changed him to the core. With the pressures of kingdom-building and the growing tension among the Seven Warriors, it was his talks with her that helped him maintain his sanity.

She curled up to him, gently stroking his chest. "Is there nothing that gives you pleasure anymore?"

Ardhios moved her dark, flowing hair from her playful smile. "For ten seasons I have tried to talk some sense into Mordher, but it is no use. Mordher refuses to deal with the men of Highwood, or anyone related to the Rion Guard."

"Perhaps my lord need only find what brings Mordher pleasure," she giggled.

Ardhios sat up. "Mordher and the other warriors care not for the domestic skill required to *build* anything."

Portina sat up as well, pulling the sheet up to her neck. "It is so cold. Will you build us a fire?"

"Of course," he answered. He rolled out of bed, pulled on his pants and boots, slipped into his shirt, and walked over to the mammoth fireplace across the room. He threw some logs on the glowing coals, stirred them with the wrought-iron poker until flames leapt around the wood. He stared at the flames, deep in thought.

"Mordher and the others have chosen war alone," he said. "And if not for that, who could say the Camonra would not have taken this kingdom from us before a single stone was laid? Even now, as we warm ourselves by this fire, Mordher watches over the eastern edge of the valley. He does not shiver in the cold. He builds an army with his iron fist, disciplining their ranks to fear him more than the cold. But they do not build—they destroy. He loves nothing else."

"Then it is good that you will show him the great works you have done," Portina said. She pulled the sheet off the bed and wrapped it around herself, settling behind him, leaning her head on his back. "Look at all that has come to pass. You undertook the building of a massive fortress in Candra, and when the small forest to the west could not supply the wood required, you went to the men of Highwood and found them willing and able, and you alone forged that bond. It was wise, my lord."

"The wisdom of it may yet be proven," answered Ardhios. "But one thing is true: without the wood from Highwood, we would never have completed the framing, flooring, or ceilings, much less the scaffolding required to raise the structure. Candra may have had hundreds of skilled masons, cutters and layers alike, but they would still have only outlined this Great Hall had Highwood not supplied the thousand laborers to support them."

"You worry too much, I think," asserted Portina. "Mordher will see."

"You don't know Mordher as I do," responded Ardhios.

Portina wrapped her arms around him and moved to his side, watching the flames with him.

"You alone have garnered the love of the people, my lord, even though you never subscribed to their beliefs in Fehamina or any of the other gods of the moon and stars. They love you, not Mordher or any of the others."

"Careful how you speak of them," cautioned Ardhios. "Such words would bring wrath from my brothers — a wrath I could not control." She looked down then, and he reached out his hand to lift her chin and placed a kiss on her cheek. "Get dressed; I must be about my business."

*   *   *

Ardhios descended from his chamber and stepped into the courtyard. Craftsmen were building carts and wagons to transport stone and sea coal; Others shaped boats for fishing. The quarrymen and smiths were having a friendly game of pins in the early light, smoking their pipes and laughing, while carpenters cut joists, floorboards, and other necessary supports for the outer rooms. Most everything was finished in the main hall and keep, and there had been talk of creating a second set of curtain walls around everything, though he had not yet approved a final design.

Maybe he had been too busy to notice, but it suddenly dawned on him that it was just as Portina had said. By bringing together the crafts and the peoples of Candra and Highwood, he had created something more than stone buildings — he had helped restore the life they lost when leaving Rion, and that semblance of their old life brought a new sense of belonging and community to all involved. He took a moment then to truly stop and look around with amazement at what he had managed to raise in the quiet valley beside the Candra Mountains.

It is time, he thought. "Page!" he shouted, and a young boy snapped to his side.

"In celebration of the Great Hall's completion, send messengers to call upon Mordher and the other Warriors to return from the eastern front. Bring me paper, pen, and wax, and I will write it in my own hand and seal it. Be quick, boy."

Within the hour, the scroll was sealed, and a rider bolted eastward.

*   *   *

A week after Ardhios dispatched the messenger to Mordher, the first winter's snow fell. Ardhios walked along the short curtain wall surrounding the central temple and pondered the beautiful night sky. He made his way down the stairs and into a domed room in the corner of the curtain walls. The room housed an olive press, and Ardhios often came there to think, for the woman who minded the donkey that turned the pressing stone rarely spoke or even seemed to notice him, and the ceaseless sound of the stone wheel crushing olives was oddly soothing.

She lightly switched the donkey's rump, then picked up the bellows to stoke the fire that warmed the room and boiled the oil in a clay jar hanging above it, scooping impurities from the surface without saying a word to Ardhios. He smiled to himself at how little mind she paid to his supposed position of authority, so dedicated was she to her craft. She shared the room with him, tolerating him, Ardhios thought, so long as he did not interrupt her work.

When her fire appeared to die down, she stepped out of the room, and a man emerged from the shadows, his hood covering his face.

"Be quick," said Ardhios. "What have you learned?"

The man glanced around and removed his hood. It was one of the acolytes of Moonledge Peak's Elder priest. "The sword of Evliit is at Moonledge Peak," he said.

"Evliit's sword is a myth perpetrated by the Guard," answered Ardhios. "Do not bother me with wives' tales."

"No, sire, I have seen it with my own eyes!" the spy insisted. "The Elder priest has locked it away for protection, and Caratacus tells no one of its existence, not even the high council of Moonledge."

There was a rustling sound outside. Ardhios fished out a small bag of coins from his coat and tossed it to the acolyte. "Keep your ears open. There's more where that came from. Now be gone." The acolyte quickly put away the coins and disappeared up the stairs just as the old woman reentered through the opposite doorway carrying several pieces of wood. She went back to tending her fire, and Ardhios was pondering the meaning of his spy's news when a page burst through the door, earning a short stare from the old woman.

"My liege, the warriors return!" the page said, winded.

"Very well," Ardhios said, and he walked up the winding wrought-iron staircase that took him to the square tower's landing above the valley. A thousand men rumbled to a standstill on the grounds below the Great Hall, and Ardhios had to admit that the sheer number of warriors following his six brethren — Mordher in the lead — concerned him. Mordher could be ruthless, but by himself, the damage might be contained. Saddle an army behind him, and Mordher might truly become totally unmanageable.

Ardhios made his way back down the stairs toward the fields east of the castle to meet Mordher and the others coming through the large wooden gates that marked the entrance to the courtyard.

"So *this* has occupied your time?" Mordher inquired in his usual gruff tone.

"Yes, brother," Ardhios replied. "This is it."

"Have the men make camp on the lawn," Mordher said to one of his soldiers, who responded with a fist to his chest.

"Yes, my lord!"

Ardhios led them through the courtyard into the Great Hall, where they removed their helmets and some of their heavier armor. He pointed out the various features of the incredible craftsmanship that had gone into the building of the hall, leading up to a massive table of polished wood. "And here we have our feasting table," he said, hoping to spread some of his enthusiasm.

"We will drink to this!" Mordher replied. The roar of Mordher's voice set the maidens into action, and they began preparing the long table at the western end of the great room. The Warriors walked into the hall, and Ardhios noticed them running their hands along the table's polished surface and admiring the eagle-claw carvings on the legs. The seven high-back chairs were padded and covered with woven upholstery bearing a symbol of seven swords. As they laid down their weapons and seated themselves, Ardhios started to take the seat at the center.

"I notice you seat yourself at the center of the table, Ardhios," Mordher commented. "Does that mean you have set yourself above us?"

In the two seasons Mordher and the others had been away, Ardhios had forgotten how much Mordher enjoyed stirring things up.

"Sit at the center, brother — there's no rank between us," Ardhios said with a slight nod.

"I wouldn't think of it, my liege," Mordher answered, and the other Warriors laughed. "Keep your seat and whatever power having carpenters and farmers bowing to you brings. I haven't the stomach for work such as this," Mordher said. Still standing, he grabbed a large piece of meat from the plate before him, ripped the meat from the bone with his teeth, then snatched up a cup of ale and washed it down.

"As we rode in, I saw that some of the craftsmen wore the colors of Rion. Were I in need of entertainment, I might have shown them how I spit upon Rion," he said, hocking up a mouthful of spit and hurling it onto the floor with the whole of his upper body to emphasize his point.

"It has taken many able craftsmen, Mordher, to build a hall such as this," Ardhios replied, ignoring the gesture.

"You have brought them from Highwood, I take it," he said. Mordher plopped down in the chair nearest the end of the table, crossing his legs on the table and letting the mud of his boots fall beside the food plates.

"I've met with the leaders of Highwood, Mordher. They wish to keep the peace between us," he answered. "They have seen the Inferiors to the east of their homes in the wood, and they see us as much less a threat than they are."

"Then they do not know *me*," Mordher said dryly. Again, a hearty laugh rang through the hall from the other warriors.

"Still," Ardhios continued. "The builders have been requested to construct a defensive wall between them and the Inferior encampments, and I have agreed to—"

"What?" Mordher asked. He slammed his cup upon the table with enough force to bend its brass base. "*You* agreed?"

"I've made many agreements for our part, Mordher — this is nothing new. The men of Highwood have seen our strength grow mightily, and they only wish to join with us against our common enemies."

"They'd better," Mordher said. "While you have been busy laying stones, I've built an army that is unmatched in this new country."

"A treaty is wise, Mordher. Many craftsmen have made their home in Highwood. We couldn't have completed so much without them."

"I despise them," Mordher said. "They swear no allegiance to anyone but the Rion Guard, the very ones that brought us the misery we now enjoy."

"Look around you," Ardhios said with a smile. "You're a lord in your own hall. You command an army that even the Rion Guard would envy. What misery indeed!"

Mordher rose from his seat and walked around the table, looking over the arched ceiling, his eyes tracing the stained beams of wood that crisscrossed the expanse of the hall's stonework. He made his way to where Ardhios sat, turned, and placed his fists on the table, knuckles down, leaning forward to look into Ardhios's face. "If you think I wouldn't trade all of this for even a moment with my wife and child, you are sadly mistaken. I will build an army that will control the new world, and neither Rion nor any of its charges will stand against us, or I will crush them—mercilessly."

Ardhios leaned toward him. "I'm not your enemy, Mordher."

"You would do well to keep it that way," Mordher replied. He leaned back from the table, walked over and picked up his cup, and emptied the goblet. "Beautiful hall, Ardhios," he said, tossing the cup into the middle of the floor as he walked toward the door. The other warriors rose to follow him.

"Wait!" Ardhios called out. "I've something you'll want to hear."

"That you have women and more drink?" Mordher scoffed. There was a round of laughter.

Ardhios was already regretting saying anything. He didn't want to lay all his cards on the table, but their lack of respect cut more deeply than he wanted to admit.

"The Elder at Moonledge Peak has Evliit's sword," he said.

The laughter stopped.

"What did you say?" asked Mordher.

"I have established a source in Moonledge, and he has informed me that Evliit's sword is under the Elder's protection," answered Ardhios.

"There is no Evliit, and there is no Sword of the Watch. These are tools to control the minds of simpletons," said Mordher.

"But if you were to *acquire* such a holy relic of the Guard, would that not shake the very foundation of their faith?" said Borian. "What better way to strike at the heart of Rion?"

Mordher seemed very pleased with that potentiality.

"Careful, Borian. A move such as that could unite all of Erathe against us," said Ardhios. "Wouldn't it be better to convince the followers of the Guard that Candra's strength would best protect their holy relic, and that the time of the Guard has passed?" It could be acquired without spilling so much as a drop of blood."

"You and your politics," Mordher sneered. "You do your talking, and I'll build an army of unquestionable strength. We'll see which path is best." Mordher turned and threw open the massive doors leading to the courtyard. He walked outside, leaving the doors open behind him. Snow spiraled across the beautifully etched floor.

The other Warriors followed him out, leaving Ardhios alone with his thoughts.

*   *   *

"Hold still!" Amphileph yelled. Citanth tried to keep his hands from shaking while he held up a sheet of thick parchment.

Amphileph used his new mastery of kinetics outside the Binding to scrawl a list of items he demanded. The pen lightly dipped into the inkwell and stroked the parchment with grace, making Amphileph's face shine with delight. With a flick of his finger, he tapped the pen upon the paper, making a strong *splat* for punctuation.

"If your idiocy were not to have so severely thinned the ranks of the Camonra, I could send them out into every land, and I would have these ingredients in no time!" Amphileph said. "Fill a clay pot from the well and bring it to me!"

"Yes, master," answered Citanth. He returned to the Binding's edge with the pot, and water sloshed out of it with his sudden stop.

"Come close," said Amphileph. "Lean the lip against the Binding."

Citanth pushed it in as far as he could, and Amphileph thrust his hand into the Binding's energy field until it would go no farther.

His ring opened, and tiny granules from a small compartment escaped, sticking to the Binding's wall as if the water pot attracted them. A thin line of them passed through the energy field and into the water; one granule at a time, they slipped into the clay jar that Citanth supported on his hip.

"Now, pour the water all around the Binding and out into the field!" commanded Amphileph, and Citanth did so. Covered in pulsating red veins, green vines the size of Citanth's thigh burst from the dirt and spread across the land, leading outward from around the Binding to the edge of Black Mountain Valley. They sprouted up over trees and buildings, bearing sacs all along their length. Opaque at first, the vines' sacs became translucent as they matured, filling with a cloudy yellow liquid, and within them, something was moving. Upon closer inspection, Citanth saw a Camon growing rapidly along the veins within the sac.

Amphileph watched them closely. "The vine will last but one season, giving me only one chance to rebuild my army, so you will tend them night and day. If any struggle to claw their way through the sacs' thick membranes, cut the sacs open to release them, and mark the weaklings with a brand. Fail me, and I will serve your guts to them."

After weeks of harvesting the Camonra, Citanth felt haggard. The sticky substance from the sacs matted his hair, and many days' growth of beard was on his face. His clothing was filthy and soiled, and he had scratched sores on his forearm until they bled. He had opened hundreds of these sacs and quickly determined that these Camon were more vicious than their predecessors, darker-skinned, and far more heavily haired. Citanth had beaten several of them away from him at birth, for they had attacked him almost immediately upon clearing their eyes of the thick, mucus-like liquid.

This new breed of Camonra was even more fearlessly obedient to Amphileph, and though they had skin like humans and their Camon brothers before them, their blood-red eyes and thicker body hair set them apart. When the sacs burst, they gathered before the Boundland, just outside Citanth's simple home. More than once their chanting had driven

Citanth mad with loathing, for they would call out Amphileph's name sometimes deep into the night. They tirelessly made weapons and armor, bred war dogs and Azrodh.

When the Camonra numbered in the hundreds, Amphileph began sending the strongest among them into the west, and one by one they returned with the ingredients he demanded. Amphileph rewarded each of them with dominion over some facet of the meager existence of the Camonra, a greater weapon, or some potion that made them stronger, faster, or healed some ailment.

They gathered his strange list of ingredients from Moonledge and Candra, Calarph and Highwood, to the edge of the deadly chasm that separated Rion from the remainder of the world, and even east into the Dark Forest of the frontiers. They killed men and Camon alike to find what their master desired, but return they did, six seasons gone, with everything he had asked.

For nearly two risings of Erathe's moon, Amphileph had stood careful watch over Citanth. He heated and stirred, separated and combined the elements, distilling a sickly black mixture that stank of death. When it was done, Amphileph ordered the Camon females into the huts of the northern camp and called the males to himself. They filled the grounds north of the Binding, but when Amphileph stood to speak, a hush fell over the warriors, and their war dogs were jerked into silence with chain or strap.

"The Creator hath given them life, these men of Rion, but they have done nothing but blaspheme the very name of the Creator whose favor lets them take their next breath! Do they honor him that hath created them?"

"No!" roared the rows of Camonra seated before him.

"All the beauties of proud Erathe have they been given, but do they respect the gift of the world around them?"

"No!" they roared again.

"They considered themselves the very embodiment of the Creator in this world, but will these faithless men reign over all?"

"No! No! No!" the Camonra bellowed.

"You are right and true, my beloved warriors! Your children will be numbered like the leaves of the great forest of Calarph! You will destroy the petulance of men upon this world! You will set right that which men have made contemptible. You will ride into the west—to the castle in the mountains that men call Moonledge, to Highwood, and to the Tower near the sea—you will go and slay every man that makes their homes there! And will you have mercy on their wives and children?"

They beat upon their chests like drums, screaming "No! No! No! No!"

"First, bring me the weak that I might make them strong!" Amphileph demanded. The majority of the Camonra separated themselves from the branded males. "You that do not bear the brand, go forth to the northern camp and join the females! Lock your doors and wait for Citanth to come for you!" When they had left, Amphileph faced the remaining Camonra that bore the brand. "And for the Watchers who have turned against me and for all mankind, I have brought about a destroyer!" Amphileph screamed. "Citanth!"

Citanth emerged from his hut carrying the culmination of Amphileph's alchemy — a single glass vial of black liquid. His face was sallow and emotionless.

The night sky was clear and cold, and Amphileph saw the bright, near planets of La, Sapath, and Denf clearly. He pointed at a line that the shining planets made between the horizon and Erathe's moon.

"They align only once in this age, Citanth! Bring forth the Aramadhi now!" Amphileph cried. His face grew deep red, and his eyes bulged in their sockets.

One of the Camonra stepped forth, and his brethren's grunts took on a rhythm with an increasingly frenetic pace. He was dressed in the ceremonial garb of the Aramadhi, a sacrifice to the Creator, the long, black feathers of the Arama birds fastened to his arm and head with bands of leather. He took the vial in his hands, and the chanting rose to a deafening volume. He uncorked the vial, drank its contents, and screamed his most defiant battle cry. All the Camonra in attendance followed with equally chilling howls and screams.

"Go now, my son! Go with all speed to the west!" shouted Amphileph.

The Aramadhi ran then, ran with the abandon of one on a holy mission.

The crowd opened a path to the west, and he sped by them, his skin showing through a pulsating blackness flowing through his veins with the pace of his racing heart. He was still running when his skin tore apart at his back with a gushing sound that opened to the birth of an Angrodha, a fearsome dragon with a near insatiable desire for destruction and the taste of flesh and blood. It shook off the skin of its dead host, trumpeting a violent screech. Citanth thought the sound of it pierced the hearts of even the brave Camonra, who for a moment stood their ground in spite of their brand. Steam rose off the leathery skin of the creature in the cold air that permeated the month of Naap, and when the creature turned its angular head toward the Camonra, they slowly moved back from it until several of them broke for cover.

Their quick movement seemed to attract the creature's attention, and it suddenly struggled to fly toward them, half bounding, half pushing itself with its wrinkled, nubile wings. It pounced upon one of the Camonra and tore him to pieces, looking up from the frayed carcass with quick jerks of its head as if it might catch another of them, then quickly fed again with its ripping teeth.

"Good!" Amphileph squealed with laughter. "Feed! Be strong! Grow!"

Citanth backed into the wall of his hut. Then he scrambled inside and slammed the door shut, laughing, then crying, then screaming at the top of his lungs as the horror of the Angrodha was unleashed on the Camonra outside. He could still hear Amphileph shouting, and he raised his head just enough to peer through the wooden slats in his window.

"Taste the flesh of your brothers, Angrodha!" Amphileph shouted, and the creature stopped for a moment as if to acknowledge Amphileph's words. "Go and destroy all that stand in your way!"

The great creature raised its head, threw back an arm of the Camon into its gullet, and then flew into the air, clumsily at first but slowly gathering skill as it disappeared west into the cold night air.

"What have you done, Amphileph?" Citanth whispered from within the security of his small room. Amphileph seemed even more emboldened by the creature, raising his hands and swirling the dark clouds that hung over the Boundland. "Rain down this misery upon all who stand against me, and on all that stand in ignorance of my power!"

Citanth watched the Camonra in horror. They beat upon their chests, the vast majority of them still standing their ground, showing their bravery and devotion.

"Run!" Citanth shouted, but they either could not hear him or did not care.

Slowly, drops of black rain began to fall upon them. Boils rose up on their flesh within seconds of contact, and any that had not made it to cover howled out in pain. Those of the Camonra that could not reach cover fell to the ground and melted into it. A foul stench rose from their blistering bodies. The spines of the fallen Camonra arched up and tore away from their appendages, forming some kind of new creature that emerged from the blackened mud and slithered away.

Citanth covered his ears, but he could still hear shrill cries, and he realized then they were war dogs. He ran to the opposite wall and moved the wooden blinds to look toward the northern camp. Hair fell from the bodies of the dogs unlucky enough to be out in the open, down in the fight pits, or in uncovered cages. They writhed in agony, chewing their way through their cages, clawing their way out of their pits, and dragging their mutated bodies into the west.

He could hear Amphileph laughing and then make a choking sound that drew Citanth back to the opposite window. The dark rain began to blot out his view of Amphileph, sizzling on the spherical orb of power that was his cage, but just before the black coating was complete, he saw Amphileph fall to the ground, foaming at the mouth and looking near death.

*　*　*

The Angrodha flew westward, ascending higher and higher into the air, circling in great arcs, drying its birthing from its wings and snorting the cooler air. It encountered the rising ash from the great tear in the land below, and it turned northward, where its coal black eyes caught a herd of deer among the wooded areas north of Tobor's camp. It folded its wings and accelerated into a dive, swooping down upon them, baring its teeth for the kill, saliva spraying from its mouth. It had already grown considerably larger, and the joy it experienced in the hunt caused it to *caw* once, scattering the herd.

It slammed one of the large bucks to the ground with its razor-sharp talons. The buck struggled against the pressure of the creature's strong jaws for a moment more, when the still-young dragon turned its neck with a jerk, tearing the buck in half. It crunched down the buck — bones, antlers,and all — then curled up upon the bloody mess and rested, waiting for the darkness of night.

*　*　*

Tobor was once again whittling on his porch when he heard the strange noise in the night. The piercing cry was like nothing he had heard before, and he laid down his carving block and placed his knife back into his scabbard. Moments later, Idhoran appeared with several warriors in tow.

"My lord, you've heard the sound coming from the north?" he asked.

"I have," Tobor said.

"What creature makes a noise such as this?" Idhoran asked.

"I know not," Tobor responded.

Adheron appeared upon the porch; the concubines in their nightclothes could just be seen behind him in the light of the torches that the soldiers carried.

"What is it, Father?" Adheron asked. "I heard a terrible shriek in the distance."

"Quiet," Tobor said. "Close the door."

Adheron reached behind him to close the heavy oak door. The concubines attempted to look around it until the latch set. For their protection, Tobor did not allow the Camon females and young to venture out at night.

"Do not alarm the women," Tobor said.

Dark clouds began blotting out the moon and stars, and Tobor could hear a murmur rising among the troops in the camp across from him.

"What's happening, Father?" Adheron asked.

"Go inside, Adheron."

"Father?" Adheron replied, noticeably upset by the command.

"Question me not," Tobor retorted.

"Yes, Father," said Adheron, the door closing behind him to the muffled sound of a litany of questions from the concubines.

No sooner was his son indoors than different strange sounds began coming from the east. At first, Tobor thought it sounded like rain, but there was more than that — a sizzling sound and animal cries of agony.

"Out of the rain!" Tobor shouted, and Idhoran and the other men shuffled inward under the porch — slowly at first, then rapidly as drops of the black rain fell upon them and awful boils appeared. They pressed with all their might against the others closer to the front wall of Tobor's home, squeezing up under the cover of the porch, crying out in agony themselves. Tobor opened the door to his home, and the group pushed inward, falling inside. Smoke rose from the sizzling pockets in their skin.

"Help them!" he yelled, and his concubines quickly covered their wounds with cloths.

Tobor jumped to his feet and stood back in the doorway. He could see the movement of the rain was westward toward the main encampment. A wave of smoke stirred from the ground as it crossed the open space between them, life sizzling like meat upon a flame, withering every plant it touched into black goo.

"Get inside!" he screamed at the top of his lungs, but there was no hearing him over the storm. In desperation, he yelled to Adheron. "Sound the alarm!"

Adheron ran to the second floor and blew his horn from their second-story window. Tobor could see the encampment clearly stirring with the sound of it. Those unfortunate enough to be outside began screaming, and then screams of agony rang out everywhere in the camp.

"I'll go to them!" Idhoran yelled, starting out from Tobor's porch, but Tobor caught his arm. Something heavier began falling right in front of them, bouncing off the roof into the yard, bursting on the path and in the grass with a *plop-plop-plop* sound.

"Birds fall from the skies in whole flocks!" cried Tobor. "It is death to go."

Tobor could see his people lighting lanterns in the huts in the main encampment, and much to his alarm, some of the males emerged from their homes to see what was happening.

The Azrodh and war dogs began crying out in agony. One of the war dogs began running toward Tobor's porch, but it flipped over and writhed on the ground as the black poison falling from the skies washed the hair from its body. It wiped its forearms over its head, removing its ears in a pile of blackened skin. Its hind legs withered as if the bones turned to mush, dragging on its belly as quills pushed out from its spine, one after another, forcing the skin into vanes between them. It clawed the earth in front of it, stretching its front legs to almost twice their original size, shaking its head and craning its neck into a mass of rippling muscles. It howled then — no longer in pain, but with ferocious anger. It seemed to notice Tobor anew, snapping at him as its claws cut furrows into the stone steps leading to the porch. It stopped for a moment and gagged, coughing up a mass of tissue, then its jaws grew larger, stretching the skin of its lips away from the gums, its growing canine teeth tearing through the skin of its face. Tobor grabbed his crossbow and fired, and the bolt entered through its open mouth, penetrating its upper soft palate, the arrowhead protruding through the snout next to its left eye. It roared in pain, crushing the bolt with its jaws and slithering away into the darkness.

For two hours the black rain fell upon the encampment, and all Tobor and the others could do was watch the misery unfold. When they did finally move down the walkway to the encampment, females and children were crying for their missing mates and fathers, and the males that remained were doing their best just to comfort them.

"Why is this happening?" the females cried. "Why has the father done this?"

Tobor winced at this reference to Amphileph.

"What father does this to his children?" Tobor yelled in desperation. "He has cursed this land! It will no longer sustain us! We move the camp northward!"

Idhoran moved toward Tobor to intercede. "My lord—"

"Today!" Tobor screamed. He turned toward his own home, but then stopped and turned back to Idhoran and the others. He could see his own son and concubines coming toward him, their terrified faces illuminated by the pre-dawn light. It was the only real home they had ever known, and after a lifetime of mastering destruction, its building may have represented the only thing that he had ever *created*. "Get them ready, Idhoran. Whatever it takes! This place will destroy us all! Send out the scouts! I must know where this black death ends."

The Angrodha's call punctuated Tobor's sentence.

"There's little time," Tobor said. "The evil of Amphileph is upon us."

By mid-morning, the scouts returned. "All manner of strange creatures wander the countryside, my lord, but the black clouds are no more."

"And how far must we go?" asked Tobor.

"This curse poisons all the fields north of Rion and east of Amphileph's temple, but it stops short of the men in the woods."

"The north wind from the fire gates of Rion must have pushed the clouds toward the northern mountains," said Tobor. "Prepare your families to leave at once," he instructed the scouts, and they signaled their respect and made haste to their own huts.

Idhoran looked at him. "What do you command, my lord?"

Tobor felt overwhelmed. "I have lost over thirty of our soldiers to this dark night," he said. "What of the Azrodh?"

"Most of the Azrodh were tied off just outside their masters' huts," answered Idhoran. "What remains of them is twisted flesh. They push around the camp on mangled legs, but all manner of teeth and claws still make them dangerous. I've ordered the soldiers to destroy them."

Tobor could hear the sorrowful cries of the infected creatures. "Such misery deserves the axe and spear," he said.

His soldiers had cornered one of the mangled creatures in the main walk that split the camp down the center.

"Clear it from the path!" Tobor cried. "We cannot lose any more time with it!"

Two soldiers drew their swords and moved toward it, when suddenly Tobor heard one of the remaining war dogs growling—a sound he knew always signaled a threat to their masters. The growl turned to wild barking and there was a scream from behind him. A rush of wind made him draw his sword.

The Angrodha had landed upon the mutated Azrodh with both claws. The sound of bone snapping signaled the strength of its grip. One of the soldiers was so startled that he fell beside the creature and began pushing himself backward on his hands and feet. The other screamed out and swung at it, his blade glancing off its chin. The Angrodha's head fell away with the swing of the sword and then snapped back, its teeth tearing away most of his attacker's chest cavity. He fell to his knees, and the Angrodha smacked down the quick meal of armor and flesh, and then snapped him up into the air by one shoulder.

"Weapons!" Tobor cried, and the females and children screamed and ran in all directions. A crossbow bolt shot into the dragon's hindquarter, and it jerked back its thigh. It grabbed the bolt with its teeth, pulled it out, and spat it aside with a low growl. It looked around—eyes narrowing with hatred. It clawed its way toward the soldier reloading his crossbow and cut him in half with a swipe of its powerful forearms.

A second shot caught it in the thick of its neckline. It roared its defiance, the sound of which was deafening, shaking their guts in their bodies.

"Take cover!" Tobor yelled, and the creature noted his location at the sound of it. He dropped the remains of the Azrodh and moved toward Tobor.

Tobor jumped through the wooden slats of the nearest hut's window. The creature tore away one side of it and pushed his head inside. Tobor tripped over something on the floor and rolled to one of the walls. The Angrodha destroyed the entire wall of the hut, pushing its body through the opening. Its wings caught upon the hut's ceiling, and its teeth snapped the air just in front of Tobor repeatedly. Tobor kicked a chair into its face, which it caught in its teeth and closed its jaws upon it, splintering the chair into pieces. The Camon general attempted to stand, but his sword caught the side of a large pot hanging over the kitchen fire, swinging the pot on the pot-hanger. The Angrodha swung down at him, hitting upon one end of the table and flipping it end over end, where it struck the bottom of the pot. The scalding hot soup pot that had been forgotten over the fire bounced off the ceiling and flew into the Angrodha's face. The winged reptile pulled its head back out of the hole in the wall in reaction to the intense pain. Tobor leapt to his feet and burst through the door on the opposite side of the hut. The creature shook its face and wiped it with its forearm.

The Camonra were yelling from all directions, and the Angrodha looked around at them with intense anger. Two more crossbow bolts struck its body, causing it to jerk back and scrape one of them away from its side with its claws. It clutched the carcass of the Azrodh with one clawed foot and the soldier with the other and pushed off the ground with a *whoosh,* up into the sky.

Tobor was so winded that he dropped to one knee. Idhoran and Adheron ran to his side.

"Father!" Adheron yelled.

Tobor stood then and put his hands on his head, still breathing heavily. He made a quick check of himself, somewhat amazed that he had escaped with but a few scratches. The hint of a smile crossed his face, and he patted Adheron on the shoulder. "I live to fight another day," he said, and then he turned to Idhoran and pointed north. "Move them out, Idhoran, immediately."

The tribe began emerging from their hiding places, and Idhoran immediately waved them in that direction. "We move northward! Move quickly!"

"Watch over your mother and the others, Adheron," Tobor said of his concubines. "And keep an eye on the sky."

"Yes, Father," Adheron replied.

Tobor drove them northwest through the swamps of what had once been the battle trails to the men of Highwood. The remaining Azrodhs' loads were heavy, strapped with everything that the Camonra could load upon them, in the fear that there would be no returning to their homes. They were moving much slower than Tobor would have liked. Nightfall was approaching. He opted for the cover of the heavy foliage that grew north of the Lake of Esoria.

The concubines had hauled his battle tent once again, as on previous journeys, but Tobor had not allowed them to pitch it—it would provide too much of a target for their flying adversary to spot. This creature changed everything he had come to know in warfare, for he had never fought with a creature of its size that could pounce upon them from the skies at any moment, rendering them into little more than prey. His years of experience as a predator suddenly felt useless against one such as this.

When the bulk of the females and little ones had curled up among the heavy-leaved plants and slept, Tobor paced carefully among them, trying to think of a strategy for defeating the winged marauder, stepping methodically over the concubines and moving out into a small clearing to see the night sky.

As he gazed at the stars, Idhoran found him.

"My liege, what are your orders?"

"I hear strange sounds in the night again, Idhoran. Have every Camon ready to sound the alert. Tomorrow, we will move northward to the mountains and make ourselves a place there in the caves, as the men have done. At least in the darkness of the stone, we might corner the beast and kill it."

"And what of the men there? Do you mean to make war on them? I count three thousand strong that will follow you and take the mountain as our own."

"The mountains have room for all," Tobor said. "We've lost brothers to this plague from the sky, and there will be more lost if the Angrodha finds us out. Our numbers are our hope of independence from Amphileph."

"The men will not stand for our presence near them," said Idhoran. "Much of what the father said of them is true; you have seen it yourself."

"They fear us, Idhoran," said Tobor. "We have lived in peace these many years since the Battle of High Wood. The unrest has been stirred by those remaining faithful to Amphileph, for they have chosen to wander into the land of men."

"They do not separate us from Amphileph—in their minds, we are one," said Idhoran.

"The father remains good at war," answered Tobor. "Those attacks break the peace and drive hatred for the Camonra into the hearts of men. He intends this, just as surely as he is behind this creature that follows us now."

"We will follow whatever orders you have given, my lord," Idhoran replied. "You are our leader, and you have proven your place."

"You are my—" Tobor began, but he heard something stirring in the brush. Idhoran drew his sword, and Tobor his own, and they began to move toward the sound.

As they walked slowly around through the underbrush, the rain began to fall again, and they moved undercover of the broad leaves of the nearest Soru bush. To their relief, the rain appeared to no longer carry the black death, but fell harmlessly on their exposed skin. Still, the damp leather vest that Tobor wore under his chainmail stuck to him, letting off a strong odor of sweat. He hesitated for a moment, and he tried to determine the direction of the wind. He did not want an enemy smelling him coming.

They were easing their way around the Soru bush with great care, when Tobor held up a hand, freezing Idhoran's movement. They could hear chewing and crunching very close to them, and Tobor was convinced that whatever it was lay just on the other side of the Soru bush's large fronds.

He moved one of the leaves back carefully with his sword. The severed foot of one of their war dogs was lying in the mud. He slowly lifted the leaf further, and he saw long fangs pushing through the skin of what remained of the hound, pulling the skin from its side like one of his concubines might lift a bed sheet from his bed. He lowered his head a bit more to see, and he saw the head of the creature. It was like the mutated war dog he had seen from his porch, its body nearly eight feet in length, its gray eyes and white pupils focused on its kill.

Tobor glanced at Idhoran and tilted his head slightly, indicating that he had found their foe.

Idhoran moved to circle around the Soru bush in the opposite direction, but his armor scraped a dead branch in the underbrush, making the tiniest sound, stopping Idhoran where he stood.

The creature stopped feeding instantly, remaining motionless except for some holes on the side of its head closest to them opening, one after another, as if straining to listen. It began to growl in a low, grating tone and quills stiffened on its face and back, their fleshy vanes quivering in the rain.

Tobor slowly stepped out from behind the Soru bush into clear sight of his present foe. The creature did not move except to extend the remaining quills on its body and swallow the bloody sheet of skin, hair and all, of the dog. It kept its head low to the ground, one eye focused on Tobor and the other twitching back and forth in the direction of Idhoran.

The creature was obviously sizing him up for the kill, and Tobor knew the time it used to do so would allow Idhoran to position himself for the ambush, for they had performed such a maneuver many times in the past. They needed no words to execute it flawlessly.

As Idhoran disappeared on the other side of the Soru, Tobor slowly raised his second hand to the hilt of his sword and prepared for Idhoran's attack. If the creature went toward him, Idhoran would strike from the side, and he would do likewise if the creature chose Idhoran.

Tobor slowly bent into a slight crouch, preparing for the ensuing attack, when he saw movement beyond the creature. Four more of them emerged from the brush behind it.

"Idhoran!" Tobor cried out in a strained whisper, but there was no response. This was not good.

"Camonra!" Tobor then shouted, calling for the aid of his fellow warriors.

Idhoran mistook his cry for help and burst through the brush on the creature's left. The creature's head turned quickly toward Idhoran, and its massive front legs dragged the remainder of its body in the direction of Idhoran's attack. Several of the other creatures also closed on him from some ten paces behind.

Tobor ran toward Idhoran and the creatures. He could hear the battle horn of the Camonra sounding behind them.

Idhoran screamed his own battle cry as the creature snapped at him. He swung his sword, its blade breaking off the lower half of one of the beast's long fangs, causing it to shake its head and back away.

"Behind!" Tobor yelled.

Idhoran looked to his right just as one of the other creatures' fangs drove up through his thigh. Tobor's blade swung across the body of the first creature, but the quills were surprisingly strong, stopping his blade from doing any real damage.

Idhoran grabbed one of the teeth that protruded from his right thigh and held on to it, keeping the creature in tow. The creature attempted to bite him repeatedly, but Idhoran bent his knee upon the ground, prying its upper jaw open.

"Aaaah!" Idhoran yelled. He flipped his blade in one hand, drove it into the neck of the creature and tore it downward. He attempted to stand with its decapitated head still hanging from his thigh.

Tobor could see a look of terror on his old friend's face, and he screamed a mighty battle cry and swung at the first creature wildly, its black blood flying through the air.

A third creature moved quickly toward Idhoran and lurched up from its legs, grabbing Idhoran by the neck. Idhoran dropped his sword and grabbed the quills on its head, pulling on them desperately until his arms fell lifeless by his sides.

"No!" Tobor yelled. The horizontal slice of his blade cut across the creature's back. He raised his blade to make another strike but saw a fourth and then a fifth creature emerging from the brush. They pounced upon Idhoran's body while a sixth and a seventh creature circled in front of it, eyeing Tobor and daring him to move among the pack.

Behind him, several of the Camonra appeared with crossbows. Tobor waded in on the creatures, and the Camonra fired their bolts in a mad panic. Tobor killed two more of the creatures before bolts made quick work of the rest, and he fell to his knees beside Idhoran's mangled remains.

"No, no!" he cried again.

"My lord, let us move back to the camp and protect the tribe!" one of the Camonra said.

Tobor knew that there could be more of these creatures. He wanted to take up his friend's body, to bury it upon the hill beside his home, as it should be done with such a mighty warrior, but instead he screamed again. The warrior hardened himself again as great warriors must, knowing there was no time to give Idhoran the honor he deserved. He stood then and took one last look at his friend's face, picked up the blood-soaked sword of Idhoran, and joined his soldiers in returning to the camp.

The sounds of strange creatures now seemed to fill the night, and Tobor roused everyone to move. Mothers pushed their crying infants to their breasts in an attempt to silence them.

"Move quickly and silently. Be sure that none fall behind," Tobor instructed.

It was decided that Adheron, Tobor's son and Idhoran's pupil, would take command under Tobor, though Tobor himself thought that the appointment might have been more in respect for Idhoran's wishes than for Adheron's abilities. The shock of Idhoran's death had cast a shadow of gloom over the entire tribe.

They made their way northeast, passing the last remnants of the Lake of Esoria, into the muddy swamps and marshes that formed there from the repeated overflowing of Esoria's banks and the high amount of rainfall. They encountered an amorphous creature, its waist-high body seemingly a mixture of mud, leeches the size of a Camon's arm, and the black film that formed on the mire itself. They lost more of their Camonra, but they remained on a course due northeast, attempting to keep some distance from Amphileph's lands and the men of Highwood.

The month of Naap passed, and most of Falingsor by the time they reached the base of the Faceless Mountains. Falingsor had brought with it a bone-chilling cold, and the entire group was completely exhausted, with little food or fresh water for the last several days of their journey. The toll was terrible, and the young ones cried and slumped in their mothers' arms, incapable of the energy to complain further.

"Send the scouts to find the humans, but keep your distance," Tobor commanded. "We want no war with them."

"Yes, Father," Adheron responded.

"Send hunters to find whatever food can be found, but keep the strongest of the Camonra here to protect the tribe should this... this dragon return."

"It will be done, Father, and what of your quarters?" Adheron asked.

The concubines began removing the poles for Tobor's war tent from the back of their Azrodh, but Tobor waved them off.

"Lurenda, bring me my pouch," said Tobor. "I will venture into the mountains to seek out the Watcher there."

"Father," Adheron said. "Do not go into the mountains alone."

"Much has passed between Watcher and Camon. To ask for help from Watchers now may do little more than invoke their wrath, but I will do what I must to protect the tribe, my son," Tobor answered. "Go now and lead the Camonra in my absence; give them hope that all is not lost."

Adheron straightened. "Yes, Father!" he said. He looked around him, and Tobor knew he could see the fear in the eyes of his people, a sight he had never seen before. "I will be strong, Father."

"I've no doubt of that, Adheron," Tobor replied. "Now go."

Tobor left the encampment of the Camonra and traveled on his mount due north through the foothills of the Faceless Mountains until a rumbling could be heard in the mountainside itself.

"You are here," said Tobor. He glanced around for any sign of the Watcher of the Mountain. "I am sure that you move the land beneath me. Show yourself, brother of my father!"

The mountainside shook until a crack began in the stone, crumbling open wider and wider until it swallowed up whole chunks of earth and stone, causing Tobor to step back. The rumble slowed to a standstill, and Tophian appeared from the depths.

"Bastard child of Amphileph, what do you want?" Tophian yelled, lowering his staff toward Tobor.

Tobor bristled in response to this form of welcome. "I am Tobor, leader of the Camonra!" he shouted.

"I know what you are!" said Tophian. "But what do you want from me?"

Tobor stepped back and swallowed his pride. "Our father has created a winged creature with teeth the size of daggers and claws that can rip a Camon in half. Our weapons barely pierce its scaly armor, and I fear that without your help, it will destroy my tribe," Tobor began.

"Your creator is mad, and his magic is as black as it is strong," Tophian said. "He's made good on his threat to unleash doom upon this world, and this Angrodha—this black-hearted dragon—it is only the beginning. The Angrodha makes no distinction between man and Camon. It cares for nothing, lives for nothing but to consume all that is not of Amphileph. It will no sooner destroy the Camonra before it makes its feast upon men."

"And there is more," Tobor said.

"Speak it," Tophian replied.

"The Father has wet the land with black poison," Tobor said. "A terrible plague has been set loose upon us all. We flee the jungles not because we want the lands of men, but to save our wives and children." Tobor looked at the ground. "I beg of you to help us."

Tophian's face softened. He walked around Tobor, looking him over.

"I have often pondered whether a soul resided in you, or if there was any redeemable quality that might warrant the mercy of the Watchers. Amphileph's deceit created you, and with such a beginning, little thought was given to your place among the Creator's creatures."

"I have thought many times of our creation and the Father's place in it," Tobor replied. "Our distance from the Father has opened our eyes to many things. If you could know the wonders we have seen in our struggles to free ourselves from our bondage to Amphileph, then you would know that we have found new meaning to our lives. We follow Amphileph no more."

"What then *is* your destination?" Tophian asked.

Tobor stopped, and his mouth came open as if to answer, but no sound emerged. His brain reeled with thoughts. He looked down almost embarrassed at his loss for words. Then he locked eyes with Tophian, and maybe for the first time in his life, he spoke boldly of a new time for the Camonra.

"Great Watcher, this is a question indeed," Tobor said. "If only answering would make it come to pass."

Tobor placed one foot upon a stone and rested his forearm on his thigh armor. He looked down the mountainside toward the Camonra camp, drawing a deep breath and exhaling as if a great weight rested upon his shoulders.

"I dreamed once that we would be a *people*, without fear of our survival, but having hope for our future. We would work a living from the land, and hunt creatures without malice for our survival. We would live in peace with men and they would live in peace with us. We would have our children have their children and their children's children, and die old in the care of our kind." Tobor looked again at Tophian. "I dreamed we would find the true Father that throws the fire from the sky, and we would know him and he would know us."

Tobor turned his face from Tophian, thinking he might wish too much.

There was a long pause, and then Tophian spoke. "Here is a creature of Amphileph's making — a brute of a being whose huge, muscular body easily hides a thinking, feeling being! Men seldom find such revelation! Now I see something more than the brute's stern gaze — now I see the weathered face of a creature clutching but a thread of hope for a better life."

Tobor turned and looked directly into Tophian's eyes.

"You have learned much in your short lives, creature," Tophian said. "You have learned much indeed."

"Could you—will you help us escape the wrath of our Father?" Tobor asked.

"Amphileph has done many a great evil. It appears to me now that the Camonra may number among those whose lives were nearly destroyed by his arrogance."

"I ask this not for me, but for all my people, Watcher," Tobor said.

Tophian walked around to Tobor's side and looked down into the valley. "I'll do this thing for you, Tobor, for I see hope in your words.

Let me go to the men of Moonledge Peak. They will have to be assured of your intentions."

"Yes," Tobor answered. "A Watcher could convince them. They would know that you speak the truth. We will stay clear of men and wait for your return."

Tobor stood up then and faced Tophian. He towered over Tophian, but the Watcher did not flinch. "It's our way to trade something, but I've brought nothing to trade."

"Remain firm in your word, Tobor," Tophian replied. "Know that this alone will repay your debt to me."

"You have my word, and the Camonra will do as I command," Tobor responded. He turned to go down the mountain, but turned back. "How am I to find you when you return?"

"We'll meet here again in four days' time. Leave your camp, and come to me here. We'll discuss what the men of the west have decided."

Tobor grunted. "It will be done." He lowered to one knee and dropped his gaze as he had done so many times before under the iron fist of Amphileph, but unlike all those times, he felt a strange difference in his heart. This Watcher was very much unlike Amphileph. This one had stood his ground without cruelty or abuse.

"I'll not forget this," Tobor said, and then he returned down the mountain.

CHAPTER TWENTY

WAR BEGINS

Making good on his decision, Tophian had proceeded directly to the men of the Moonledge caves, but they received him with great angst. The people had swarmed the council in a panic.

"Lord Tophian, we cannot do battle with this flying creature! And what of the warriors of Candra? Will they not frown greatly on a pact with the Inferiors? This could lump us with our enemies in the eyes of our allies."

Tophian knew as much to be true. "I'm not suggesting that the Camonra live in your midst. Let the Camonra make their camp far away, in the eastern part of the mountains. I could make great caves for them to stay until the threat of the Angrodha has ended."

"My lord, these are the creatures that brought the wrath of the Creator upon us; these Inferiors destroyed our homeland. It is because of them, we are exiled, and because of them, we may never see our families and kindred again. It is a mighty thing that you call upon us to do!"

"Yes," Tophian replied. "A noble thing for sure. These creatures are but pawns in the Watcher's War—it is Amphileph that merits your hatred."

There was a rumbling from the crowd, and Caratacus adjusted his collar; beads of sweat began to form on his now pasty white face.

"My lord, even if we say these things to be so — that these... what do you call them?"

"Camonra," replied Tophian with reserve.

"That these... Camonra... will live in peace with us," Caratacus continued, "we cannot change the minds of the world around us by simply saying that something is decreed to be so!" Our people will live in fear, and that fear will be our decree's undoing. And when that day comes, many will die, I'm afraid."

The rumble of the crowd swelled again, enough so that Caratacus rapped his gavel and commanded quiet in the room.

Tophian thought about the logic of the council's words. Though he wanted it not to be true, the Watchers' War had rippled through all humanity. Here, first hand, were its effects. Tophian looked at each of the councilmen's faces, and the fear and anguish were palpable. He knew then that the deep caves of Moonledge were still too close. "Evliit's heart is broken for the despair of men," he said. "I've made my request as I've promised to do."

Tophian turned slowly around, looking each of them over one last time for a change of heart. He did not storm out with flair. No, Tophian walked out from them quietly, letting the next of the arguments begin before a stunned council, who had expected him to demand his way. He moved to the exit, looking at the faces of the crowd. Only the ignorant among them did not notice the eyes of the Watcher. He wandered out from the council chambers, searching their faces for hope, and acknowledging his own responsibility, however small it might be, for their plight.

As Tophian left the High Council's chamber, the crier announced that the Candrians were arriving from the south. Apparently, a contingent of warriors had been set to defend the construction of an additional outer fortress at the Moonledge caves. Tophian moved up against one of the walls just outside the chamber and waited, straining to hear their conversation over the rumble of the chamber.

Mordher and Borian entered, arguing.

"What's needed is a great wall to separate us from the Inferiors," Mordher said. "We would hold the high ground and hold back any against us, and I should control the weapon."

"The creatures that move against us are foul, brother," Borian replied. "We would need a great wall indeed. And of this weapon — this Sword — does Ardhios have other news?"

"Bah! The fool fears its possession!" Mordher laughed. "He would have this lot of politicians keep it! Let him find like-minded fools that will lay stone. Let him build our wall! Let him build it for the rest of his days!"

"He'll do it just to spite you!" said Borian, laughing in return.

Tophian took the opportunity to move to them, and his quick movement into their space caught their attention. Tophian noticed that their hands found the hilts of their swords and their faces lost their smiles.

"I apologize for my intrusion," he said. "My name is Tophian, and I've come to ask for your help."

Mordher and Borian relaxed only slightly. Mordher looked over Tophian's clothing, and he bristled. "What's that to us, wizard?"

Tophian tolerated Mordher. It was necessary, to achieve his objectives. "The Camonra of the east have asked me to intercede on their behalf," Tophian said. "They've come to the land of men to escape the new dangers to the south. They wish to live in peace."

"They've a strange way of showing their intentions," Borian said. "There's word that they terrorize the people in the eastern valley, and we've also heard tell of them attacking here in Moonledge."

"There are apparently factions within their tribe. This Camon goes by the name of Tobor. I've met with him, and he's assured me that his tribe has separated themselves from Amphileph and wishes a peaceful coexistence with men."

"The Camonra? They are *all* but minions of Amphileph!" exclaimed Borian. "Are they not the very ones that attacked Rion?"

"Tobor and his warriors were once deceived by Amphileph, attacking Rion in his name, but that has been years past, warrior. Their situation has changed. They no longer swear allegiance to him."

"Bred to kill, those were," Mordher said. "What kind of peace can you make with such savages?"

"The Camonra are under attack themselves," Tophian interjected. "They have called on me to enlist the assistance of men to defend their tribe against an Angrodha."

"An Angrodha?" Mordher replied. "What manner of creature is this?"

"A winged raptor, a dragon — it is yet another of Amphileph's abominations."

"So their master finds no love left for them?" Mordher laughed. "He has created something to destroy another of his own making? It's either genius or madness—hard to say which."

"Amphileph is the source of this evil, not the Camonra, and the Angrodha represents a threat to men and Camonra alike," answered Tophian.

Mordher eyed Tophian. "Then these . . . Camonra . . . would be indebted to us?"

Tophian did not like the tone of the inquiry, but it represented a break in the ice. "All the people would be indebted to you, warrior. Your names would be heralded far and wide."

"But the *Camonra*—they would be indebted to us, yes?" Mordher repeated.

"Yes, I suppose they would," Tophian acquiesced. Tophian could see the wheels turning in Mordher's head. His desire for power obviously drove his decision-making, and Tophian knew that such a man's loyalties change without warning, but he was resolved to move forward.

"We will kill this creature, this Angrodha, if the Camonra swear allegiance to Candra!" said Mordher.

Tophian did not think that there was much chance of either, but he could present it to Tobor. "I will make your offer known to the Camonra," he replied.

"Let them draw out the creature, and our archers will fill the sky with arrows, and we will hack it to pieces!" Mordher said.

"We'll see if such a creature will stand against the Army of Candra!" echoed Borian. Their bravado did little to impress Tophian, for the potential danger they so easily accepted told volumes of their understanding of the Angrodha. Nevertheless, their offer represented possibly the only chance he had to stop whatever Amphileph was attempting with the attack on the Camonra.

"When could your warriors be ready to travel east?" Tophian asked.

"We'll gather our supplies and be ready to move tomorrow. Borian, have the captains bring fifty men to carry supplies back to the camp."

Borian nodded. "With your leave," he said.

"Make haste," Mordher said, and Borian marched away.

"I'm going to find a hot bath and love among the wenches of Moonledge, wizard!" Mordher said, with a wily smile. "Would you care to join me?"

"No, warrior," Tophian replied. "I'll join you and your soldiers in the valley tomorrow."

"You don't know what you're missing, wizard," laughed Mordher. "The women of Moonledge could show you some real magic!"

"I go to rest in the cool of the caves, warrior. Tomorrow, then," Tophian said. He made his way up the hill toward the caves of Moonledge.

Mordher walked the opposite path toward the brothel on the western side of Moonledge Keep until Tophian had made his way up the long row of steps leading into the darkness of the cave entrance; then he turned and hurried to the valley below.

He neared the outer edge of the warriors' encampment. "Soldiers of

Candra!" he called out, surprising the two soldiers on watch. They immediately went for their swords, but Mordher raised his blade under the chin of the one closest to him. "If I had been the enemy, you'd be dead!" Mordher said. "Let me get that close again before you question my approach and I'll kill you myself!"

"Yes, my lord!" they replied in loose unison. "Forgive us!"

Mordher dragged the blade under his chin, nicking him, and then put it away. It was a small cut, but it began to bleed, and the soldier pinched the cut together with his fingers.

Mordher squatted and tore a piece of goat from a spit over the small fire. "Get Borian!"

"Yes, my lord!" the lower-ranking soldier said. He pulled a torch from one of the holders and ran toward the encampment.

"Bring me some salt," Mordher commanded. He tore away a steaming chunk of the hindquarter with his teeth, attempting to avoid burning his lips, and then wolfed it down.

"Yes, my lord," the soldier replied. He let go of the clotted cut and pulled a small leather pouch from his belt, handing it to his commander. "And we've ale for you, my lord."

Mordher dipped his fingers into the pouch, sprinkled the meat with salt, and handed it back to the soldier. Then he tore off another chunk. "One can never underestimate the value of salt," he added.

"No, my lord," the soldier replied, handing the commander a wooden mug of ale he poured from a keg sitting upon a small cart that some of the town's wenches had brought down from Moonledge. The black, tar-like ale ran slowly from the spigot, thick as pitch.

Mordher sniffed it, grimaced, and took a long swallow anyway.

"Moonledge brew," he muttered, wiping his mouth with the back of his hand. "If the gods wanted to punish a man, they'd make him drink this."

Borian appeared, adjusting his armor as if woken from a sleep. "You called, my lord?" he asked.

"The wizard will take us to the Inferiors tomorrow, so that we might kill this creature that hunts them," Mordher said.

"Yes, my lord," said Borian.

Mordher slugged another gulp of the ale, eyeing Borian as if waiting for him to say more. "The wizard will take us to the very heart of our enemy, yes?"

"Yes, my lord."

"Maybe the Inferiors have more than one enemy to worry about, eh?"

Borian looked at him for a moment, and then he raised his brows in recognition of where Mordher was leading.

"Have the archers ready their bows, and the fighters their swords," Mordher said. "Surely, the wizard gives us an opportunity to claim the Sword of Evliit for our efforts. I think tomorrow will be a glorious day!" A large smile slowly formed on Mordher's face, mirrored by Borian.

"Glorious indeed!"

*　*　*

The following morning, Tophian met Mordher and his warriors in their encampment below Moonledge. Mordher insisted that Tophian take one of the horses and ride with them. Tophian agreed, wanting to conserve his spiritual energies for the encounter with the Angrodha, though he really did not care for riding.

He led them around the mountain range east, until on the fourth day, just as Tophian had promised Tobor, they arrived at the foothills near the Camonra encampment.

"I will go alone to the Camonra camp," said Tophian. "With tensions what they are, let me tell them of our plans."

"As you wish," Mordher replied. "We'll wait here for you."

"We'll not tarry," said Tophian. "When the last of the sunlight tips the crest of the Black Mountains, come to the eastern end of this mountain range. The Camonra encampment is just around the bend. We'll group together with their forces, and take the attack to the Angrodha."

"We look forward to it," Mordher said.

As Tophian rode away, Borian leaned in close to Mordher. "What do you make of it, Mordher?"

"The Camonra are weakened, running. This Watcher has their trust. We are at the crossroads of a new era, Borian," Mordher said.

"What are your orders?" asked Borian.

"Gather the captains," Mordher said.

*　*　*

Tophian rode first to the path leading up the little plateau where he and Tobor had met, but Tobor was not there. He waited for a short time, and then he became concerned, so he began his descent into the valley below him further east. The sun was at the point where the Candrian warriors would be on the way.

The last few days had been taxing. The Angrodha was strong and agile, and it would continue to grow in size without greatly affecting that agility. It was no foe to take lightly, even given his powers as a Watcher. He debated getting Mategaladh involved, but his dear friend might have expended more than anyone else in binding Amphileph, so great was his commitment to stopping that madness. Involving Mategaladh now might serve only to get him killed, for Tophian knew that if Mategaladh had recovered even half his powers, he would never back down from a fight. He did not want to chance it. He would have to stop the Angrodha.

Tophian reined in his horse and bowed his head in prayer.

"*Creator... how could things have gone so wrong? Forgive us, mighty One, if our actions have in any way turned one so brilliant — one once so devoted to You — into an enemy of Your creation.*"

He let the words drift into the cold mountain air, then exhaled slowly, as though releasing a weight he could no longer bear. With a gentle nudge of his heel, he urged the horse toward the ridge, hoping for a clearer view of the valley below.

Such brilliance suffered little from the imperfections of men, Tophian thought. Amphileph had once been the most gifted among them — sharp of mind, fierce of spirit, unwavering in purpose. But when he began to claim that men had become a blight upon creation, when his intolerance hardened into certainty, he grew steadily bent on their destruction... and on cleansing the world of their existence.

And when the Spellmakers declared they would end the time of men and usher in the reign of the Camonra, the ancient bond between Watchers and Spellmakers shattered in an instant.

Amphileph had crossed the line with Evliit the moment he created the Camonra — his *warriors*, his "superior race." Evliit would not tolerate such arrogance. The notion that Amphileph could fashion a superior race, a replacement for humankind... these were matters for the Creator alone.

Who did Amphileph think he was?

Tophian could see the Candrian warriors approaching from the southwest. He met them at the foot of the mountain. Mordher pulled his horse's bit back with enough force that the horse whinnied in pain.

"What of the Camonra?" Mordher asked.

"Tobor wasn't there," Tophian replied. "I fear the worst." Tophian thought he saw a smirk on Mordher's face, but dismissed it. "We go to the

Camonra camp."

"Of course," Mordher responded. "Candrians!" he cried, and the rumble of their horses signaled their presence at his side like a storm.

"Follow me back up the mountainside!" said Tophian. "We'll take the high ground."

As they rounded the mountain, the Camonra camp came into view below. The Angrodha circled high above it — and just below Tophian's position — so close that he ducked behind an outcropping of stone to avoid being seen. But with two hundred Candrians on horseback behind him, concealment was impossible. The Angrodha had spotted them.

It wheeled once more and descended, landing on a narrow ledge along one of the ridges of the Faceless Mountains, just beneath Tophian and the Candrians. It screeched — a piercing, metallic cry — and the echo rolled through the valley twice before fading.

Tophian leaned out, trying to get a clearer view of the Camonra camp.

Several of the Camonra had already taken cover among the foothills, while others remained in the open — one of them unmistakably Tobor.

"Archers! Dismount!" Mordher shouted.

About fifty archers swung off their horses in practiced motion and drew their bows, eyes fixed on the ridges below.

*   *   *

In the failing light, Tobor could just see the riders upon the ridge and yelled encouragement to the Camonra. "The Watcher has found us!" he cried. "Let them draw the Angrodha's attention!"

Tobor's excitement ended quickly, seeing Adheron's eyes widen and turn skyward.

"Father!" Adheron yelled. "Run!"

Tobor ran for cover in the brush, and Adheron moved to his father's aid. The Angrodha swooped down upon the clearing, clipping the treetops with one of its hind legs. The trees exploded into splinters, and a heavy branch slammed into Adheron's face and chest, hurling him to the ground. He vanished beneath the crashing debris.

"No!" Tobor roared, sprinting toward his son. His massive arms strained as he heaved at the fallen branch, desperate to reach Adheron, oblivious to the Angrodha's looming shadow.

"Camonra!" Tobor bellowed, hoping their assault might distract the predator long enough for him to free his son.

The Camonra responded instantly, shouting war cries as they loosed a volley of crossbow bolts into the creature's scaled hide. Tobor seized the moment, wrenching the branch aside.

Adheron lay bruised and battered, motionless beneath the debris. A deep gash split his brow and lips, blood pouring freely. Tobor reached for him—but the Angrodha had endured all the bolts it intended to. It attacked.

Its vast shadow engulfed Tobor. The creature's wingspan had grown to nearly fifty feet since their last encounter. It beat its wings once, a thunderous gust that blasted dust into Tobor's mouth and eyes, blinding him.

He wiped his eyes just in time to see the Angrodha lift briefly into the air, then crash down among the attacking Camonra. They scattered in panic as the beast lowered itself onto its forearms and sniffed the ground.

It snorted, then cawed — a harsh, triumphant sound — as though pleased to have found their scent.

*　　*　　*

"Do you have torches?" Tophian asked Mordher.

"Yes," Mordher replied. "Torches!" he shouted.

"Light them and draw the Angrodha to me!" Tophian commanded.

Tophian dismounted and stepped into a clearing on the mountainside. Ten or so men pulled black, tar-soaked stumps of wood from their saddlebags and struck flints to ignite them. The moment the torches flared to life, the Angrodha's head snapped toward the light. It cawed sharply and leapt skyward.

"Come to me!" Tophian shouted. Mordher waved the torchbearers forward.

Tophian lowered his eyes, pressing his hands together at his chest. Then he lifted them — and the mountainside trembled. A murmur rippled through the Candrians.

"What is this?" Borian whispered.

"I know not," Mordher answered, backing away with the others as loose stones shook free and hovered above the ground. One massive stone drifted beside Mordher; he tapped it with the tip of his sword. It rotated, weightless yet immense, and he quickly stepped back.

Above them, the Angrodha folded its wings into a killing dive.

"Stand clear, but be ready!" Tophian called.

"The creature comes!" Mordher shouted, pointing as the Angrodha plunged toward them, claws opening, wings spreading wide enough to blot out the moon.

"Ready!" Mordher cried to his warriors — but many had already lost their nerve. Torches fell from trembling hands, igniting patches of winter grass as men fled in panic.

The Angrodha screamed.

In the blaze of torchlight, Mordher saw Tophian's face — calm, resolute, unflinching.

Tophian slammed his hands together.

The stones shot forward like thunderbolts. Smaller ones punched clean through the Angrodha's leathery wings; a massive stone struck its face with a sickening crack, snapping its head back and sending the creature reeling.

The Angrodha folded in on itself and crashed down upon Tophian. One enormous wing struck him full-force, hurling him violently against the mountainside. His body slid off a sheer ridge and disappeared into the darkness below.

Mordher saw Tophian's body lying lifeless below and called to his warriors.

The Angrodha twitched and kicked, struggling to regain its bearings. "Attack!" he roared.

Battle cries erupted around the clearing as the Candrians loosed their arrows, but the creature's scales were too thick; the shafts lodged only in the softer flesh of its forearms and legs.

The stinging pricks only roused the Angrodha further. It heaved itself upright, and the soldiers rushed in with swords drawn — only to be swept aside as the beast lashed out with a single forearm, flinging a dozen men off the mountainside.

The pikemen surged forward, thrusting at its less-scaled underbelly. The Angrodha roared in fury, rolled onto its belly to shield itself, and clawed at the mountainside, kicking four more soldiers into the air.

From the encampment below, Tobor saw the chaos unfolding above — torn between carrying Adheron to safety and joining the assault.

"Camonra!" he bellowed.

He sprinted toward the foot of the mountain, and his warriors thundered after him.

Twice the Angrodha tried to take flight, but the Candrians swarmed it, hacking and stabbing. Enraged, the creature turned on them, snatching up attackers and tearing them apart. Bodies continued to fall from the mountainside.

"We take too many losses!" Borian shouted to Mordher.

Mordher's face twisted — disgust at the creature, and at the retreat he knew must come. But Borian was right; his army meant more than his promise to the Watcher.

"Retreat!" Mordher bellowed.

The order was met with relief. The remaining Candrians broke and ran for their lives.

Mordher could see that the Angrodha was bleeding from several wounds, but it looked more enraged than weakened. Instead of taking to the air, it turned on his warriors, snapping them up with claw and teeth.

Just when it seemed the Candrians would be wiped out entirely, the Camonra reached the mountainside. Mordher watched in astonishment as their massive crossbows punched through the Angrodha's thick hide far more effectively than Candrian arrows ever had — especially at such close range.

They fell upon the creature with a ferocity Mordher had only ever seen them unleash against men. The Angrodha shrieked, wheeled, and turned its fury toward the Camonra, abandoning the fleeing Candrians altogether.

"We must flee now while we have the chance!" Borian yelled to Mordher, who had stopped to watch the melee.

"Wait, brother!" Mordher snapped. "Wait and see!"

He and Borian ducked behind a head-high outcropping of igneous rock.

Borian called for the Candrians to regroup as the Angrodha traded wound for mangling with the Camonra.

Though the beast snapped at him again and again, Tobor bounded from rock to cliff to boulder, narrowly escaping its clashing teeth — a spectacle no warrior of Candra had ever witnessed. The Angrodha killed many of his warriors, until Tobor leapt onto its back and drove his great axe deep into its spine.

He twisted, straining to free the blade from the dragon's thick scales. The Angrodha shrieked in agony and lurched skyward, carrying Tobor with it. He tried to cling to its shoulder and swing again, but the creature soared into the night. Tobor slipped away, and he and his axe crashed onto the mountainside with a sickening thud.

Several Camonra rushed to him, lifting him from the ground. Though shaken, Tobor lived. The Camonra howled their defiance at the fleeing creature, clanging their weapons and cheering their general's courage.

"I must go to Adheron!" Tobor shouted, forcing them to set him down.

Mordher watched the Angrodha vanish into the southern dark. He watched the Camonra celebrate — and his blood boiled. He snatched a bow from one of his archers, drew it so hard that several horsehairs snapped, and loosed the arrow.

It flew between two Camonra and struck Tobor just beneath the right scapula.

Tobor staggered, turned, and locked eyes with Mordher. The arrowhead protruded from his chest. He raised a hand to point at Mordher — then collapsed. Two or three Camonra tried to catch him, but he slipped through their hands and slid down the slope in a heap. They scrambled to turn him over, but Mordher knew from their faces that his arrow had done its work.

The remaining Camonra screamed their battle cries and charged toward Mordher, who still held the bow before him.

"Archers!" Borian shouted, and a rain of arrows fell upon the Camonra, killing many — but the rest came on, heedless of their wounds.

"Ride!" Mordher roared.

The Candrians mounted and fled down the mountainside. The Camonra leapt among them, ripping soldiers from their saddles, flashing across Mordher's vision like shadows with teeth. He spurred his horse without mercy, and the Candrians raced toward Moonledge until the Camonra's battle cries finally faded behind them

*　　*　　*

Tophian regained consciousness only minutes after Tobor fell. He woke to the war cries of the Camonra chasing the Candrians west. Forcing himself upright, he heard the wailing of the females and children in the camp below. They were sifting through the wreckage of the Camonra encampment and had found the profusely bleeding, unconscious Adheron — and they had assumed the worst.

The younger warriors emerged from their hiding places, eyes fixed on the sky, fearing the Angrodha's return. Then they found Tobor's body, and mourning erupted into chaos.

They surrounded him, lifted his body above their heads, and carried him toward the center of the camp. The concubines screamed in grief, and from his vantage point Tophian could clearly see the arrow jutting from Tobor's chest. More Camonra returned from the chase, shouting Mordher's treachery and mistakenly claiming the attackers were soldiers of Highwood.

The camp's grief turned instantly to hatred, and Tophian knew the mob would not listen to reason — not now, not from him.

His injuries were life-threatening, and the spiritual force he had used to hurl the stones had drained his ability to heal. He prayed for strength, trying to clear his mind of the pain, but the nerves in his back burned like fire, and the bruising across his ribs made every breath a struggle.

Drawing on every shred of concentration he had left, Tophian pushed his aura outward. He felt — and heard — the bones in his back shifting, popping back into place.

The earth loosened beneath him, parting to let him sink into the mountain's core. He moved through the stone, deeper and deeper, until he slipped into the hollow of a cavern. There, on the cool, wet floor, he collapsed in darkness.

His aura flickered out, and the mountain sealed itself behind him.

*　*　*

Far to the north, Mategaladh woke with a jolt, seized by the unmistakable sense that something was terribly wrong. He pushed himself from his bed and made his way to his prayer room. The incense burning there wrapped around him like a balm, easing the ache in his bones.

On the wall hung a woodcutting of the original Watchers. Mategaladh paused before it.

It was sadly happy, he thought — carved just after the Calling, when nineteen mortals had begun their discipleship under Evliit. A time before the divisions of Watcher and Spellmaker. A time when faces shone with hope.

His strength had been returning these past weeks, and Mategaladh knew he had been spared from death at Amphileph's Binding for a purpose. Now, he felt that purpose stirring.

"Creator, thank You for the life I breathe today," he began. "I thank You for the Binding of evil, for the bountiful harvest when the moons of Sapath are in the house of Ardidhus. I stand ready to use every power

You have given me to save mankind from destruction, and to carry on the good work of Evliit.

"I renew my strength in You, my Creator, and once more I claim the power You have promised. Let me be the force You have made me to be, in this time, according to Your plan — to command all things that grow upon Erathe.

"Show me that I might—"

He stopped.

A sudden pressure filled his mind. Images flickered — Tophian, the Camonra, the mountains.

"Tophian?" he whispered, narrowing his eyes, trying to focus the vision.

Then a sharp, electric pain shot through him.

"Oh!" he gasped, as though pricked by a needle. "Spirit, come to me now! I must come to Tophian's aid."

The moment the words left his lips, power surged through him. The weakness that had plagued him evaporated. Warmth blossomed in his gut and spread through his limbs, sweat breaking across his brow.

Tophian was in danger. Grave danger. Something had gone terribly wrong south of the Faceless Mountains. Mategaladh could feel it — in the land, in the air, in the trembling of the spiritual fabric itself.

Amphileph had done something they had not foreseen. And though Mategaladh could not yet judge the Binding's integrity, he knew with certainty that something… some evil… had slipped free.

"Keep him safe," he prayed, rising to his feet. He looked around the room for his things.

He had to leave at once.

Tophian was in dire trouble.

*　*　*

Adheron woke to the wailing of the concubines — all but Lurenda, who knelt beside him, carefully stitching his torn face. She paused often to wipe away the silent tears that blurred her vision.

"The Angrodha!" he gasped, jerking forward, stopped only by her steadying hand.

"My son," Lurenda whispered. "Everything has changed."

He searched her face — and saw a sorrow deeper than he had ever known in her.

"It has taken Father?"

She lowered the needle he had caused her to pull back, tears welling again.

"Let me finish," she murmured. She leaned close, tying the knot with practiced care, biting the horsehair thread she had scavenged from the bows of fallen Candrian archers.

"The bowstring makes a fine stitch, my son." She set her hands in her lap.

Adheron touched the fresh seam, feeling the torn flesh beneath.

"Tobor… Father!" he cried, the words strained by the tight pull of the stitch.

"Yes, my son. Tobor is gone."

Adheron turned his head away to hide his tears, but the pain — of body and spirit — overwhelmed him. His chest heaved, and a cry tore from him for all to hear.

"The Father has struck at us even from his prison!"

"No, my son," Lurenda said firmly. "The arrow that killed your father flew from human hands — as surely as the Angrodha was meant to kill us all."

Adheron pushed himself upright.

"What do you mean?"

"The humans of Highwood have betrayed us. It was seen by the Camonra — by our own eyes. They struck down your father even as he saved us." Her voice trembled.

"They fled west. We know not where."

Adheron screamed, the force of it reopening his wound so that blood ran anew.

"They have gone back to their Highwood!"

He drew his sword.

"Camonra!"

The warriors gathered instantly, their rage drowning out the cries of the females until Adheron raised his blade for silence.

"We go to Highwood!" he roared. "We will go to Highwood, and we will kill the humans!"

A thunderous roar answered him — but Lurenda's voice cut through it.

"Will you not stay and bury Tobor?"

Adheron's eyes burned.

"Give my father to the heavens with fire! Let his embers mix with the blackness of night! Let the Camonra remember great Tobor and avenge his death! Bring me fire!"

A warrior thrust a torch into his hand. Adheron tore a dead branch from a nearby tree.

"A pyre for him — our worthy leader!"

The Camonra ripped branches free, piling them over Tobor's body. Adheron cast the torch upon the kindling. Flames leapt high, forcing them back from the heat.

"We go to Highwood!" Adheron cried. "Bring me my father's mount, for I command the Camonra now! Have the females and children follow! We leave this land and make our revenge on the humans!"

He pointed his sword westward and strode toward Highwood.

And the Camonra — warriors, females, and children alike — followed him.

CHAPTER TWENTY-ONE

COSTLY PROTECTION

Citanth attempted to communicate with Amphileph within the Binding, but nothing reached him. Amphileph had lain in his own vomit for days, and Citanth had begun to fear he was dying. His breaths came in short, ragged bursts, and insects crawled freely across his skin.

The black rain had nearly halved the Camonra in the northern camp. Citanth estimated fewer than three thousand loyal remained.

Though the twisted mutations had slithered westward, the Camonra were convinced the horror could begin again at any moment. Amphileph's zealots seized on that fear, binding the survivors to him with fanatic devotion. They cried out for forgiveness, unable to understand what sin had earned them their Father's wrath. They sacrificed doubters, burning them in Amphileph's name, but he did not answer.

Citanth watched their twisted faith with growing despair. They believed they had caused Amphileph's sickness — that their penance might restore him. Day and night they beat themselves with whips, carved their chests with knives, and wailed for absolution.

He watched until he could bear no more. Their misguided love hollowed him out, stealing the last hope he had for forgiveness from the true Creator. His mind frayed under the strain, and the days blurred into a nightmare of flames, sacrifices, and howling.

On the fifth day, Amphileph rolled over.

The Camonra erupted in frenzied celebration. They crowded the Binding's edge — just as lightning exploded within the dome. Forks of white fire rippled across the inner surface, growing brighter and brighter. A storm cloud gathered at the top of the dome, swelling until it blotted out everything inside. The flashes intensified until they burned exposed skin and blinded the onlookers. The thunder became a continuous roar, driving the less faithful fleeing to the northern camp.

Just before dawn, the storm ceased. The dark vapor thinned. Amphileph's body was gone, and the door to his great Temple was sealed. A thin wisp of smoke drifted from the vents in the dome. The Camonra slowly returned, sleeping on the ground around the Binding, fasting until their Father reappeared.

Three days passed.

Then Amphileph stepped from his Temple.

His garments shimmered with such splendor that Citanth could hardly look at him. The Camonra fell prostrate around the Binding. Citanth emerged from his hut, shielding his eyes with his good arm.

"Citanth!" Amphileph's voice boomed.

"Here, Lord Amphileph!"

"Our brother Tophian remains behind."

"Lord?"

"Not all the Watchers perished making this cage!" Amphileph thundered.

"I have seen Tophian through the eyes of the Angrodha. He hides in the mountains to the north."

"What do you command?"

"I must finish what I began — but the old fool stands in my way. Take the faithful and destroy him. He is weak. Vulnerable. Strike before he regains his strength."

"Yes, my lord."

Amphileph's voice rose, echoing across the camp.

"Go forth into all the lands of Erathe. Destroy this pestilence that is mankind wherever you find it. They flee into mountains and hills, into wood and dale, for they cannot return to Rion. Hunt them. Kill them. And if you find any who once called us brother, kill them as well — for they brought this fate upon themselves by standing against me. Do these things and bring me the Sword of the Watch! For I alone am worthy to wield it!"

He gestured toward the Camonra.

"These, my children, will aid you. There is purity in the Camon heart. Use the Angrodha. Kill the man Galbard. Have one of the creatures bring the Sword to me."

Citanth opened his mouth to speak, but Amphileph cut him off.

"Do not test me, Citanth! Have I not shown you how I deal with ineptness?"

The memory of his slaughtered brethren — their bodies rotting in the sun — flashed through Citanth's mind.

"I restore you to your position over the Camonra," Amphileph said. "But fail me again, and you will join them."

Citanth turned to the Camonra, still prone before the Binding.

"Arm yourselves!"

They scattered to their huts. Citanth did the same, returning moments later in armor. The Camonra assembled in ordered ranks.

He adjusted his breastplate, donned his helmet, and climbed onto a half-built retaining wall meant for Amphileph's coming colonnade. He raised his good hand.

Silence fell.

"Camonra!" he shouted. "Make ready for war!"

The ranks erupted in ecstatic fury, clanging weapons until the sound nearly drowned out Amphileph's cackling laughter.

Citanth bowed low. The Camonra fell silent again.

Amphileph stepped to the edge of the Binding.

"Yes! Yes! War!" he cried. "Will you tarry in killing the infidels who have abandoned their maker?"

"No!" the Camonra roared. "The infidels will die!"

"Fear not!" Amphileph screamed. "I will send the Angrodha to protect you! Go first to the mountains and destroy the Watcher!"

"Yes, Father!" the Camonra bellowed.

Citanth mounted an Azrodh and rode out before them. The Camonra ranks fell in behind him, marching west.

*　*　*

Mordher and Borian arrived at the entrance to Moonledge Peak, startling the craftsmen of Rion with the thunder of their horses' hooves on the rocky foothills.

"How can this be?" Mordher demanded of one of them. "How have you set such stone?"

The arched temple entrance towered eighty feet high. Six dozen steps rose into three monumental openings, each seventy feet tall, carved into the mountainside. The immense stones seemed impossible — beyond even Ardhios's greatest feats.

"We have done so with the aid of the Watcher called Tophian," one mason replied.

The name tightened Mordher's throat.

"The wizard?" Mordher asked.

"You know of him?" said another. "His power is beyond compare."

Mordher and Borian exchanged a wary glance.

"So we have heard," Mordher said. "But we had not seen these works with our own eyes."

Borian stepped forward.

"We must speak to your lord at once. Can you arrange an audience?"

"Our council oversees the Keep of Moonledge," the mason replied. "I will go to them immediately. Whom shall I name?"

"The Candrians, Mordher and Borian," Borian said. "It is urgent."

"At once, my lord. My men will show you where to water your horses."

The remaining masons guided them through the sally port on the right side of the thick curtain wall. The Candrian soldiers dismounted and watered their horses at a well in the center of the craftsmen's courtyard. The masons kept silent, and when Mordher and Borian passed, they looked away.

Mordher pulled Borian aside.

"We have set things in motion that cannot be undone, brother."

Borian's face tightened.

"That we have. What now is our play?"

"The Camonra will seek vengeance — that is certain," Mordher said. "But these people may be persuaded to thin their ranks."

"How so?"

"We warn their council of the coming attack. I will demand the Watcher's weapon for their defense. Then we return to Candra while they make war upon the Camonra. We test our strength best from behind our own walls — and against a weakened foe."

Borian stared at him.

"You would set the Camonra upon Moonledge? You go too far, brother."

Mordher seized him by the collar and yanked him close. Borian's hand flew to his weapon in reflex.

"You are in this as well," Mordher hissed.

Several Candrian soldiers turned at the commotion, eyes widening. Mordher noticed their attention and barked at them. "Be about your business or deal with me!"

The soldiers scattered, suddenly very interested in anything that wasn't their commanders' quarrel.

"Let go of me," Borian hissed through clenched teeth. "Or will your temper foul even this chance?"

Mordher released him with a shove and spat on the ground.

"Don't pretend I stand alone in this. Or I'll make it so."

Before Borian could answer, a mason pushed through the Candrian ranks.

"The council is assembling," he said. "This way."

"Of course," Borian replied, straightening his tunic. He followed the mason, Mordher close behind.

They crossed the courtyard and ascended the steps into the Keep's opening — a vast, covered hall of soaring arches and carved stone. Sculptures of fallen Rion warriors stood in various stages of completion. Apprentices swept dust and stone chips from beneath the master sculptors' feet.

"Follow me," the mason said, guiding them behind another stairway that climbed toward an upper deck hidden by scaffolding.

"Careful — construction is constant these days. Everyone is excited about the new apse."

He gestured toward the hemispherical dome carved into the mountain, its curved walls opening into four long naves lit by torches. Their footsteps echoed through the stone corridors as they continued deeper until they reached the entrance to the council chamber.

The chamber buzzed with movement and hushed voices. The council was already assembled.

The crier's voice rang out:

"Mordher and Borian of Candra!"

Caratacus sat at the head of the table.

"I am Caratacus, and I welcome you to Moonledge."

Mordher and Borian halted before the council.

"We bring sad tidings," Borian said. "The Camonra march toward you. They bring war."

A ripple of alarm swept the chamber — a rising murmur like locust wings. Caratacus raised his hand.

"Silence."

The room stilled.

He fixed his gaze on Borian.

"How is it you know this, Candrians?"

"We traveled east," Borian said, "to the valley that splits the Faceless

Mountains. There we saw the Camonra with our own eyes. They come toward you — and they mean you harm, as they did when they marched on Rion."

"It has been said that the Camonra live in peace in the southern part of Etharath, and that the time of Amphileph's reign is past," said Caratacus. "What could bring them north to this place?"

"Conquest, still, my lord — but there is more," Borian replied. "A creature of the ancients — an Angrodha — accompanies them. My brothers and I have come to warn your people."

At this, the chamber erupted in alarm. Caratacus rose sharply to his feet, eyes narrowing — not in disbelief, but in the grim recognition of a truth he had hoped never to hear spoken aloud.

"Silence!"

He slammed the gavel against the stone tabletop, the crack echoing through the hall.

"You have seen the Angrodha?"

"Yes, lord," Borian said. "And I wish I had not. The ancient stories do not begin to describe the terror it brings. Our weapons were useless against it."

Mordher paced the length of the council table, meeting each councilor's eyes. He saw fear — and opportunity tightening around him like a snare he himself had set.

"If only we had a greater weapon," he said, voice low and deliberate. "Something truly powerful. Then I would strike down this monster for you."

Caratacus chewed his lip, thinking.

"What if I could give you Evliit's sword?"

Mordher spun toward him. The chamber erupted again until he raised a commanding hand.

"If this is true, then now is the time to produce it. In my hands, it could mean the difference between victory and defeat."

The chatter swelled once more.

"Quiet!" Caratacus roared, pounding the gavel until Mordher feared it would splinter. At last the room stilled.

"How much time do we have?"

"A day, perhaps two," Borian answered.

Caratacus exhaled heavily.

"You leave us little time to act. You would take up Evliit's Sword to aid us in our defense?"

"Of course!" Mordher cut in. "I would wield the mighty blade against all who make war upon men!"

Caratacus looked around the council, jaw tight. Then:

"Bring the Sword."

Mordher's pulse hammered. After all his maneuvering, they were simply going to hand it to him.

Two acolytes moved behind the council table. A Rionese Elder stepped forward, facing a great tapestry. He lifted his hands, and the acolytes drew the tapestry aside. Another curtain rose, revealing a marble alcove lined with carved figures of the Watchers. At its center stood a statue of Evliit, hands open over a marble chest resting on an altar. A faint hum — or perhaps the echo of the priest's chant — seemed to vibrate through the alcove as the chest was revealed.

The priest began to chant in the ancient tongue. Four warriors retrieved long poles from either side of the alcove, sliding them through rings on the chest. With effort, they lifted it to shoulder height and carried it before the council table. An acolyte placed a golden stand beneath it, and the warriors lowered the chest with reverence.

"Behold, Evliit's sword," Caratacus proclaimed.

Everyone in the chamber fell to their knees. Mordher and Borian stepped forward.

"You have chosen well," Mordher said. "With this weapon, I will crush the Angrodha, the Camonra — and Amphileph himself."

He reached for the marble lid—

"Wait!" the priest cried.

He signaled an acolyte, who brought forth a basin of water. The priest dipped a small canister on a wooden dowel into it and flicked droplets onto Mordher. The former Guardsman bristled with irritation as the priest continued chanting and held the basin toward him.

"What does he want?" Mordher muttered.

The priest stopped, annoyed.

"Cleanse yourself."

When Mordher hesitated, the priest lifted the basin under his hands. Mordher splashed the water over them, and an acolyte dried them with a cloth. The priest stepped back.

Mordher placed his hands on the marble lid.

In that moment, he believed the Sword would yield — that destiny itself bent toward him.

Then the pain struck.

His arms jerked taut. His muscles seized. He could not lift it. The numbness in his hands flared into searing heat.

"Barothma!" he snarled.

The chamber gasped.

The priest stepped forward, voice solemn and resonant.

"The Sword chooses," he intoned, "and it destroys those it rejects."

"It is said that I destroy any who cross me!" Mordher snarled. "Don't try me, priest."

He seized the lid again, gritting his teeth as the burning in his arms surged through his entire body. The pain was so intense it made him tremble — but Mordher forced the lid open and looked inside.

When he looked upon the Bhre-Nora's adorned case, he lost his sight for a sliver of time. He was transported back to the mountainside, the site of the Angrodha's attack, but — he *was* Tobor, watching from Tobor's point of view as he drew back the arrow. He saw it loose in slow motion, felt the arrowhead pierce Tobor's skin, shatter his rib, and drive through his heart. The agony was real, immediate, overwhelming.

He dropped the marble lid and clutched at his chest, but there was no arrow — only the pain. His knees buckled.

"Mordher!" Borian shouted, catching him as he pitched forward.

Mordher fought to stay conscious. Borian's face blurred in and out.

"It is cursed," Mordher gasped.

"When have we needed magic?" Borian said. "Steel is enough to end our enemies. Leave this thing be!"

"No…" Mordher mumbled. He reached toward the chest again, but his arm fell uselessly to his side. He could still feel the phantom shaft lodged in him, and his breath came shallow and ragged.

"Get me away from that thing."

Borian dragged him back.

The priest stepped between them and the Sword.

"Return the Sword to its resting place!"

The acolytes hurried to lift the chest, carry it back into the alcove, and draw the tapestry closed.

Caratacus's concern deepened.

"We do not control whom the Sword chooses. Surely you do not hold this against the people of Moonledge. Your friend is right — you have no need of this magic. Let our healers tend to him."

"I don't need your healers!" Mordher barked, struggling upright with Borian's help.

"We mean no offense, warrior," Caratacus said gently. "Let us stand together against Amphileph. Will you not join us in this fight?"

Borian answered before Mordher could speak.

"We will — but we must first return to Candra to warn the valley. Unlike Moonledge, we have no mountain to shield us. We must bring our people into the Warriors Hall. What would stop the Angrodha and Amphileph's army from moving on to us after seeing your defenses?"

Caratacus considered this carefully.

"You are right. The great caves of the Keep will protect us. The Camonra may ravage what lies outside, but no creature will easily breach our walls. Go, then. Warn the people of Rion in the west. There is no time to bring them here, though we would gladly take them in."

"Your offer is generous, my lord Caratacus," Borian said. "But our best defense is to warn the valley and Highwood. We ask your leave to ride west."

Mordher pushed away from Borian and forced himself to stand straight.

"May you ride like the wind," Caratacus said. "We will meet the enemy when they come and buy you what time we can."

"Your courage inspires us," Borian replied. "May you wound them so deeply they dare not continue."

"We will give our finest efforts," Caratacus said, dismissing them with a gesture.

"Fare thee well," Borian added.

Mordher said nothing. The two left the chamber and returned to the troops waiting in the outer court.

Mordher pressed a hand to his chestplate.

"Are you all right?" Borian asked.

Mordher shot him a glare.

"Ready the troops."

"With your leave, my lord," Borian said, riding off to give the order.

He returned moments later. Mordher still clutched his chest, though he tried to hide it. Borian's eyes flicked to the hand, then back up.

"The troops are ready," he said.

"I meant to say 'well done' in there," Mordher said to Borian. "You almost convinced *me* we intended to help Highwood."

Borian's jaw tightened.

"It would cost us little to spare a rider to warn them."

"I'll not waste any of our men on Highwood — though your words were elegant," Mordher replied.

Color rose in Borian's cheeks.

"Then you should not have let me speak them. If we do not honor our promises, they become worthless to every future council."

"I'll not spare a rider for Highwood," Mordher repeated.

Borian wheeled his horse to face him.

"I thought as much."

The look he gave Mordher carried all his disappointment.

"What?" Mordher snapped.

"I'll not speak for you again, brother. Make your own commitments."

Borian paused, then added, "And you should know — I have already sent a rider to Highwood."

He turned his horse and rode west toward the Hall without waiting for a reply.

"You did what? Borian!" Mordher roared after him.

"I will kill you with my own hands!"

Borian never looked back.

"To Candra!" Mordher shouted, and the Candrians rode from Moonledge Peak toward their fortress in the valley.

*　*　*

Adheron gathered his fighters in the fields east of the great line of trees.

"Camonra!" he roared. "The humans have shown their true nature in the killing of Tobor! Amphileph was right — they are a plague upon Erathe!"

A thunder of voices answered him.

"If the Angrodha hungers, then let us line the roads with human bodies, that it may feast upon their flesh!"

"Yes!" the Camonra howled.

"Fill your quivers! Sharpen your swords and axes! The Camonra have blood on their minds!" Adheron bellowed.

He turned to the females, who were already stoking the frenzy — slaughtering an Azrodh, heaving it onto the spit, and dancing wildly around the rising fire. Sparks spiraled into the night as they taunted the Angrodha itself, daring it to descend upon them.

"Let their scouts see us dancing in the dark!" Adheron shouted.

"Let them prepare for war — it will not save them! Tonight we will add their heads to our belt rings!"

He spurred his Azrodh forward and rode toward Highwood. Runners darted through the moonlight. Lamps flared in doorways. The settlement stirred awake — but Adheron cared nothing for stealth.

"I shall take what I want with only a hundred Camonra!" he cried.

Torches flickered in the distant trees as Highwood scrambled to respond. Adheron gathered his warriors close and pointed toward the shifting lights.

"Look at their fear," he said. "They should be afraid! They have made war with the Camonra!"

*   *   *

A runner burst into the commander's quarters in Highwood, where several officers stood over a map of the lands around Moonledge Peak.

"What is the meaning of this?" his superior demanded.

"My lord, the Camonra are here!" the runner shouted.

"What?" the commander snapped.

"Did not the rider from Candra say the Inferiors would strike at Moonledge?" another officer asked.

"That was his message," the first commander replied. "Are they forming ranks?"

"No, my lord. They've built a bonfire. They're shouting and dancing around it — as if they want us to see them."

The commander stared down at the map, then let out a long, frustrated breath.

"We prepare to march to Moonledge's aid... and the Camonra come here instead."

*   *   *

Ardhios waited outside the Seven Warriors Hall. Runners had warned him of Borian's approach, and he had lined the path with warriors — thousands of them, standing in disciplined ranks.

Borian reined in his horse and dismounted.

"You've been busy, brother," he said. "You greet us with an army of your own?"

"There is fear among the people, Borian," Ardhios replied. "Rumors of dark creatures and Camonra on the move. They expect the Hall to protect them for their fealty — and I mean to do that."

"*You* mean to?" Borian echoed.

Ardhios didn't flinch.

"Yes. *I* mean to — since it appears my brothers are indisposed."

Borian gestured toward the valley.

"You've set lamps along the road nearly to the valley's edge. I hope you've spent your time on more than lighting the way for our enemies."

Ardhios lifted his chin.

"For the Hall!"

The ranks on either side thundered the cry back at him, spears stamping the earth in near-perfect unison.

Borian's brows rose.

"I see," he said wryly.

Ardhios saw Mordher approaching over Borian's shoulder. Mordher rode hard until the Hall came into view; then he and his warriors slowed to a controlled trot as the lamplight lined the path.

"Look at him," Borian muttered. "He sees your army outnumbers his."

Mordher reined in, dismounted, and strode straight toward Borian — striking him to the ground with a single blow. Borian sprang up, sword drawn, and Mordher's blade flashed free in answer.

Ardhios descended the Hall's steps at once.

"Oh, Mordher... will you never change?" he breathed, then shouted, "Cease this at once!"

Soldiers shifted around them, hands on weapons, forming a tightening ring. Mordher and Borian noticed the movement and held their ground.

"Mordher, what is it now?" Ardhios demanded.

"We will continue this later," Mordher growled at Borian.

Borian said nothing, but both men — grudgingly, stiffly — sheathed their swords and turned their attention to Ardhios. The tension between them still crackled, but at least the blades were down.

"What of my proposal to connect our strongholds to Moonledge Peak's southern walls? Did Caratacus accept that such a union would allow us to migrate north beyond the Candra Mountains under the protection of our joint armies?"

"We did not discuss those matters," Borian said. "There was an incident—"

"An incident?" replied Ardhios.

"I killed the leader of the Camonra, and the beasts didn't like it very much," Mordher said.

"What?" Ardhios asked. "You did what?"

"The opportunity presented itself to eliminate the leader of the Camonra, and I took it," said Mordher.

"Our plan was to complete the wall with Moonledge Peak and strengthen our alliance with the people of Highwood," said Ardhios. "Was it not agreed that you would defend the lands north of there until the builders could connect our outpost to their southern wall?"

"The opportunity presented itself," Mordher repeated.

Ardhios paced the floor.

"I'm working to establish rule within the kingdom, Mordher — a sense of safety that might create the wealth we need for growth and prosperity. Have you no idea that the Camonra—"

"The Inferiors!" Mordher snapped.

"The *Inferiors*... will only be stirred to attack us? What you've done serves only to bring war upon us before the advantage is ours," Ardhios said.

"I was strong enough to draw the bow and bring him down like a great elk," Mordher replied, flashing a smile at Borian. "One less Inferior to trouble us."

Ardhios threw up his hands.

"Borian, can you not talk sense into this one? Instead of drawing treaties with Moonledge and Highwood for a wall to keep them out of our lands, I'll now be begging for soldiers. Do you not understand?"

Mordher stepped to the side, circling.

"We will not beg for soldiers. We'll demand them."

Ardhios let out a dry, incredulous laugh.

"Demand them? And by what authority — that I represent the warrior who killed the leader of the Inferiors?"

"This will be a war none of them can survive alone," Mordher said. "They will join us, or they will fall." His voice rose.

"You wanted to unify the west? Then this is the beginning of that union — a new union that will bring all mankind together against the prophets of old and the world they have made for us. This is the beginning of a new kingdom of the west!"

Ardhios stopped pacing and faced him squarely.

"You gamble everything," he said. "You've set in motion things that cannot be undone."

"The old ones have controlled us long enough," Borian said.

"There *will* be a Western Kingdom," Mordher declared. "It will rise on the ashes of Rion. Never again will the prophets of old direct the affairs of men, waging wars for this god or that one. We will destroy the Inferiors, and then the evil one in the east. After that, men alone will determine their destiny."

Ardhios's voice was low, steady.

"You may have determined our destiny, Mordher — but it may not be the destiny you imagine."

"You said it yourself, Ardhios: it matters not now. None of it!" Mordher shouted. "What has begun will end either in a new kingdom… or the end of men."

"Everything is black and white, is it?" Ardhios replied.

"And even then, I cannot choose — because you have chosen for us."

He stood firm, posture straight, expression controlled. He knew how Mordher thrived on provocation, so he held his anger in check, projecting only cold, immovable resolve.

"Very well. I will send for soldiers."

He lifted his hand.

"Riders to Highwood!" he shouted, and runners sprinted off at once.

"May the Creator be with us."

"He is with us!" Mordher snapped. "And you would do well to show that you know it."

Ardhios didn't rise to the bait.

"You would do better to keep your temper in check, brother, before you—"

"Before I what?" Mordher stepped forward, pointing at him.

"That one is frightened," he said to Borian. "I prefer my leaders fearless."

Ardhios didn't flinch.

"You know less of me than you think, brother."

With that, he turned and ascended the stairs into the great hall — not retreating, simply ending the conversation.

Borian watched him go, then looked back at Mordher.

"Ardhios is a good man. We have plenty who want our heads without you stirring up our own camp."

Mordher snorted.

"Very well. Let them come for my head. I look forward to sticking them like fatted hogs."

*　　*　　*

Mategaladh rode to the northern edge of the Faceless Mountains and dismounted. He could feel Tophian deep within the stone, a distant pulse in the bones of the mountain. He struck his staff against the rock.

The end of the staff unfurled like fingers, burrowing into the mountainside. Stone crumbled away until the staff suddenly straightened, latching onto something hidden within. Mategaladh wrenched backward and tore a chunk of black stone free. He righted the staff, and its tendrils curled tightly around the stone, compressing it until it glowed with a fierce inner light.

Roots erupted from the place he had struck, rising into the air around him. They hung suspended for a breath, then plunged deep into the mountainside, prying the rock apart.

Mategaladh stepped toward the opening as the roots drove upward and outward, binding the loosened stone to the surrounding earth. The swelling timbers groaned under the strain, widening the passage enough for him to enter the central cavern.

The roots continued their work, pushing deeper into the mountain and weaving themselves into a living lattice that forced the earth aside, carving a tunnel into the mountain's heart. Mategaladh walked on until he reached the largest of the inner caves.

A great popping of stone echoed through the chamber, followed by the crash of shifting earth. When the noise faded, he thought he heard a low groan from somewhere ahead.

He lifted his staff high, its glow spilling across the cavern walls, and squinted into the darkness to see as far as the light would reach.

"Tophian!" Mategaladh cried.

He hurried to his friend's side and eased an arm beneath him, gently rolling him over. One of Tophian's eyes sat out of alignment with the other, and his breathing was shallow. Mategaladh brushed the dried, flaking blood from his face and whispered a prayer for consciousness to return.

A swelling along Tophian's lower ribs caught his eye — several were clearly broken. Mategaladh laid his hand upon them and prayed again. A crackling sound answered him as the bones shifted beneath his fingers.

Tophian's eyes flew open. He stared up at the cavern roof, at the thick tendons of roots crisscrossing the stone.

"What are you doing, you old fool?" he sputtered.

"Are you trying to bring the whole mountain down on our heads?

You cannot shift the stone like this — these vines of yours! Stop this at once!"

At his command, the roots recoiled, and the tunnel behind them collapsed in a thunder of falling stone. Dust billowed through the cavern until Mategaladh's light was nearly swallowed. Tophian raised a hand, and the dust swept aside.

"Tophian!" Mategaladh said, joy breaking through his worry.

"What in the name of the Creator has happened to you?"

"I have much to tell, Mategaladh," Tophian murmured. "Much indeed."

"Rest, friend. I have you," Mategaladh said.

At once, Tophian's eyes closed, and he drew a long, relieved breath. Mategaladh felt a weight lift from his own heart.

"That's right, friend. Rest," he whispered.

*　　*　　*

Mategaladh tended to Tophian for the better part of two days. When Tophian finally regained his strength, he recounted the story — the waking of Tobor's mourners in the valley, and the beehive of hatred that swirled around the fallen warrior's body.

"The arrow was Candrian. There is no mistaking it," Tophian said.

"The Camonra were out of their minds with rage. That much I heard before I crawled away."

"There was no stopping it," Mategaladh replied.

"Even though we bound Amphileph, his creation had already spread too far to gather back in. It was a fleeting hope that such a day might never come. The Camonra and Man were never meant to coexist so easily."

Tophian shook his head.

"It could have been. I was close — so close — to moving them east, until the fools from Candra ended any chance of it. At times like this, when I see such treachery, I can almost understand Amphileph's loss of hope for men."

Mategaladh rummaged through Tophian's bag with growing irritation.

"Why don't you carry the herbs I gave you? Why must I always find you half-dead and without so much as a single good herb? Bah!" He dropped the bag and dug into his own, producing a dark, bulbous root and thrusting it toward Tophian's face.

Tophian wrinkled his nose.

"You know I hate Erdwara."

"Oh, you old ingrate! Take it and eat it!" Mategaladh snapped.

Tophian muttered under his breath but pushed himself upright against the cave wall. He took a large bite of the Erdwara root and, for a moment, looked ready to spit it out — until a quick glance at Mategaladh's watchful eye changed his mind. He exhaled slowly through his nose and resumed chewing with a grimace.

"There. That will make things better," Mategaladh said.

Tophian extended his left arm. A deep indentation marred the muscle and bone, and a bulge along the forearm suggested a break. As the herb took hold, the bluish bruising faded toward pink. Tophian straightened his arm, and the swelling began to recede. He tossed another piece of Erdwara into his mouth.

Mategaladh pulled three more roots from his bag.

"I've not enough to heal you as I would like," he said, "but here is the last of it."

"Absolutely not," Tophian replied.

He shifted his battered body into a more comfortable position.

"I was unable to destroy the Angrodha, my friend. You'll need far more of that herb before *your* day is done."

"The Angrodha sought to kill even the Camonra, you say?" Mategaladh asked.

"It was clear to me it meant to kill us all," Tophian replied.

"Never in my life would I have imagined standing beside the Camonra in a fight for survival. I would never have dreamed I would say such a thing, brother — but I see them differently now that they have turned from their worship of Amphileph."

Mategaladh gave him a strange look.

"What?"

"I did not say their creation was not an abomination," Tophian continued.

"But I spoke with their leader — Tobor, the one who was slain. He bore no malice toward mankind. And when he told me they no longer followed Amphileph's desire to destroy us, I believed him."

He drew a slow breath.

"As a Watcher, I have sworn to protect the world of men. But I tell you, Mategaladh — that moment changed me. I saw the Camonra for what they truly were: pawns Amphileph shaped to serve his ends. Living, breathing creatures, as we are. And Tobor... Tobor sought peace with men."

Tophian's voice softened.

"They feared the Angrodha as much as we do. Amphileph sent it to destroy them every bit as surely as he sent it for us."

Mategaladh started to respond, then pressed his lips together and looked away.

"If the Candrian has killed their leader, those hopes are dashed," he said.

"The Camonra will exact swift and terrible justice, without regard for their losses. We must move to protect the people who will be caught in the middle. Can you travel?"

"Yes… though I doubt I'll be much good to you if it comes to a fight," Tophian answered.

The tortured look on Tophian's face told Mategaladh more than words could. His spirit was willing, but his body was broken, his power drained to embers. Mategaladh scanned the cave for an exit, but the darkness swallowed every feature. He focused, and the stone at the end of his staff brightened.

"I will go alone, Tophian. You must regain your strength."

The light revealed more of the cavern walls, but not enough to show a clear path.

"You know these mountains, brother. Can we follow the caves to the surface, or must I force our way out?"

"No, no!" Tophian said sharply.

"The caves will not endure much more of your tinkering. You could bring down the weight-bearing members of the catacombs. It is not far."

They moved slowly upward along the smooth walls, crystals in the stalactites catching the glow of Mategaladh's staff like scattered stars.

"Quiet, Mategaladh. Listen," Tophian whispered.

They rounded a curtain of stone. Faint trickling water echoed ahead, and a thin wash of moonlight spilled through a narrow break in the cave's ceiling.

"There is a way to the surface just ahead," Tophian said.

"Follow the ridge to Moonledge. The depths of the mountains will care for me. I will rest here a moment, then descend to the inner catacombs. I know my way in my own home, Mategaladh. You must go. Go to Moonledge."

He grabbed his side and winced as the last words left him.

"Then go to your home and rest there. I'll warn the people of

Moonledge Peak and Highwood, and you should recover all that you can. I may very well have to call upon your aid in short order, whatever your strength."

"When you call, I will come," Tophian said — but the look in his eyes chilled Mategaladh. He could not remember the last time he had seen fear in Tophian's face.

"Farewell, friend," Mategaladh said, and turned toward the surface.

Once above ground, he climbed to the highest point he could reach along the southern face of the mountain — and the sight before him staggered him.

To the south, dozens of torches burned in the plains before Highwood. To the west, hundreds more clustered around the Keep of Moonledge Peak. And then, crossing the face of the moon, the Angrodha shrieked its malice — a jagged silhouette flashing against the stars before vanishing into the night.

Mategaladh's mouth fell open.

"Creator of Erathe… help us," he whispered.

*   *   *

Adheron prepared to ride into Highwood with a hundred warriors— fifty cavalry and fifty foot soldiers. His revenge-driven fury made him oblivious to Citanth and his warriors gathering to the north, but his scouts were not so blind.

One of them came racing in from the north.

"Lord Adheron! Lord Adheron, forgive me!"

"Speak!" Adheron barked.

"My lord—Amphileph's army moves on Moonledge Peak!"

Adheron yanked the Azrodh's reins, and the great beast lumbered around until he faced the scout.

"Amphileph?" Adheron dismounted, pushing through the ring of captains to hear the scout over the shrieking females around the bonfire and the warriors shouting for battle.

"My lord," the scout said again, breathless, "the Angrodha and four thousand Camonra attack Moonledge Peak!"

Adheron's expression hardened.

"You have done well," he said.

The scout bowed and withdrew from the circle of his superiors.

This news gave Adheron great pause. He turned toward Moonledge

Peak, then back to Highwood, the torchlight flickering across his face as he weighed the choice before him. Through the branches of the massive trees, he could see the torchlights of Highwood's warriors flickering like restless spirits. He waved away his servant and the Azrodh, then gathered with his captains, questioning their strategy with a patience that would have made Idhoran proud.

"Our scouts tell us that Amphileph's army moves on Moonledge Peak, and the Angrodha attacks at their command," Adheron said.

"We stand ready to follow you," the captains replied.

A second scout approached the circle and dropped to one knee.

"What news have you?" Adheron asked, and the captains parted to let the scout speak.

"My lord, archers line the trees of Highwood. The men have set man traps and spikes to stop our Azrodh from entering the forest."

"Very well," Adheron said, and the circle closed around him again.

His newfound authority pressed heavily upon him. He longed for the judgment of his father and of Idhoran — but neither stood beside him now. He knew he must rise to their measure on his own.

"Amphileph means to destroy the men of Moonledge Peak," Adheron said, thinking aloud.

"But they could take heavy losses attacking the stronghold."

The captains exchanged uneasy glances. One stepped forward.

"My lord, if Amphileph's army turns on us — as surely it will — we cannot afford great losses fighting the men of Highwood. No warrior fights as fiercely as he does upon his own land, and they hold the height of the forest above us. If we ride into their midst, we will lose many warriors. Then our families may stand alone against the victors at Moonledge."

A wind rose from the northwest, and thunder rolled across the plains east of Highwood. The Rainland seemed to prod them onward with its unwelcome breath.

Adheron's head spun. He looked toward the distant orange glow pulsing over the rift that separated them from Rion. He looked at the anxious faces of his captains, lit by wavering torchlight. Then he looked back at the blackness of the Rainland — and remembered the creatures of Amphileph. The Angrodha's cry echoed faintly on the wind.

"We go west," Adheron said at last, "around the southern edge of the forest. Then we strike from their rear."

His voice hardened.

"I will avenge my father's death. Put the torches out. We travel under cover of darkness — as swiftly as we can."

"Yes, my liege!" the captains answered, and the entire tribe gathered their things once more and moved out.

*   *   *

The soldiers of Rion scrambled through the trees of Highwood, watching with mounting intensity as the Camonra gathered on their very doorstep. Then a deeper trepidation seized them. One by one, the Camonra's torchlights winked out, swallowed by the blackness of the night.

They had already sent the women and children southwest along the Highborne River toward the villages in the Dales of Shinetower. Now an eerie silence settled over Highwood, broken only by hushed orders and the distant rumble rolling out of the Rainland. Lightning flashed now and again, offering only momentary glimpses of movement in the grasses. Every soldier grew hypersensitive to the slightest sound, the faintest shift of shadow.

"Can you see them?" one of the Rionese soldiers whispered.

"No," came the reply. Then suddenly—

"To the right. To the right."

*   *   *

Adheron and the Camonra could see torches moving in the trees, gathering in their direction. Faint shouts drifted from the woods.

"The grass is higher there," Adheron said. He moved the group farther south from the tree line. He glanced back to see the females and children moving that way—then an arrow hissed past his ear.

"They've found us!" Adheron shouted.

Bedlam erupted. Torches descended from the trees, moving toward them.

"Epar! Locra! With me!"

His two captains rushed to his side. They pushed toward the tree line—Adheron with his sword drawn, his captains with crossbows—arrows slicing the air around them.

"Bring light!" someone yelled, and a man burst from the high grass. Adheron struck him with the hilt of his sword, splitting his chin open.

"Ready!" Adheron called to Locra—

—but an arrow struck Locra in the side of the neck. He staggered, clutching the shaft, his crossbow falling from his grasp.

A gust of wind bent the grass, giving Adheron a clear view of the Highwood men—bows drawn, swords ready, closing fast. He dragged Locra back into the cover of the grass.

"Be still!" Adheron urged, but Locra writhed in agony.

"They're here!" a man with a lamp shouted.

"We must go," Adheron whispered—

—but Locra's gurgling breath stopped. Adheron eased him to the ground and took up his crossbow.

The Highwood soldiers were nearly upon him and Epar.

"Here! They're here!"

"For the Camonra!" Epar roared. He surged from the grass, arrows striking him as he charged. He fired his crossbow into the ground before collapsing.

Adheron circled low through the grass and sprang up beside a young squire. Terrified, the boy raised his lamp. Adheron's blade crashed down, shattering the lamp in a burst of fire that engulfed them both and ignited the tall grass.

The squire screamed, running aflame through the field. Fire crawled up Adheron's clothing. He dropped his sword, beat the flames from his head, then threw himself to the ground to smother the rest. Half-blinded, he snatched up his sword and watched the squire collapse twenty paces away, a burning trail marking his path.

The wind seized the flames, whipping them into a wall of heat that drove Adheron south and forced the Highwood soldiers back toward the trees. He sprang away from the inferno and ran toward his tribe. Arrows hissed past him; cries of "Fire!" rang out.

The night brightened as the flames spread. Adheron saw Highwood men hauling water from forest wells, archers forming a protective line against the Camonra.

He burst from the darkness beside his warriors.

"Adheron!" one cried. Their relief lasted only a heartbeat before discipline returned.

"Hold still, my liege." Cool water splashed over Adheron's burned face. He tried to clear his right eye, but it was useless.

The flames rose higher, forcing them back.

Adheron caught his breath.

"The soldiers are coming! Move the families farther south!"

"But my lord—look!" a warrior said, pointing.

Adheron turned. Flames crawled into the great forest, lighting the sky.

"The northwest winds carry the fire straight to Highwood, my lord."

The heat grew unbearable. Smaller trees burst into flame. Fire raced into the branches and wooden structures built by the Rionese. Ash drifted like snow. Superheated air roared upward through the canopy, igniting tree after tree like tinder.

Men trying to fight the blaze choked on smoke and collapsed. Others fled west, desperate to outrun the heat—many could not.

"My father is avenged!" Adheron said, collapsing to the ground in exhaustion, watching cinders spiral upward in the curling heat above Highwood.

"My liege, your captains stand ready for whatever you command!" a soldier called.

"Your allegiance humbles me… but there is nothing more for us here," Adheron murmured.

He turned again toward the roaring flames devouring the human structures woven through the branches of Highwood.

"Even if the forest is reduced to ashes, the humans will build again."

He grasped the soldier's arm and let himself be pulled to his feet. Several captains regrouped before him in the field southeast of Highwood.

Adheron sheathed his sword.

"Gather the women and children. We go south to find new lands. My father was right — we must avoid the humans. Their evil is like the poison that runs in the waters of the Rainland."

"We are with you, Adheron, as we were with Tobor before you," one captain said.

Adheron nodded, though his gaze drifted toward the burning forest.

"Perhaps Amphileph was right. Perhaps the humans are beyond saving. Let him destroy them if he will — but my father gave his life to protect the clan. I will honor his memory not with vengeance, but by ensuring our survival."

He raised his voice so all could hear.

"Move the Camonra southwest to the jungles, far from this evil! We will drive Amphileph's creatures from our lands and live free of his corruption. We will live free of it — or die fighting for our place in this world, just as Tobor wished."

And so the Camonra followed him southward into the darkness.

*　　*　　*

Mategaladh saw the flames of Highwood roar into the night sky far below the southern ridge of the Faceless Mountains.

"Oh, no… no!" he breathed, helpless before the loss of life and the destruction of one of his beloved forests.

"You'll pay for this, Amphileph!" he cried, and hurried along the ridge toward Moonledge Peak, ever watchful for the Angrodha overhead.

In the valley southeast of him, at the rear of Amphileph's vast column, Citanth also saw the glow rising in the west.

"A great fire rages in Highwood!" Citanth shouted. "Hold your positions!"

The order rippled down the ranks until thousands of Camonra halted on the fields outside Moonledge Peak's Keep.

"Back away!" Citanth commanded, raising his withered hand to the sky.

The Camonra cleared the area at once — and not a moment too soon. The Angrodha swooped down into the clearing, now fully grown, its wingspan stretching nearly fifty feet. It shrieked twice, a piercing, bone-deep sound that made the Camonra flinch and cover their ears. Citanth strode toward it as the creature shook its head, muscles rippling down its long neck. The Angrodha lowered its face until its hot breath washed over him.

"This is most opportune!" Citanth shouted up at the beast.

"You, my pet, will remain here and kill anything that attempts to come or go from Moonledge Peak! They cannot hide in their Keep forever!" Citanth laughed, and the Angrodha cocked its head, lips curling to reveal a row of clenched teeth.

"The men of Highwood flee their precious woods!" Citanth crowed.

"We could march our full army into the Dales of Shinetower! Feast upon these weaklings, and I will summon you when it is time to strike the men of the Dales!"

The Angrodha snorted, then spread its massive wings and launched itself into the air above Moonledge Peak.

"Turn, great army — turn!" Citanth shouted.

"The Creator has smiled upon us! Soon we dine in Shinetower!"

The marching drums thundered, and the Camonra wheeled southward.

*   *   *

Deep within Moonledge Peak's caves, Caratacus tried to assure the masses that the Keep was impenetrable. But the soldiers who had remained outside to delay the Camonra had been nearly wiped out by the Angrodha's assault. Those who survived had fled into the courtyard, slipping between buildings, desperate to avoid being seen.

Outside, the Angrodha landed among the structures with a thunderous impact. It ducked its head and folded its wings tight against its body as it stepped toward the temple entrance on the outer face of the Keep. Its claws carved deep furrows into the stone steps. Then it pressed its massive head against the lockdown doors and unleashed a roar that vibrated through the thick stone walls.

The beast sniffed along the door's edges, searching for the scent of men, pausing only to snort dirt and dust from its nostrils.

*   *   *

Mategaladh watched Amphileph's army march toward Highwood and hurried down the mountainside. The sun might rise and set a dozen times before Citanth reached the Northern Bridge across the Highborne River, and another day before he reached the Dales of Shinetower.

This is my chance, he thought. Facing both the Angrodha and the Camonra would be suicide. But facing the Angrodha alone—this might be the only moment he would ever have.

He climbed the hillside toward the temple grounds and nearly stumbled upon a Rionese soldier hiding between two buildings.

Mategaladh stepped beside him.

"Ah!" the soldier yelped. "You scared the life out of me!"

"I didn't mean to startle you, my friend. I've come to do battle with the creature."

The soldier stared, then laughed in disbelief.

"You? Alone? That monster carried off twenty armed men in moments, sir!"

"Stay here," Mategaladh said, moving along the building's wall.

"No problem there, sire," the soldier muttered, pressing himself flat against the adobe stone, halberd clutched to his chest.

Mategaladh rounded the corner—and saw the Angrodha's massive back. He stepped into the center of the courtyard and closed his eyes in prayer.

The Angrodha froze mid-snort. Slowly it drew its head back from the Keep's doors and fixed both eyes on him. Its lips peeled into a snarl, revealing teeth still stained with Rionese blood.

Mategaladh's eyes snapped open just as the Angrodha launched itself from the doorway. It bounded once, then hurled itself through the air on its wings, jaws spreading wide for the kill.

Mategaladh raised his hand.

A blue aura erupted from his body, engulfing both himself and the Angrodha. The beast slammed into the field of energy and slowed, thrashing violently, claws and teeth raking at the shimmering barrier as it inched toward him.

"You are an abomination!" Mategaladh cried, lifting both hands to hold the field steady. The aura wavered, pushing the Angrodha back—

—but the creature roared and clawed its way forward again.

With a shout, Mategaladh forced the aura outward. The Angrodha shot backward, smashing into the temple stone. It collapsed to the side, dazed, then shook its head and lunged again, shattering a statue of a Rionese soldier with a single swipe.

It coiled and sprang. Its claws tore at the aura, bolts of energy crackling wherever it touched. The Angrodha shrieked as blue fire clung to its wings. It slammed its burning wing into the dirt, trying to smother the flames, then pounced again, jaws driving closer and closer to Mategaladh's outstretched hands.

The entire valley flashed with blue and white light.

"I draw my strength from the Creator Himself!" Mategaladh cried.

The flashes merged into a single blinding radiance. The aura exploded outward, hurling the Angrodha against the outer wall of Moonledge. Stone collapsed as the creature crashed through it and fell back into the ruin.

The aura faded. Mategaladh dropped to one knee, breath ragged. He knew the truth all Watchers feared: channeling such power through flesh and blood came at a terrible cost.

The Angrodha's wings fluttered madly as it clawed at the broken wall, trying to pull itself upright. More stone collapsed under its weight. It rolled forward with a shriek, smashing a section of the wall into fragments before dropping to all fours. Then, with a lurch, it charged at the small figure of Mategaladh standing in the center of the courtyard.

Mategaladh drove his staff into the ground. A massive vine erupted upward, then plunged back down between him and the creature. The earth shook violently around him. Splinters flew as the Angrodha tore at the weaving vine. More vines burst from the ground in rapid succession, forming a thick cocoon around Mategaladh. The Angrodha clawed and bit at the living barrier, unable to rip it free from its deep roots.

It bit into the cocoon again—then recoiled, shaking its head violently as if the taste itself were poison. With a furious roar, it struck again, tearing away great chunks of vine with teeth and claws. Then, all at once, it staggered back and gagged.

The Angrodha choked again. Its left hind leg began to quiver uncontrollably. It squinted its eyes and coughed up a gush of black liquid writhing with larvae. A mournful cry escaped it as it vomited dozens more, propping itself on its forearms while its hind legs folded beneath it.

The larvae split open, revealing small leathery winged creatures that flopped in the filth, shaking the muck from their bodies, clicking their mouths. They crawled, squirmed, and leapt through the thick black regurgitation, latching onto the Angrodha like ticks.

Desperate, the Angrodha tried to fly. It managed one great push into the air, but lacked the strength for a second. It crashed back down the mountainside, sliding into the buildings where a soldier hiding nearby fled screaming.

The creature rolled to its feet—then its belly split open. Hundreds more larvae spilled out in its dying lunge. They burst into their winged forms almost instantly and, one by one, took to the air. They circled Moonledge in the pre-dawn sky for nearly an hour before turning south and flying toward Shinetower

As the morning light revealed the extent of the carnage, the fearful soldier crept back to the cocoon. It had withered almost as quickly as it had formed. He touched it cautiously, afraid it might still hold some poison, but it crumbled beneath his fingers like a rotted tree limb. Heart pounding, he searched for any sign that the old wizard might still be inside.

Peeling away the last of the layers, he saw Mategaladh's face — pale, still, lifeless. Yet the soldier kept tearing at the cocoon, clinging to the faintest hope of rescuing the one who had saved him.

When he split open the side, Mategaladh slid into his arms. The young man lowered him gently to the ground and pressed his ear to the Watcher's chest. Nothing.

He checked for breath — and Mategaladh gave the faintest moan.

The soldier's eyes widened. He hoisted Mategaladh over his shoulder and sprinted toward the temple, shouting for help.

Chapter Twenty-Two

Attack on Shinetower

Aleris tried the door on Rendaya's cottage, but it was barred, so he got a good running start and flew through her kitchen window with a crash of glass. He ran headlong into and bounced off a pan that was hanging from the ceiling, fell straightway to Rendaya's chopping block that doubled as a general storage area for her herbs and whatnots.

He lay flat on his back in the center of the block, scattering several of her glass containers to the floor. The clamor shot Rendaya straight up from her bed. A blue aura appeared to cover her skin and then migrate to her open hand in the shape of a sphere, its blue glow filling the room.

"Not my window!" Rendaya cried. "Aleris! Ebert made me that!"

Aleris propped himself up on one arm and rubbed his head. "I'm truly sorry, Rendaya, but there's a great fire in Highwood! You must come at once!"

"What?" Rendaya repeated. "A fire?"

""Yes, yes!" Aleris said. He flew to her side and grabbed her sleeve as if he would pull her up from bed. "I fear that Amphileph is moving upon the west!"

"Yes, of course, let me dress at once," Rendaya said, and she threw back the blankets. She opened her armoire and grabbed some of her clothes, throwing them across the chair before unceremoniously beginning to remove her nightgown.

"My lady!" Aleris said. He hovered and turned to face the kitchen window. "I will wait outside!" he said, and he quickly exited back through the missing pane.

When Rendaya stepped outside, she was already sure that there was a real problem. She could see smoke rising to the sky above the Southwood treetops.

"We must go to Shinetower; it is time!" Aleris said.

A twinge tightened in Rendaya's midsection. Would she truly have to cross paths with the Watchers again? It had been a long time, but old wounds ran deep.

"I'm coming," she said.

She pushed aside her doubts, focusing on the present moment. Her aura flared outward from her core, enveloping her in a vibrant blue glow, and she shot upward. She opened her eyes as she cleared the tops of Southwood Forest, fixed her mind on Shinetower, and her trajectory arced toward it with the mere thought.

She landed smoothly in the crop fields south of Shinetower and waited. Aleris arrived moments later, wings beating the last of the night air from his path.

"They fear you, Rendaya," Aleris said. "Let me speak to them first."

"I'll wait here," she replied.

Aleris nodded and flew toward the gates of Shinetower, stopping short when he spotted a familiar wagon. Jalin sat at the reins, and Ro was helping Tiamphia down. Her slightly rounded stomach made Aleris certain she was pregnant.

"I feared my friends were in danger."

Aleris turned toward the voice and saw Galbard approaching. His hair had grown long and unruly, and his beard was full.

"Galbard?" Aleris said.

"I saw the flames of Highwood and thought my friends might be in trouble," Galbard replied.

"I meant to bring only Ro, but Tiamphia and Jalin wouldn't hear of it. They wanted to stand at our sides as we stood at theirs. I may not be the Swordbearer, but if the armory can spare good steel for an ordinary man and his son, we will raise it for Shinetower and the Dales, old friend."

He hesitated, eyes misting.

"I cursed my Creator once…" Galbard said quietly.

"Today I ask only for the strength to fight for the people of the Dales."

"Galbard!" Aleris cried, hovering before him.

"We'll surely find two swords for such good company!

"I've heard riders arrived this morning," Galbard said, "reporting the Camonra's attack on Highwood. Nothing stands between them and the Dales now."

"Then let us go to the upper deck and speak of war," Aleris said.

"Tiamphia and Jalin's rooms remain untouched. Let them take refuge there."

"Very well, my friend," Galbard answered. "Lead the way."

*　　*　　*

Seeking order and security, frightened townspeople had roused Cayden in the deep of the night. He left Nara to sleep a little longer while he spoke with the town council beneath a street lamp outside their home. A rider brought the news: the Inferiors had set fire to Highwood, and its people were fleeing toward Candra. Cayden rode for Shinetower at once, stopping only long enough to send a messenger back to Nara, instructing her to be ready to leave the Dales at a moment's notice.

By the time he arrived, the sun was rising in the eastern sky. Galbard stood with Aleris and Ro on the upper deck of the great tower, all three fixed on the massive column of smoke rising from Highwood — and on the strange flock of creatures weaving through the black plume. Footsteps sounded behind them, and Galbard turned as Cayden emerged from the stairwell.

"Cayden! Good!" Galbard said. "I feared I might not have the benefit of your counsel before things got out of hand here."

"Galbard?" Cayden asked. "Do my eyes deceive me?"

"Hello, my friend."

Cayden dropped to one knee.

"Sire, we are ready to fight for you."

"Now, now — none of that," Galbard said. "Rise, man. We are brothers."

He looked out over the smoke-choked horizon.

"This is it, then. Reminds me of the first time I ever set foot in Shinetower, so many years ago. I was convinced the Camonra were right behind me."

A weary breath escaped him.

"I suppose they always were."

"Yes, lord," Aleris said. "This is our destiny."

"What have we, then?" Galbard asked.

Aleris answered.

"Shinetower's defenses are of no use without the Sword, but it remains a formidable structure. The Bhre-Nora stand ready to fight for you. And the people of the Dales will be greatly encouraged by your return. They will rally to your cause."

Galbard tried to smile, but the weight of the world pressed heavily upon him.

"Then let those from the Dales who can fight be ready to meet our enemy at the Northern Bridge of the Highborne River. We've no room for everyone within the tower, and we must give the people time to flee as far as they can."

He turned to Cayden.

"Have you a map?"

Cayden produced a scroll of parchment and rolled it out upon the altar of the Sword. Galbard watched him do so, thinking of the power that had once rested there. He shook his head, as if to fling such thoughts away — there was no time for that kind of longing.

"We will take the fight to them in waves," he said, "falling back through the Dales and finally to Shinetower."

"There is another who can aid us," Aleris said. "With your permission, I will retrieve her."

"By all means," Galbard replied, puzzled but trusting.

Aleris took flight, diving over the tower's edge to signal Rendaya. Moments later he returned and landed among them.

"She's coming."

Rendaya touched down in the center of the upper deck, her blue aura still visible even in the full daylight. She stood tall, composed, assessing.

"Galbard, this is Rendaya," Aleris said.

"Who is this?" Galbard asked. "A Watcher?"

Cayden's eyes widened.

"My lord — this is the one they call the Witch of Southwood! The being who landed on the *Merrius*! She told us to build the tower and protect you!"

Galbard studied her.

"Clearly you know more of me than I do of you, Rendaya."

Rendaya looked at each of them in turn.

"I'm no Watcher," she said. She walked to the edge of the deck, gazing toward the smoke rising from Highwood.

"I meant no offense," Galbard said. "You wield abilities I have only seen in Watchers."

Rendaya turned back, her expression softening just slightly.

"A new creature flies above Highwood," she said. "Unnatural — Amphileph's work, without question. Do you have archers?"

"Yes," Galbard answered. "We've archers."

Rendaya faced Aleris.

"The tower's defenses were built to repel a ground assault. Defending from the air will be... difficult."

"We will do what we can," Galbard said. "To the last man."

Rendaya paced from the altar to the parapet, scanning the skies.

"It is wise that you sent your people north," she said. "The Dales are abandoned?"

"Only the warriors and our healers remain," Galbard replied.

"The Camonra will not give chase to them as long as they believe the Sword is here," Rendaya said.

"But there is no sense tempting the likes of Amphileph with easy bloodshed, no matter if their objective lies elsewhere."

"Cayden, I entrust the first wave to your command," Galbard said.

"Let them know they have found the Dales."

"I'll be about that now," Cayden replied. "With your leave, my liege."

Galbard placed a hand on his shoulder.

"Protect your numbers, Cayden. Lead the people to the warriors in Candra if you must."

"Yes, sire!" Cayden bowed and hurried down the stairs.

Rendaya turned back to Galbard.

"The Sword lies deep within the Keep of Moonledge?"

"Under the protection of Caratacus," Aleris answered.

Galbard exhaled.

"Now I wish I had it close. I feel the fool."

"You did what Evliit asked of you," Rendaya said.

"I would never have believed a man could outpace Amphileph's pursuit. But now the next challenge is upon you: keeping the Sword from him."

"We will give Amphileph the sting of defeat," Galbard said.

"If we can thin his ranks, the warriors of Candra and Moonledge may yet drive them back into the east."

Rendaya's gaze sharpened.

"Do not underestimate the Bhre-Nora. Their size is no measure of their ferocity. You've seen them build — I've seen them make war. We will give the Camonra a proper welcome."

Galbard squinted toward the distant movement on the horizon.

"So you believe they will attack by land and air?"

"Yes," Rendaya said. "You should arm yourself."

Galbard hesitated. He had not taken up a weapon since leaving Shinetower — years spent farming, building, living quietly.

"Indeed," he said softly. "That time has come, hasn't it."

Rendaya nodded.

"What of your own family?" she asked. "Have they left for Candra?"

"They would not hear of it," Galbard said.

"Aleris has seen to them. No one has ever taken over our rooms here in Shinetower. My wife, my son, and his wife are there now."

"Please pardon my frankness, my lord," Rendaya said, "but you should convince them to leave with the others. Your line should not end here."

Galbard absorbed her words in silence, then turned and descended the stairs.

*   *   *

Far below the tower, Cayden ran without stopping until he burst through the door of his and Nara's home in the Dales.

"Nara!" he cried, breathless. "Nara!"

She pulled back the drape to their bedroom.

"What is happening? The people are all leaving their homes!"

"Galbard is asking everyone to flee to Candra Valley!" he shouted. "Are you ready to leave?"

"Yes, I'm ready — but what of you? Where will you be?"

"The warriors will set out for the Northern Bridge. We'll hold them there as long as possible, then fall back to the Dales and finally to Shinetower. We hope to thin their ranks before they reach us."

"Will the warriors in Candra come to our aid?" Nara asked.

"That is our hope," Cayden said.

"We will beg them to protect the women and children and send soldiers to strengthen us."

Nara's composure broke.

"I will not leave you!" she cried.

"Oh, Nara…" Cayden stepped forward, voice softening.

"You must take refuge in the valley, away from these monsters. I'll come for you when they're defeated and the Dales are safe again."

But she shook her head, tears spilling.

"I cannot leave you!"

Cayden pushed his scabbard aside and pulled her into his arms.

"How can I fight while fearing every moment for your safety? You must go — for both our sakes."

She gasped at the words, looking up into his eyes. Her forehead fell against his chest, and she wept openly. He held her, kissed her hair, and gave her a moment to breathe.

Then he lifted her chin gently.

"The others will need to see your example," he said.

"Be strong, Nara."

She swallowed hard.

"I will go. I'll go because you have asked me."

They embraced once more. Cayden led her outside and helped gather her things. Women and children were already heading toward the northern end of the Dales, and he urged her to join them.

"When you reach the valley, stay with our people," he said.

"The Highborne will block the Inferiors from crossing from the north. They'll follow the river to the Northern Bridge."

Nara's voice trembled.

"Cayden, I'm afraid for us."

Her expression tore at him.

"I've told the leaders to keep to the western trails," he said.

"They know the road to Candra well."

"It's not getting lost that worries me," she whispered.

Cayden wrung his hands.

"I must join the other men at the Northern Bridge. Riders have already gone to the Candrians. Galbard has asked for their aid."

"But what if the Candrians refuse?"

"How can they? Our downfall is theirs. The Inferiors do not distinguish Candrians from the people of the Dale."

Something in her posture shifted — resignation, or perhaps courage. She bent to gather her things. A tear slipped down her cheek, but she wiped it away quickly.

"Please be careful," she said.

"You must go now," Cayden said — then pulled her into his arms again, looking deeply into her eyes.

"I love you, Nara."

"I've never doubted that," she said softly.

"Return to me soon, my love."

Cayden knew that if she asked to stay, he would have let her — but she didn't. She stepped into the line of people leaving the Dales, looked back at him once, and then disappeared into the crowd.

Cayden looked at their small cottage in the Dales one last time. The chances were good it would be destroyed in the coming attack. A tug of anxiousness pulled at him — the urge to go back inside, to look around one more time for something precious he might have forgotten. But he resisted. There was no carrying anything with him, no time to hide it. Everyone was gathering in the fields west of the Northern Bridge over the Highborne River, and he needed to be among the first to arrive.

He made his way to the eastern end of the Dales, where the men were assembling their weapons. They had torn down sections of the retaining walls along the bridge walks to gather stone for the six catapults they had labored over for days to bring into working order.

"The Inferiors will be forced to narrow their lines to cross the bridge," Cayden said.

"We'll release the catapults as they funnel inward."

"They'll move on us quickly," one of the men replied.

"Yes, they will," Cayden said.

He walked among them, listening to their nervous chatter. These were masons and craftsmen, not warriors. Cayden could see in their faces the terror of meeting an Inferior in hand-to-hand combat.

He decided a clear directive might steady them.

"I've divided the archers into two groups," he said.

"The first group will release their arrows immediately after the catapults' volley. Reload the catapults and fire as many times as you can — but the first group of archers will fire only once more before they flee. I suggest one or two more volleys at most before abandoning the catapults."

He pointed toward the cobblestone stretch of road leading to the bridge.

"When the Inferiors reach that point, the second group of archers will fire while we all retreat into the Dales. Don't tarry, my friends. Your only advantage may be that you know these streets better than our foes. Our task is to thin their ranks as best we can and give our people time to get as far from Shinetower as possible."

"Yes, sir!" the men answered.

"Well, let's be about it, then!" Cayden commanded.

They moved quickly into position, the catapults forming the front line.

*　*　*

Citanth watched the strange creatures circling in the sky north of Highwood. He had expected to see the Angrodha, and its absence gnawed at him.

The Camonra marched along the edge of Highwood as rain began to fall. The forest's blackened, twisted trunks reminded Citanth of the withered flesh of his right hand — the constant reminder of his last encounter with the Sword. He longed to return that cursed object to Amphileph. Amphileph would use it to reshape the world and raise Citanth to the status he deserved. Once he delivered the Sword, everything — even his ruined arm — would be made right again.

"Where is the Angrodha?" he shouted to his troops.

The flames still raged on the eastern side of the Highborne River, but the river's width had spared the western growth from catching fire. Little remained of the Rionese tree-fortress — only ash, charred beams, and the scattered remnants of those who had stood their posts to the bitter end.

"Look!" Citanth cried.

"Look at what remains of the fools who opposed Amphileph's power! The men of Rion have only delayed their fate!"

In the distance, Shinetower rose above the horizon.

"There it is!" Citanth laughed.

"We march to Shinetower unopposed, my warriors!"

Then the wind shifted violently, stirring the smoke into a rising wall. It twisted, thickened, and shaped itself. Even over the thunder of marching feet, Citanth was certain he heard Amphileph calling his name — distant, layered with the rumble of thunder rolling through the darkening clouds to the east and south.

Citanth straightened in his seat, scanning the horizon. Among the ashes he saw the broken weaponry of Rion, scattered beside the bodies of those who had refused to flee. The voice grew louder. The wind whipped the smoke into a towering form — Amphileph, floating above the ruins of Highwood, arms outstretched toward him.

"Bow down!" Citanth screamed, rising in his carriage.

The Camonra halted mid-stride and dropped to one knee. The captains reined in their Azrodhs and followed suit. Citanth leapt from his carriage and ran toward Highwood, falling to one knee before the smoky apparition.

"My lord, we do your bidding!" Citanth said. He looked down at the ground, but not before he managed another glimpse of Amphileph's wispy form, shifting in the wind.

Amphileph's voice drifted in and out on the winds. "The Angrodha is no more," he said. "Mategaladh has destroyed it."

"My lord?" Citanth responded.

"Silence!" Amphileph said. "It is no matter. His powers were not great enough to end its life force, only alter it. I anticipated as much! What remains now are the Syra, and they will come to your aid in destroying my enemies. Behold!"

The form of Amphileph mixed with the wing wash of hundreds of Syra, swirling above the heads of Citanth and his soldiers. Hundreds of the tiny winged creatures landed among them and spread their mouths open to show their rows of circular teeth, making that clicking sound that drowned out all else. The intensity of their calls rose until the Syra became so agitated that they began to fight among themselves all around the soldiers.

One of the Azrodhs became spooked and rose up on its hind legs. Its rider rose to grab for its reins, and the sudden movement caught the attention of the Syra. A wave of leathery flesh washed over rider and Azrodh and engulfed them. Their tails squirmed in the pile, the awful clicking noises rising and falling with the howls of the Azrodh and the screams of the rider beneath them. The Camon shot up from the pile, throwing half a dozen of the Syra off. The Azrodh shook off the Syra with a twisting quiver that ran the length of its scaly hide.

One of the Syra had driven its spear-like tail into the rider's spine and whipped its body forward, sinking its teeth into the back of his head. The soldier screamed and flailed, and the wings of the Syra flapped madly around his face. The Syra's lower jaw unhinged, and its circular row of hook-shaped teeth stretched the scalp across the top of his head. The Syra's body arched up and its eyes blinked; then the sound of crunching bone could be heard, and the soldier's arms relaxed and fell to his side.

The sound of collective awe caused Citanth to look slowly toward the chaos, when he saw his soldier's torso twitch like a dog shaking water from its coat. His head bobbed, and the Syra seemed to gag. Its eyes rolled back in its head, and its eyelids fluttered closed. The Syra's torso collapsed against the back of the soldier's neck, and it appeared to push its internal organs into the soldier's skull cavity.

The Camon soldier fell to one knee and then to the side, his hand barely stopping his toppling over. The sides of the Syra shuddered, it exhaled, and the soldier seemed to gain some bearings and stood back up on two feet. He rose, and the Camonra surrounding him looked in horror at his face. His eyes were lifeless and his mouth was agape, blood drooling its way down the side of his neck.

Citanth could see the makings of panic. The Camonra began moving back from their comrade, exciting the Syra into an even more frenzied state. The winged parasites swirled into the air and back to the ground, shuffling again and making that awful clicking sound.

The Camon with the Syra parasitically attached began to walk toward Shinetower. His comrades cleared him a path, and he continued without acknowledging their existence.

The ethereal form of Amphileph folded its arms. "Enough!" he said, and the flock of Syra swirled into the sky.

Citanth let his eyes look up to the mist. "My lord, Amphileph, what is your command?" he asked.

"Make your camp here. I will see through the Syra's eyes as I did through the Angrodha. Let the creatures make their way into the land of men. I'll search them out, and then I will issue your next command." The Syra dove back down, crossing just over their heads in a swarm, and then the creatures shot through the mist that was Amphileph and disappeared into the sky.

The mist dissipated and the figure of Amphileph was gone.

*　*　*

Ardhios woke to the smell of wood burning. He gently moved Portina's head from his shoulder, rose from the bed, and stepped onto the balcony. From the window he saw smoke rising from Highwood. His heart lurched. He dressed quickly and hurried downstairs.

Several workers from Highwood stood in the courtyard outside the Seven Warriors Hall, their distress unmistakable.

"My lord, riders come from Highwood!" one cried.

"The Camonra have attacked our people — burning them out of their homes, killing many of our kin! Large numbers of them have camped southeast of the ruins!"

Ardhios seized a runner.

"Get Borian at once!"

The runner took flight, and within minutes Borian arrived in the courtyard.

"The Camonra are moving on Highwood and the Dales," Ardhios said.

"What would you have me do?" Borian asked.

"Gather your troops and join us. The people of the west must stand together."

Mordher emerged from the Hall.

"A meeting without me?"

Ardhios pointed toward the southern road.

"Look, Mordher! Look what is happening!"

A great number of Highwood's people were approaching — soldiers, families, elders — all fleeing north toward the Seven Warriors Hall.

Ardhios's voice cracked with fury.

"What in the Creator's name have you started, Mordher?"

A servant appeared with his horse, and Ardhios practically leapt into the saddle.

"We must defend these people!"

He didn't wait for Borian or Mordher to answer. He spurred his horse forward, galloping toward the oncoming crowd. Soldiers and civilians shouted as he approached. Many bore burns; their clothes and faces were blackened with soot.

"Help us, sire!" they cried.

The crowd pressed in around him. Ardhios reined in his horse, calming it as best he could.

"The Inferiors have burned us alive!" another shouted.

"Come to the Great Hall!" Ardhios called.

"We have supplies and healers. You are welcome here!"

He turned his horse and rode back toward the courtyard.

"The Camonra are attacking the people of Highwood," Ardhios shouted.

"We must ride out to meet them! We will combine our forces and drive the Camonra back!"

"My warriors follow no one but me!" Mordher barked.

Ardhios felt fury rise, but he forced himself to think. The people of Highwood were watching him — *needing* him.

"Mordher, have you not seen how I've amassed an army equal to yours?" Ardhios said.

"Join me in defending these people, and all will see that I follow you."

Mordher smiled, slow and poisonous.

"Now you need me? Now you need to fight, and suddenly I'm in your favor again?"

Ardhios bit his tongue.

"Borian, will you join me?"

Borian blinked, stunned — then extended his hand.

"Yes, my brother. I will take the fight to the Inferiors."

Mordher snorted.

"What are you without me?"

"Gather your army, then," Borian shot back.

"Show me how a true warrior fights."

Mordher's eyes narrowed.

"I will show you how to kill Inferiors!" he roared.

He turned to his soldiers.

"Get my horse!"

Ardhios turned to the refugees.

"Go to the Warriors Hall!"

"Every soldier stays!" Mordher shouted.

"Let the women and children make their way to Candra!"

"They're worn and tattered, Mordher! What good will they be to us?" Ardhios countered.

"They'll make fine fodder for the Inferiors if they don't obey!" Mordher snapped.

"Foot soldiers — that's their place!"

Ardhios glared at him.

"Depart!" he commanded the soldiers.

"Join the others in the camp. There's water and food — gather your strength."

The Highwood soldiers exchanged uneasy glances.

"Yes, my liege," they said, and headed toward Mordher's encampment.

Once they were out of earshot, Ardhios rounded on Mordher.

"Is this what you wanted?"

Mordher sneered.

"What can you expect from people who build their houses in trees?"

"What?" Ardhios stared at him, then turned to Borian.

"Has he lost his mind?"

"I'll not speak for him," Borian said.

"He lies happily in the bed he's made."

Ardhios stepped closer, voice rising.

"You've started a war! The whole of the Spellmaker's army is set against us. We must band together — the survivors of Rion — or they'll destroy us one by one. With Highwood gone, we have no choice but to go to Moonledge Peak and plead for their aid. Mordher, this battle could be our undoing!"

He turned to Borian.

"I cannot trust him with my army. But I would turn them over to you. Will you lead them in my stead until I return?"

Borian allowed himself a brief moment of satisfaction at Mordher's scowl.

"Yes," he said.

Mordher leaned forward in his saddle, jaw jutting in contempt.

"Let them come!" he shouted.

"Take your people to the valley, Ardhios, and leave the fighting to the men."

Ardhios drew his sword, and Mordher mirrored him.

"Be still!" Borian barked. Both men turned toward him, weighing his loyalties.

"Be gone, Ardhios. There is no shame in being savior to the homeless. Ignore him — and go."

"I didn't survive two years in a Rionese prison to listen to such madness!" Ardhios shouted.

"I will take fifty of my men to escort Highwood's survivors. Then I ride for Moonledge!"

"Take them," Borian said.

Ardhios spurred his horse toward the townspeople.

"People of Highwood!" he cried.

"Listen to me! Women and children — follow me! Soldiers of Highwood — form up here!"

He circled left, and the people obeyed. Then he swung back toward Borian and Mordher.

"May the Creator protect us!"

He drove his horse forward and raced toward the Seven Warriors Hall.

"Captain!" Borian called.

"Separate the women and children from the men!"

"Yes, my liege!"

Soldiers began herding the weak toward the Hall. Borian addressed the remaining warriors.

"Soldiers of Highwood, you are hereby conscripted to fight for Candra! The women and children will follow Ardhios to safety. You will fight the Camonra with us!"

Mordher thrust his sword skyward.

"Soldiers! Form up! We march for the Northern Bridge!"

Ardhios watched his army follow Mordher and Borian, wondering if he had done the right thing. He called to his captain:

"Take them to the Seven Warriors Hall. I ride to Moonledge Peak and will return as soon as possible!"

He spurred his horse and galloped away.

*　*　*

Six hours later, Ardhios stopped at Highborne Falls to rest his horse and refill his water. He walked the animal around the base of the Candra Mountains, the Faceless Mountains rising in the distance. Then he mounted again and rode through the night. Just as dawn broke, he reached the outskirts of Moonledge Peak.

The damage from the Angrodha was everywhere. The Keep stood

open, and soldiers were piling brush and debris onto the creature's carcass to burn away its stench. The mood was tense.

"Who goes there?" a soldier called.

"His colors are Candrian," another said.

"Looks like they've sent but one soldier to aid our cause!"

A ripple of laughter followed.

"I am Ardhios of the Seven Warriors!" he shouted.

The laughter died instantly.

"Take me to Caratacus!"

"At once, my lord!" the soldier said.

Ardhios dismounted.

"Wet down my horse and water it. I've little time before I must ride again."

He strode up the Keep's stairs. Women were carrying flowers in armfuls.

"What has happened here?" he asked.

"A Watcher lies near death in our walls," a woman said.

"He gave his life to destroy the monster."

"A Watcher?"

"Yes, my lord — Mategaladh."

Ardhios pushed forward into the council chambers. Caratacus and the council were deep in discussion while healers spoke urgently of bleeding, herbs, and remedies for the dying Watcher.

"Caratacus!" Ardhios called.

Caratacus turned.

"I am Caratacus. You wear the colors of the Candrians. What news have you?"

"My lord, I am Ardhios of Candra. The war is far from over. We need warriors to drive the Camonra from our lands. Amphileph's army marches on Highwood and the Dales — and when they are finished there, they will march on Candra."

"We've no warriors to spare," Caratacus replied.

"We've troubles enough here."

"But my lord—"

Caratacus cut him off.

"You Candrians. What gall! Was it not enough that we allowed your brethren to attempt taking the Sword of Evliit? What more do you want from us?"

Ardhios frowned.

"The Sword of Evliit? Who tried to take it?"

"The one called Mordher," Caratacus said.

"But the Sword rejected him. We will keep it until Evliit himself returns. Allowing Mordher even to see it was a mistake — one made in fear for our lives, and one we will not repeat."

"My lord, I have little time. Surely you could—"

"It is of no use to argue, Ardhios. Our decision is—"

A commotion erupted at the side entrance. Priests hurried in, whispering urgently to Caratacus — but before they finished, a figure appeared in the doorway.

Mategaladh, pale and trembling, stood propped on his staff.

The hall fell silent. People dropped to their faces.

"Praise the Creator!" Caratacus breathed.

"We thought you dead, Watcher! We never—"

"I am near enough to death," Mategaladh said, cutting him off, "but not ready to let the people of Highwood, the Dales, or Candra fall to Amphileph."

He pointed a shaking hand toward Ardhios.

"Give this man his chance with the Sword. It goes nowhere it does not wish to be."

His knees buckled. Priests caught him.

"You must rest!" the high priest urged.

"I must defend the people of Erathe!" Mategaladh cried.

"Give him the Sword — now!"

He coughed violently, struggling for breath. The priest nodded to the guards. They pulled back the tapestries and brought forth the chest.

Before the ceremonial words could begin, Ardhios stepped forward, opened the chest, lifted the case, and drew out the Sword in its scabbard.

A collective gasp filled the hall.

Mategaladh's voice softened.

"You are worthy, Ardhios."

He steadied himself against the priests.

"Listen to me. You will need a Calarphian horse to reach Shinetower with all speed. One named Galbard there will know what must be done. Will you do this?"

"I will," Ardhios said.

"There is no time to lose..." Mategaladh whispered — and collapsed into the priests' arms as they carried him away.

Caratacus straightened, shaken but resolute.

"Bring this man a horse!"

The hall erupted into motion.

*   *   *

For two days, Citanth waited for word from Amphileph about the Syra's movements along the Highborne River, but there was no word. He had ordered the Camonra to sift through the ashes of Highwood, but there was little to nothing that they could salvage for war. He walked to the edge of the Highborne River and looked across at the trees on the other side. Items were scattered along a path leading south to the Northern Bridge, but other than the occasional decomposing body, there was no sign of the humans. He knelt over a small eddy and looked at his reflection, almost gathering back some of the humanity he had lost in Amphileph's captivity, but letting it slip away in the next moment.

There was no escaping what he had become, and when he focused on the water's reflection, it began to change, and an image of the Camon appeared, his Syran parasite bored into his head, distorting his facial features. The decaying Camon's mouth hung open, and the Syra pushed its tongue through the opening and lapped at the water. It shifted inside the Camon's head, twitching the wings that protruded out of the back of the Camon's crushed cranium. It too had come upon the river's edge and found no crossing in sight for its host. The Camon's body was still strong, and the Syra knew it could still feed off it for days, pushing it day and night, up and down the riverbank in search of a crossing. Citanth struck the surface of the water in his frustration, and the vision ended. The wait was driving him mad.

He returned to the main body of warriors, who were also impatient, waiting around a fire they had made from a ten-foot high pile of partially burned remains. The wind rose up suddenly and stoked it into a whirlwind of flame that began to consume the gruesome fuel. It became so hot that those surrounding it had to shield their faces and push back from it. Then, all at once, the Camonra began to shout and chant, for Amphileph's form had appeared in the flames.

"The men protect a bridge that crosses into their lands south of Highwood." Amphileph's voice could be heard coming from the fire.

"Destroy them!" the voice wailed. The fire suddenly intensified and then just as suddenly snuffed out, cold. The Camonra leapt to their feet and screamed for battle.

They quickly assembled into a column to march westward. "To the bridge!" Citanth cried. "Destroy them!"

"Destroy them!" the Camonra shouted in response.

*　　*　　*

Ardhios rode around Highborne Falls in little more than half the time it had taken him the day before. He pushed through the Candra Valley at breakneck speed, at times fearing exhaustion would drop him from the saddle — only to find strength again in the thrill of carrying the Sword of Evliit at his side.

He shot past a line of soldiers marching from Candra, and by midafternoon Shinetower rose on the horizon. Within the hour he reached its gates, where warriors of the Dales labored to build barbicans around the courtyard walls. He pulled the proud Calarphian horse to a halt and dismounted, his legs trembling from the ride.

"I must find a man by the name of Galbard!" he called.

The soldiers exchanged a single look and answered together: "This way!"

Ardhios followed them into Shinetower, keeping the Sword wrapped in a long rawhide bag until they reached the upper deck, where Galbard and the others were bent over a map, drawing the lines of battle.

"My lord, this is Ardhios of Candra," the soldier announced.

"I've no time—" Galbard began, not looking up.

"Unbelievable! Galbard, look!" Aleris exclaimed.

Ardhios had dropped to one knee, holding the Sword of the Watch before him, head bowed.

"I bring this Sword to its rightful bearer, in the name of the Watcher Mategaladh."

Footsteps approached. The Sword lifted from his open hands. Ardhios looked up to see Galbard's face — stern, resolute, transformed.

"It seems I cannot escape my destiny," Galbard said.

The others stared in stunned silence.

"How can we ever repay your efforts, Ardhios? We owe more than we can say."

"Help me protect my people," Ardhios replied.

"This is all I ask, good sire."

"You look exhausted. Rest a while in Shinetower."

"I cannot rest until this evil is driven from our lands," Ardhios said.

"I leave the Sword in your capable hands. I must return to the Seven Warriors Hall. My brothers will not understand why I brought the Sword here, and the people of Highwood need sanctuary. My place is there."

Galbard placed the Sword upon Ardhios's shoulders.

A surge of spiritual energy coursed through him, making his eyes widen and his back arch.

"May the Warriors of Light protect you," Galbard said.

"Rise, Ardhios — the first knight of Shinetower."

Ardhios rose, fully energized despite the impossible ride.

"The power of the Sword in your hands is miraculous," he said.

"I bid you well."

"Fare thee well, Ardhios," Galbard answered.

*　　*　　*

"Someone's coming!" a voice cried from Cayden's front lines.

The warning rippled down the ranks. Cayden pushed forward.

"What do you see?"

"A Camon, I think."

Cayden peered into the early-morning gloom. A lone figure was running toward them, slightly left of center. He clapped the nearest soldier on the shoulder.

"Good eye, brother."

He raised his voice.

"Four archers — ready!"

Four bowmen stepped forward and lifted their bows.

"Steady…"

They drew.

"Fire!"

The arrows arced into the dim sky. Cayden tracked them until they vanished against the firmament. The lone figure kept running — until three arrows struck him in the neck, shoulder, and chest. He collapsed.

"Scouts! Front and center!"

Two slim runners approached. Their fear was plain.

"See what you can find. Don't tarry — there may be more scouts behind him."

"Yes, my liege!"

They sprinted toward the fallen Camon. They were two-thirds of the way there when the body moved. The soldier pushed up to one knee, arrows still jutting from his flesh.

The scouts froze and looked back.

"Hold!" Cayden shouted, waving them back.

They sprinted for the bridge.

"Archers!"

The bowmen raised their weapons again.

"Fire!"

All four arrows struck true — one above the knee, two in the chest, one in the abdomen. The figure twisted with the impact, and the men could see the arrows had passed clean through.

The Camon dropped to one knee.

Then the flurry began.

A winged creature tore itself free from the back of the soldier's head, beating its wings hard as it ripped loose and shot into the air. The body fell face-down and did not move again.

The scouts ran out once more, circling the corpse cautiously before kneeling to inspect it. They returned at a run.

"It's an Inferior, sire," one said.

"But whatever that creature was — it ripped open the back of his head getting out."

The second scout swallowed.

"I rolled him over, sire. His face… he looked like he'd been dead for some time. I don't understand it."

"Well done," Cayden said.

"Move to the rear — no. You—return to Galbard. Tell him what you've seen. Inform him that we are ready: catapults and archers in place."

The older scout stepped forward.

"My lord… my brother Antio is younger. If it please you, let him go."

"Of course."

The younger scout touched his chest in salute and sprinted away.

"Move to the rear, son," Cayden told the remaining scout.

"It'll get ugly up here."

"Yes, my lord." He ran.

A shout rose from Cayden's left.

"My lord! Riders from the north!"

The men saw the Candrian banner cresting the hill and erupted in cheers.

Borian reined his horse to a sharp stop. Mordher halted behind him, raising a fist to stop the army.

"Who's in charge here?" Borian called.

"I am," Cayden answered.

Borian dismounted and clasped Cayden's forearm.

"We've come to kill Inferiors."

"We're glad to see you!" Cayden said.

"We've been charged with delaying their march until our people have fled. Then we fall back to the tower and make our stand. We've reinforcements and man-traps there."

"Retreat is your plan?" Mordher sneered as he thumped down from his horse.

"Why would we retreat?"

"We've no idea of their exact numbers," Cayden replied.

"But the Inferiors have mounted an impressive force. We've seen them from the tower's height. They mean to make war upon us."

"Who speaks of war without armor?" Mordher scoffed.

"Mordher—" Borian cut in, giving him a stern look.

"Forgive my friend. He means no disrespect."

"We are masons and craftsmen, hunters and farmers," Cayden said.

"But we defend our land — and that should not be underestimated."

"If they cross the Northern Bridge, they'll march straight to Shinetower," Mordher said.

"We must break their lines and scatter them here."

"We've sent the people of the Dales to Candra," Cayden answered.

"We'll draw the Inferiors toward the tower so the women and children are furthest from the battle. The soldiers of Candra will be the last defense if the worst happens. Pull your soldiers back and meet them in the northern fields if you must. At the very least, we'll have thinned their ranks."

"We might flank them as they attack the Dales, brother," Borian said.

Mordher grunted.

"Flanking sounds good."

"But if you meet them here, who protects our people if they turn north?" Cayden asked.

"We are four thousand strong," Borian said.

"They'll not easily overrun us."

Mordher jabbed a finger toward Cayden.

"So what is it, then?"

"We'll do as Galbard commanded," Cayden said.

"But nothing in that prevents your plan of attack. Let us seek the Creator's will."

"You seek the Creator's will," Mordher growled.

"I'll sharpen my sword and axe."

He turned to leave — but a shout rose from the front lines. A runner burst into their midst, breathless.

"My lord Cayden! Thousands of Inferiors approach! And something flies above them — hundreds, maybe thousands of bat-like creatures! Or vultures — I don't know, sire — but they're creatures of the evil one, by the very sight of them!"

"Spread the word!" Cayden commanded.

He turned to the runner.

"Ready the catapults and archers!"

The runner sprinted away.

Cayden faced the Candrians.

"What say you?"

Mordher raised his weapons high.

"Ready the cavalry! Archers! Shields, spears, spikes! We kill Inferiors today!"

His battle cry electrified his soldiers — as if he had been born for this moment.

Borian pointed north.

"We'll wait just over that hill."

He called to Cayden:

"Give them your catapults and arrows. Flee, and let them give chase — just as you've been commanded. We'll be watching. When you take flight, we'll flank them!"

The two Candrian leaders mounted their horses. Cayden watched them ride back to the main army, leading their forces over the hill and out of sight.

Cayden took one knee and called to the heavens.

"Creator!"

At that single word, the whole of the Shinetower fighters knelt with him. Cayden lifted his voice in prayer:

"Holy Creator! We give thanks for Your many blessings — for family we may call our own, and for neighbor who stands beside us in our time of need.

Thank You for the special blessing of our wives and children, our brothers and sisters.

Protect us, that we may rejoin them in a time of peace.

Give us victory over the evil that presses down upon us.

May our enemies depart our lands and return to their homes defeated, never to return."

He drew a breath, and his voice deepened.

"And if this be the day we join our ancestors in the Third Domain, may it be with such a valiant stand that the warriors who have gone before us will smile at our arrival, knowing that we have died well and right."

Cayden rose, and his men rose with him. He tightened his swordbelt, turned toward the lines, and shouted:

"Catapults!"

Cayden pulled glass pieces and a thick leather sheet from his pocket. He set the glass at either end, wrapped the leather around them to form a spyglass, and peered through it. What appeared to be the Camonra leader was shouting something—then a swarm of winged creatures dove past him, streaking toward the Shinetower fighters.

"The flying creatures attack!" Cayden shouted. He stowed the spyglass and pointed.

"Archers, fire!"

A hail of arrows tore into the oncoming swarm, dropping hundreds of Syra from the sky. Bodies tumbled and skidded across the ground—but the vast majority spiraled around the arrows, weaving through the volleys and closing the distance.

Cayden felt the plan unraveling.

"Fire!" he screamed.

Another wave of arrows filled the air. The Syra scattered outward, clearing his view—and revealing the Camonra charging behind them. Thousands. His men saw it too. Terror rippled through the line.

"Hold! Hold!" Cayden shouted.

"Fire catapults!"

The catapults hurled their stones through the haze of wings, smashing Syra midair—but the drag of flesh and wing slowed the projectiles, and they fell short of the Camonra ranks.

Then the Syra hit the archers.

They descended in a frenzy—hind legs gripping, claws slashing. Cayden watched helplessly as his men were overwhelmed. They were dying in droves. Standing their ground wasn't valor—it was suicide.

"Run!" Cayden cried.

The men tried to flee, but the Syra were everywhere. Panic shattered the line. Packs of the creatures landed among them, dragging men down.

*   *   *

"Form ranks!" Mordher cried, and the Candrian soldiers flooded the hillside overlooking the Northern Bridge. Even Mordher paused at the sight of the sheer number of Camonra spreading out from the bridge into the Dales.

"Cavalry to the front!" he shouted, and the archers broke ranks to let the horses thunder past.

Approaching the bridge, Citanth saw the shift in formation. The Candrians were not preparing to defend — they meant to attack.

"Syra!" he screamed.

"Arm yourselves!"

The Syra swooped down upon the dead. Many found suitable hosts, and a hundred or more corpses lurched upright, joining Citanth's foot soldiers. The Camonra kept their distance as the Syra armed their hosts with weapons scattered across the battlefield. Now the living and the dead turned their attention toward the Candrian army.

"What is your bidding, master?" the Camonra captain asked, eager for blood.

Citanth pointed toward the Candrians.

"Let the Syra deal with them. We move on the Dales."

The monstrous horde — the dead men of the Dale — shuffled forward.

The Candrians met them with a barrage of arrows. A few struck true, killing the parasites by piercing their hosts' skulls, but most only maimed the corpses without stopping them.

With each passing moment, the Syra grew more lethal. They drew their hosts' swords and advanced without hesitation, unfazed by the second and third volleys that struck them before they crashed into the Candrian cavalry.

"Kill them all!" Citanth roared.

Three and four Syra-ridden corpses swarmed each rider, clawing, slashing, biting, stabbing — often striking one another as much as the Candrian — but dragging horse and rider down all the same.

"We're losing the cavalry!" Mordher shouted.

"Infantry, attack! Archers to the front!" Borian commanded.

The hillside shook with the roar of battle cries and the thunder of boots. A wall of foot soldiers charged down to meet the Syra-hosts, while the archers formed a line before Borian and Mordher.

The Syra and their hosts tore through the cavalry until the infantry crashed into them, overwhelming them with sheer numbers. Several Syra tried to escape by tearing free of their hosts, only to be shot down by Candrian arrows.

The battle raged in the valley between the two rolling hills. Borian saw the Camonra leader continuing to funnel soldiers into the Dales. When more than half had crossed the Northern Bridge, he watched him signal the two companies already on the western side to join the Syra's assault.

Borian leapt from his horse.

"Inferiors!"

Mordher did the same.

"Lose the horses! This is going to be up close and personal!" Mordher shouted.

As the two hundred or so Camonra stormed the battlefield, the two thousand Candrian soldiers tightened their formation, shields locked and swords raised, bracing against the sheer size and strength of the enemy. Some of the Camonra simply plowed into the line, battering men to the ground and picking them off one by one.

"Come to me, offspring of Amphileph!" Mordher roared at the nearest Camon.

The creature's head snapped toward him, and it bellowed back, spittle flying.

"Come closer, and I'll give you your chance to honor the Creator! I'll parade your head on a pike!"

The Camon charged, swinging its great axe in a wide lateral arc that narrowly missed Mordher's face. A backhanded return swing swept upward across his body — another near miss. On the third strike, Mordher caught the blow on his shield, driving it into the ground and forcing the Inferior to overreach. Mordher stepped in and rammed his sword into its throat to the hilt, ripping it free at an angle that nearly severed the head.

"Let me get to their leader!" Mordher shouted.

"I'll rip out his heart with my bare hands!"

Borian rode down the line, trying to reach him.

"Twenty companies have already made it into the Dales of Shinetower," Borian warned.

"We are no match for those numbers!"

Even as he spoke, the bulk of the Camonra marched southwest toward the villages.

"The Camonra go to Shinetower!" Mordher snarled.

Only two companies remained to face the Candrians. A brief lull settled between the armies, each side giving the other a few paces of space.

"They mean to hold their ground — to hold us back!" Mordher growled, and he and the Candrians hurled curses and taunts across the gap.

"We've taken heavy losses," Borian said.

"We must pull back, Mordher. The Dales are on their own now."

"No!" Mordher shouted.

"We can take them!"

His defiance ignited the tension. One of the Camonra answered the taunts by charging straight into the Candrian line, swinging his great axe and launching three men into the air. The display emboldened the rest, and the Camonra surged forward, smashing into the Candrians, breaking their lines, and cutting them down left and right.

*　　*　　*

The Candrians fought bravely, but even with their superior numbers, they won the field only at a terrible cost. More than half their army lay dead or dying. The last of the Camonra fell beneath Candrian blades and arrows — and still Mordher screamed for more.

"Cavalry, mount up!" Mordher bellowed.

Borian, bleeding heavily, was being helped back to his horse by two soldiers.

"Are you mad?" Borian shouted.

He pushed the soldiers aside long enough to cinch a strip of cloth around the deep gash in his thigh.

"We lie in ruin at the hands of a fraction of their army, and you want to follow them? We go to Candra and bar our doors, praying the fighters of Shinetower finish what we cannot!"

"I turn away from no one!" Mordher roared.

"Then you go that way alone, brother!" Borian answered.

He turned to the remaining Candrian troops.

"We go to Candra!"

"You do not give the orders, Borian!" Mordher snarled.

Borian met his gaze once — a cold, exhausted stare — then turned his horse toward the Candra Valley and began a weary trot. One by one, the Candrian warriors turned their backs on Mordher and followed their wounded commander.

Mordher snapped. He seized the nearest soldier and hurled him to the ground.

"You don't leave unless I give the order!" he screamed.

Borian wheeled his horse and galloped back. Several warriors rushed in, forming a ring around Mordher.

"Leave him be, Mordher!" Borian shouted.

"Leave him be — or deal with all of us!"

Mordher drew back his sword, ready to drive it through the fallen soldier — but the sound of two dozen blades being drawn froze him. He looked up. The men were closing in, slowly, deliberately.

"You would dare challenge me?" Mordher cried.

"I will kill you all!"

"Leave him be," Borian repeated, voice iron-hard.

"We are not the enemy — but we will not let you kill our own."

Mordher saw fear in their faces — but something stronger beneath it: resolve. If he pushed this further, he would not survive it.

He released the soldier's armor, letting him fall. He whistled sharply, and his horse trotted to his side. Mordher sheathed his sword, swung into the saddle, and glared at them all.

"This will not be forgotten!" he shouted, and he galloped away toward Candra.

*　　*　　*

Cayden and the remaining Shinetower fighters sprinted into the outskirts of the Dales, scattering into alleyways and side streets, hoping only to hide long enough for the Syra to pass overhead. Seeking cover, Cayden kicked in the door of a small cottage and stumbled inside. His lungs burned, his heart hammered against his ribs, but he managed to shove a table in front of the door.

Through the window he saw young Antio race past, screaming in terror, before disappearing into the alley behind the cottage.

You need to hide, boy, Cayden thought.

He moved to the back window, but Antio was nowhere in sight.

"Antio? Antio, are you there?"

"Cayden?" came the reply.

"Is that you?"

"Yes, it's me."

"Did you see them? Are they still coming?"

"They're just behind us," Cayden said.

"We need to find a way out of the Dales, but right now you must get out of the open."

"I saw those flying creatures carry away my brother Marcus," Antio said, voice breaking.

"Several of them latched onto him and carried him away!"

Cayden heard the desperation — the edge of panic. If the boy lost control, he was dead. Cayden forced calm into his voice.

"Have you any arrows left?"

There was a pause as the clicking of Syra wings passed somewhere overhead.

"Four in my quiver… and one on my bow," Antio answered.

The clicking faded.

"What are we going to do?"

"We must get back to the tower," Cayden said.

"Have you seen the others?"

"They're scattered through the village," Antio replied.

Shouts of Inferiors echoed in the distance.

"We'll never make it to the Gates of Shinetower!"

"We've got to keep moving, Antio," Cayden called — but there was no answer.

He strained to listen. The clicking returned, louder now, circling overhead. Cayden scanned the cottage and spotted a back door leading to the alley. He moved toward it — then froze.

The clicking stopped.

Then came a single click.

Then another.

Then several more, each louder than the last, each cutting off abruptly.

Cayden heard the patter of feet on the wooden roof above him.

"Antio! On the roof!" he hissed.

The clicking erupted all around them.

Antio screamed.

Cayden fumbled with the latch, threw open the back door, and burst into the cobblestone alley.

Shoulder-high stone walls lined the narrow passage. Antio was pinned against one of them — a Syra crouched atop him, his arrows scattered across the ground, one of his hands trapped in its jaws while the other clawed desperately at the barbed tail embedded in his shoulder.

"Antio!" Cayden hollered — but another Syra shot past him, skidding across the cobblestones before rolling to its feet. It leapt, its barbed tail slicing the air where Cayden's head had been a heartbeat earlier. He dove to the ground, and the creature vaulted back over the cottage roof and vanished.

"Help!" Antio cried.

He released the Syra's tail and drew a short blade, hacking through the tail halfway. The creature shrieked and clamped its jaws down on his hand, ripping away his pinky, his ring finger, and half his middle finger. Antio stabbed it again and again, long after it stopped moving.

"Antio!" Cayden shouted, rushing to him.

"Get up, boy!"

Antio was in shock. He jerked his blade up as if to strike Cayden, splattering the wall with black blood.

"Wait!" Cayden said.

"It's me, Antio — it's me!"

"Help me..." Antio gasped.

He stared at his mangled hand, then back at Cayden, tears brimming.

"Help me..."

Cayden scooped up the scattered arrows and shoved them into Antio's quiver, then slung the bow over his shoulder. Screams echoed from the north.

"We have got to go now!" Cayden said, hauling the young scout to his feet.

Out of the corner of his eye, he saw the temple the Bhre-Nora had built over the escape tunnel that surfaced in the Dales.

The temple door stood ajar.

"Come, Antio!"

"I can go no further," Antio whispered.

Cayden wrapped an arm around his waist.

"Hold onto me!"

Syra swarmed to the east, rising high into the evening sky before diving into the rooftops. Cayden and Antio climbed the temple steps as the shouts of Camonra soldiers filled the town square.

A lone Camonra scout appeared from nowhere.

"Humans!" he cried.

He fired a crossbow bolt — missed — and charged, reloading as he ran. Cayden set Antio on the steps and shoved open the massive wooden door.

"Humans!" the scout screamed again, closing the distance in great bounds.

Antio had managed to draw an arrow. With his chewed-off hand he strained to pull the bowstring, tears streaming down his face. He and the scout fired almost simultaneously — the bolt struck Antio through the heart, and Antio's arrow drove upward through the Camon's neck.

"No!" Cayden cried.

He lurched toward the doorway before realizing Antio was already gone. He slammed the temple door shut. Inside, he found a locking mechanism — but he couldn't make sense of it.

Panic clawed at him. The Camonra battle drums thundered outside, closer and closer.

He turned, trying to recall Aleris's words. The temple housed the entrance to their world — *but where?*

He ran to the nearest door and flung it open. Inside stood a towering statue of Rendaya. There was no time to marvel. He circled the room, searching for any hidden passage, any seam in the stone — nothing.

Desperate, he crouched behind the statue's base. The war drums pounded just outside. He edged forward to peer toward the entrance, expecting the doors to burst inward at any moment.

Then he saw it — a Rionese inscription carved into the back of the statue's base.

"For Her Love the War Began," Cayden read aloud.

The stone beneath him shifted. With a grinding rumble, it dropped away, revealing a stairway descending beneath the statue's massive pedestal.

"May the Creator bless your name, Aleris," Cayden breathed — and he descended into the caves of the Bhre-Nora.

*   *   *

Rendaya looked down at the shadows stretching across the Dales.

"They've taken the Shinetower Dales," she said.

"They'll reach the Gates of Shinetower by tomorrow afternoon."

"I cannot see the Candrians anywhere," Galbard replied, his voice flat.

"It seems we are alone in this."

Ronan stepped onto the deck.

"I hope I'm not interrupting, Father."

"Not at all," Galbard said.

"Rendaya, this is my son, Ronan."

"I'm pleased to meet you, Ronan," she said.

"Though I wish it were under different circumstances."

"I've heard you've come to help my father."

"We work together to keep the Sword from Amphileph," Rendaya answered.

Ronan bowed.

"I thank the Creator that you are here. One with your powers is a blessing indeed."

"It will take the sacrifice of many to succeed today," she said quietly.

Galbard pointed toward the swirling mass of Syra, their wings glowing orange in the evening sun as they circled over the town.

"A great many of the flying creatures remain."

"You've good archers, you say?" Rendaya asked.

"Deadly accurate archers."

"Then we must keep the Syra away from the altar. You must pour the Sword's power into the altar stone. Use it well, and Shinetower will defend you."

Galbard turned toward the stone altar.

"It has been so long. Releasing the power into the stone… that was easy once."

"And it will be again," Rendaya said.

"You and the Sword remain one. Focus on an even flow. Keep control."

"At the altar, I can't see the courtyard—"

"Worry not about the tower's defenses," Rendaya said.

"Only the Bhre-Nora know them. Aleris will command them. I will defend you with all my strength."

"May I have a moment with my father?" Ro asked.

Rendaya studied him briefly, then nodded.

"Of course. I'll speak with the archers. With your permission, I'll spread them among the balconies and bring the finest to the deck."

"Yes, of course," Galbard said.

"I'll return shortly. With your leave."

She descended the stairs.

Galbard turned to Ro.

"What is it?"

Ro hesitated, searching his father's face.

"I fear for you, Father. We're placing everything in the hands of Rendaya and the Bhre-Nora, and here on the deck… there's nowhere to go if things go badly. I know you trust Aleris, but being cornered like this—it doesn't seem wise. We should take the Sword to the Candrians, join forces with them. Together we might push the Camonra back."

Galbard watched the Syra swirling over the Dales, their wings catching the dying light. He closed his eyes and let the wind brush his face. "I've tried to outrun my destiny, Ro," he said softly.

"But I know now this is where I should be."

"Father—"

"Signal the Bhre-Nora," Galbard said, turning to him.

"And ask your mother and Tiamphia to join me on the upper deck with all haste. I would speak with them."

"Yes, Father."

Ro bowed and descended the stairs to the outer balconies. He gave the trumpeters the signal, then turned toward the family quarters. Before he reached the landing, Jalin and Tiamphia emerged.

"We heard the trumpets," Tiamphia said.

Jalin's eyes widened.

"May the Creator keep us. Your father has called upon the Bhre-Nora?"

"Yes, Mother. Please — both of you — he needs you at once."

They ascended together. Through the window slits, Ro saw the Bhre-Nora approaching in formation. Aleris alighted on the upper deck just as the family stepped onto it.

"It's time, Galbard," Aleris said.

"Yes, Aleris. It is time."

He turned to his family.

"Please take Jalin and Tiamphia to the tunnel to Candra. Ro will go with you."

"What?" Ro said.

"Father, I am not leaving you."

Galbard's expression tightened with pain, but he held his son's gaze.

"Take your mother and your wife through the tunnel. There is a leader in Candra named Ardhios. He will give you sanctuary. I have the Bhre-Nora and Rendaya to protect the Sword. Now I need you to protect the line of Shinetower."

Ro looked at Jalin and Tiamphia — their fear, their trembling hands, Tiamphia instinctively cradling her swollen belly.

"It will be done, Father," Ro said.

"Come," he urged them, and they moved toward the stairs.

"Jalin?" Galbard called.

"May I speak with you?"

She stepped aside with him. Galbard took her hands.

"I had wished for us so much more," he said quietly.

"I still remember the day you said you'd marry me."

He searched her eyes — a thousand unspoken things pressing at the back of his throat.

"I'm not sure I ever told you," he said, voice trembling, "but that was the most wonderful day of my life."

Her hands shook.

"Oh, Galbard... don't tell me these things."

"I have to tell you..."

"Tell me later, when all of this is past us."

Galbard looked down at her hands, his thumb brushing over her wedding ring.

"The Camonra are—"

"No." Her voice was firm, though her lower lip trembled.

"Tell me when we're together again."

"Of course."

He leaned in and kissed her cheek, narrowly missing the tear that slid down.

"When I see you again, we'll have much to talk about."

She wiped the tear away and stepped back. Her ringed hand lingered in his until the last possible moment, then slipped free as she rejoined Aleris, Ro, and Tiamphia at the stairwell.

"Fare thee well," Galbard said.

He lifted the Sword of the Watch, placed it upon the altar, and knelt before it in prayer.

"And may the Creator keep you, Father," Ro whispered, before taking Tiamphia's hand and following the others down the stairs.

Galbard prayed. Rendaya placed her hands upon him and prayed as well. A blue aura rose around him and the Sword, shimmering like heat above stone. When the glow steadied, she stepped back and looked over the chest-high wall to gauge how far the Camonra had pushed into the village.

The Sword of the Watch brightened on the altar. The stone beneath it grew hotter and hotter.

Aleris paused as he led Jalin, Ro, and Tiamphia downward. He could already feel the heat rising through the central shaft of the tower, overtaking the cool draft that whistled through the window slits.

Warm air surged upward.

"We must hurry!" he said, and they raced down the stairs.

*   *   *

Cayden ran through the tunnel beneath the statue of Rendaya until he reached a clattering maze of brass piping in every imaginable size, twisting and turning like veins around bone through the adjoining passages. Smaller pipes lined the walls, each feeding into tiny glass housings that glowed with an eerie green light. Cayden couldn't tell whether the glow came from magic or some kind of burning fuel. The whole place reminded him of the alchemist's shop in the village — all hissing and banging and trembling — but on a scale far beyond that little laboratory.

He followed the piping tunnels away from the Camonra, though he had no sense of direction. All he knew was that he needed to reach Shinetower, and he remembered the stories of the Bhre-Nora tunnels stretching for miles beneath the land.

The hissing grew louder. Then came the grinding of stone against stone, chains pulling and straining somewhere inside the walls. The pipes rumbled and knocked and whooshed as something surged through them — and then an explosive bang struck the elbow joint beside him, shoving it nearly halfway across the tunnel before it snapped back into place. Cayden sprinted past, half expecting the pipes to leap off their mounts or burst in his face.

The heat from the steam became unbearable. He stopped to wipe the sweat stinging his eyes — and heard voices ahead.

The tunnel opened into a vast cavern filled with gears and pistons. The noise was deafening.

The Bhre-Nora scurried everywhere, darting in and out of tunnels, adjusting valves and throwing levers on the pulsating pipes. Water sprayed from joints, feeding brass tubes that spun around the massive stone shaft rising through the center of the cavern. It was a storm of hissing, banging, dripping, spraying, and steam.

"Aleris!" Cayden bellowed from a catwalk stretching toward a central platform where pipes and levers converged around the stone column.

One of the Bhre-Nora zipped past him, then hooked around and hovered in front of him.

"Lord Cayden?" he said.

"You should not be here! It is very dangerous! How did you get here?"

"I came through the temple in the Dales! I'm trying to reach Shinetower!"

"Follow me!" the little sprite cried, shooting past him.

"Hurry — I must get you out of here!"

Cayden scrambled across the catwalk, and several Bhre-Nora gasped in astonishment at the sight of him.

"The Dales have been breached!" the little creature shouted to others who streaked past Cayden, racing in what he assumed was the direction of the temple.

"That way! Hurry!" he cried again, pointing up a long, steep stairwell carved straight through the bedrock beneath Shinetower.

*   *   *

Citanth swept through the Dales in short order, finding no resistance. By evening, the Camonra crested the last of the rolling hills that stood between them and Shinetower.

They assembled about a league from the outer ring walls, which zigzagged through the stone walkways leading to the tower's base. Torches dotted the paths, their flickering light casting leaping shadows that made the stone floors seem to shift beneath their feet. Periodically, steam blasted from large ports along the tower's sides, and a deep rumble trembled through the ground. The barbicans appeared abandoned.

"Master, they run and hide!" a Camon captain shouted.

"Quiet," Citanth said.

"They wait for us. Stay together."

The Camonra advanced through the gateway into the courtyard and onto the stone path leading toward the tower, where Citanth stood with his acolytes and a dozen soldiers. The Syra landed around him, clicking and shifting, awaiting his command.

Citanth looked up at the torchlit rise of the tower. Its upper reaches vanished into darkness, save for a faint blue glow hovering near the apex. He was studying the glow when movement caught his eye — a soldier approaching through the Syra.

"Come!" Citanth ordered.

The Syra parted. The soldier dropped to one knee.

"What is it? Be quick."

"My lord, we have discovered an entrance to an underground tunnel in the village."

Citanth's eyes narrowed.

"Interesting. Tell your captain to take twenty Camonra and investigate."

"Yes, my lord!" The soldier struck his chest with his fist, then retreated through the Syra.

Citanth lifted his arms.

"Fly, children of Amphileph!" he commanded.

"Find where the humans hide!"

*　　*　　*

Cayden's calves and thighs were burning, and he wheezed from the frantic climb through the bedrock toward Shinetower's ground floor. Just when he thought he could go no farther, the smooth tunnel walls widened into a landing lit by the same tiny green lamps he had seen beneath the Dales. He felt along the opposite wall until his fingers found the faintest seam in the stone. There was no handle, but when he pressed against it, the wall swung inward to reveal the alcove behind the famous statue of

Galbard's *Realization*.

The sight steadied him. He still had the tower's remaining stairs to climb.

"Creator, help me," he muttered, stepping into the alcove and pushing the hidden door closed.

He turned—and nearly collided with Aleris, who was leading Ro, Jalin, and Tiamphia toward the escape tunnels at Galbard's command.

"What are you doing?" Aleris asked.

"I came through the tunnels," Cayden said.

"You did what—"

A thunderous ruckus cut him off. At the tower's base, soldiers were dropping heavy timbers across three steel mounts, barring the great wooden gate. Others hammered angled posts into place with sledgehammers.

An archer rushed down the stairs.

"They're coming!" he shouted.

Eighty or ninety Shinetower fighters stood ready on each floor, bracing to stop the Camonra's ascent at any cost. Outside, the Syra circled the tower's base, weaving through the staggered walls like hunting hawks.

"Cayden, please see to my mother and Tiamphia," Ro said.

"I must stay here and defend the tower."

"Now wait one moment, Master Ro—" Aleris began.

Ro ignored him. He kissed his mother's cheek.

"I love you, Mother."

Then he turned to Tiamphia and kissed her deeply, holding her gaze.

"Your husband is no coward."

"I never thought it for a moment, my love," she whispered.

She pulled him close again.

"Please, Ro… be careful."

Ro stepped back.

"Go now. Go and be safe."

Cayden exhaled sharply.

"What do we do?"

"Come with me—now," Aleris said, already descending the stairs.

Cayden's legs screamed in protest, but he pushed on.

"Of course."

He followed them through the secret door and back down into the tunnel stairway.

Ro stepped out of the alcove and shouted to the soldiers.

"We're ready, men of Shinetower! Fill your hearts with courage!"

One of the fighters spotted him.

"Ro!" he cried — and Ro's presence visibly lifted the spirits of the men.

A bell clanged violently.

"Syra! Syra!"

Ro sprinted along the outer walls of the tower floor. The Syra were clawing at the window slits in the lower levels, scraping at the stone, pausing only long enough to press their heads against the openings, their black eyes searching for prey. The men backed away from the riotous clicking that echoed through the tiny slits.

A pounding began at the thick wooden doors — slow at first, then faster, harder. The clicking grew deafening.

Ro lunged to the nearest window slit and drove his sword through it. Something jerked the blade, nearly pulling him into the opening. Bracing a foot against the wall, he wrenched it free. Black blood coated the steel, and two barbed tails wriggled through the slit, stabbing wildly at the air. Ro swung and severed one of them.

"Be ready!" he shouted.

Their claws were chipping away at the stone.

"Kill any that pass!"

A Syra forced its head through the slit, and Ro rammed his sword through its face.

"Be not afraid! We can do this!"

He raced back toward the main gates.

"Hold the gates!" he roared, throwing his weight against the supports.

A rapid pecking and clawing sound rose from the other side — then a Syra's stinger punched through the wood.

"They're destroying the gate!" Ro shouted.

"Archers! We need the archers! Hold the gates!"

Several men braced the supports with their shoulders.

Ro sprinted up the stairs to the first level — and found chaos there as well. The archers had erected spiked wooden barbicans across the balconies, and the Syra had impaled themselves upon them so thickly that no arrow could pass. Ro hacked at the mass of bodies, carving a narrow opening.

"Archers, fire!" he bellowed.

"Clear the barbicans with your short swords if you must — but fire on the Syra at the main gate!"

The order echoed up the stairwell. Archers hacked through the carnage and loosed their arrows, crisscrossing the swarm attacking the gate. The rain of arrows was relentless, and hundreds of Syra fell from the sky.

But the Syra's encircling fury climbed the tower, rising level by level until it reached the balconies. The first row of archers fell under the assault.

Those above them continued to fire, but Syra landed on the second-floor balcony — then the third, then the fourth — while the rest hammered the main gate below.

Citanth saw that the archers were cutting down the Syra — but more importantly, the Syra were keeping the archers occupied. This might be his only chance to storm the tower gates.

"Attack!" he roared, and the better part of seventeen companies of Camonra surged into the Shinetower courts.

They had barely cleared the outer walls when a deafening burst of steam blasted from the tower's sides. The Syra that could flee from the superheated torrent did so quickly, but several were caught mid-flight, igniting and arcing across the sky as writhing balls of flame.

The Camonra smashed through the abandoned barbicans and into the maze of the first three barrier walls — but then the ground trembled beneath them. The earth shifted. The Camonra halted, struggling to keep their footing.

"What's happening?" Citanth shouted.

The barrier walls tore free of the turf, sliding on hidden foundations with the grinding shriek of stone on stone. Openings realigned, slamming shut to form concentric rings around the tower's base.

Suddenly the Camonra could neither advance nor retreat.

"What trickery is this?" a Camon captain cried. He pressed along the wall, searching for an exit. When he stepped onto a stone slab, it flipped upward, pitching him into a nest of spinning gears. They seized him instantly, dragging him under with a truncated scream and a spray of entrails. The slab snapped back into place — leaving only a smear of blood to show he had ever existed.

Panic rippled through the Camonra.

A post shot up from the courtyard floor. With a hiss of steam, it spun, flinging out a horizontal arm at head height. The blow shattered the skulls of four Camonra before the arm retracted, folding neatly back into the post, which sank flush with the stone.

Spikes erupted from random patches of ground, impaling Camonra cleanly before vanishing again. Half a dozen warriors collapsed at once, dead before they understood what had struck them.

Another explosive burst of steam — and the walls shifted again, creating new openings that looked like exits or hiding places. But as soon as Camonra rushed toward them, massive stone pistons slammed shut, crushing any who had stepped inside.

The survivors tried to flee, clawing at the outer walls, leaping for the edges to climb over. Scalding steam blasted from vents along the base, burning their legs and feet, filling the maze with a choking fog so dense they could see only inches ahead. The steam robbed the air of oxygen, leaving the winded Camonra gasping.

In the blinding haze, the Bhre-Nora man-traps devoured them like ravenous beasts.

"No! No-ooo!" Citanth screamed.

"Stay back!" he shouted to the remaining Camonra, helpless to save their comrades.

The screams echoed between the stone walls — cries for help, cries of agony — until the courtyard became a chamber of death.

"Where is it?" Citanth screamed.

He looked up the tower's height and saw flashes of blue light flickering at its summit.

"Syra — to the top of the tower!" he shrieked.

The remaining Syra broke off their battle with the archers and surged upward toward the upper deck of Shinetower.

"Here they come!" Rendaya shouted.

The Syra hurled themselves at the blue aura expanding from Rendaya, the field now enveloping the entire upper deck. They dove again and again, piercing the outer plasma shell, folding their wings tight and clawing through the crackling energy as they fought to reach Rendaya and Galbard.

"Remember, Galbard! Let nothing stop the Sword's power from flowing into the altar!"

Galbard's eyes stayed closed, but Rendaya saw him give a sharp, determined nod. The Sword of the Watch pulsed, and the altar stone beneath it glowed faintly.

Syra bodies piled atop one another, their teeth and claws snarled in the pulsating field. Rendaya tried not to notice the weakening shimmer of the aura — but they were closing in. She could now clearly see the truth of their gullets: rows of teeth behind the teeth, a second crushing set snapping hungrily as they fought to latch onto her.

They tore at each other in their frenzy to break through, shoving the dead aside and spilling them over the tower's edge. Bodies splattered across balconies and stone walkways far below. Still, their numbers pressed in.

"Ah!" Rendaya cried as the outer aura collapsed.

Several Syra crashed onto her at once. She slammed her fist into the deck, releasing a shockwave that blasted them back in a spray of black blood. The survivors scrambled, slipping and flopping on the gore-slick stone.

Black blood rolled down the sides of the protective aura still surrounding Galbard. Through it, Rendaya could just make out his face — grimacing, but unmoving, still kneeling in prayer.

A Syra leapt at her. Rendaya seized its life-force midair, ripping it from the creature in an instant. It fell dead at her feet.

"Creator!" she gasped.

For a heartbeat, the veins in her arm darkened, pulsing black beneath her skin. Pain lanced through her body.

*   *   *

Cayden, Jalin, and Tiamphia emerged from the descending stairs with Aleris into the main cavern, where the Bhre-Nora were still frantically scrambling over pipes and levers to maintain the tower's defenses.

"You must hurry!" Cayden called to Jalin and Tiamphia.

Aleris buzzed back and forth, utterly beside himself, clearly distressed at being away from the controls for even a moment. He pointed toward a tunnel on the far side of the cavern.

"That way leads to the western shores!" he shouted.

The cavern was blisteringly hot now, and the roar of steam nearly drowned his voice.

"I must return to my duties, Cayden! Follow the tunnel toward the western shores!"

Cayden pulled Jalin and Tiamphia toward the tunnel, urging them forward. He turned to signal his thanks to Aleris — and caught movement out of the corner of his eye behind the pressure-control deck on the central core.

A Camon soldier was emerging from the tunnel leading back to the Dales.

"Go now!" Cayden shouted to Jalin and Tiamphia.

"Here!" the Camon bellowed, and a distant reply echoed from the tunnel behind him.

Every Bhre-Nora in sight turned toward the intruder, drawing their tiny, razor-edged swords. The Camon ignored them entirely, drawing his own blade and bounding across the catwalk toward Cayden, Jalin, and Tiamphia.

Cayden stepped between the Camon and the women, fumbling for his sword.

The Camon raised his blade to strike — but two Bhre-Nora streaked past Cayden's face, slashing across the Camon's eyes. The creature screamed, stumbled, and toppled over the catwalk railing, bouncing off pipes before vanishing into the darkness below.

Aleris zipped back to Cayden.

"Go now! More of the Camonra will be here any second!"

"But—" Cayden began.

"Protect Jalin and Tiamphia! Go now before it's too late."

Aleris rose over Cayden's shoulder, looking past him at the terrified women.

"Remember us, miladies," he said softly.

Then his face hardened. He adjusted his goggles.

"Bhre-Nora!" Aleris cried.

"Attack!"

He shot toward the center of the cavern.

Tunnels all around them erupted with motion as the tiny warriors poured out in swarms. The air filled with Bhre-Nora, a living cloud of wings and green-lit lamps. A mass of them converged on the eastern tunnel entrance, clinging to walls, pipes, and catwalks. Their lamps tinted the entire cavern an eerie green.

For a moment, Cayden could only stare — a sight no human had likely ever witnessed.

Then he tore himself away and sprinted toward the western tunnel.

"Go! Go! Go!" he shouted, pushing Jalin and Tiamphia into the dim passage.

They disappeared into the darkness beyond.

*　　*　　*

The Syra were recovering from Rendaya's blast, shaking the muck from their bodies as they closed in around her and Galbard.

One of them streaked past from behind. Rendaya barely dodged, drawing its life as it passed. Her heart lurched. That same wave of despair and bone-deep fatigue washed over her.

"Archers!" she cried.

From their hiding places just below the upper deck, the archers rose, snatching arrows and firing at will. Three Syra fell in the first volley — but Rendaya and the archers were still hopelessly outnumbered.

A Syra's tail struck her arm, numbing it from elbow to little finger. It tore her garment at the shoulder before she drew its life force — but the cost was the same. Her body slowed. Her own life ebbed.

Another Syra cut down an archer. Rendaya ripped the creature's life away in a desperate attempt to save him. She fell to one knee. Her lips turned purple.

Galbard's aura dimmed — thinned — and the Syra sensed it instantly. They hurled themselves at the remaining barrier around him with renewed fury.

One Syra looped high, then dove with all its strength. Its tail pierced the inner aura and struck Galbard in the upper back, just behind the heart.

"No!" Rendaya screamed.

She drew the life from every Syra in sight. One after another they dropped lifeless to the deck — and then she collapsed as well. The aura around Galbard vanished. He toppled to the ground. The glow of the Sword faltered.

The tower's defenses stalled. Pistons froze mid-stroke. The Camonra who had survived the courtyard's traps hesitated, bewildered. Some scrambled for the outer walls, hauling survivors over the edge. Others might have done the same — if not for the sudden grinding of stone, the shifting of walls, the reopening of exits.

Below, in the eastern tunnels, the Bhre-Nora clashed with more than a dozen Camonra and several Syra. The Bhre-Nora slashed relentlessly, carving hundreds of cuts — but in the cramped tunnel, a single Camon killed a hundred of them before collapsing in a bloody heap.

The Bhre-Nora threw themselves at the Syra, sacrificing their bodies to destroy the creatures who devoured them whole or in pieces, snapping wildly to the last.

"Pull back!" Aleris commanded.

They fell back toward the cavern, fighting bravely, but the Camonra forced them out of the tunnel. A group of Bhre-Nora shoved a support column free from the cavern wall above the eastern tunnel, snapping the catwalk loose in a rain of debris and dropping three Camonra into the depths. Two more tried to leap the gap to the central deck — and fell to their deaths.

"We must protect the Sword!" Aleris cried.

The Bhre-Nora swarmed up the stairwell to Shinetower. They forced the secret doorway open just enough for Aleris to burst through into the statue room and onto the main floor.

"Ro!" he shouted.

"Ro, come quickly!"

Ro and the men were peering through the window slits, trying to understand why the defenses had stalled, when Aleris shot past him and back again.

"The Camonra are within the tower walls!" he cried.

"Something has gone very wrong on the upper deck! We must see to your father!"

"Father?" Ro breathed.

"No!"

He ran to the stairs.

"Warriors of Shinetower — our time has come!" Ro shouted.

"Go, master! May the Creator keep you! Save your father!" a captain called.

"Yes, go, master!" the men echoed.

"We will hold them! Go to Galbard!"

"May the Creator be with you!" Ro answered.

For the first time since the battle began, fear brushed his spine — not fear of death, but fear of failing those who depended on him. He raced up the stairs.

When Ro reached the upper deck, the sight hollowed him.

Rendaya lay motionless, her hair drifting in the breeze. Galbard lay beside her, unmoving.

Ro fell to his knees and rolled his father gently onto his back.

"Father!"

Grief tore through him.

Galbard's eyes fluttered open.

"Ro... I cannot move. The stars fade from the sky."

"Lie still, Father. I'm with you."

Ro cradled him in his lap. The world narrowed to Galbard's eyes.

"We must protect the Sword," Galbard whispered. Then suddenly, his fingers tightened weakly on Ro's arm.

"Ro... look over the edge. Tell me if the Camonra have been driven back."

Ro shook his head. "Father, I won't leave you."

Galbard's breath trembled, but his voice found a thin edge of the authority Ro had obeyed since childhood.

"Go now, son," he whispered. "I need your eyes. We must know if they've taken the gate."

He gave Ro the faintest hint of a smile — not strength, but reassurance, a father's last gift.

Ro swallowed his grief.

"Yes, Father."

He eased Galbard down and ran to the edge.

Below, the Camonra were climbing the walls, a mass of bodies rocking the great gate. With a final heave, they broke it inward and poured into the tower's lower floor.

Ro sprinted back.

"They are coming, Father!"

But when he knelt beside him, Galbard was gone.

The world tilted. The battle sounds faded to a distant hum.

"No…" Ro whispered.

He pulled his father close and kissed his forehead. Tears streaked his face. A groan of pure agony escaped him.

He laid Galbard gently upon the deck and rose. He walked to the edge of the upper deck.

Below him lay the mayhem of the courtyard — scattered bodies, black blood smeared across stone, man-traps frozen mid-motion — a nightmare tableau.

It was overwhelming.

He squeezed his eyelids shut, and when he opened them again, the sounds of battle surged back into his ears.

Aleris and a dozen Bhre-Nora burst from the upper-deck stairwell.

"Master Ro!" Aleris cried.

"The Camonra have broken through!"

They saw Galbard's lifeless form. They saw Rendaya lying among the Syra corpses. As one, the Bhre-Nora flew to her side, pushing the bodies away.

"Rendaya!" Aleris cried. He brushed her hair aside, gazing into her face with aching tenderness.

"She has taken the poisonous souls of the Syra. Her spirit is weighted down by their darkness."

Below them, the screams of battle rose — men fighting in the stairwells, Camonra flooding the tower floor by floor.

"She will never enter the Third Domain with such darkness upon her soul!" Aleris cried.

"Bhre-Nora — my brothers — right this injustice!"

The Bhre-Nora gathered around her, placing their tiny hands upon her, eyes closed in prayer.

Aleris glanced up and saw Ro standing alone at the parapets.

He flew to Ro's side.

"Ro! Ro!"

Ro seemed distant, hollowed.

"All is lost, Aleris."

"No!" Aleris slammed into Ro's chest, pushing him back from the edge.

"Do not let them die in vain! Use the Sword! Call upon its power!"

His voice softened.

"We are leaving now. You must defend the Sword of the Watch."

Ro stared at him.

"Leaving? What do you mean, leaving?"

Aleris pointed to the circle of Bhre-Nora around Rendaya.

"We give up our spirits to purify her. Goodbye, Ro."

Ro watched as Aleris returned to the circle. A black mist lifted from Rendaya's body. One by one, the Bhre-Nora released their spirits — soft white vapors rising from their tiny forms. Rendaya's face changed: the blackened veins faded, the purple lips softened, and her pale beauty returned. A pure white vapor rose from her as well.

Their spirits spiraled upward like embers on a sacred wind.

Stillness followed — a stillness that shook Ro to his core.

Ro moved to the altar and placed his hands upon it. His fingers traced the veins in the stone, then brushed the silky steel of Evliit's sword. A jolt shot through him. Memory surged — the day his father first tested him. Pain pierced his heart, but it was swept aside by a sudden warmth, a certainty that his father renewed his vow now through his son.

He knew what he must do.

"Creator, you have blessed me beyond measure, for my father's blood runs through me."

He leaned over the stone, motionless. He felt the vibration of war below — steel ringing, men and Camon roaring.

This was his path.

This was his calling.

There was *no one else*.

He called upon the Sword.

"Creator, pour Your spirit through me! Use my flesh to impart Your power into this, Your servant's sword!"

He thought of Tiamphia and their unborn child. There would be no peace for them if Amphileph gained the Sword. A heat bloomed in his core, racing through his limbs and into the altar.

A glowing blue mist flowed from his fingers, dancing across the altar stone, pooling around the sword, spilling over the edges. It rose around him, muffling the world as though he were submerged underwater. The aura swelled into a sphere ten feet wide. Lines of electricity leapt between the sword, his body, and the sphere's inner wall. His face glowed. Light poured from the sword, blinding him to the Camonra bursting onto the deck.

They hacked at the sphere. Each strike drew bolts of energy from Ro, ripping through their bodies and blasting through stone.

Far below, the altar stone glowed deep red. Cracks of molten light split its surface. Copper tubes percolated. Gears turned. Shinetower's outer walls slammed together in an explosion of stone. Relief vents roared white plumes into the night.

The upper deck flooded with Camonra. They pushed into the aura, heedless of its deadly rejection.

Below, deathtraps spun off their shafts. Courtyard stones erupted skyward. Steel whined under impossible pressure.

In the Bhre-Nora cavern, steam hissed from every direction. Tanks exploded. Pipes ruptured. Rivets ricocheted like bullets. The catwalk tore free and fell, dragging Aleris's control panels into the abyss.

Ro's vision adjusted. The Camonra appeared as ghostly shapes drifting in the aura. They slowed, suspended, their faces clear — some lifeless, others snarling as they fought to reach him. More climbed from the stairwell, crawling over the dead, clawing toward him through the dense field.

Light unfurled from him in sweeping arcs, each one like the herald of a new age. He closed his eyes and saw Tiamphia beside the calm waters of Highborne Falls, the faint sweetness of flowers in her hair.

His head snapped back. Light burst skyward from the Sword. When he opened his eyes, he saw the beam parting the clouds in a widening circle, revealing the heavens with impossible clarity. They were beautiful beyond words.

He lifted his hands. Arcs of electricity rose from the altar in their wake.

"Tiamphia!" he cried—

—and the core of the tower exploded.

A shockwave tore down its length, hurling massive stones from Shinetower deep into the Dales.

When the last stone settled, silence gathered like a shroud — and the world slipped from one age into another.

*   *   *

Citanth had been staring directly at the tower when the white-hot flash erased his sight. The concussion followed an instant later — a thunderous force that hurled him and his acolytes from their feet. The blast killed the acolytes outright, but Citanth lived, swallowed in the sudden darkness of blindness.

A wall of dirt and debris swept him nearly half a league to the north. When he finally awoke, broken and blind, he dragged himself upright. The world was nothing but heat, dust, and ringing silence. He staggered forward, hands outstretched, and stumbled into the night.

*   *   *

Steam and fire tore through the tunnels, collapsing long stretches of earth in every direction. The tower's courtyard sank beneath the Dales of Shinetower, swallowed into the fiery chasm left by the explosion.

Earth poured like water into the cavernous wound, dragging the turf from beneath two-thirds of the Dales as if pulling a carpet from under a table. Buildings toppled. Fires erupted in what little remained standing.

In moments, the Dales — as anyone had ever known them — were gone.

*   *   *

In the tunnel, Cayden felt the earth shudder beneath them before the sound of the explosion reached their ears.

"Get down!" he shouted to Tiamphia.

She pressed a hand to her belly, whispering a promise she could not finish before the world fell in.

The tunnel walls collapsed. Dirt slammed him to the floor. He tried to picture where each of them had been, tried to move, to carve out pockets of space he could widen — but the earth kept falling. It pinned his limbs. Then his head. Then it filled his eyes, his ears, his mouth.

Silence followed.

*   *   *

"Over here! There's someone over here!" a man of Highwood shouted.

They clawed at the dirt with their hands, lifting Cayden's head, wiping his eyes and nose and mouth with their fingers. More people converged, pulling debris away in frantic handfuls.

Cayden lay motionless.

They freed his body from the collapsed tunnel and laid him beside the furrow that had been their escape route. Someone splashed water over his face—

—and Cayden gasped, jerking upright.

The world swam in and out of focus, as if reality itself were struggling to reassemble around him. He screamed, eyes wide with terror, and it took minutes before his breathing slowed.

"Another one here — but she has passed," a searcher said.

Cayden turned his bloodshot eyes to see Jalin lifted from the earth. They laid her gently down and crossed her arms.

Her body was curled protectively, as if she had died still shielding someone.

"There's someone beneath her!" another cried.

They dug again and pulled Tiamphia free. Her head had been wedged behind Jalin's knees, forming a small void — an air pocket.

As they lifted Tiamphia to the surface, Cayden looked toward where Shinetower had stood. Nothing remained but scattered fires burning across a collapsed valley.

"Is she alive?" Cayden asked.

"Yes… barely."

He closed his eyes at the words — and slipped back into unconsciousness.

EPILOGUE

An aging man and woman stood in the doorway.

"We are here to see Tiamphia," the man said. "Is she here?"

A young man in his early twenties opened the door.

"Yes, sir. I am Strad, son of Tiamphia."

"And of Ro," the man added gently. "Your father was Ronan of Shinetower."

Strad froze, stunned into silence.

"How… how do you know that name?"

The man smiled softly, the expression carrying decades of memory.

"I am Cayden, and this is my wife, Nara. We knew your family long ago. May we speak with Tiamphia?"

"My mother has gone to the market… but how—"

"We have much to talk about," Cayden said.

Strad stepped aside quickly. "I'm sorry — please, come in."

Cayden helped Nara to a seat. The kitchen was modest, with only one table and two chairs, so he remained standing out of respect for Strad, the man of the house.

Strad pulled out the chair for him.

"No, sir — sit, please. I've a stool I'll be quite comfortable on."

He fetched the stool and sat, motioning for Cayden to take the chair.

"Thank you," Cayden said.

"Would you like something to drink? Something to eat?"

"No, no, we're fine," Nara said warmly.

"We appreciate your hospitality, Strad," Cayden added, "but we've come a long way to see your mother."

"How do you know her?" Strad asked.

Nara glanced at Cayden — a small, unspoken exchange passing between them.

"I once escorted your mother when she traveled to the southern kingdom," Cayden said. "Before the Wall. Long before you were born."

"My mother will be thrilled to see you, I'm sure. From where are you traveling?"

"I've been searching for old artifacts of Shinetower," Cayden answered. "Nara and I have lived most of our years in Southwood."

"In Southwood? Word is that Southwood is haunted."

"Don't believe everything you hear," Nara said with a smile. "Our home was a little paradise."

Before Strad could reply, the latch clicked and the front door opened. Tiamphia stepped inside, speaking about the market — then stopped cold at the sight of Cayden and Nara.

"Mother?" Strad asked, alarmed by the look on her face.

"Cayden! Nara!" Tiamphia gasped. She steadied herself against the doorframe, color draining from her cheeks before slowly returning.

They rose to greet her. Her expression softened into a warm, trembling smile.

"Have we aged that much?" Nara teased gently.

"Yes, my dear… I'm afraid we have," Cayden said, smiling in return. "It's good to see you, Tiamphia."

He embraced her, then Nara did the same. They all sat, quiet for a moment, simply taking in the years.

"I have something we must discuss," Cayden began.

Tiamphia's heart tightened — the old ache she had carried alone for decades.

"Strad, would you mind getting us more bread from the market?"

"But you just came—"

He caught the look in her eyes and understood: *she was dismissing him like a child from the adult table.*

"Of course, Mother."

In that moment, she saw Ro's eyes in her son's face, and the years folded like paper.

"Thank you, dear," she said softly.

When the door closed behind him, she leaned forward.

"You've found it, then."

Cayden paused. He and Nara exchanged a look.

"Yes," he said.

"But how? The Candrians searched for decades. I heard they finally gave up."

Cayden smiled faintly.

"Bellows."

Tiamphia blinked. "Bellows?"

"Rendaya's cat," Nara said, laughing softly at the memory.

"Rendaya…" Tiamphia whispered. "I had almost forgotten that name."

Her mind flashed back to the upper deck of Shinetower — the strange sorceress, the chaos, the light.

"The Witch of Southwood."

"'Witch' was never the right word," Nara said. "But it was all we knew. So we went to Southwood searching for clues to her devotion to the Sword of the Watch. We wandered for days before we found a black cat crying in the forest. He wouldn't leave us alone."

Cayden chuckled. "I nearly tripped over him. When I scolded him, he ran off — so I followed. That's when I saw it: a well-worn path deep in the forest. We followed it… and met a woman walking toward us."

"When we asked about Rendaya," Nara said, "she laughed and offered to show us where Rendaya had lived."

"We reached a small cottage," Cayden continued, "but she said she could not enter. 'The Bhre-Nora have restored my soul at their own expense,' she told us. 'I must rejoin them in the Third Domain.'"

Nara shivered at the memory. "It still gives me goosebumps. We suddenly realized who she was. It had been Rendaya walking with us all along."

"'I knew from the moment we met that you would protect the Sword,' she told me," Cayden said. "'Finish that good work, Cayden. Return the Sword to the line of Galbard.'"

"I told her I didn't know if the Sword had survived the fall of Shinetower," Cayden said. "But she insisted: 'Return the Sword to Galbard's line. Hide it well. For though many generations may pass, a descendant of Galbard will be called upon to carry it again.'"

"Nara wiped her eyes. "She apologized to me — for frightening the people when we first arrived on the Western Shore. She said she knew no other way. She asked my forgiveness… and gave us her cottage. She said it held answers to the questions that had haunted us."

Cayden nodded. "She warned us again: 'Amphileph will not rest until he has the Sword. He is even now plotting his return.' Then she told us where to find it — buried deep in the ruins of Shinetower."

"And then," Nara whispered, "she called to Bellows. He leapt into her arms. She held him close… and the two of them dissolved into a soft radiance that rose into the night sky."

Cayden placed his hands over Nara's, then looked at Tiamphia.

"The cottage was filled with scrolls, books, letters — all describing what Rendaya called *The Watchers' War*, and the absolute importance of keeping the Sword from Amphileph. We found the plans Nara had seen in her visions — the plans for Shinetower, the Bhre-Nora tunnels… everything."

"And?" Tiamphia whispered.

"And there was a map," Cayden said. "A map showing exactly where the Sword lay buried."

Nara continued. "We knew we were meant to find it. But the Candrian Mordher had soldiers guarding the ruins. For twelve years they scavenged the site. We waited. We watched. The ground grew unstable — collapses everywhere. Eventually they gave up."

"When they left," Cayden said, "we began digging. It took years. Rockslides set us back again and again. But we never gave up."

He reached beneath his cloak and placed a leather pouch on the table. He opened it.

The Sword of the Watch gleamed softly in the lamplight.

"Hide it well, Tiamphia," Cayden said. "Just as Rendaya asked. Amphileph will never stop searching."

Tiamphia stared, breath caught in her throat. With trembling hands, she folded the pouch closed.

"But what will I tell Strad? About the Sword… about his father?"

Cayden's voice softened.

"Tell him the Sword is an heirloom. Tell him nothing. Tell him whatever you must — but hide it, and tell no others."

"And his father?" she whispered.

"Tell him the truth," Cayden said. "Tell him his father was a brave man who saved a doomed world. Tell him that without Ro, there would be no Western Kingdom."

"Come with me."

Tiamphia led her father-in-law's old friends to her bedroom, where she cleared a keepsake chest her father, Caratacus, had given her. Her fingers brushed the worn wood, and she smiled, remembering Strad carving his initials into it as a boy — and Caratacus scolding him for it.

She removed the contents and took the Sword from Cayden, laying it gently in the bottom of the chest. For a moment she imagined Galbard's hands upon the hilt, steady and sure, and the memory steadied her own trembling. She covered the Sword with a dress, some folded fabric, and a few harmless whatnots. Then she closed the lid and locked it.

"I will tell Strad when the time is right," she said.

Cayden helped her set the chest at the foot of her bed and draped a quilt over it, as if it had never been touched.

When Strad returned, they shared wine and fresh bread and told stories of the Dales and Shinetower, of Galbard and Ro. Strad seemed renewed by their words. They talked late into the night, until he finally fell asleep, overwhelmed by the weight of the past. Yet as he drifted off, the stories of Shinetower settled in him like long-buried embers stirred to life — rekindling pride in the father he had lost and whispering of the place he was meant to take in the Watch.

In the morning, Cayden and Nara were gone.

*　　*　　*

Tiamphia kept her secret until she was very old. Then, when Strad's own son reached sixteen years of age, she told Strad that the chest would be his upon her death — and her single request was that his son, and his son after him, keep the Sword forever in the family of Galbard.

She told him then of that fateful day at Shinetower, and of his father's bravery. She told him that he could bestow no greater honor upon Ro than this: when Evliit returned, the line of Galbard would deliver the Sword to him, just as Galbard himself had sworn.

After she died that winter, Strad never forgot the oath he had given his mother. And so the Sword — and the promise bound to it — passed from father to son, generation after generation, even as the legend of Galbard and the stand at Shinetower faded into myth and was, at last, forgotten.

And so began the Sword's long wait for the next to awaken its power.

A Final Word

For generations, the Dales of Shinetower stood as a quiet corner of the Western Kingdom—until the night the ancient tower awakened, unleashing a battle that shattered an age. As Syra, Camonra, and the forces of Amphileph converged, a handful of unlikely defenders made their final stand: Galbard, the humble mason who bore the Sword of the Watch; Rendaya, the mysterious guardian whose power came at a terrible cost; and Ro, a son who had to rise in the moment his world fell apart.

When Shinetower collapsed into legend, its survivors scattered—carrying secrets, scars, and a single oath that had to endure. Decades later, a chance encounter in a quiet village rekindled the embers of a forgotten war, revealing a truth long buried beneath ruin and time: the Sword of the Watch survived.

And though the world has forgotten the stand at Shinetower, the Sword has not forgotten the world.

Continue the Legacy

The world of the Sword of the Watch spans generations — from the forging of the Sword to the rise of the Swordbearers.

Discover the other books in the saga:

- *The Watchers' War* — Book 1 of the Sword of the Watch
- *The Fall of Daoradh* — Book 3 of the Sword of the Watch

Author's Note

Stories are bridges between generations, and this one has been a long time in the making. I'm grateful you chose to cross it with me. The world of *The Sword of the Watch* continues to grow, shaped by the courage, sacrifice, and quiet strength of its characters. I hope their journey stays with you long after the final page.